SOLDIER'S PROMISE

BY
CINDI MYERS

MILLS &
BOON®

First Published in Great Britain 2018
By Mills & Boon, an imprint of HarperCollins*Publishers*
1 London Bridge Street, London, SE1 9GF

© 2017 Cynthia Myers

ISBN: 978-0-263-26457-9

46-0118

MIX
Paper from
responsible sources
FSC™ C007454

FSC
www.fsc.org

This book is produced from independently certified FSC™ paper to ensure responsible forest management.

For more information visit: www.harpercollins.co.uk/green

Printed and bound in Spain
by CPI, Barcelona

Carmen pulled away from him.

Carmen pulled away from him, resisting the urge to rub the place on her arm where he had touched her, where she imagined she could still feel the heat of his hand.

"You can insist all you want, but I'm not going to help you."

"One thing I learned reading Metwater's writings is that he hates cops," he said. "What do you think he'll do if I tell the cult leader he's got one living with him, lying about who she is and spying on him?"

"I could have you arrested for interfering with an investigation," she said.

"You could. But you'd have to deal with Metwater first." He removed his sunglasses and she found herself held by the intensity of his sapphire-blue eyes. His voice was a low, sexy rumble she was sure was intentional. "I'm thinking maybe you would prefer to deal with me."

Cindi Myers is the author of more than fifty novels. When she's not crafting new romance plots, she enjoys skiing, gardening, cooking, crafting and daydreaming. A lover of small-town life, she lives with her husband and two spoiled dogs in the Colorado mountains.

For Morgan and Erik

Chapter One

Jake Lohmiller raised the binoculars to his eyes and studied the group of women who moved along the rim of the canyon. Wind sent their colorful cotton skirts fluttering, so that they reminded Jake of butterflies, flitting among the wild roses that perfumed the air. The women were gathering rose hips and wild raspberries, the murmur of their voices drifting to him on the wind, their words indistinct.

He shifted his elbow to dislodge a pebble that was digging into his flesh and trained the glasses on a dark-haired woman. Her long, straight black hair, high cheekbones and bronzed skin set her apart from the mostly fair-skinned redheads, blondes and brunettes around her. She seemed out of place, not just because of her appearance, but because of the way she carried herself. She moved slightly behind the other women, her movements both deliberate and graceful, her bearing wary. Jake sensed a tension in her, like a cat poised to spring.

She stopped at the corner post of a falling-down fence that ran alongside the path the women were following, and turned to stare across the high desert landscape of rock, cactus and stunted trees, one hand raised to shield her eyes from the sun's glare. Jake ducked down behind the rock outcropping he had chosen as his vantage point, though he knew she couldn't see him. Not at this distance. Not when he had been so well-trained to not give away his position.

He had been in the Curecanti National Recreation Area in southwest Colorado for three days, watching the women, learning their routines and habits, and planning his next move. The dark-haired woman turned away and hurried to catch up with the others, and Jake shifted his attention to the oldest woman in the group—a slight, very fair blonde with almost-white hair and light blue eyes. She went by the name Phoenix these days, the latest in a string of names and nicknames she had gone by over the years. He tried to read her mood, to guess what she was thinking or feeling, but at this distance he could tell nothing except that she looked fairly healthy—something that hadn't been the case the last time he had seen her. He clenched his jaw, struggling against the mixture of love and anger that warred in him whenever he thought about her.

He shifted again, focusing this time on the youngest member of the group, and his jaw relaxed. Sophie was growing up to be a pretty young woman, her long brown hair plaited in a single braid that hung to her shoulder blades. She laughed at something one of the others said, and Jake's heart clenched, aching at the sound. The last time he had seen her, she had been ten and crying. Four years had changed her in so many ways, but it cheered him to see her looking so happy, especially since he hadn't expected it—not here.

The women moved on until they were out of the visual field of his binoculars. The silence of the wilderness closed in around him, with only the rattle of the wind in dry tree branches reminding him that he hadn't suddenly gone deaf. He put away the binoculars, then stretched out on his back, the shadow of the boulder keeping the sun off his face. He ignored the hardness of the dry ground and focused on reviewing all the information he had gathered so far. It was time to complete his mission. He had to make contact with Phoenix and Sophie and persuade them to leave with him. But he had to do it without raising alarm. And preferably without attracting any attention from the local cops.

A shadow fell across his torso, and the crunch of a leather sole on gravel had him lurching to his feet, reaching for the weapon at his side. "Keep your hands where I can see them!" a woman's voice commanded.

He held his hands out from his sides and stared at the dark-haired woman. Obviously, she had left the group and circled around, but how had she managed to sneak up on him? Had he gotten so rusty in the months since he had left his unit in Afghanistan? He must have, because, in all the time he had been watching her, he had never noticed the handgun she was aiming at him now.

CARMEN REDHORSE KEPT her weapon trained on the man who stood opposite her, thankful that he was cooperating with her orders. He was a big, powerful-looking man, young and strong, and he seemed at home here in this rugged environment. He held his hands at his sides, and his gaze remained focused on her, his manner calm, though it struck her as the calm of a predator who doesn't feel a threat from a weaker opponent rather than that of a man who has nothing to worry about. "Who are you, and what are you doing out here, spying on us?" she asked.

"Who are you, and why should I answer your question?" His expression and the tone of his voice betrayed nothing. She judged he was about six feet tall, lean and muscular. His erect posture, close-cropped hair and deep tan pegged him as a military man—either still on active duty or only recently discharged. An officer, she guessed—he had the air of a man who was used to being in charge.

"I'm the woman who has a gun trained on you," she said. "Trust me, I know how to use it." Until she knew more about him and what he was up to, she wasn't going to let him distract her. "I need you to very slowly remove your weapon from the holster and place it on the ground in front of you."

He hesitated, then did as she asked, his attention focused on her, though she couldn't see his eyes clearly behind the dark aviator sunglasses he wore. He straightened, some of the stiffness gone out of his posture. "What is a cop doing way out here?" he asked.

"What makes you think I'm a cop?" she asked.

"I'm right, aren't I? Everything from your choice of weapon to the way you handle it—not to mention the way you bark out commands—says law enforcement. And not a rookie, either." He shifted his weight, still keeping his hands in view. "So what are you doing in Daniel Metwater's cult?"

His word choice—*cult* instead of *group* or, as Metwater preferred, *Family*—told her he wasn't a fan of the trust-fund millionaire turned itinerant preacher, who was camped with his followers on public land. The women she had been foraging with were part of Metwater's faithful. "What I'm doing here isn't your concern," she said. "And you haven't answered my question—what are you up to? And I'll need to see some ID."

"My wallet is in my back pocket," he said.

"Take it out slowly, and hand it over."

He did as she asked. She studied the Texas driver's license. "Jacob Lohmiller," she read. Twenty-seven years old, with an address in Houston. She glanced across at the Veteran ID. Army—so she had been right about that. And he had been discharged only four months before. "You're a long way from home, Mr. Lohmiller."

"Are you conducting some kind of undercover operation with Metwater's bunch?" Lohmiller asked, accepting his wallet from her and returning it to his pocket. "Are they involved in something criminal?"

The Ranger Brigade—a multidisciplinary task force charged with law enforcement on Colorado's public lands—had suspected Daniel Metwater's involvement in more than one crime, but so far they had found little evidence to support their suspicions. Carmen was ostensibly with the group now, posing as a new convert in order to verify that the group's women and children were not subject to any kind of abuse. She had lobbied hard to take a closer look at the group after a young woman who had been associated with them had died. Her commander had agreed to give her a week, all the time he could spare from the Rangers' other duties. Four days of that week had passed, and Carmen was just beginning to win the other Family members' trust. She couldn't afford to have Lohmiller blow her cover.

"What are you doing here?" she asked again. "Why were you watching us just now?"

"As you said, this is public land. Maybe I came out here for a hike."

She glanced at the pack that lay in the shade of the boulder he had been stretched out beside. "So you were hiking, and you saw a group of women and decided to take a closer look."

He shrugged. "Maybe."

"How long have you been in the area?" she asked. "Where are you staying? Do you have a vehicle, and where is it parked?"

"Why all the questions?" he asked.

"A man focused on a group of women, a man who refuses to account for himself, makes me suspicious. I wonder what I would learn if I brought you in for questioning."

"I flew in to Montrose four days ago," he said. "I've been hiking and camping out here ever since. I have a truck parked at my campsite not far from here."

She nodded. "So, again—why were you watching us?"

"How did you know I was watching you?" he asked.

"I had that sensation of being watched," she said. "I saw a bird startle from your hiding place and decided to take a closer look."

He looked away and mumbled what might have been a curse word. She waited, the gun pointing toward the ground now, but still in her hand.

"I came here to check on a couple of Metwater's followers," he said. "To make sure they're all right."

"Which members?" she asked.

"A woman who calls herself Phoenix and a girl, Sophie. I don't think she's taken one of their loopy nicknames yet."

"You know Phoenix and Sophie?" She knew of a couple of families who had sent private detectives to check up on their loved ones at the camp, but the forty-something blonde and her fourteen-year-old daughter had never mentioned any other family to Carmen.

Lohmiller squared his shoulders. "Phoenix—her real name is Anna—is my mom. Sophie is my half sister."

It was Carmen's turn to be surprised. "Phoenix is your mother?" The woman looked scarcely old enough to have a son Lohmiller's age, and he didn't resemble her at all.

"She had me when she was sixteen."

"There's nothing to prevent you from walking into camp and visiting your mother and sister," Carmen said. "Why skulk around in the wilderness?"

"I needed to assess her situation, determine the lay of the land and formulate a plan for getting them away from here."

Again, his choice of words was telling. He spoke like a man on a mission. "What exactly did you do in the service, Mr. Lohmiller?" she asked.

"Army Rangers."

She might have guessed. "Your mother is an adult, free to make her own decisions and, by extension, decisions for her daughter," she said. "I'll admit, a wilderness camp with no running water or other facilities is not my first choice for a place to live, but it's her choice. Neither she nor Sophie are in any danger that I've been able to determine. Or are you aware of something I'm not? Some circumstance you believe puts them in danger?"

"No particular circumstance, no. But my mother doesn't have a history of making wise choices."

"*Wise* and *dangerous* are two different things."

"As you said, my mother is free to make her own decisions, but my sister is not. And the so-called wilderness paradise Daniel Metwater likes to brag about is no place for her."

Carmen thumbed the safety on her weapon and shoved it into the waistband of her skirt. Later, she'd replace it in the holster strapped to her thigh beneath the long, loose skirt. For all his obvious agitation and coiled energy, she didn't sense that Jake Lohmiller was any threat to her. "I've talked to Sophie, and she's not unhappy. She's being homeschooled, she's healthy, and she seems to have a great relationship with her mother." So far, nothing Carmen had learned in her time with the Family had pointed to any abuse or neglect, though she couldn't shake the feeling that life in the camp wasn't as rosy as Metwater and his followers liked to paint. The truth was, a week probably wasn't long enough to get a real picture for what was going on. She didn't look forward to returning to her commander with nothing to show for her efforts.

Lohmiller scowled. "What about that creep, Metwater?"

"What about him?"

"I've checked him out. I've read his blog and newspaper articles about him—everything I could find online. And I've been watching him for a few days now. He collects beautiful women the way some men collect cars. How long before he starts eyeing Sophie?"

His words sent a shiver through Carmen. "I'm sure your mother would never let anything happen to Sophie."

"You don't know my mother like I do."

"When was the last time you spoke to her?"

"Four years ago. Sophie was ten."

"People can change a lot in four years."

"My mom is still making poor decisions. Bringing Sophie out here proves it."

Carmen couldn't argue with that. Though Sophie seemed content enough, following an itinerant preacher didn't seem the best way to bring up a child. But before she could think of a reply, Lohmiller said, "You don't strike me as the typical Daniel Metwater follower."

Knowing that he had been spying on her long enough to feel qualified to make such an assessment annoyed her. "Who do you see as his typical follower?" she asked.

"Disconnected, discontented, idealistic. Young, white and, as far as I can tell, mostly well-off and well-educated. I'm not questioning your education, but the people who flock to someone like Metwater are searching for some idealistic world that he's promising them."

Okay, so he had done his homework. But she couldn't resist goading him. "You don't think I'm those things?"

"You have a job and a purpose. I doubt if most cops stay idealistic for long, even if they start that way. You seem too down-to-earth and practical to fall for all his mumbo jumbo."

"And I'm not white."

She ignored the pleasant tremor that swept through her as his gaze assessed her. "That, too. Are you Native American?"

"You got it in one."

"So, if you're not one of his followers, that means you're here as a cop. Possibly undercover. What are you investigating?"

Time to get her head back on the job. "I'm not going to discuss my purpose here with you."

"Fine. You don't have to. You can at least give me

your name—or whatever name you're going by out here."

Fair enough. "My name is Carmen. Carmen Redhorse."

"Well, Officer Redhorse, the fact that you're here means something is going on in camp that has the cops suspicious. And that means my sister and my mother don't belong there."

"Then you need to talk to your mother and stop lurking in the wilderness," she said. "Some people might get the wrong idea."

"You're the only person who knows I'm here. I can't control whether your ideas about me are wrong or not."

Had he meant the comment to sound vaguely sexual? Was he trying to provoke her, or was it just his nature? She glanced toward the canyon rim. The other women were long out of sight now. She had told them she wanted to walk back alone, to think about some things, and had promised to catch up with them later. But how long could she stay away before someone came looking for her? "Are you going to talk to your mom?" she asked Lohmiller.

"I'll talk to her," he said. "And what do you think she'll tell me?"

"I have no idea."

"Yes, you do. You've been hanging out with her for at least three days. You must have made some judgments about her. So, tell me what you think she'll say when I ask her to leave Metwater's little cult and come live with me?"

"She'll tell you she and Sophie are happy here, that Daniel Metwater changed her life and she doesn't want to go with you."

He nodded. "Exactly. So talking to her isn't going

to be enough. I have to find a way to convince her to leave—with Sophie."

"That's between you and your mother. I can't help you." She started to turn away, but his hand on her arm stopped her.

"I think you can help me," he said. "In fact, I insist."

She pulled away from him, resisting the urge to rub the place on her arm where he had touched her, where she imagined she could still feel the heat of his touch. She might have known he was the type who thought he could boss her around. "You can insist all you want, but I'm not going to help you."

"One thing I learned reading Metwater's writings is that he hates cops," he said. "What do you think he'll do if I tell him he's got one living with him, lying about who she is and spying on him?"

Metwater would be furious if he learned she was a cop, but that didn't mean he would do anything more than kick her out of his camp. But even though she didn't have any proof that he was involved in anything illegal, everything she knew about him told her he was capable of violence. Still, she was a cop. She knew how to look after herself. "I could have you arrested for interfering with an investigation," she said.

"You could. But you'd have to deal with Metwater first." He removed his sunglasses, and she found herself held by the intensity of his sapphire-blue eyes. His voice was a low, sexy rumble she was sure was intentional. "I'm thinking maybe you would prefer to deal with me."

Chapter Two

Jake knew his words had gotten through the tough attitude she wore like a shield. A rosy flush burnished Officer Redhorse's cheeks, and he could almost see the sparks of anger in her eyes at what he could admit was his clumsily delivered threat. He wasn't sure if she would scream at him or go ahead and shoot him, so he hastened to try to repair the damage.

"Look, all I'm asking is for you to help me out a little," he said.

"I can't help you," she said.

"You can talk to my mother. Tell her you think it's a good idea for her and Sophie to come with me."

"I hardly know your mother," she said. "Why would she listen to me? And I know even less about you. I have no way of knowing if going with you is a good idea or not."

Couldn't she see that he was a good guy? Well, maybe not. "Check me out," he said. "You'll see I don't even have a traffic ticket."

"Just because you've never broken a law doesn't make you a good guy. Daniel Metwater doesn't have any traffic tickets, either."

He winced. Then another idea occurred to him. "Does Metwater trust you?" he asked.

She looked as if she had tasted something sour. "I'm not sure *trust* is the right word."

"But he likes you," Jake said. "He's attracted to you. You're a beautiful woman, and you're a novelty."

"Because I'm not his usual white and desperate type?"

Because that tough, don't-touch-me attitude of yours is sexy as all get-out. But he thought better of saying that. He was already in enough trouble here. "From what I've seen and heard, the Prophet likes pretty much all young, attractive women—at least, the ones who follow him around and hang on his every word. If you're working undercover in his camp, I assume you're playing the part of devoted disciple."

She pressed her lips together but didn't comment.

"Maybe I can help you out," he said.

"I don't need your help."

"I might be able to find out things you can't. I could talk to the men in camp, let you know what I hear."

She shook her head. "Talk to your mother, but leave me out of it." She turned and walked away.

He watched her leave, her back straight and her confident stride quickly lengthening the distance between them. Should he follow her? He was going to have to go to Metwater's camp sooner or later to confront his mother. He would have liked to have had the pretty cop on his side. The meeting with Phoenix wasn't going to be an easy one, and it would have been good to have an ally. But, if he had to, he'd do the job alone. He was used to working solo—he'd been on his own since he was a teenager. And he knew how to tackle tough jobs.

He had already let his sister down once. He wouldn't let that happen again.

He waited a moment to let Carmen get ahead of him, then started to follow. He would see what she did when she got to camp, then make his decision about when to approach his mother.

Before they reached camp, however, Carmen caught up with the other women. He was too far away to hear what was said, but it appeared that a couple of the women greeted her. Then a figure broke from the group and ran up to Carmen. Though Jake couldn't hear what the girl was saying, he recognized Sophie, and she was clearly agitated. Carmen put a hand on the girl's shoulder, listening, then she and Sophie turned and headed back toward Jake.

He walked out to meet them. Sophie stared at him, eyes wide. "Jake? Is that really you?"

"It's me, sis." He held out his arms, and she ran to him and buried her head against his shoulder. The feel of her—bigger than the last time he had seen her, but still so slight and vulnerable—sent a tremor through him. He loved her so much. Why had he stayed away so long?

"Thank God you're here," she said.

He pulled her away a little, so that he could see her face. "What's wrong?" he asked. "Why are you so upset?"

"It's Mama. Something's really wrong with her." She grabbed his hand and started leading him forward. "We have to hurry, before it's too late."

CARMEN FOLLOWED BEHIND Jake and his sister. If she had had any doubts about telling Sophie of her brother's arrival, she knew now she had made the right decision.

Sophie walked with one arm wrapped around Jake's waist and looked up at him as if she couldn't believe he was here. For his part, Jake studied his sister as if he couldn't get enough of looking at her.

"Tell me exactly what happened," he said as they headed toward Metwater's camp at the foot of Mystic Mesa.

"We were walking back to camp, and Mama just collapsed," Sophie said. "I mean, one minute she was fine, and the next she just—fell over." The girl looked back at Carmen. "Starfall and Sarah got a couple of the men to carry her to the Prophet. They said he would know what to do for her."

"Has Phoenix complained of feeling bad lately?" Carmen asked.

"No. She's just acted, you know, normal." Sophie turned back to Jake. "I still can't believe you're here. What are you doing?"

"I came to see you." He tried to smile, but the expression didn't reach his eyes. "You're growing up fast."

Sophie hugged him tighter. "I've missed you so much."

"I've missed you, too." His eyes met Carmen's over Sophie's shoulder, as if challenging her to deny that his sister loved him and was glad to see him.

"Mom's going to be so happy to see you, too," Sophie said.

"Is she? She wasn't very happy with me last time we spoke."

"She was just worried about you joining the military. But she's in a different place now. A better place." Sophie frowned. "Or she was, until this."

"Maybe the heat got to her," Carmen said. "I'm sure

she'll be fine." She touched Jake's arm. "You need to hide your gun before we get to camp. Walking in with it visible like that will only cause trouble." She had already tucked hers back into the holster on her thigh.

She expected him to argue, but he nodded. "Okay." He unstrapped the holster from around his waist and stuffed it into his pack. Sophie watched, wide-eyed and silent.

The US Forest Service allowed dispersed camping for up to two weeks outside of designated campgrounds. Through mysterious political connections, Daniel Metwater had wrangled a permit for his group to settle for an extended period in this remote area, near a natural spring at the base of a rocky mesa in the high desert landscape of Curecanti National Recreation Area. This was the third such camp the group had occupied in as many months. Like the others, it consisted of a motley collection of trucks, campers, tents and makeshift shelters, grouped in a rough oval around a central campfire.

A large, late-model motor home was parked at one end of the oval, solar panels winking from the roof. "That's where the Prophet lives," Sophie whispered to Jake.

"Starfall." Carmen called to a woman with dark, curly hair who was wiping the face of a naked toddler outside a large, white tent. "Where is Phoenix?"

"She's with the Prophet," the woman said. She stared openly at Jake. "Who is he?"

"This is my big brother, Jake," Sophie said. "He wants to see Mom. Is she okay?"

"She'll be fine," Starfall said. "She's resting now and shouldn't be disturbed."

"Is your Prophet a doctor?" Jake asked.

Though Starfall was at least a foot shorter than Jake, she managed to look down her nose at him. "He is a spiritual healer."

Jake started toward the motor home, but Sophie held him back. "We're not supposed to go into the Prophet's home without an invitation," she said.

"I'm not one of his followers," Jake said. "I don't have to play by his rules." He gently uncurled her fingers from around his arm and started for the motor home again, Carmen close behind him.

Sophie caught up with them as they climbed the steps to the RV. Jake pounded on the door.

He had raised his fist to knock again when the door eased open, and a pale blonde peered out. Andi Matthe-son—who now went by the single moniker Asteria—was one of the reasons Carmen had joined Metwater's Family. The daughter of a former US senator was eight months pregnant and, as far as Carmen could deter-mine, hadn't seen a doctor in months. So many of the Prophet's followers were young women who were ei-ther pregnant or mothers to small children that Carmen wanted to determine if they were receiving the neces-sary care. Andi frowned at the tall, imposing man lean-ing over her, then looked past him to Carmen. "What do you want?" she asked.

"We're here to see Phoenix," Jake said.

"This is Phoenix's son, Jake Lohmiller." Carmen stepped up beside him. "Sophie told us her mother had fainted and, naturally, he's concerned."

"She's fine," Andi said. "She just needs to rest." She started to close the door, but Jake flattened his hand against it, holding it open.

"I want to see her," he said.

"The Prophet—" Andi began.

Jake didn't let her finish. He shoved past her into the motor home. Carmen and Sophie followed. "Phoenix?" he called.

"Mama?" Sophie echoed.

Daniel Metwater, dressed in his usual outfit of loose, white shirt and trousers, his dark, curly hair framing the intensely handsome face of a male model, appeared in the doorway that led to the back of the RV. "What is the meaning of this disturbance?" he asked.

"I'm here to see Phoenix." Jake started to move past Metwater, but the Prophet blocked him.

"Phoenix is resting," he said.

"I'm going to see her anyway." He took Metwater by the shoulders and shoved him aside. One of the muscular young men Metwater kept near him as bodyguards rushed forward, but Jake ignored him and charged into the bedroom. Carmen followed, one hand hovering over the weapon under her skirt. She didn't want to blow her cover by drawing the gun, but Jake might not leave her any choice.

Phoenix lay on Metwater's bed and, with her whitish hair and her face so pale, she almost blended with the sheets. As Jake reached her, the bodyguard grabbed his arm. "No!" Phoenix sat up, one arm outstretched. "Don't hurt him, please!"

Jake's thunderous expression softened. He sat on the edge of the bed and took Phoenix's hand. "Hello, Mom."

Her smile transformed her face. "Jake. What a wonderful surprise!" She cupped his face in her hands, as if needing to reassure herself he was real. "What are you doing here?"

"I came to see you. How are you feeling?"

"I'm fine." She managed a wavering smile. "I just got too hot out there or I didn't drink enough water or something." She wrapped both of her hands around his. "It's so good to see you. How did you ever find me?"

"It wasn't easy," he said. "I talked to a lot of people. One of your old friends from Denver mentioned you'd taken up with some millionaire turned preacher. I did some more digging and heard about this group and came out here to see if you were with them."

"I kept meaning to write and let you know Sophie and I were okay and that you shouldn't worry. You always were such a worrier."

"You shouldn't disappear that way," Jake said. "What were you thinking?"

Phoenix licked her pale lips. "Do your grandparents know I'm here?" she asked.

"No. Not yet."

She lay back on the pillows and closed her eyes. "Don't tell them, please. There's really no need for them to know."

He looked as if he wanted to argue that point but pressed his lips together and said nothing.

Metwater moved to the other side of the bed and took Phoenix's hand. "What are you doing here?" he asked Jake.

"I came to see my mother."

"This is my son." Opening her eyes, Phoenix struggled to a sitting position once more. "Jake, this is the Prophet. The man who saved my life." She beamed at Metwater, the adoration making Carmen a little sick to her stomach. Frankly, the Prophet, for all his good looks and charm—or possibly because of them—gave her the creeps.

"You need to leave now," Metwater said. "You're obviously upsetting your mother."

"Oh, no!" Phoenix protested. "We haven't even had a chance to talk. And I'm feeling much better, I promise." She started to get out of bed, but Metwater pushed her back against the pillows once more.

"I can feel your pulse racing," he said. "All this excitement isn't good for you." He turned to Jake. "You can see your mother later. Tomorrow, after she's had a chance to rest."

"Or I could take her with me now," he said. "To a doctor who can check her out. Someplace safe."

"Jake, I don't need a doctor," Phoenix protested. "And why wouldn't I be safe here? The Prophet has given me his own bed. I don't deserve such an honor."

"Mother, I came to take you away from here. You and Sophie."

Carmen winced. Not the way to approach this.

Phoenix laughed. "Don't be silly, Jake. This is my home. Our home. We're not going anywhere."

"That's right," Metwater said. He smiled and beckoned toward Sophie. "Come here, child. Don't be shy."

Sophie flushed and walked very slowly, head down, to the side of the bed where Metwater sat. He put his arm around her and pulled her close. "You're happy here, aren't you?" he asked, his lips practically brushing the girl's cheek.

She stood frozen, avoiding his eyes.

"Of course she's happy." Phoenix stroked her daughter's hand. "You love it here, don't you, dear?"

Sophie nodded, though she still didn't look up. Carmen swallowed the sour taste in her mouth. She had to fight to keep from ordering Metwater to take his hands off the girl. The muscles bunched along Jake's jaw as he glared at the Prophet.

Metwater met the glare with a challenging look of his own. "Your mother and sister are well cared for here," he said. "You don't have anything to worry about."

Carmen wasn't so sure about that. She couldn't decide whether Daniel Metwater or Jake Lohmiller was likely to cause the most trouble.

Jake glared at Metwater. "Get your hands off my sister," he said, and there was no mistaking the menace behind his words.

"Sophie doesn't mind, does she?" Metwater snuggled the girl closer.

"Get your hands off her, or I'll break them off!"

"Jake!" Phoenix grabbed his arm. "That's no way to talk to a holy man."

"There's nothing holy about the way he's holding Sophie."

Phoenix sent her daughter a worried look. "Maybe Sophie should leave us now," she said.

Metwater unwrapped his arms from around the girl. "You may go now, daughter," he said.

Sophie ran from the room without looking at any of them. A moment later, the door to the motor home slammed behind her.

Phoenix turned to Jake. "Now look what you've done," she said.

"What *I've* done?" Jake stood. "This charlatan has pulled the wool over everyone's eyes. Can't you see this is no place for a child? This is no place for you."

"Enough." Metwater clapped his hands together. "You may not come into my home and insult me this way."

Jake took a step toward the Prophet, fists clenched.

Carmen had seen enough. She moved forward and took his arm. "Come with me," she said softly. "We'll figure something out."

"You're not welcome in my home or my Family's home," Metwater said. "Leave, and don't come back."

The guard stepped forward and took Jake's other arm. His muscles tensed beneath Carmen's hand, but she held on, even as he shook off the guard. "I'm leaving," he said. "But this isn't the last you've seen of me."

Chapter Three

Jake wrenched from Carmen's grasp and stalked out of the room. She started after him, but Metwater's voice stopped her. "How do you know this man?" he asked.

"I don't," she said. "He approached me while we were out gathering fruit. He told me he was Phoenix's son and that he wanted to see her. Then Sophie ran up and told us her mother had collapsed."

"It was just too much sun," Phoenix protested. "I'm fine." She looked to Metwater. "Jake always did have a hot temper, but he doesn't mean anything by it. He's a good boy. He was just worried about me, that's all."

Metwater kept his gaze fixed on Carmen. He had dark, piercing eyes that dared you to blink first. "I don't want you associating with him," he said. "He strikes me as dangerous."

Carmen nodded. Not that she was agreeing with Metwater, but she was anxious to get out of the motor home and find Jake before he caused any more trouble.

"You may go now," Metwater said.

She ground her teeth together. Reminding him she didn't need his permission to walk away wouldn't fit with her cover of the new, meek disciple. She kept her head down until she was out of the RV, then looked around for Jake.

She spotted him with Starfall and another woman, Sarah, outside a lean-to that served as the camp's communal kitchen. "We were just telling Soldier Boy here that we could use a man like him around," Starfall said. She gave Jake an appreciative once-over.

"Your Prophet doesn't agree," Jake said.

"He doesn't like people who disagree with him," Sarah said. When the others looked at her, she flushed. "But it's his camp, so I guess he gets to make the rules."

"Phoenix never let on she had a good-looking son like you," Starfall said, looking Jake up and down.

"She doesn't talk about her past," Sarah said. "Most people here don't."

"They don't," Starfall agreed. She turned to Carmen. "For instance, we don't know anything about Carmen here, except that she heard the Prophet at a rally in Grand Junction and fell in love with his teachings."

"There's nothing to know," Carmen said. She touched Jake's arm. "Where is Sophie?"

"I don't know." He frowned. "I need to find her."

"She's probably at Phoenix's trailer," Starfall said. "You know teenagers. They're always in a snit about something."

"I'll take you there," Carmen said.

Jake followed her away from the two women. When they were out of earshot, Carmen said, "We have to hurry. Metwater will send someone to make sure you left camp, and Starfall will probably tell them where you went."

"Does everyone here do what Metwater tells them to do?" he asked.

"That's part of the deal when you join up with his *Family*," she said. "You turn over all your worldly goods to him and agree to live by his rules."

"You did that?" he asked.

"No. I'm still on probation. I get to hang around for a couple of weeks and decide if this is what I really want."

Jake looked around them. Women and children were everywhere, along with a handful of men. Everyone was young and attractive. "I don't get it," he said. "What do people see in this kind of life?"

"They're unhappy and looking for something," she said. "Some meaning or purpose. They want to be part of a special group and feel special themselves. Metwater promises that."

His eyes, as intense as the Prophet's, met hers, but with a warmth she had never found in Metwater's gaze. "What does he get out of it?" he asked.

"All their property, for one thing, though for most of them that's just a little cash and maybe a vehicle. A lot of adoration and ego strokes. Power."

"And nothing he's doing is against the law?"

She shrugged. "As long as the people involved are competent adults and they hand over everything willingly, there's not a lot we can do."

"Which brings me back to my original question," he said. "Why are you here?"

She glanced around, as much to buy time to formulate her answer as to make sure they couldn't be overheard. "There are a lot of women and children here. We want to make sure there's no abuse involved."

He stiffened. "Have there been reports of abuse? Rumors?"

"No." She pressed her lips together. "It just seems the potential is there. We wanted to be sure."

"*We* being what organization? Child Protective Services?"

"No. The CPS is satisfied that everything is fine here." He had already pegged her as a cop—her refusal to acknowledge that hadn't changed his mind. Maybe it was better to let him know she had real authority behind her. "I work for the Ranger Brigade."

He considered this. "That's a federal group, right? Multi-agency take force working on public lands? I think I read something in the paper about you. But there can't be many people out here. Is there much crime?"

"You might be surprised. People think they can get away with a lot when there aren't many people around to watch."

"But you're watching," he said. "What crimes do you think Daniel Metwater and his bunch are committing?"

"Why should I tell you? I don't know anything about you."

"You know my name. You know I'm a veteran."

"What have you been doing since you were discharged from the Army?" she asked.

"I've been looking for my mother and my sister. And I just want to protect them. If you know something about Daniel Metwater that bears on that, please tell me."

The man was either an Emmy-worthy actor, or he was being straight with her. He had already had the chance to blow her cover and hadn't done so, and his concern for his mother and sister was genuine. Maybe he could even help her in some way, if she gave him a little more information.

"He hasn't done anything that we can link directly to

him," she said. "But he attracts the kind of people who bring trouble. A couple of weeks ago, we arrested a serial killer who was one of his hangers-on. Not a follower, exactly, but someone who visited the camp often and was close to Metwater. There have been other incidents around the camp." She shook her head. "I shouldn't even be talking about this. I'm on really thin legal ground here. The local DA has asked us to back off. Metwater's lawyers have accused us of targeting the group and harassing Metwater and his followers."

"But you're federal, right? You don't have to comply with the DA's orders?"

"Right. But we're trying to keep things low-key. I'm here to compile a census of the group and to make sure everything is above-board." Not exactly a dangerous undercover mission.

"And he was really harboring a serial killer?" He shook his head. "All the more reason to get Sophie and my mother out of here."

They had reached the turquoise and white vintage travel trailer Sophie shared with her mother. "I don't think your mother and sister are in any danger," Carmen said.

"You saw the way Metwater held Sophie. The guy's a creep."

"Yes. It was…unsettling. But as free as he is with the women in camp, I've never seen him make any kind of unhealthy gesture toward the children. And that includes Sophie. He refers to all the children as his own. And I'm watching him very closely."

Jake looked over the trailer. "So this is where they live?"

"It's really very comfortable inside," Carmen said. "I'm sure Sophie will be happy you came after her."

She started to turn away, but he touched her arm. "Will you come with me?"

The request surprised her. "I would have thought you wanted to see your sister alone."

He grimaced. "Until a few moments ago, we hadn't seen each other in four years. The last time I saw her she was just a little kid. Now…" He shrugged. "I'm not sure I know what to say to her. It might be less awkward with you along."

This was the first chink in his armor he had shown, and it touched her. "All right." Maybe hearing what he had to say to his sister would help her figure him out.

Jake knocked on the door, but there was no answer. "Sophie, it's me, Jake," he called. "Can I come in?"

The door opened, and Sophie peered out at them, her expression wary. "What do you want?" she asked.

"I just want to see you," he said. "It's been a long time."

She looked past him to Carmen. "All right," she said and held the door open wider.

The little trailer was crowded but neat, despite Sophie's schoolbooks scattered across the dinette table and the kitchen counter covered with jars of dried herbs, a bowl of the wild raspberries they had picked that morning and a tin can filled with purple and yellow wildflowers. "Are you okay?" Jake sat on a small sofa next to his sister.

"Sure." She shrugged. "I'm just worried about Mom."

"Has she fainted like this before?" Carmen asked.

"A couple of times—" Sophie worried her lower lip

between her teeth "—that I know about. And she's been tired a lot lately."

"When was the last time she saw a doctor?" Carmen asked.

"She doesn't believe in doctors," Sophie said.

"I'll talk to her and see what I can find out," Carmen said.

Sophie brightened. "That would be great. She won't say anything to me 'cause, you know, I'm just a kid."

"Did that guy, Metwater, upset you?" Jake asked.

Her expression clouded once more. "You upset me. Going all caveman and arguing over me like I was, I don't know, a dog or something. It was embarrassing."

Jake looked at Carmen, desperation in his eyes. "I wasn't trying to embarrass you," he said. "I didn't like the way he was holding you. I didn't think you liked it, either."

"I don't like him because he keeps saying he's my father now and stuff like that."

"He hasn't ever, like, touched you, um, inappropriately, has he?" The tips of Jake's ears were red, but he marshaled on. "You know what I'm talking about, right?"

"Yes, I know." Sophie looked miserable. "And he hasn't done anything like that. I'd call him on it if he did. I'm not afraid of him like some of the people around here."

"Why are they afraid of him?" Carmen asked.

"Well, maybe *afraid* isn't the right word. Mom is just in awe of him and thinks he really is this holy man. And he has those bodyguards he orders around to enforce his rules, so I guess that makes some people nervous."

"What kind of rules?" Jake asked.

"Oh, just stuff like you're not supposed to have guns in camp, and we don't eat meat on Mondays and Fridays—stuff like that. It's no big deal."

"What did Mom mean when she said Metwater had saved her life?" Jake asked.

"He got her off heroin. I thought you knew that."

"I wasn't sure she was off," Jake said.

"She is." Sophie looked around. "I mean, where is she going to score drugs out here? Anyway, the Prophet got her to quit, and he gave her her new name." She looked at Carmen. "She was Anna before. Now she's Phoenix. You know, that mythical bird that rose from the ashes. Mom loves that kind of thing."

"I take it Grandma and Grandpa don't know where you are," Jake said.

Sophie's eyes widened. "No, and you can't tell them."

"Why not?"

"Because the court awarded them custody of me, back when Mom was still doing drugs—right after you left to join the military."

Jake scowled. "Why didn't anyone tell me about this?"

"I don't know. I guess because you and Mom argued before you went away, and she figured you would side with Grandma and Grandpa against her."

"She was probably right," he said. "If you were with Grandma and Grandpa now, you'd be living in a real house and going to school and having friends your own age."

"And where would Mom be? If you make me go live with Grandma and Grandpa, she'll be all alone."

"Sophie, it isn't your job to look after Mom," he said. "She's supposed to look after you."

"She's doing that. We're fine here."

"Except you're hiding from our grandparents."

Sophie pushed her lips out in a pout. "I don't want to live with them. I want to stay with Mom."

"Then she should go to court and get legal custody of you. I could even help you with that."

Sophie looked skeptical. "Mom would never do that. She hates lawyers and cops and people like that."

"A lot of times people like that are on your side," he said. "Don't ever be afraid to go to the police if you need help." His gaze met Carmen's over the top of Sophie's head and a warm thrill ran through her. She really didn't want to like this guy as much as she was starting to—not when she still had so many unanswered questions about him.

"Promise me you won't tell Grandma and Grandpa we're here," Sophie said.

Jake looked stubborn. "Mom is breaking the law by keeping you here with her," he said.

"You don't understand!" Sophie's face twisted, the picture of teenage angst. "Mom needs me."

Carmen put a steadying hand on the girl's shoulder. "Your brother is just trying to understand the situation." She gave Jake a hard look. He needed to tone it down and stop putting Sophie on the defensive. "He wants what's best for you *and* your mom."

"Of course I do." His smile looked a little forced, but Carmen appreciated that he was trying. "I want you both safe and happy."

"We're safe and happy here."

Jake opened his mouth as if to argue but wisely thought better of it. Instead, he stood. "I'll come back to see you as soon as I can," he said.

"Promise?" Sophie's eyes were shiny, as if she was holding back tears. "You won't leave us again, will you?"

"No, I won't leave." He gave her a last, desperate look before leaving.

"Will you be all right here by yourself?" Carmen asked Sophie. "You can come stay with me if you like." The tent she had brought with her wasn't that big, but she would make room for the girl.

"Mom will be back soon." Sophie smoothed her hand over the seat cushion. "She's going to be all right, isn't she?"

"We'll make sure of it." Carmen gave the girl's shoulder another reassuring squeeze. She was so young and trying to be so strong. Carmen wanted to pull her into her arms and hold her tight, but she sensed Sophie would resist. After all, Carmen was a stranger to her, and the life she had led so far had probably taught her not to trust strangers. She wasn't even sure she could trust her brother.

"Will you talk to Jake?" Sophie asked. "Convince him that Mom and I are fine here. We don't want to go back to Grandma and Grandpa."

"Why don't you want to go back to them?" Carmen asked.

"Because Mom is happy here. Her old friends and the drugs and everything aren't here. She's safe here. I want her to be safe."

"I'll talk to him," Carmen said. "But I doubt he'll listen to me." Jake struck her as a man who made up his own mind, without relying on the opinions of others.

"He likes you," Sophie said. "That will make him listen."

Carmen might have argued with that but let it pass.

"You come to me if you need anything," she said and left the little trailer.

Jake was waiting outside, frowning at a couple of men who were watching him from beneath a tree across the clearing. "More of Metwater's goons?" he asked, as Carmen came up beside him.

Carmen studied the two shaggy-haired young men, boyfriends of a couple of the women she had met. "They're not part of his bodyguards," she said. "But they've probably heard you're not supposed to be in camp."

"Maybe I should hang around a little longer, to show Metwater what I think of his trying to order me around," he said.

"Don't." She gripped his arm. "You're not going to help your sister and mother by raising a stink like this. Let me handle this. I promise I'll make sure Phoenix and Sophie are all right."

His eyes met Carmen's, and the intensity of his look burned into her. "Looking after them isn't your job," he said. "It's mine. And it's my fault they're here right now. If I had stayed home, instead of leaving them to run off to the military, Sophie would be safe in Houston with our grandparents. She'd be enrolled in school and worrying about boys her own age, instead of living here in the wilderness with a phony prophet and his whacked-out followers."

"Or maybe things would be worse, and your mother would still be an addict or dead of an overdose." She faced him, toe to toe. "You won't accomplish anything playing the blame game."

He clenched his jaw. "You're right. But I'm not going

to let you or Metwater or anyone else keep me from looking after Sophie and my mom now."

"Where is Sophie's father?" Carmen asked.

"Who knows? He was another free spirit Mom hooked up with for a few months during one of the periods when I was living with my grandparents. He's a musician out in California—a real flake. I think he's seen Sophie twice in her whole life."

"That must be hard on her." Carmen saw her own father at least once a week.

"Probably, but you adjust."

The tension in his voice tugged at her. "Who was your father?" she asked.

"Another guy who ran out on her when she needed him," Jake said. "A high school classmate—apparently a senior who was headed to college. His plans didn't include her and a kid." He shrugged. "I never met him. Never wanted to."

Was that true? Carmen wondered. Surely a boy would want to know his father. Her own dad was an anchor in her life, a source of love and guidance and so many qualities that made her who she was. Being rejected by a parent must have hurt Jake deeply, even though he didn't show it. "None of you have had it easy, then," she said.

His jaw tightened. "We did all right. Most of the time. And I'm going to take care of Mom and Sophie now."

"There's nothing more you can do today," she said. "You should go before there's trouble."

"I'll leave camp—for now. But I promise, I'll be keeping an eye on this place—and on you."

He turned and stalked away, leaving her breathless

in the wake of this pronouncement, a feeling curling up from her stomach that was part fear and part attraction she really, really didn't want to feel.

Chapter Four

Jake hiked back to his camp in a secluded copse, just off a dirt road. The sun beat down, hot on the top of his head. A soft breeze brought in the smells of sage and pinion, and the trill of birds. Such a peaceful, idyllic scene. Some of Metwater's followers probably saw it as a kind of Eden. The Prophet no doubt painted it that way. But Jake sensed something rotten underneath all that beauty.

Carmen must have sensed it, too. He wasn't sure if he bought her story about being undercover in the camp to check on the conditions for the women and children. Why carry concealed if you were only doing a welfare check?

He hadn't made her as a cop when he'd first seen her, walking with the women. Did that make him sexist? Or was it only because his attraction to her had sidetracked his thinking? Her cool, reserved attitude intrigued him. He liked that she didn't rattle easily, and he'd be a liar if he didn't admit that her slightly exotic beauty added to her appeal. She was the type of woman he'd want guarding his back in a fight—and by his side in bed.

The odds weren't good either of those things would happen. Officer Redhorse didn't trust him—not even to look after his own mom and sister. Maybe her instincts were better than his, and she sensed he wasn't entirely leveling with her. But he had plenty of good reasons for keeping secrets just now.

In any case, he didn't have room in his life for a relationship right now—he hadn't had that kind of room for a long time. Before the army, family drama had stolen all opportunity to get close to anyone else. He'd been caught between his concern for his mom and sister, and his anger that they were always so needy. His mother was over forty, and she seemed incapable of looking after herself. She was always in trouble—trouble with creditors, trouble with the law, trouble with drugs.

Four years ago, he had told himself things weren't that bad. His leaving might even be the kick in the pants she needed to accept her responsibilities and get clean. When he had finally gotten over his anger enough to touch base with her, six months after he'd enlisted, he had been more annoyed than worried when he discovered she had left town. He told himself she would turn up again. She always did.

Then he had been deployed, and time had gotten away from him. It had taken him months after his discharge to find her, months during which he had decided he had been a coward for running out on Sophie the way he had. He had been so eager to escape his problems, he hadn't thought of anyone else. The knowledge hurt, like a punch in the gut. He wouldn't make that mistake again. He wouldn't let her down this time.

He approached the camp he had made in a secluded wash, screened from the road by a tumble of red and gray boulders and a clump of twisted pinions. He froze when he spotted the Jeep parked next to his pickup, secluded behind some trees. He doubted anyone had accidentally chosen that place to park. As carefully and soundlessly as possible, he reached back and eased the gun out of his pack, then unfastened the pack's straps and let it slip to the ground.

Unencumbered, he moved stealthily toward the camp, keeping out of sight behind the screen of boulders. Warmth from the rocks seeped into his palm as he braced himself to look through a gap into the camp.

An older man with a barrel chest, dressed in khaki shorts and a white, short-sleeved shirt that billowed over his big belly, bent over to peer into Jake's tent. When he straightened, Jake studied the jowled face with mirrored aviators perched on a bulbous nose. This guy was no cop—he didn't have that aura about him, and he was seriously out of shape. Jake could hear him wheezing from across the camp.

The man spotted the cooler that Jake had shoved deep into the shade of a pinion and waddled over to it and popped the top. Smiling, he pulled out a beer, condensation glinting on the brown glass. Nope, not a cop. Just a common thief. Jake rose from behind the rock, his gun trained on the intruder. "Put that back where you got it," he barked.

The man inhaled sharply, and the bottle slipped from his hand, shattering on the rock below, beer fountaining up and onto the man's hiking boots. He looked down at the mess, frowning. "Shame on you for making me waste a good beer," he said in heavily accented English. Was he German? Austrian?

"What are you doing in my camp?" Jake asked.

"I was looking around." The man was red-faced from too much sun, but he didn't look nervous.

"And you were helping yourself to my beer," Jake said.

"I was thirsty. Isn't that the rule of the outdoors—to always offer refreshment to a fellow traveler in need?"

Jake took a step closer, keeping the gun trained on the intruder. "You don't walk into someone's camp and help yourself. That's called theft."

The man spread his hands in front of him. "I did not mean to offend. Perhaps things are done differently here in the wild west of America." He nodded toward Jake's gun. "You are making me nervous, waving that around."

"Keep your hands where I can see them, and turn around."

The man hesitated. "Why do you ask this?"

"I'm not asking. Do it."

The man slowly raised his hands and turned to present his back. Jake moved from behind the rock and checked the man's pockets and waistband. No gun. He relaxed a little and lowered his weapon, though he kept it in his hand. "You can turn around now."

The man did so. Up close, he looked even older—close to sixty. "What are you doing out here?" Jake asked.

"I am on vacation."

"From where?"

"From Germany. Munich. I come to the United States every year."

Jake looked around at the austere landscape. Not the kind of thing he would expect a city guy from Munich to be attracted to. "Why?"

"I embrace the wild beauty of this land." The German spread his arms wide. "I find it endlessly fascinating."

"Really?"

He dropped his hands. "Also, I have a great interest in the flora and fauna of the American wilderness."

"Are you a botanist or something?"

"I am a hobbyist. My name is Werner Altbusser." He extended his hand, but Jake didn't take it. He didn't for a minute believe this guy was as innocent as he pretended to be.

"Where are you camped?" Jake asked.

If he had been on the receiving end of these questions, Jake would have told the guy his campsite was none of his business, but Werner had no such qualms. "I am staying in a motel in Montrose," he said. "I do not enjoy camping. And I realized when I was out here that I had not brought enough water with me, hence I was doubly glad to see your camp."

Werner hadn't just "seen" Jake's camp. Jake had made sure it wasn't visible from the road, and there were no nearby trails. "So you figured you'd wander over and take a look," Jake said.

"I hoped someone would be home, and I could ask for a drink."

Jake opened the cooler and took out a bottle of water. "Here you go."

If the German was disappointed not to receive a beer, he didn't show it. He twisted the lid off the water bottle and half drained it in one gulp. So maybe he was thirsty. Jake took out a bottle of water for himself.

Thirst slaked, Werner looked around the camp. "This is a remote location," he said. "What brings you here? Are you, like me, a lover of nature?"

"I have business in the area."

Werner's eyebrows arched in unspoken question, but Jake didn't elaborate.

"I met some other people camped in the area," Werner said. "A group of young people, who said they are part of a large family who live here."

Jake stiffened. Was he talking about Metwater's bunch? "Where did you meet them?" he asked.

"Oh, while I was out walking." He waved his hand vaguely. "Very nice young people." He grinned, showing white teeth. "Very pretty women. Do you know them?"

"No," Jake lied.

Werner drained the rest of the bottle, then crumpled it and set it on top of the cooler. "Thank you for the water. I will be going now."

Jake couldn't think of a good reason to detain the man. "Next time you come across an unoccupied camp, don't wander in and help yourself," he said. "The next person you meet might not be as understanding as me," he said.

"I will remember that." He gave a small bow, then turned and walked unhurriedly to the Jeep. After a few moments, the engine roared to life and trundled back to the road.

Jake waited until the vehicle was out of sight, then retrieved his pack and carried it into his tent. Out of habit, he checked the contents, searching through the spare shirt and socks, extra ammo, energy bars, sunscreen and water. But the item he was looking for wasn't there.

He upended the pack on his sleeping bag, and emptied out the side pockets as well, the sinking feeling in his stomach growing to Grand Canyon proportions. The folder with his credentials and badge were gone. Whoever had taken them now knew he was a Fish and Wildlife officer. His cover was blown before the sting had even begun.

Chapter Five

Starfall cornered Carmen after breakfast the next day. "Heard from Soldier Boy?" she asked, smirking.

Carmen started to pretend she didn't know who Starfall was talking about, but why play dumb? "I haven't heard from him," she said.

"Hmm." Starfall twirled one long curl around her index finger. "I was hoping he'd stop by today to visit."

"You know the Prophet told him he wasn't welcome here." Metwater had made a point after dinner last night of announcing that he wanted everyone to be more vigilant about keeping out uninvited visitors. He passed it off as a concern for the safety of the group, though he had specifically mentioned Jake as an example of someone who could disrupt the harmony of the group.

"Roscoe said he spotted a bunch of berry bushes south of here," Starfall said. Roscoe was the Family's mechanic. He made extra money by collecting rusting metal and the remains of cars that had been dumped in the wilderness, and selling them to scrap dealers in town. "Want to come pick with us this morning? If we get enough fruit, we can make jam."

Carmen actually liked picking berries. The weather was pleasant, the scenery beautiful and it was one of her best opportunities to mingle with all of the women and many of the children in the group. She was learning about their backgrounds and getting a good picture of their relationships to the Prophet and to each other. Though some of them looked a little more ragged and dirty than others, she hadn't found any real signs of neglect. A little more attention to schooling and health care would have been warranted, but she couldn't see that Metwater and his followers were breaking any laws. Another day or two, and she would have to wrap up her investigation and get back to more pressing matters, so she might as well make the most of the time she had left. "Sure, I'll come."

When the women assembled with their buckets and baskets, Carmen was surprised to see Sophie and Phoenix. "Are you sure you're well enough to be going out?" she asked Phoenix.

"I told her she should stay home and rest," Sophie said.

"I'm fine." Phoenix smiled. She looked pale but, then, she always looked pale. "And I like berry picking. I wouldn't want to stay behind and miss it."

"Come on, let's go," Starfall called. "I don't want to wait around all morning."

They set out, a motley collection of half a dozen women and an equal number of children. Some women had chosen to remain behind, including Asteria. But most enjoyed the opportunity to be away from camp, enjoying the nice weather. They found the raspberry bushes Roscoe had told them about, the thorny, fruit-laden canes clustered along the edge of a small canyon. Carmen began filling a plastic ice-cream bucket with the sweet, red fruit, careful to avoid the sharp thorns which continually caught and tugged on her clothes. She had worn jeans for the work and a billowing blouse that hid the gun tucked into her waistband.

Except for the gun, she was reminded of other berry-picking expeditions when she was a girl, with her relatives on the Southern Ute Reservation south of here. Aunt Veronica would try to scare them with stories about bears that would try to steal the fruit, and her mother would promise a reward for the child who picked the most berries. Smiling at the memory, Carmen paused to stretch her back and sample some of the juicy berries. She was sucking juice from her fingers when she noticed Starfall had moved away from the others and was searching the ground some distance away.

While most of the women had welcomed Carmen to the Family, Starfall had kept her distance. Carmen was still trying to figure out where the slight, curly-haired woman fit into the group dynamic. She wasn't one of Metwater's favorites—women who hovered around him at every meal and ceremony, like groupies around a rock star. She shared a tent with Asteria next to Metwater's motor home and had a little boy whose father had accompanied her to the Family, but who had left after less than a month. All this Carmen had learned from other women, not Starfall herself. There was something sly and grasping about the young woman that made Carmen always on edge around her—and curious to know what she was hiding.

She moved away from the berry pickers and toward Starfall. The other woman straightened at her approach. "What are you looking for?" Carmen asked.

Starfall swept her mass of curly, brown hair back from her forehead. "Do you know anything about cactus?" she asked.

"Not much." Her grandmother had taught her how to cook the green pads of prickly pear—removing the thorns and cutting the flesh into thin strips to sauté as a vegetable—but it wasn't one of Carmen's favorite dishes, and she doubted Starfall was interested in the recipe.

"I'm looking for this." Starfall thrust a piece of paper toward her. Carmen took the paper and studied it. Obviously printed from the internet, it showed a squat, barrel-shaped cactus with wicked-looking spines and a soft pink flower.

"Where did you get this?" Carmen asked, returning the paper.

Starfall folded the copy and tucked it in the pocket of her skirt. "I met a guy in town who said he'd pay me twenty bucks for every one of these I found and brought to him." She studied the ground again. "He said they grew around here, but they wouldn't have flowers this time of year."

"Isn't it against the law to take plants from public land?" Carmen asked. She knew it was, though enforcement was lax, considering the other crimes the Rangers had to worry about.

"This place is full of cactus," Starfall said. "Who's going to miss one?"

"Who was this guy?" Carmen asked, joining Starfall in searching the ground.

"Some old German. A tourist. He said he collects cactus. It sounded like an easy way to earn twenty bucks. But maybe not. I've been looking all morning and haven't seen any of these."

"Starfall!"

Sophie ran to them. "I think I found one of those cactus you're looking for," the girl said.

"Really?" Starfall brightened. "Show me."

Carmen followed the two of them to a spot near the canyon rim but away from the berry thicket. Sophie squatted down and pointed. "It's not very big," she said. "But it looks like your picture."

Starfall pulled out the paper and held it beside the cactus. "I think you're right." She patted Sophie's shoulder. "Thanks, honey." She straightened, then put up her hand to shield her eyes as she stared in the distance. A sly smile spread across her face. "Well, what do you know?"

Carmen followed the other woman's gaze and recognized the tall figure striding toward them, just as Sophie shouted "Jake!" and began running toward her brother.

Jake hugged Sophie, then the two continued arm in arm toward Carmen and Starfall.

"What are you all looking at?" he asked when he joined them.

"Why, you, Soldier Boy," Starfall said, while Carmen said nothing.

"Hello, Carmen," he said.

"Hello." She kept her expression and her voice cool. She still hadn't made up her mind how she felt about Jake. On one hand, she admired his devotion to his sister and mother, and his courage and determination to do the right thing. But he also struck her as quick-tempered and a little mysterious. She appreciated a strong man, but she didn't want to have to wonder if he was on the right side of the law.

"I told Mom you'd come back," Sophie said.

"Where is she?" Jake looked past his sister toward the other women, who had moved down the rim of the wash to pick more berries.

"I talked her into sitting down under a tree and resting." Sophie pointed to a shady spot where Phoenix sat. Just then, the older woman looked over to them, smiled and waved.

"How is she feeling today?" Jake asked.

"She says she's better." Sophie shrugged. "I guess she is. She came back to the trailer about suppertime and went straight to bed and slept all night, so maybe she was just really tired."

"Uh-huh."

"What brings you to see us, Soldier Boy?" Starfall lightly touched Jake's shoulder and smiled.

"I was out hiking and saw you all picking berries and thought it would be a good opportunity to visit with my mom and sister away from the camp."

"You're not afraid of the Prophet's enforcers, are you?" Starfall said. She squeezed his bicep. "You look like a man who knows how to handle himself."

Jake shrugged away from her. "What were you ladies looking at just now?" he asked.

"We were looking at cactus," Sophie said, ignoring Starfall's frown.

"What kind of cactus?" Jake focused on the ground where Sophie pointed.

"Starfall knows," Sophie said. "Show him the picture."

"I don't think so." Starfall hugged her arms across her chest. "Why don't you go back to your mother, and let us adults talk?"

Sophie pouted. "Jake's my brother. I want to stay with him."

Jake put his arm around her. "Sure, you can stay with me."

Starfall tossed her head. "I was hoping I'd run into you again soon," she said.

"Why is that?" he asked.

She glanced at Carmen. "I wanted to talk to you. Alone."

"You can say whatever you need to say here," he said.

Now it was Starfall's turn to pout. But Jake's expression sent the clear message that he wasn't budging. "I have something that belongs to you," she said. "Something I found when I was out walking yesterday."

He tensed, and it was as if the temperature around him dropped a few degrees. "What is it?" he asked, the three words sharp with anger.

Starfall twirled a lock of hair. "Something you wouldn't want to fall into the wrong hands."

"Give it back."

Sophie cringed at his sharp tone, but Starfall only laughed. "Oh no," she said. "If you want it, you'll have to pay for it. Or I could hand it over to the Prophet. He might be very interested in it."

"What are you talking about?" Sophie asked before Carmen could voice the question.

But neither Jake nor Starfall answered. They glared at each other, then his expression cooled, and he seemed to shrug off his anger. He turned his back to Starfall and squatted to get a closer look at the cactus. It was a clear dismissal. Starfall glared at him, hands fisted at her sides, and Carmen braced herself to pull the other woman off him if she decided to attack.

Jake had to be aware of Starfall's anger, but he continued to ignore her. "I think that's a Colorado hookless cactus," he said to Sophie.

Starfall glared at Carmen, then moved over behind Jake. "Don't you want to know more about this item I found?" she asked.

"Right now I'm more interested in this cactus."

"How does a guy like you know anything about cactus?" she asked.

"It's a hobby of mine."

"That's the same thing the guy said who asked me to find these for him," Starfall said. "Since when are cactus such a big hobby?"

Jake stood. "You might be surprised," he said. "Who was the guy?"

She opened her mouth to answer, but her words were drowned out by the loud *crack!* of gunfire. Granite shards exploded from a nearby boulder. Sophie screamed, and Carmen reached for her weapon but was shoved hard as Jake forced her and Sophie to the ground and then pulled Starfall after them. "Stay down," he ordered, even as he drew a gun.

Chapter Six

Jake fought to slow his breathing and control his racing heart as a second shot struck the dirt in front of the boulder he and the women were sheltering behind. Movement from an outcropping of rock fifty yards distant caught his eye, and he aimed his pistol and fired. No return fire came, and seconds later a car door slammed and an engine roared to life.

Staying low, he moved from behind the boulder and raced in the direction of the shooter's hiding place, cresting a small rise just in time to see the rooster-tail of dust that trailed the vehicle's retreat. Cursing his bad luck, he kept moving toward the rock outcropping where he thought the gunman had been positioned.

He had knelt to examine the area when the pounding of footsteps announced he was not alone. "It's just me," Carmen called before he could raise his weapon once more. She came around the largest boulder, holding her own gun and a little out of breath from running. "Did you get a look at the license plate?" she asked.

He shook his head and shoved his gun back in the waistband of his jeans. "No. And I didn't get a look at him, either." He picked up a stick and nudged a brass casing. "Some of these are still hot."

She moved in beside him, and he caught the clean herbal scent of her hair. "A .223-caliber," she said. "Probably an AR-15."

"That's what I thought," he said. "Pretty common ammo. Tough to trace."

He didn't have to look to know she was pinning him with the kind of gaze designed to make guilty suspects squirm. "What are you doing out here?" she asked.

"I'm here to get my sister and mother away from Metwater, to someplace safer and more suitable for a child."

"And you carry a gun to do it? And what did Starfall mean—she has something of yours? What is she talking about?"

He blew out a breath. He'd known this was coming. In fact, he'd planned to tell her as soon as he had clearance from his supervisors. There wasn't time for that now. He needed help, and she might be the only one he could turn to. He met her gaze with a hard look of his own. "Can I trust you?" he asked.

"I guess that depends on which side of the law you're on."

He liked that answer. "I'm on the right one. I'm a cop, too."

She sat back on her heels, her expression telling him she hadn't seen that one coming. But she recovered quickly. "Let me see your badge."

"That's the problem. I don't have it with me. Someone stole it out of my pack yesterday after I left Metwater's camp. I think it was Starfall."

"How did she manage to steal it out of your pack? What were you doing?"

He checked their surroundings to make sure they couldn't be overheard. Sophie and Starfall were back at the canyon rim, surrounded now by the other women. "Is Sophie okay?" he asked. He had been in such a hurry to pursue the shooter he hadn't had a chance to check on his sister.

"She's fine," Carmen said. "More excited than scared. Tell me how Starfall could have gotten your badge."

"I came back to my camp yesterday after I left you and found an old German guy rifling through my things. I took off the pack and left it on the ground so I could sneak up on him. Starfall must have followed me and gone through the pack while I was dealing with him."

"She said an old German guy was the one who wanted her to collect the cactus for him," Carmen said. "He told her he'd pay her twenty dollars apiece for them."

"They're worth hundreds on the collectible market. Even thousands."

Her eyes widened. "For one little cactus?"

"It's an endangered species. Collectors—especially in Germany and Japan—are fanatics about adding rare specimens to their collections." He stood and offered his hand. After a moment's hesitation, she took it, and he pulled her to her feet.

"Why didn't you show me your badge when I asked you for your ID yesterday?" she asked.

"Because I'm undercover and the fewer people involved the better," he said. "I'm a special agent with the Fish and Wildlife Service. I'm part of a team that has been tracking the German, gathering evidence. He's part of what we suspect is an international team of smugglers. We're hoping he can lead us to some of his partners. When he gets ready to leave the country, we'll confiscate his collection and file charges."

"Where do your mother and sister come in?"

"I volunteered for this job when I learned they needed an agent to come here and follow the German around. I had heard Sophie and my mom might be with Metwater, and this was the perfect opportunity to see if the rumor was true. I had a week's personal time saved up, so I took it before my duties started."

"Are you on the job now?"

"I wasn't supposed to start tracking my suspect for another two days, but obviously he's changed his itinerary and showed up earlier."

"When were you planning to tell the Ranger Brigade about your investigation?" she asked. "You can't operate in our jurisdiction without us knowing about it."

"That part is up to my supervisors, not me," he said. "Though I'm sure you'll tell your bosses about me now."

"I will, but not right away," she said. "Unless there's trouble, I only check in by phone when I can get close enough to town to get a signal."

"You're not worried, being out here on your own?" he asked.

"I told you, this isn't a high-risk assignment. I'm just observing, making sure everything is on the up-and-up with the women and children. Now about your suspect, is he the one who fired on us?"

"I don't know." He looked down at the shell casings again. "This really isn't his style. He hasn't shown any tendency toward violence before."

"And why would he shoot, if he's the one who offered to pay Starfall for the cactus he wanted?" she asked. "Then again, when there's money involved, even passive people can turn mean."

He nodded. "I need to go after him. But I need my

badge and credentials. I can't risk them falling into the wrong hands."

"Maybe you should just pay Starfall to give them back."

"I'm not exactly rolling in funds here, and I need the savings I have left to look after Mom and Sophie."

"So, what are you going to do?"

"I was hoping you would help me."

She folded her arms across her chest. "Do you want me to arrest her?"

"Wouldn't that blow your cover?"

"It would. But I'm about done here. I haven't found any evidence of mistreatment of anyone in the camp— by Metwater or anyone else. They aren't living the way most people would probably think is safe and hygienic and all that—but people always said the same thing about Native Americans, and they managed to survive okay." She flashed a smile, her teeth very white against her tanned skin.

"I could arrest her," he said. "But I'd rather use her contact with Werner—the German collector—to build my case against him."

"What do you want me to do?"

"I want you to steal my badge back."

She blinked. "How am I going to do that?"

"You live in that camp. You know where she lives. There can't be many places for her to have hidden something like that."

"And what are you going to do while I'm rifling through her belongings?"

"I'm going to distract her."

"How?"

He shrugged. "She's obviously been flirting with me. Maybe I'll let her think I'm interested."

Did he imagine the spark that fired her eyes at this suggestion? She looked away before he could be sure. "That would probably work," she said.

"Does that mean you'll help?"

"It's my duty to come to the aid of a fellow law enforcement officer." She spoke with a perfectly straight face, but he thought he caught a glimpse of teasing in her eyes.

"When do you think is the best time to do this?" he asked.

"Tonight. There's a bonfire at dark. Most people are away from their homes then. It would be easier for you to lure her away then, and easier for me to slip into her tent."

"I'll see you tonight, then."

She started to turn away, but he stopped her. "Have you had a chance to talk to my mom about coming with me?" he asked.

"No. She isn't going to listen to me."

He looked past her, toward where his mother and Sophie now sat together in the shade. "I'm going to talk to her. She should at least see a doctor."

"I agree that's a good idea," Carmen said.

A few of the berry pickers looked up when Jake and Carmen approached, but no one said anything as he joined his mother and sister in the shade. He sat beside Sophie and patted her hand. "Are you okay?" he asked.

She nodded. "Who was shooting at us?" she asked.

"I don't know. But they're gone now."

"Maybe it was a poacher who mistook you for a deer," Phoenix said.

Jake could have pointed out that he and the others with him in no way resembled deer or any other game animal, but he kept quiet. If it made his mother feel better to believe the shooting was an accident, he wasn't going to try to dissuade her.

"Too many people have guns who shouldn't," Phoenix said. She scratched her neck. "The Prophet is wise to ban them."

Jake ground his teeth together to keep from telling her what he thought of her Prophet. "How are you feeling today?" he asked instead. "Did something bite you?"

She stopped scratching. "It's nothing. And I'm feeling much better. I'm sure it was just too much sun yesterday. You see I'm being careful today. I'm staying in the shade and resting."

"Maybe you should see a doctor," he said. "Sophie said this wasn't the first time you've fainted recently."

"Sophie is like you—she worries too much."

"But Mom, I—"

Phoenix waved her hand to cut off her daughter's words. "I'm feeling a little hungry," she said. "Why don't you pick some berries for me?"

Jake could tell Sophie wanted to protest but, after a moment's hesitation, she rose. "I'll come with you," Carmen said and earned a grateful look from the girl.

Phoenix watched them leave. "Carmen is a good young woman," she said. "She has a very peaceful aura."

Jake wouldn't have described Carmen as *peaceful*. If anything, being around her made him feel more unsettled. "About the doctor, Mom," he prompted.

"I don't need a doctor. I don't trust them."

"If Sophie was sick, you'd take her to the doctor, wouldn't you?" he asked.

"Sophie is never sick. We live a very healthy life here. Much healthier than if we lived in the city."

"But you obviously aren't well. Well people don't faint for no reason."

"If you think you're going to use my health to try to take Sophie away from me, it isn't going to work." She shoved to her feet and stood glaring down at him. But even this stance failed to make her look strong. She was so small and pale she made him think of a child—or a ghost.

"I don't want to take Sophie away from you," he said gently. "I want us to all be together again. As a family." Not the pretend family Metwater had made in the wilderness but a real one where he could keep her and Sophie safe.

"I want us to be a family, too." She squeezed his hand, excitement lighting her eyes. "I'll ask the Prophet if you can come live with us here," she said. "I know you got off on the wrong foot with him, but I'm sure if you apologize and promise to work on controlling your temper, he'll allow you to stay."

He stiffened and struggled to conceal his annoyance. Hadn't she gotten the message that he didn't want anything to do with her so-called Prophet? "I don't want to stay here," he said. "I don't want to live in the wilderness or follow your Prophet. You need to be where you can have proper medical care—where Sophie can go to school and have friends."

Phoenix released his hand. "We can't leave here," she said. "We have to stay, for Sophie's sake."

"What do you mean?"

"While I was alone with the Prophet yesterday, he told me a secret." She wore a dreamy expression he knew too well—an expression that meant she was caught up in one of her fantasies that had little relation to reality.

"What are you talking about?" he asked.

"You have to promise not to tell Sophie. Not yet."

He said nothing, his eyes locked on hers, tensed for her next words.

"The Prophet told me he wants Sophie to be his wife," she said.

"She's only fourteen!" The words exploded from him and, as several of the others looked in his direction, he forced himself to lower his voice. "That isn't a good thing, Mother. That's one more reason to get her out of here. Why can't you see that?"

"Don't be so reactionary, Jake. He isn't going to marry her right away. He'll wait until she turns eighteen. In the meantime, she can begin studying, learning all the things she needs to know in order to be a good helpmate to him."

"The only thing she needs to learn is how to be a normal teenager. For a grown man to even think of a fourteen-year-old that way is sick."

"No, it's not," Phoenix insisted. "It's a great honor." Her expression grew dreamy again. "Imagine, my daughter married to such an important man."

"No." Jake wouldn't let it happen. Maybe it was too late to save his mother from Daniel Metwater's clutches, but he would protect his sister at all costs.

Chapter Seven

Flames leaped from the pyramid of dry logs, orange light painting eerie shadows across the faces and bodies of the men and women who danced around the bonfire to the hypnotic beat of a deerskin drum. Daniel Metwater, with his chiseled body stripped to a loincloth, and his muscular chest and back gleaming with oil, led the procession of dancers, head thrown back, eyes closed in an expression of either pain or ecstasy—Carmen couldn't tell.

She stepped farther into the shadows, wary of being seen and pulled into the line of dancers. Starfall wasn't dancing, either. Moments before, she had slipped away from the group around the fire, her figure merging with that of a man at the edge of the woods. Jake had shown up right on time—Carmen had recognized his broad shoulders and military stance, even in the dimness. She ignored the churning in her stomach at the sight of the two of them together. Jake was every bit as devious as Starfall, since he hadn't bothered to tell Carmen— a cop—that he was also law enforcement. And he had stormed off this afternoon after talking to his mother without saying good-bye to her or his sister. So, as far as she was concerned, he and Starfall deserved each other. The only reason she was helping him was because he was a fellow cop. She believed in loyalty to the badge, even if he didn't.

She hurried away from the fire, into the deeper shadows behind the tents and trailers. She moved carefully, guided by memory and instinct more than by the faint light from a quarter moon and the now distant glow of the fire.

The tent Starfall shared with Asteria showed pale in the darkness, a white cocoon illuminated from within by a battery-powered lantern that sat on a TV tray near the tent's entrance. The white-walled tent was the kind favored by hunting outfitters, tall enough to stand and move around in, and big enough to house a crowd for a meal or a poker game. The two women had furnished the space with colorful rugs, cots, a folding table and chairs, and a crib for Starfall's six-month-old son.

Carmen didn't spot a lot of potential hiding places in the sparsely furnished space. She switched off the lamp and made her way to Starfall's cot and dug a small penlight from her pocket. Shielding the light somewhat with her body, she swept the beam over the cot, stopping at the foot of the bed and the metal trunk that sat there.

A black-and-silver padlock secured the hasp of the trunk. Carmen tugged, but the lock held tight. She added *buy Starfall a new lock* to her list of things to do as she took out a penknife and went to work on the cheap security measure. The lock popped, and Carmen eased up the lid of the trunk.

The items Starfall felt the need to keep under lock and key were pitifully few—a small photo album with old pictures of people Carmen didn't recognize. Her son Hunter's birth certificate shared an envelope with a certificate for someone named Michelle Munson—probably Starfall's real name.

A tattered envelope held a faded Polaroid photograph of a little girl with a mass of brown curls—Starfall? With it was a postcard showing a beach scene on one side and a scrawled message on the other. *Hope you're being good for Aunt Stef. Love Mom.* Costume jewelry and old clothing filled most of the rest of the trunk. Carmen found a manila envelope tucked in the bottom, full of newspaper clippings. With a start, she realized the articles were about Daniel Metwater—not Metwater the Prophet, but Metwater the son of a wealthy industrialist. Carmen read through the first article—a description of the finding of his brother David's body. One sentence was underlined: *The body was identified by a distinctive tattoo on his left shoulder.*

Why would Starfall be so interested in articles about the Prophet's life before he began his preaching? Had she known his brother David? Or was it merely the case of a fan collecting every bit of information she could about her hero?

Carmen replaced the clippings in the envelope and tucked it back into the bottom of the trunk. She felt along the sides and in the lining of the lid, checking for any place Starfall might have hidden Jake's badge and law enforcement ID. She might have slipped it under one of the rugs or sewn it into a tent flap, but neither of those options seemed as secure as a locked trunk.

She replaced everything in the trunk and started to close the lid, then stopped and took out the photo album again. The pink, embossed cover of the album looked old—maybe something Starfall had inherited from someone. The hairstyles and clothing in the pictures inside dated from the 1990s and earlier. The only image Carmen recognized was the eight by ten photo that filled the album's last page. Starfall smiled out from the photo, which might have been a school photo from high school. Carmen turned the page over—it felt heavier and thicker than the others in the album.

She eased her fingers between the photograph and the album page and felt a surge of triumph as she brushed what felt like leather. Working carefully, she snagged the edge and dragged the item out. Bingo! The solemn face of Special Agent Jake Lohmiller looked out at her, across from a gold shield on the other side of the leather folder's crease.

"What are you doing in here, snooping through Starfall's things?"

She slipped the ID into the waistband of her jeans seconds before the flashlight beam lit her up. Pivoting on her heels, she glared at the man who had spoken and shielded her eyes with her hand. She could just make out a pale, bearded face and relaxed a little. "Starfall asked me to get something for her," she lied, rising.

"No, she didn't." The speaker, a lean, athletic blond who went by the name Reggae, lowered the flashlight and frowned at her. He was one of a handful of men who hung around the younger women, flirting and offering to do errands, though Starfall usually ignored him.

"Believe me or don't, I don't care." Carmen started to move past him, but he put out a hand to stop her.

"I saw her just now with that new guy—Phoenix's son," he said. "They looked pretty cozy." His scowl told her he wasn't pleased about this.

"Then what are you doing here?" Carmen asked.

"I was waiting for her to come back."

"Why? So you could spy on her and her new boyfriend?"

"You heard the Prophet. That guy isn't supposed to be here. I was going to warn her she could end up in trouble if she let him hang around."

"What kind of trouble?" Carmen asked. Metwater talked about "consequences" for people who disobeyed the rules but, other than kicking them out of the group altogether, what kind of power did he really have over these people?

"I don't know, but it can't be good. The Prophet might make her leave."

"I'll let her know you're concerned." She tried to move past him, but he grabbed her wrist, his grip surprisingly strong.

"Hey!" She tried to pull away, but he held her tight.

"What were you doing in here?" he asked. "And don't lie to me this time."

JAKE HAD NO trouble persuading Starfall to slip off into the woods with him. Was she so trusting, or merely overly confident of her own powers? "I want that badge," he told her when they were out of earshot of the crowd around the bonfire.

"I'm sure you do." She turned toward him and pressed her hand to his chest. "And I'll be happy to give it to you, but you'll have to pay me for my trouble."

"Is that why you took it?" he asked. "For money?"

She moved in closer, her body pressed to his. "I like knowing people's secrets," she said. "I especially wanted to know what makes you tick, Soldier Boy."

"So you went through my pack?"

"It was just lying there." She walked her fingers up his chest. "Finders, keepers."

"The man in my camp—was that the man who asked you to collect cactus for him?"

"What man?" She sounded annoyed. "I didn't see any man. I followed you because I wanted to talk to you. When I saw the pack, I decided to take a look, and I found the badge." She slid her hand around the back of his neck. "I never cared for lawmen before, but for you I could make an exception."

He pulled her hand away. His first instinct was to tell her he had no interest in thieves, but he didn't want to scare her off. He had to keep her occupied until Carmen could get out of the tent. Besides, this might be his best chance to find out more about Werner Altbusser. "How much do you want for the badge?" he asked.

She took a step back. "I figure it ought to be worth at least a thousand dollars to you."

"What if I decide to arrest you instead?"

"I'm a very good liar. I could convince your superiors that you planted the badge on me after I turned down your advances. After all, what competent law enforcement officer loses his badge?"

He winced, grateful she couldn't see him in the dark. He had the feeling this wasn't the first time she had played this particular kind of poker game. He had to be cautious about his next move. He wasn't going to pay her the money. And he wasn't going to arrest her. Doing so would possibly destroy the undercover operation he was assigned to—a project which his agency had spent a great deal of money and time putting together. He had pulled out every persuasive argument he could think of to keep his supervisor from taking him off the case altogether, when he had called in to report his encounter with Werner in his camp that afternoon. He had managed to convince his bosses that Werner saw him as just another camper, which would make it even easier for Jake to follow him. His supervisor had admitted they had no one else to put on the case right now, but Jake knew if he screwed up again he'd be out—ordered back to Texas and away from Phoenix and Sophie before he could do anything to help them.

Starfall was right—the embarrassment she could deal out to him might be enough to wreck his career.

"I thought the whole point of living in a group like this was that you don't need money," he said. "Everyone pools their resources, and the Prophet provides the rest."

She made a snorting sound. "Everyone needs money. And the Prophet provides what he wants us to have— not necessarily what we need."

"Why are you here if you don't embrace the lifestyle?" he asked.

"I'm getting what I need right now," she said. "And you might be surprised at the opportunities living like this provides a resourceful person."

"Like selling cactus to an old German?" He still hoped she would give him more information about Werner, but she didn't bite.

"Or selling a badge back to a lawman," she said.

"I don't have a thousand dollars on me."

"I can wait. But not long. Bring me the money tomorrow."

"All right. Tomorrow." With a little luck, Carmen would have the badge, and Starfall would be disappointed.

"In the meantime..." She moved in closer. "Sure you don't want to come back to my tent with me?"

"Don't you have a baby to look after?"

"He's staying with Sarah tonight." She smoothed her hand down his arm. "I told her I had plans."

"I'll walk you back, but I won't come in." He needed to make sure Carmen was safely out of there before he let Starfall go in.

"At least give me a chance to change your mind." She took his hand, and he let her lead him back into camp. The bonfire had dwindled to glowing embers, and the drum had long ago fallen silent. No one took note of them as they strolled toward the white tent.

They had almost reached the entrance to the tent when Starfall halted. "I always leave a light burning when I go out at night," she whispered.

"Maybe your roommate came back early and put it out."

"She wouldn't do that." She clutched his arm. "Someone's in there. Don't you see the movement?"

He did see movement. In fact, at that moment, the tent flap flew back, and two people tumbled out. They appeared to be struggling—fighting. Jake pulled a flashlight from his pocket and aimed the beam at the combatants. Carmen was holding onto a skinny blond dude, one arm bent behind his back. "Let me go!" the young man shouted.

"Reggae! What is going on?" Starfall raced forward.

At her approach, Carmen released the young man, who fell forward. She straightened. "Hello, Starfall. Jake."

"She was in your tent," the man said. "She was snooping around in there, and I tried to stop her."

"I was only getting that item you had in your trunk,"

Carmen said. "The one you needed me to retrieve for you." Her eyes met Jake's, and she gave an almost imperceptible nod. He felt muscles he hadn't even known he'd been tensing relax.

"I didn't ask you to get anything," Starfall said.

"The item you wanted to give to Jake." She lifted the hem of her shirt and pulled a leather folder from the waistband of her jeans and handed it to Jake.

He checked the folder—everything was in order. "Thanks," he said and pocketed the credentials. He wouldn't let them out of his sight again.

"You went through my things!" Starfall charged at Carmen, but Jake caught her around the waist and held her back.

"She took back something you had that didn't belong to you," Jake said.

"I didn't disturb anything else," Carmen said. "And I'll buy you a new lock."

"You can't just go through someone's things," the man—Reggae—said.

Starfall glared at Carmen. "You're going to be sorry you ever crossed me," she said, then shoved past her into the tent.

Reggae looked after her. "Maybe I should go in," he said. "And, you know, comfort her."

"Why don't you do that?" Jake said. He didn't care one way or another, but he wanted to get rid of the young man.

Reggae lifted the tent flap and ducked in after Starfall. Jake took Carmen's arm. "Let's get out of here while we can," he said.

She looked back over her shoulder as they moved away from the tent. "That didn't go so well."

"Not the best timing," he said. "Now that she knows I'm a cop, she might figure out you're one, too."

"It doesn't matter," she said. "I'm leaving here tomorrow. I didn't find anything useful and I need to get back to more pressing cases."

"Such as?"

She stopped and faced him, moonlight illuminating her face. "I want to help you with your case—if you still have one."

When her eyes met his, he felt a jolt in his gut that had nothing to do with being a cop, but he forced his mind back on work. "Why wouldn't I have a case?"

"Your cover is blown. As soon as Starfall figures out you're tracking Werner, she'll tell the German you're a cop."

"She could, but she's motivated by money. I'm thinking I can get my bosses to agree to pay her as an informant. We can use the evidence she provides to strengthen our case."

"That's taking a big risk," Carmen said.

"I don't think so. I think she's bored. The chance to play secret agent would appeal to her."

"The chance to get closer to you, you mean."

No missing the snide tone in her voice. He suppressed a smile. "Are you jealous?"

"Of course not!" She folded her arms over her chest. "I just know when another woman has her eyes on a man."

And who do you have your eyes on? he thought. "Why do you want to work with me on this case?" he asked.

"If this plant theft and smuggling is on public land, the Rangers should be involved anyway," she said. "In fact, we have an agent working on plant smuggling in the national park."

"We know about that investigation, and that isn't related. This is bigger—international."

"I still want to help you."

"Why?"

"Because I think it's important. And because, if Starfall is involved, she'd give me a remaining link to Metwater's group. I can't be undercover here anymore, but I still want to keep an eye on things. And you'll give me another link through your mother and sister."

"They both like you a lot," he said. "Even if you stop pretending to be one of the Prophet's faithful, I hope you'll help me persuade my mom to leave here. I think she'll be more inclined to listen to you."

"Maybe not, when she figures out I'm a cop. But I'll do my best to continue to be her friend. And your sister's, too."

"And me?" He moved in closer.

"I'm still trying to figure you out," she said. She rested a hand on his shoulder. "I'm not sure I trust you."

"You can trust me." He slid his arm around her and snugged her closer. "Give me time to prove how much."

She tilted her head up, and he brushed his lips across hers. When she made no protest, he deepened the kiss. She held herself very still at first, as if waiting for him to prove himself. He slid one hand beneath the heavy fall of her hair and savored the heat of her body against his, the softness of her mouth and the earthy, herbal scent of her. The tension left her, and she angled her mouth more firmly against his and tightened her hand on his arm, keeping him with her, though he indicated no desire to leave. She kissed him the way he had seen her do everything else—with strength and confidence and a command of the situation that took his breath away.

She broke off the kiss but held him with a steady gaze. "I'll give you a chance to prove I can trust you," she said.

"You won't be sorry," he said as she stepped away.

"I hope not. Just remember—I don't give second chances."

She walked away. He stared after her until she was no longer visible in the dark, feeling as if he had just been sucker-punched—and wanting to be hit again.

Chapter Eight

Carmen made it back to Ranger headquarters the next morning in time for the commander's briefing. She had packed up her tent and slipped out of camp without saying good-bye to anyone, though she'd left a note, taped to the door of Phoenix's trailer, saying she had decided to go back home but that she hoped to stay in touch. She planned to keep her work as part of the Ranger Brigade secret for as long as possible, since she still hoped to visit the camp to check on Phoenix, Sophie and the others. Once Daniel Metwater and his followers learned she was a cop, he would try to keep her from what he saw as interference with their way of life.

It felt good to be back in uniform, seated at her usual place to the commander's left in the utilitarian conference room. "Welcome back, Sergeant Redhorse," Commander Graham Ellison said after he'd called the meeting to order. "I think we should start with your report."

"To summarize—I didn't find anything actionable at Daniel Metwater's camp," she said. "No signs of abuse or neglect. As far as I could determine, the children and pregnant women in the camp aren't receiving any kind of regular medical care—which we already suspected.

But they all appear to be healthy." She frowned, remembering Phoenix's fainting spell and unnatural paleness.

"Why do I sense an 'except' at the end of that statement?" the commander asked.

"There was one incident while I was there—a woman named Phoenix fainted. She didn't look well but insisted she was fine." She shrugged. "You can't force an adult to see a doctor, and I didn't get the sense that Metwater would prevent her from going to a clinic if she wanted to."

"And Andi Mattheson seemed fine to you?" Agent Simon Woolridge asked this question. He had been Carmen's biggest supporter when she had suggested the undercover investigation. A former Emergency Medical Technician, he suspected the young woman who now went by the name of Asteria might be suffering from diabetes or some other complication of her pregnancy and felt the Rangers should intervene.

"She seemed fine," Carmen said. "Though she spent most of her time closeted with Metwater."

"We'll keep an eye on things in the camp, as usual," Graham said. "But for now, we'll turn our attention to other matters."

"Something else did come up while I was at the camp," Carmen said. "It's not related to Metwater. Only peripherally to one of his family members." She was about to tell them about Jake and his investigation into cactus smuggling, when a knock on the conference room door interrupted her.

"Come in," Graham called.

One of the administrative assistants stuck her head around the door. "There's someone from Fish and Wildlife here to see you," she said. "He says it's urgent."

"Then you'd better show him in," Graham said.

Carmen wasn't surprised to see Jake Lohmiller step into the conference room. But the sight of him in uniform did give her a jolt. The man she'd first met as a slightly scruffy camper in the backcountry was now the picture of a spit-and-polish officer of the law, from his clean-shaven face and freshly trimmed hair to the gleaming toes of his boots. The combination of authority and sex appeal unnerved her a little more than she wanted to admit.

"Hello." He nodded to the officers gathered around the conference table. "I apologize for interrupting your meeting, but I didn't think this could wait." He stepped toward Graham, who had risen to greet him, and offered his hand. "Special Agent Jake Lohmiller, Fish and Wildlife."

"Graham Ellison, Ranger Brigade." The two men shook hands. "What can we do for you, Agent Lohmiller?"

"I'm working an undercover operation, shadowing a German tourist who is suspected of smuggling thousands of dollars of rare cactus out of the country for sale to collectors in Europe," Jake said. "It's a sensitive case we've been building for more than a year."

"We've had some trouble with plant smugglers in the national park." Lance Carpenter, the Montrose County Sheriff's representative on the Ranger Brigade task force, spoke up. "Not cactus, but ornamental plants. A local landscaper was digging them up without a permit and offering them for sale to customers."

"This case has a much bigger scope," Jake said. "These stolen cactus go to hobbyists, primarily in Germany and Japan, who will pay a premium for wild-gathered rare species. We know, for instance, that this

German is targeting the Colorado hookless cactus, which is on the endangered-species list. Its scarcity makes it a prize for collectors. We believe the man I'm following is a fairly low-level player in an international smuggling ring."

"What do you need from us?" Graham asked.

"I've learned that the German is paying locals to dig the cactus for him. If they're caught, they pay the penalty, while he gets away. My assignment is to shadow the German, so I'm asking your help in making contact with these locals."

"Why weren't we made aware of this investigation before now?" Graham asked. Several heads around the table nodded. The Rangers were responsible for law enforcement on public lands, but not every agency believed in sharing information about their cases.

"The fewer people who know about an undercover investigation like this, the safer for everyone," Jake said. "The idea was that I would follow the German and document his activities for the few days he's supposed to be in the area. I'd be in and out before you even knew I was here. But that was before this new development. I contacted my supervisor this morning, and he is supposed to be getting in touch with you."

Graham could have insisted he needed to wait to speak to Jake's supervisor before he agreed to help the Fish and Wildlife agent. Carmen resisted the urge to confirm that his story was legitimate—then she would have to explain how she knew him and why she hadn't mentioned him and his case before now. Never mind that she had been about to tell all before Jake interrupted—it still looked bad.

"I can spare someone for a few days," Graham said.

"Lance, since you worked on the other plant-theft case, you can work with Deputy Carpenter."

Carmen ordered herself not to react. Yes, she had wanted to work with Jake on his case, but saying so now would only arouse suspicion about her motives. Since when was she so interested in cactus? And, since every time she and Jake looked at each other she imagined sparks arcing between them, her co-workers might pick up on that. It was tough enough being the only woman on the team, without confirming any suspicions any of the men might have that she was ruled by her emotions. She was as tough as any of them when a case got difficult, but some men always had doubts, and she didn't want to do anything to strengthen those.

"If you don't mind, I'd prefer a woman for the job," Jake said. He avoided looking at Carmen, though she felt as if every other eye in the room was on her. *Way to be subtle*, she thought.

"Why is that?" Graham asked.

"The person the German has contacted to dig cactus for him is a woman. She lives with a group that's camping in the Curecanti Recreation Area—they call themselves *the Family* and are some kind of commune or something."

While the ability to lie was a good talent to have for undercover work, Carmen couldn't help thinking Jake was a little too good at it. What was wrong with admitting he knew Metwater and his followers? Or was it simply ingrained in him to never reveal more information than he had to? Whatever the reason, it didn't make him any easier to trust.

"Or something," Simon muttered.

"I think a female officer would have better luck getting this woman to confide in her," Jake said. "If we could persuade this woman to work with us, we could build a stronger case against the German."

On the outside, Carmen was Jane Cool, but inside she was groaning and covering her face with her hands. No one was going to believe that, were they?

"You're going to a lot of trouble to nail one plant collector," Simon said. "Why?"

"He may be only one man, but we suspect in the past year he's shipped over two thousand specimens, many of them rare and irreplaceable, out of the country," Jake said. "Some species have already been wiped out in the wild by similar collectors. My agency wants to send a strong message that this kind of destruction of resources won't be tolerated. In addition, if he can lead us to the dealers he supplies, we already have agreements in place with law enforcement in Europe that could enable us to shut down the market for these cactus."

"Officer Redhorse, do you have any objection to working with Agent Lohmiller?" Graham asked.

Yes, because the man tells the truth only when it's convenient, and he's too sexy for his own good, and I have a hard time keeping my mind solely on the job when he's around. She cleared her throat. "No, sir. It sounds like an interesting case."

"Officer Lohmiller, if you'll wait in the other room until we're done here, you can meet with Officer Redhorse," Graham said.

"Of course." He looked at Carmen at last. She hoped she was imagining the wink he gave her—and that no one else around the table had seen it.

The commander waited until the door had closed behind Jake, then returned to his seat at the head of the table. Carmen held her breath, hoping he wouldn't ask her if she had known about Jake and his cactus-smuggling case. She would have to admit the truth, and that would look very awkward.

"What were you saying before our interruption?" Graham asked.

She blinked. What had she been saying?

"Something else that happened while you were undercover in Metwater's camp," he prompted.

Right. She'd been about to tell them about Jake. But she couldn't do that now without looking guilty of something. Which she wasn't. She searched her mind for anything else plausible she could say and settled on the other curious thing she had made note of last night. "One of the women in camp, who goes by the name Starfall, has a big file of newspaper clippings about Daniel Metwater—not his writings as a prophet or anything like that, but articles about his life before he decided to wander in the wilderness. Quite a few of the articles are about his brother's death."

"The brother who was murdered," said the man next to Carmen, Marco Cruz with the DEA.

"Right," she said. "The police in Chicago suspected a hit by organized crime but weren't able to pin the murder on anyone."

"Why is this woman so interested?" Simon asked.

"I don't know," Carmen said. "But I thought it was odd. Something worth adding to the other information we have about Metwater and his group." And probably not worth bringing up, if she hadn't needed something to answer the commander's question.

"Be careful around the minnow Mountie," Simon said.

She stiffened at Simon's use of the slang term for a Fish and Wildlife officer. "Why do you say that?"

"I think it's suspicious that he didn't want to involve us until he needed help," Simon said. "And asking for a woman, when you were clearly the only woman in the room—I think he's up to something."

"Come on, Simon, would you want to work an undercover op with Lance, when you could have our resident beauty queen as your partner?" Marco asked.

Carmen tensed. Last month her mother had mailed a package to the office that included the crown and sash from her brief stint as Miss Southern Ute—a not-so-subtle reminder of Carmen's place in the tribe and part of an ongoing campaign by her parents to encourage her to leave the Ranger Brigade and sign on as a member of the Ute Tribal Police. She had made the mistake of opening the box in front of some of the guys, and now she might never hear the end of it. Carmen had even wondered if the teasing had been part of her mother's plan, too. Wilma Redhorse was a sharp attorney and a brilliant strategist, so Carmen wouldn't put it past her mom to foresee this development.

"Some people might consider that a sexist remark," Graham said.

Marco sent her an apologetic look. "No offense intended."

"I don't take offense," she said. "I take revenge."

"You're in trouble now," Lance said.

"I think we've said enough on the topic." Graham consulted the notebook in front of him. "Just a few updates on current cases to take care of…"

Carmen turned her attention back to the commander,

but part of her mind was on the case ahead and the con-
founding, intriguing man she'd have to work with. Even
though Jake made her uncomfortable, his case and its
environmental and international implications interested
her. This was the kind of case she had joined the Ranger
Brigade to work on—something much bigger than keeping order on her family's reservation. Why couldn't her
mother see that?

Half an hour later, Carmen stood with Jake in the
parking lot behind Ranger headquarters, next to a battered and very dusty pickup truck, the bed piled with
camping gear. "This definitely doesn't look like an of-
ficial vehicle," she said.

"That's the idea."

She nodded toward the headquarters building. "Was
all that really necessary in there? You couldn't have
told the truth—that we met at Metwater's camp and
you thought I could be useful to your case?"

"I wasn't sure you'd want your co-workers knowing
we'd met before. After all, I'm the untrustworthy Cactus Cop."

His teasing tone almost made her smile—almost. But
she wasn't about to let him think she was going soft. "I
hope you don't really think I'm going to persuade Starfall to do anything for you—she hates my guts."

"I have faith in you."

"You don't need me to persuade her—make her think
you've fallen for her charms, and she'd probably do anything for you."

"Then maybe you can make her think agreeing to help
me is the best way to catch my attention."

"I'd be better off persuading her you're going to pay

her a lot of money. The woman is seriously motivated by cash. When I was going through her trunk, searching for your badge, I came across a couple of things that made me wonder if she was holding other people's property hostage. Or blackmailing them." For instance, was there something in those articles she had collected about Daniel Metwater that she was using to blackmail the Prophet? She was the one woman in camp who didn't fawn over him, and yet she seemed to hold a position of privilege. It might be worth looking into…

"I'll leave it up to you to decide how best to approach Starfall." Jake brought her attention back to his investigation. "Whatever you can find out about her relationship with the German could be helpful, but I hope you'll also try to persuade my mom that she and Sophie need to leave Metwater's group—the sooner, the better."

"You left in a hurry yesterday afternoon," she said. "And Phoenix wouldn't say anything when I asked if the two of you had had a nice visit."

"She told me that Daniel Metwater told her that he wants to marry Sophie!" His voice strained with agitation. "What kind of man says that about a fourteen-year-old?"

"Do you think she was telling the truth?" Carmen asked. "I mean, I'm not saying your mother is a liar, but that seems so preposterous."

"She said he intends to wait until Sophie is eighteen, but in the meantime she can prepare to be his *help-mate*." His look of disgust mirrored her own emotions. "I have to get her out of there," he said. "And I need to get Mom away from there, too, if I can. I stopped by to see her this morning, and she was still in bed—Sophie said she was resting, but when I saw her, she looked ill. They told me you'd left and showed me your note. That's when I decided to come to Ranger headquarters and plead my case."

"Did you really talk to your supervisor and ask him to bring me in?"

"Yes. I do sometimes tell the truth, you know. Most of the time, actually."

"All right. I'll talk to Starfall, but don't expect much. And I'll talk to Phoenix, too. If she really is ill, maybe I can persuade her to visit the clinic in town. And I'll try to find out more about this marriage proposition of Metwater's. If she still thinks I'm one of his followers, she might give me more details."

"That's what I'm hoping. When you talk to Starfall, make her think I really need her help."

"Or maybe I should tell her she shouldn't trust you as far as she can throw you."

The barb earned her a smile that sent heat curling through her. "You only say that in a feeble effort to resist my charms."

Flirting with him was too dangerous, so she focused on the job. "What are you going to do while I'm back in Metwater's camp?" she asked.

"I'm going to follow Werner Altbusser."

"Where is he right now?"

He checked his watch. "He told his waitress at breakfast this morning that he was going to spend the day at a local hot springs and spa. Apparently, smuggling endangered species is stressful, and he needed a break. I double-checked, and he had an appointment for a day full of treatments. Just in case he didn't show up or decided to leave early, I charmed the attendant at the spa into giving me a call. I told her he was my uncle, and I was planning a surprise party for him."

"And she believed you?"

"I can be very convincing."

She bet he could. One smoldering look from those blue eyes and a roguish smile, and the poor attendant had probably been weak at the knees. "Are you sure he's not just an ordinary tourist on vacation?" she asked, a little more sharply than she had intended.

"We've got video of him pocketing thousands of dollars' worth of rare cactus in four different states."

"Then why not arrest the guy now? Why go to all the trouble and expense of following him, when you already have plenty of evidence?"

"One count of plant theft doesn't carry much weight. The more evidence we can gather against him, the better chance we have of getting jail time and a really big fine—enough to make similar criminals take note and maybe think twice. And we still hope he can lead us to the really big fish—the dealers who purchase his finds."

"Carmen?"

She turned to see DEA agent Marco Cruz striding toward her. The muscular Latin officer wore a grim expression that immediately put her on alert. "What is it, Marco?"

He stopped in front of them. "We just had a report come in of a dead man in a tent over in the South Rim campground. He was reportedly shot in the back of the head."

"I guess a murder investigation trumps my plant case," Jake said.

"This might be part of your case," Marco said. "Supposedly, this guy had a whole backpack full of cactus in his vehicle."

Chapter Nine

Carmen stared down at the body of the young man she had known only as Reggae. He lay on his side a few feet off the trail, a faded, blue pack at his back.

"That's not my guy." Jake moved in behind her.

"No." He wasn't the German smuggler. He was just a kid who was searching for a place to belong. So why was he lying here dead?

"He doesn't have any ID on him." Marco said. He had brought Carmen and Jake here from Ranger headquarters. "Ethan thought he looked like the type who'd hang around Metwater."

"He was one of Metwater's followers," Carmen said. "He went by the name of Reggae." She squatted down for a closer look. His face in death looked very young and surprisingly peaceful. A small black hole above his right temple was the only sign of violence.

"A .22-caliber, close range." Marco crouched beside her and pointed to the wound. "You can see the powder burns."

"You said that pack is full of cactus?" Jake asked.

"Right." Marco stood. "No identification, no food or clothes or camping equipment, just an old garden trowel and about two dozen cactus plants."

"Mind if I take a look?" Jake asked.

"Go ahead." Marco glanced at Carmen. "Simon and Ethan processed the scene, since you were tied up with him." He jerked a thumb toward Jake, who was already kneeling beside the pack.

She nodded. As a member of the Colorado Bureau of Investigation, she usually took lead in processing crime scenes, but all the Rangers had the experience and training to handle the job. She turned to Jake. "Are those the cactus your collector is interested in?" she asked.

"Not the rare ones he asked Starfall to find for him. There are a few that might bring in a few bucks, but most of them are too common for Werner and his buyers to be interested in." He opened his palm to display a golf-ball sized round cactus, covered with hairy, pinkish spines. "If Werner hired this guy to gather specimens for him, he either didn't give him very good instructions, or Reggae ignored him."

"Maybe he wasn't working for Werner." Carmen stood also. "He was always hanging around Starfall, trying to impress her. Maybe he heard she was looking for cactus and thought gathering a bunch would be a good way to catch her attention." She glanced down at the dead man again and fought back a wave of sadness. Reggae had been trying to do something sweet for a woman he liked, and the gesture may have cost him his life.

"Any ideas who killed him, and why?" Marco asked.

"It wasn't Werner." Jake closed the pack and dusted off his hands. "He wouldn't want to call attention to himself, especially for a bunch of plants he couldn't use."

"A rival smuggler?" Marco asked.

Jake shook his head. "We haven't heard of anyone

else operating in this area but, even if they were, why kill a dumb kid over plants you can't use?"

"Maybe it was a warning for Werner and his people to stay out of the rival group's territory," Carmen said.

Jake looked skeptical. "I'll check with my office, but I'm pretty sure we haven't heard of any other smugglers active in the cactus trade internationally. Werner and the few people he worked with have made a name for themselves with buyers."

"Maybe someone new is trying to take over the operation," Marco said. He looked down at the dead young man. "This doesn't have the feel of a random shooting. More like a deliberate hit."

"Do we have any witnesses?" Carmen asked. "Did anyone hear or see anything suspicious?"

"No one has come forward," Marco said. "The hiker who found the body called it in about two hours ago. The medical examiner estimates time of death at around five hours ago. He'll have a better estimate for us after the post mortem, but it rules out the guy who called it in. Five hours ago he was having breakfast in Montrose with three friends."

"Five hours ago would make it about seven a.m.," Jake said. "Werner was at his motel then. Somebody was out and about early."

"We'll have to talk to Metwater," Carmen said. "Try to find out Reggae's real name, and if he has any family."

"Metwater will swear he doesn't know anything," Marco said.

"We need to talk to Starfall, too," Jake said. "I want to know who she told about her cactus-selling sideline. And I want to find out if she knew what Reggae was up to."

"We'd better double-check where Werner was this

morning," Carmen said. "In case he does have something to do with this."

"I'll stop by the spa and confirm his appointments," Jake said. He checked his watch. "I'll need to call my supervisor and report this latest development. Even if it's only coincidentally linked to my case, he'll want to know."

"We'll try to track down the people who signed the trail register this morning and question them," Marco said. "There are only three names, and one of them is the man who found the body."

"Who is he?" Jake asked.

"A geology professor from Ohio," Marco said. "He's completely freaked out about this."

"Maybe Reggae has an enemy we don't know anything about," Carmen said. "Someone from his past who tracked him down and decided to kill him."

"Let's hope Metwater or someone else in camp can tell us Reggae's real name, and we'll dig deeper into his background," Jake said.

"What should we do with the cactus?" Marco asked.

"Hold on to them as evidence until we're sure they have nothing to do with my case," Jake said.

"And if they don't?" Carmen asked.

He shrugged. "Usually we destroy them. Most of them wouldn't live if replanted. Cactus look hardy, but they're pretty difficult to transport and grow—another reason viable specimens are so valuable."

"So the murdered man collected the wrong type of cactus and ended up dead," Marco said. "Maybe because he made an enemy, and maybe because he was simply in the wrong place at the wrong time."

"Maybe the person who killed him was upset about

the cactus theft itself," Carmen said. "A militant environmentalist."

"Those groups usually try to send a message and make a public statement," Marco said. "Killing one guy on a remote trail doesn't get them the kind of attention they want."

"It's worth checking into," Jake said. "But I agree, this doesn't fit that kind of scenario. To shoot a man up close, on a remote trail, feels personal."

"So we need to find out who wanted Reggae dead," she said. "And why."

"It could be because of something Reggae did," Jake said. "Or because the killer wanted to send a message to someone close to him."

"What kind of message?" she asked.

"I'd say when someone is killed, the message is almost always, *watch out—you could be next.*"

JAKE LEFT CARMEN with the crime-scene team and drove back to Montrose to check on Werner at the spa and to report in to his boss. He had agreed to pick Carmen up in a couple of hours on his way back to Metwater's camp.

Werner Altbusser was dozing under a mud mask, his rotund figure swathed in seaweed, when Jake looked in on him at the spa. The attendant reported he had been at the facility since eight that morning.

"I would have called if he left early," she said, her lips forming a pretty pout. "Don't you trust me?"

"This way I get to see you again." The words rolled off his tongue, but he felt guilty as soon as he said them. Flirting was second nature to him, especially when it netted information he wanted. But he could almost see Carmen frowning and shaking her head, dismissing him as shallow and manipulative. He shrugged off the image. He was doing his job, and who was she to judge him, anyway?

He called his supervisor, Resident Agent-in-Charge Ron Clark, from the parking lot of the spa and made his report. "I met with the Rangers, and they've assigned an agent to work with me on the local angle," Jake said. "Werner isn't collecting today—I get the impression he's waiting for something. Maybe he's expecting someone else to arrive—one of his fellow hobbyists." That was how the smugglers always characterized their activities, as an innocent hobby.

"Or he's lying low because he's worried about you." Agent Clark, a forty-year veteran who wore his cynicism as a badge of honor, had already lectured Jake about screwing up years of investigative work when he confronted Werner in his camp. Jake figured he was in for round two and braced himself for another tirade. But his boss kept his words brief. "We're pulling you off the case. We're sending another agent in this afternoon to take over the tail."

"I thought you said you didn't have anyone else to work the case," Jake said.

"A field agent from Grand Junction, Tony Davidson, has agreed to take over for the moment. You can return to Texas."

Being pulled from the case was bad, but being ordered back to Texas before he had had time to help his mother and Sophie was a disaster. "There's been another development that may be related to our case," Jake said. "A young man was murdered in the wilderness area where Werner was collecting yesterday. He had a backpack full of cactus. He may have been working for Werner."

"Why was he killed?" Clark barked the words.

"That's what we need to find out. I was going to head out this afternoon to question some people who knew the young man. He's a local, and part of the hippie group I was telling you about. He's a friend of the young woman Werner hired to collect for him, so it's possible Werner hired this young man, too. His killing could be the work of a rival smuggling group or a radical environmental group."

"Is that what the Rangers think? Are they aware of such groups operating in the area?"

"All they'll tell me is that they're considering a number of possibilities. You know how these other agencies are—very closemouthed. I think if we're going to learn anything useful, I really need to stay here as a part of their investigative team."

He held his breath, gripping the phone so tightly his fingers ached.

"All right." Clark sounded tired. "I can spare you for a few more days. Adding murder to the list of charges against Werner would lend some serious weight to our case."

"That's what I thought, sir." He didn't really think the German had anything to do with Reggae's death, but he would play up any possible link to gain more time to work on his mom. If he had to, he could turn her in to the local cops for violating Sophie's custody order, then he could take Sophie back to their grandparents. But he wanted to help his mom, not hurt her more. He wanted to persuade her and his sister to come with him willingly. She could get the medical help she needed, and the three of them could start rebuilding their family.

Also, he wasn't ready to leave Carmen Redhorse just yet. The strong, sexy sergeant had awakened something in him he had thought long dead—the desire to be with someone not just physically but also as a part of her life. He wanted more time to see where those feelings went and decide what he should do about them.

He picked her up at Ranger headquarters. As she slid into the front seat of his pickup, the intoxicating aromas of beef, onions and spices hit him, and his stomach growled. "Have some lunch," she said, handing him a foil-wrapped packet.

"What is it?" he asked, leaving the vehicle in Park and unwrapping the foil, inhaling the amazing scents.

"Indian taco." She unwrapped her own packet, then handed him a plastic fork. "You'll probably need this."

He took a forkful of the bean-and-meat mixture and all but moaned at the taste. "Did you make this?" he asked after he'd swallowed.

She shook her head. "My mom. She stopped by with enough for the whole office."

"If she does this regularly, you must be the most popular person on the team." He took another bite. "Amazing!"

"She's convinced I'll wither away without home cooking. And she likes to remind me what I'm missing by not moving back home to the reservation."

"She really wants you to move home? And do what?"

"Work for the tribal police." She stirred the fork around her taco but didn't take another bite. "She thinks I should be using my education and training to help my people the way she and my dad did—she's a lawyer, and my dad has served on the tribal council."

"Sounds like a lot of pressure," he said.

She drank from a bottle of water and nodded. "My family has always had high expectations. When I was a kid, I didn't dare screw up. It wasn't allowed."

"My family had no expectations at all for me," he said. "It didn't matter what I did." Though in some ways that had felt freeing when he was younger, he had felt the lack of anyone rooting for—or even expecting him—to succeed.

"You seem to have done all right for yourself," she said. "Military veteran. Cop. Your mom should be really proud of you."

"I'm not so sure about that," he said. "Cops aren't her favorite people and, as a pacifist, she doesn't much approve of the military."

"So why did you go that route—army, then Fish and Wildlife?"

He had asked himself the same question more than once. "I think my life growing up was so chaotic that I gravitated toward organizations that were all about order." And that was enough of talking about himself. He turned the conversation back to her. "Do your parents expect you to marry someone from your tribe?" he asked.

"Oh, yes. Mom even has the man all picked out."

Her frown told him she didn't think much of the idea. "Seriously?" he asked. "Who's the lucky guy?"

"Rodney Tonaho. Tribal police chief. Former high-school basketball star, class valedictorian and all-around great guy."

"But not your guy?" He hoped he didn't sound too anxious about her answer to this question.

She slid her gaze over to him. "I prefer to pick my own men."

What were his chances of her picking him? She had kissed him last night at Metwater's camp, but that could have merely been curiosity or responding to the moment. She had made it pretty clear she didn't trust him. He had spent most of his life in situations that demanded he live by his wits. Sometimes that meant lying or pretending to be something he wasn't. He wasn't even sure he knew how to reveal his true self to another person.

He turned his attention away from such dangerous thoughts and focused once more on the food. "Thanks for sharing the bounty," he said. "I've never had an Indian taco before."

"Neither did the Utes, until they ended up on the reservation." She finished off the last of her lunch and crushed the foil into a ball. "We started making them to sell to tourists. They're tasty, but not something you'd want to eat every day—too much white flour and grease. If you want a real Native dish, you'll have to try some of my aunt Lucy's venison stew."

"Sounds good." He finished the last of his taco and wiped his hands on a napkin before putting the truck into gear. "Ready to reveal your true identity to Metwater and his followers?"

"I am," she said. "I'm looking forward to seeing the expression on Daniel Metwater's face when he finds out he was hosting a cop."

"You'd think a prophet would have seen through your disguise," Jake said.

"I'm sure he'll have an explanation for his followers."

Her expression sobered. "Though I hope Sophie and your mom will understand why I kept the truth from them."

"My mom isn't going to be happy to find out I'm a cop, either." He glanced at her. "In her past, she had more than a few run-ins with the police, none of them pleasant." One of the toughest parts of his screening for his job had been admitting that his own mother had a record for drug possession, solicitation and theft. He might have had a tough time in some city police departments but, being a Fish and Wildlife officer, he rarely dealt with drug crimes and prostitution.

"Phoenix gives Daniel Metwater credit for getting her off drugs," Carmen said. "Whatever else he's done wrong, we have to applaud him for that."

"Yeah, good for him," Jake said. "But she needs to move on now. And she needs to let Sophie move on. Whether her story about Metwater wanting to marry Sophie is true or not, nothing good will come of the two of them staying with him."

"I agree," Carmen said. "And I'll do what I can to help you, though I don't see how I can have much influence."

"I want to talk to her first," he said. "Before we speak with Metwater and Starfall."

"Sure. It might even be good if they think she's the reason for our visit. It might cause them to let down their guard."

No one challenged them as they walked into camp from the parking area. "There's almost always a guard," Carmen said. "I wonder why no one is on duty today."

"Maybe it was Reggae's turn to keep watch," Jake said.

Almost everyone in the camp openly stared at them as they moved among the tents and trailers. Jake knew they were focusing on the uniforms more than the people in them—it was both a positive and a negative about the apparel. It marked officers as figures with special power, which some people respected, and most people feared, at least a little.

Starfall jumped up from the folding chair she had been sitting in by the door of the white tent and openly gaped at them, then ducked into the tent—was she hiding or merely going to tell her tentmate, Asteria, about this latest development?

Sophie stared, too, when she opened the door of the trailer she shared with Phoenix. She took in Jake's dark brown pants and khaki uniform shirt, and the khaki pants and shirt Carmen wore, with her sergeant's stripes and blue Ranger Brigade patch. "Jake, why are you dressed like that?" she asked. "And Carmen—what's going on?"

"May we come in?" he asked. "You don't have to be afraid. You're not in any trouble."

She stepped back and let them move past her. Phoenix sat up from where she had been lying on the daybed and pushed a knitted afghan aside. She, too, stared at the uniforms. "Jake, please don't tell me you're a cop!" she all but wailed.

"I'm an investigator with the US Fish and Wildlife Service," he said. "My job is to protect our plant and animal resources."

His explanation did little to change the expression of disgust on her face. She turned to Carmen. "And you're one of those Rangers—the ones who are always hassling us. You weren't here as our friend at all. You were spying on us."

"I was trying to learn more about the group," she said. "Trying to understand you."

"And to think I thought of you as my friend." She looked away. "You can both leave now."

"We're not leaving," Jake said. "We're both here because we care about the two of you." He sat beside Phoenix and took her hand. "Mom, you're clearly not well. Look at you—having to lie down in the middle of the day. That isn't like you."

"I'm not as young as I used to be." She pushed her limp hair back off her forehead. "I've been taking a tonic I'm sure will help me, but herbal medicines take a while to work."

"What are your symptoms?" Carmen asked. "And what are you taking for them?"

"I'm taking molasses and apple cider vinegar to strengthen my blood, and dandelion root for fatigue," Phoenix said. "It's all very healthy, nothing narcotic or illegal."

"You need to see a doctor, to make sure it isn't something more serious," Jake said. "There's a clinic in town. I could take you."

"You won't bring me back here," she said. "You hate the Prophet—you're afraid of his power." She turned to Carmen. "He told me that's why the Rangers are always bothering us—they know that the Prophet is more powerful than they are, that if everyone followed the peaceful way he preaches, it would put them out of work."

Jake saw that this twisted logic made perfect sense to her, but Sophie wasn't buying it. "Some people don't want to be peaceful," she said. "Jake and Carmen will always have work trying to protect the rest of us from them." She touched his shoulder. "Why are you here today?"

"We have some sad news," he said. "One of your members, a man named Reggae, was killed early this morning. It may be related to a case I'm working on."

Sophie's eyes widened. "Reggae?"

He took both her hands in his. "Yes, but you can't say anything to anyone until we've told Metwater. We're hoping he can tell us how to get in touch with Reggae's family."

She nodded, her eyes bright with tears. "He was always nice to me," she said. "I'm sorry he's dead."

"What kind of case?" Phoenix asked.

"An illegal smuggling operation." He squeezed her hand. "I can't say more."

"And you think the Prophet had something to do with this?" Phoenix looked indignant. "Well, you're wrong."

"We don't have any reason to believe he's involved," Carmen said. "Why do you think we would?"

"Have there been any strangers in camp lately?" Jake asked. "People with foreign accents?"

"Don't be ridiculous." She folded her arms across her chest and looked away again.

Jake turned to his sister. "Have you seen or heard anything unusual in the past few days?"

She shook her head. "No. No one has visited—just you and Carmen. What kind of foreign accent?"

"It doesn't matter." He stood. "We'd better go see Metwater now."

"You can walk with us to his motor home," Carmen said to Sophie. "If it's okay with your mother."

"I'll go with you," Sophie said, jumping up and running out before her mother could object.

"The clinic in town is very good," Carmen said to Phoenix. "The nurse practitioner is a friend of mine, and the fees are on a sliding scale."

Phoenix said nothing and kept her gaze fixed out the window. As soon as they were out of the trailer, Jake put his arm around his sister and pulled her close. "How are you doing?" he asked.

"Okay." She shrugged. "I'm worried about Mom."

"She doesn't look very well," Carmen said. "Is she eating?"

"Not much." Sophie shook her head. "She said everything upsets her stomach. She sleeps a lot. The Prophet excused her from work duties." She looked up at Jake. "He even tried to get her to see the doctor. He's not all bad."

"I'm glad to hear it," Jake said. "Try not to worry too much. That's my job."

"I can't believe you're a cop," Sophie said. "Mom hates cops." She flushed. "Only because she got in so much trouble with them when she was doing drugs and stuff."

"Your mom isn't in any trouble with us," Carmen said. "We only want to help."

"I know," Sophie said.

They reached Metwater's motor home. "Go back to Mom," Jake said. "I'll try to check in with you again tomorrow, but, if you need anything at all, here's my number." He took one of his cards from his shirt pocket and handed it to her.

She studied the card. "We don't have a phone. No one does. They don't work out here."

"Get someone to bring you to Ranger headquarters," Carmen said. "You can call from there, or I'll help you."

She nodded and slipped the card into the pocket of her jeans. "I guess being a wildlife officer is a good job, huh?" she asked.

"I think so."

"Good enough to support all of us if we came to live with you?"

"Definitely good enough for that."

She hugged him, then hurried away, back toward Phoenix's trailer. Jake and Carmen climbed the steps of Metwater's RV. The door opened before Jake could knock. Asteria looked out at them. "The Prophet wants to know why you're here," she said.

"We came to inform him of the death of one of his followers," Jake said.

She looked startled but said nothing and held the door open wider for them to enter. Metwater sat in a recliner across the room, feet up, posture relaxed. He, too, remained silent as they entered, though Jake could read the contempt in his expression from across the room.

"One of your followers, Reggae, is dead," Jake said. "We need to know his real name so that we can contact his family."

"I wondered where he was this morning," Metwater said. "It wasn't like him to shirk his duties."

"Aren't you curious as to how he died?" Jake asked.

"I assume you'll tell me."

"He was murdered," Jake said.

Still, Metwater's expression betrayed nothing. It was the face of a statue—handsome and unfeeling. He turned to Carmen. "Why are you here?"

"I knew Reggae," she said. "I came to tell his friends what happened to him and to find out what I could about him—to try to find the person who killed him."

"And you think it was one of us, don't you? That's what the Rangers always think." He shifted position, bringing the recliner upright with a thump. "Get out of my house. I welcomed you in because I thought you were a believer, yet it was all lies. You came here as a spy and my enemy. Get out."

Carmen didn't flinch, though Jake sensed her tension. He wasn't sure he could have withstood Metwater's raging without firing back, but she kept calm. "I have a job to do," she said. "One that includes protecting all the people in this camp—and you. Do you know anyone who would have any reason to execute Reggae with a bullet to his temple?"

Metwater's face had been flushed with rage, but now it was drained of color. "Why did you use that word— *executed*?"

"Because that is what Reggae's death reminded me of," she said. "He was shot in the temple with a small-caliber weapon, the gun so close there were powder burns. His hands were tied behind his back. We can't be certain, but my guess would be more than one person was involved. They probably made him kneel in the dirt and killed him there."

Metwater looked ill. Asteria moved over to put a hand on his shoulder. "You should go," she told Jake and Carmen. "The Prophet is deeply affected by violence. It's because he's a man of peace."

"That's not the reason, is it?" Jake asked. Metwater hadn't reacted at all to news of Reggae's death, only to the specific manner of that death.

Metwater shook his head. "Go," he said, the single syllable a croak. "Just…go."

They left. Outside the motor home, Jake turned to Carmen. "What do you make of that?"

"He looked terrified," she said.

"Like someone who got a message he didn't want to receive," Jake said. "Let's see if anyone else in camp can shed any light."

"Starfall," Carmen said. "She has a whole file on the Prophet. Almost like a dossier. I found it when I was searching for your badge."

Starfall had returned to the folding chair outside her tent. "I knew there was a reason you two were so cozy," she said as they approached. "You're just a pair of pigs."

"I thought that slang went out of fashion years ago," Jake said.

"We're a little behind the times here," Starfall said. "Haven't you noticed?"

"I'm afraid we have some bad news," Jake said.

"The only bad news is that you two are here," Starfall said.

"Reggae is dead," Carmen said. "Someone killed him this morning."

Starfall stared. "No."

"I'm sorry, yes." Carmen squatted down in front of her chair. "We're trying to find out who killed him. Did he ever mention any enemies to you? Anyone who might want to harm him?"

Starfall shook her head. "Not Reggae. He was a nice guy." She blinked, her eyes shiny. "A really nice guy."

"This wasn't an accident," Jake said. "He had a backpack full of cactus. Was he collecting them for you?"

"For me?" She swallowed. "I told him a guy would pay for cactus, but that was all. He never said anything about wanting to get in on the deal."

"Maybe he wanted to surprise you," Jake said.

"That would be just like him." She gave a ragged laugh. "He was always trying to impress me. If I said I wanted wild strawberries, he'd pick a big bowl full. Or if we needed something repaired, he would always volunteer." She swallowed, tears streaming down her cheeks. "I was pretty awful to him, really, and he was so nice to me."

"I'm sorry," Carmen said. "I know he was your friend."

"How did he die?" Starfall said. "I mean, you said he was shot, but how?"

"A bullet in his temple," Carmen said.

"You mean, like an execution—like a mob hit or something?"

"Why do you say *mob*?" Jake said.

Starfall shook her head, as if trying to clear it. "It's just funny, that's all."

"What's funny?" Carmen asked.

"For him to die that way." Her eyes, without their usual guile, met Jake's. "That's the same way Daniel Metwater's brother was killed."

Chapter Ten

A search of Reggae's tent revealed that his real name was Donald Quackenbush, from Pocatello, Idaho. He had no criminal record, and the only family the Rangers could locate was an older sister who reported she hadn't seen her brother in five years and didn't have the time or money to come get him now.

Carmen hung up the phone from that conversation feeling a too-familiar mixture of anger and disgust. At least Starfall had truly grieved the young man's death, and Daniel Metwater had sent word half an hour ago that he would pay for Reggae's cremation if the ashes were returned to the Family, so that they could give him a formal memorial.

"The sister says she has no idea what her brother has been doing all these years," Carmen told Jake. He had pulled up a chair to the opposite side of her desk and was sharing the workspace with her. On the way back from Metwater's camp, he had revealed that he was no longer assigned to tail Werner Altbusser but would work with the Rangers on the murder investigation.

"I found a couple of articles about David Metwater's death," he said, looking up from his laptop. "Starfall is right—he was shot in the right temple with a .22-caliber pistol. His hands were tied behind him, and he was dumped in the river."

"It could be a coincidence," Carmen said. "Or maybe the mob is branching out into cactus smuggling."

"Or maybe someone is sending a message to Daniel Metwater, and Donald was the unfortunate means of delivering the message."

"Metwater was certainly affected by the news," Carmen said. "I can see how it would be a shock to hear about someone else he knew dying the same way as his brother, even if Reggae's murder has nothing to do with Metwater."

"I'm having a hard time seeing a connection," Jake said. "David Metwater died almost two years ago. Daniel Metwater hasn't made any big secret of his whereabouts or what he's been doing. Why would the mob decide all of a sudden to come after him?"

She ran both hands through her hair. "I don't know. And I'm too beat to come up with any good theories tonight. Let's pack it in until tomorrow."

"Good idea." He powered down his laptop. "Want to grab a bite to eat?" he asked. "You provided lunch—it's only fair I should buy you dinner."

She should say no. Getting involved with a co-worker was a bad idea, even if he was only temporarily liaising with the Rangers. And part of her still wasn't sure she could trust him. "Okay," she said. They would talk about work, she promised herself. Two co-workers reviewing the day.

She directed him to a café in town with good soups and salads and a choice of entrées that included, but wasn't limited to, burgers. "I like this town," Jake said as he settled into a booth across from her. "I wish I had more time to stick around and explore the area."

"It's a lot different from Houston," she said. "I was there once, visiting cousins. I remember heat, humidity and very flat terrain."

"It's great if you like big cities," he said. "But I'm thinking I should move Sophie and Mom someplace quieter. Maybe where Mom won't have so many temptations to slip back into her old life."

The mention of Phoenix sobered Carmen. "She doesn't look well," she said. "Even Metwater noticed. Maybe we can persuade him to order her to see a doctor. She might listen to him."

"I'm willing to try anything at this point." He set aside his menu. He looked beat—fatigue in his eyes and weariness in the set of his shoulders. She had to resist the urge to lean over the table and squeeze his hand.

Instead, she searched for a safe topic of conversation. "What's going to happen with Werner?" she asked.

"The other agent will tail him and get the photographs we need for our case. I met the agent—Tony—a couple of times at training seminars. He seems like a good guy—he'll do a good job."

"And you? Is this a setback for you?" His supervisor couldn't have been happy about Jake making contact with their suspect.

"It depends on what else I can turn up. We know Werner isn't working alone. He has partners overseas, and we suspect here in the States also. People who cover for him and maybe do some collecting for him."

"Maybe one of them got into an argument with Reggae. Maybe we're looking at this wrong, and he didn't collect those cactus—he took them from someone else."

"Except the cactus in that pack were worthless," Jake said. "And the way Reggae was killed wasn't an argument gone south."

"Right." The waitress took their orders—Thai chicken salad for her and blackened trout for him.

"I don't understand how the smugglers get enough rare cactus to make it worth their while," she said when they were alone again. "There are millions of acres of public land, but they can't possibly search every inch of that space for a type of cactus that may only be a few inches across."

"No, they can't. They have to have help. They can study terrain through things like Google Earth and isolate the most likely habitat. Sometimes they contact private landowners and ask permission to collect on their land. Most people don't realize it's illegal. Some of them see it as a good thing, getting rid of a nuisance."

"Or maybe sometimes they trespass," she said. "That happens on tribal land all the time. People think it's just empty land, so it's okay for them to camp or hunt arrowheads or whatever. The tribal council has spent a lot of money on fences and signs and efforts to educate the public."

"I envy you," he said. "Being part of a cohesive group like that. I imagine it's like an extended family. That's something I don't have. Maybe that's why Metwater's bunch appealed to my mom. She wanted that sense of belonging."

"A tribe is a family," she said. "It's a connection to a people and a heritage, and also to land where my family has lived for generations."

Jake sat back in the booth, studying her. "How did you get into law enforcement?" he asked.

"I was going to be a teen counselor," she said. "To pay for my schooling, I took a job at a youth detention center. Talking with the officers who worked there got me interested in law enforcement. I went through the police academy and decided I wanted to focus on investigations. I went back to school for more training, got on with CBI, then, when the federal government decided to form the Ranger Brigade to police public land, I applied and was accepted." She shrugged. "I like being closer to home."

"But not too close," he said. "Otherwise, you'd take the job with the tribal police."

"Right." She traced a bead of condensation down the side of her iced-tea glass. "I love my parents, but I need space to live my own life. They have this whole plan for my life, but I need to figure out my own direction. It's like—no matter what I do, they think I could do better."

"That kind of pressure would make some people give up," he said. "Seems to me you've done the opposite and worked hard to excel."

"Yes, I have." But sometimes she wondered if all her striving had been worth the cost. She had focused so much on being the best in an arena dominated by men that she hadn't even had one serious relationship, at an age when so many of the girls she had gone to school with were married with children. If she had bent to her parents' wishes and returned to reservation life, would she, too, be married with babies of her own?

The server brought their meals, and they ate in silence for a while. What Jake had said earlier about the smugglers taking advantage, coupled with her own stories about reservation life, had planted an idea in her head.

"Would you like to come with me to the reservation to-morrow?" she asked.

He paused with his fork halfway to his lips and stared at her. "You're inviting me to your reservation?"

"There are a couple of people I want to talk to," she said. "They might be able to help us with this case."

"How?" he asked.

"It's complicated. And it may lead nowhere." She stabbed at a chunk of lettuce. "We don't have to go. It was just an idea."

"No. I'd love to come with you." He grinned. "I want to meet your parents. I promise to be on my best be-havior."

JAKE FELT LIKE a guilty man facing cross-examination by a prosecutor who had never lost a case as he sat across the desk from Wilma Redhorse in her offices in the Southern Ute Tribal Council Center. The glass and con-crete high-rise was not the reservation architecture he had expected, but the briefest tour of the Southern Ute Reservation near Ignacio, Colorado, showed him that his ideas about reservation life, at least for this tribe, were sadly outdated. In addition to the building that housed the tribal council, there was a high-rise hotel and casino, expansive cultural center and museum, business center, fitness center and more.

"Carmen tells me you two are working on a case to-gether," Wilma Redhorse said. She was a slightly older version of her daughter, her black hair hanging loose about the shoulders of her stylish red business suit, black eyes piercing behind chic square-framed glasses. "But you're not a member of the Ranger Brigade."

"No ma'am. I'm conducting an investigation for Fish

and Wildlife, and the Rangers have a case that may be related to mine. It made sense to work together." He wished he had listened to his instincts and worn his uniform. The brown and khaki combination gave him authority and identified him as one of the good guys. Instead, at Carmen's request, he had dressed in jeans and a western shirt and boots. She also wore jeans and a sleeveless blouse that showed off her toned upper arms. Of course, she had no need for an identifying uniform here—everyone already knew her and everything about her.

"Where are you from originally?" Mrs. Redhorse asked. "Where is your family?"

"We moved around a lot when I was a kid," he said. "Right now, I live in Houston, but my mother and younger sister are in Montrose County."

"No family in Houston?"

"No, ma'am." He sensed his lack of kin made him lesser in her eyes, but that might have been his own self-consciousness putting thoughts into his head. "I'm trying to persuade my mother and sister to come live with me," he added.

She nodded. "Families should be together, but not everyone sees it that way." She looked over his shoulder at her daughter when she spoke.

"Mom, what about the cactus collectors I asked you about?" Carmen asked, her voice crisp and business-like. "Has anyone like that asked to collect on tribal land or been caught trespassing?"

"If they have, I haven't heard of it," Wilma said. "They haven't asked permission and, if they had, it wouldn't have been granted." She turned to Jake. "We're trying very hard to preserve all our resources. The only reason we have this land is that the government thought it was useless. When oil and gas were discovered here, the mineral rights provided opportunities for our people. If we have valuable cactus, we'll decide what to do with it, not a bunch of European collectors."

"Would anyone else know if someone had asked about cactus?" Carmen asked.

"You should talk to Chief Tonaho. If anyone was caught trespassing or trying to dig up any cactus, he would know. And he would like to see you. He always asks me when you are going to come work for him."

"I like the job I have," Carmen said, with the weary tone of someone who has given the same answer many times but knows the words aren't really heard.

Wilma's gaze shifted to Jake. "The tribal police chief and Carmen grew up together. He knows how smart she is. He could use someone like her helping him. I always tell her they would make a great team."

"I'm certainly happy to have her as my partner," he said. Let her mom make of that remark what she would. Not that he and Carmen were partners in anything but a professional sense, but it wouldn't hurt to keep Wilma guessing.

"We'll go talk to Rodney," Carmen said. "I'd like him to meet Jake. Then we'll stop and talk to Aunt Connie."

Wilma frowned. "You're not sick, are you?" She leaned closer to study her daughter. "You look tired."

"I'm fine. We only want to ask Aunt Connie's opinion on something."

"What do you need an opinion on?" Wilma asked.

"I have a medical question for her," Carmen said. "Nothing to do with me, I promise." She moved to the door. "Come on, Jake."

He stood. "It was nice meeting you, Mrs. Redhorse," he said.

She nodded. "Good luck with your case, Agent Lohmiller."

Jake let out a breath as the door to the office closed behind him. "Notice she didn't say it was nice to meet me," he said.

"Hurry," she said as they walked back to her car, a gray Camry she had insisted on driving instead of his filthy pickup. "She'll call Rodney and tell him we're coming. Later, she'll call him and Connie before we're even off the reservation and find out everything she said to us."

"I'm a little jealous," he said.

"Of Rodney? Don't be. He's a nice guy, but not my type."

Some time he might ask her what her type was, but he didn't want to derail the conversation. "I can see how your mother's concern could be a bit oppressive, but my mom has always been so involved in her own problems that half the time she had no idea where I was or anything that was going on in my life."

Carmen looked over the top of the Camry at him. "Your mother loves you," she said. "I'll never forget the look on her face when you walked into Metwater's RV that first day and she realized it was you."

"I know she loves me," he said, opening the passenger side door of the car. "I'm just pointing out that having a parent who is concerned about you and the choices you make isn't all a bad thing."

She nodded and ducked into the driver's seat. "You're right. I know my mom wants the best for me, I just wish we were on the same page more often about what that is."

She started the car and turned left out of the parking lot. "Tell me about Rodney Tonaho," he said. "What should I expect?"

"Aside from being a high-school basketball star and the class valedictorian, he won every award there was, went off to college and it was pretty much a repeat performance. He's the youngest police chief we've ever had."

"No wonder your mother loves him."

"Everyone loves Rodney," she said. "He's very charming."

"Charm is overrated."

She laughed. The sound relaxed him a little. At least she hadn't fallen under Mr. Perfect's spell.

Rodney Tonaho greeted them at the door of his office. "It's good to see you again," he said, shaking Carmen's hand. "Your mother called and said you were coming." He turned and offered his hand to Jake. "You must be Agent Lohmiller."

The handshake was firm but not painful. Perfect, like everything else about the man, from his starched and pressed uniform to his movie-star good looks. Jake reminded himself that just because the man had apparently never had to struggle for anything in his life didn't mean he wasn't a nice guy and a good law enforcement officer. But he was going to have to prove himself before Jake would trust him.

"We're investigating a case that involves smuggling rare cactus," Carmen said when she and Jake were seated across from Rodney's desk in his office.

Rodney steepled his fingers and nodded. "So Wilma said. I don't know of anything like that going on on the reservation."

"The guy I'm tracking is a German named Werner Altbusser," Jake said. "He, or someone representing him, might contact you about collecting cactus on tribal land. Or they might simply trespass and dig up what they want without permission."

Rodney scowled, which only made him more rugged and handsome. "If they try that, they won't get away with it. We view trespassing and theft very seriously."

"Let us know if anything like that happens," Carmen said. "And be careful. One man who may have been working for Werner has already been murdered."

Rodney's expression relaxed. "Of course I'll let you know if anything comes up."

"Thanks." She stood. "We won't take up any more of your time."

"I'm always happy to see you," he said.

Jake heard the truth behind his words, and glimpsed the longing in Rodney's eyes that set off alarm bells in his head. His hands tightened on the arm of his chair as he stared at the man across the desk. Carmen might think the chief wasn't her type, but Rodney definitely had feelings for her.

"It was a long shot, but I thought it was worth checking out," she said as they set out in her car again.

"It was a good idea," Jake said. "Will he really call if he hears anything?"

She glanced at him. "Of course he will. Why wouldn't he?"

He shrugged. "I don't know. He would want to help you, but maybe not me?"

"Why wouldn't he want to help you?"

"He might see me as a rival for your affections."

She slammed on the brakes, throwing him forward,

then pulled to the side of the road and stopped the car. "What are you talking about?" she asked.

He forced himself not to squirm in his seat. "I like you," he said. "I'm attracted to you. And I'm guessing by the way you kissed me the other night that you're attracted to me, too."

She looked away, but he didn't miss the flush that warmed her cheeks. "It was just a kiss," she said. "We work together."

And people who worked together sometimes got involved. That was life. But if she wanted to play that game, he could, too. "Fine. Forget I mentioned it. Tell me why we're going to see your aunt." he asked.

"She's a nurse practitioner at the tribal clinic." She glanced at him. "I wanted to ask her about your mom, if that's okay with you."

So much for keeping things strictly business. He couldn't explain why her concern for his mom moved him so—maybe because, on some level, it felt like she was caring about him, too. "That would be great," he said. "I'd love to get a professional's opinion."

Connie Owl Woman was a short, round woman who wore her silver hair in a long braid coiled at the back of her head. Her blue eyeshadow matched her blue scrubs, and she squealed with delight and gathered her niece in a crushing hug when Carmen and Jake walked into her office at the clinic. "Your mother already called and told me you were on your way over," she said. "And you must be Jake." She pumped his hand, her fingers squeezing all the feeling out of his. "Wilma said you and Carmen are working together."

"It's good to meet you," Jake said, reclaiming his hand and flexing his aching fingers.

"What can I do for you two today?" Connie beamed at them. "You both look healthy enough to me."

"We wanted to ask you about Jake's mother," Carmen said. "She's been ill."

Connie's face sobered. "What kind of illness?"

"I don't know," Jake said. "She refuses to see a doctor. She's very pale and tires easily. She's fainted a few times, and she says nothing agrees with her when she eats."

"Any history of health problems?"

"Not really." Jake hesitated, then added, "She has a history of drug use. She was addicted to heroin, though she's been clean for a while."

"Hepatitis is always a risk with a history of drug use," Connie said. "But what you're describing could be almost anything—anemia or something more serious—even cancer." She shook her head. "Impossible to tell without an examination and probably some blood work."

"That's what I was afraid you'd say," Jake said. "She's very stubborn about seeing a doctor, thinks she can cure herself with herbal remedies."

"There are some excellent herbal remedies out there," Connie said. "I have patients who rely on them. But there are times when modern medicine is just the thing." She patted his arm. "Your mother is probably afraid. I see it all the time. Especially if the sick person believes the disease is somehow their own fault. Your mother may believe her past behaviors led to her current illness, and she has the attitude she's only getting what she deserves, and she deserves to suffer. Which is ridiculous, but people believe ridiculous things every day. Some of us are more prone to it than others."

"Do you have any advice for getting her to see a doctor?" Jake asked.

She shook her head. "You might remind her that knowledge gives her power. Finding out what is going on with her health will give her the information she needs to make the right decisions. Sometimes framing it as a way of gaining control, when the person is afraid of having control taken away, can help."

"I'll try that. Thank you."

Connie reached over and patted Carmen's shoulder. "It is good to see you," she said. "You should come back for the powwow next month. Bring your friend here with you. Stay the weekend so he can get to know everyone."

Carmen smoothed back her hair and avoided looking at Jake. "I imagine he'll be back in Houston by then."

Connie shook her head. "Oh, I don't think so." She patted Jake's shoulder now. "Come back next month."

"Maybe I will."

They left the clinic, and he waited until they were in the car again before he spoke. "Why doesn't your aunt think I'll be in Houston by next month—and why do you think I will be?"

"You're here on temporary assignment," she said. "You're from Houston. When the case is over, you'll go back." She gripped the steering wheel with both hands but didn't turn the key in the ignition.

"I need to settle my mother and sister in a place that's good for them," he said. "I already told you I don't think a big city like Houston is that place. Maybe this is."

"What about your job?"

"There are other jobs. I could transfer or work somewhere else. I'm used to going where the next opportunity takes me."

She didn't relax her grip on the wheel. "I can't imagine living like that," she said. "I've always had a plan for my life—a next step to get where I want to go."

"If that works for you, that's great," he said. "It never worked for me." Life was full of too many variables. If his mom didn't pay the rent, they might have to leave in the middle of the night and find a new apartment across town, or in another town altogether. If she ended up in jail, Jake had to drop everything and look after Sophie. If he missed work to babysit his sister while his mother was roaming the streets in search of drugs, he might lose his job and have to find another one. All that uncertainty had taught him how to think on his feet. It had taught him not to rely on other people. Maybe to someone like Carmen, it made him seem unreliable. Someone she couldn't trust.

She dropped her hands to her lap and sighed. "Aunt Connie likes to make predictions about people," she said. "She says she's a good judge of character."

"Is she? Do her predictions come true?"

She shrugged. "Sometimes." She shifted the car into gear and flipped on her blinker before turning onto the road. "She liked you, so that's something in your favor."

"I liked her, too."

She pulled the car back onto the highway. "Do you want to see where I grew up?" she asked.

The question surprised him. The offer felt somehow intimate. Another acknowledgment that maybe not everything between them was strictly professional. "Yes, I'd like that."

She nodded and turned the car away from the clinic and the casino and office buildings toward country that quickly grew more rural—housing developments and shopping strips gave way to hayfields and pasture. She turned onto a gravel lane that led through an open iron gate, past white-fenced paddocks and a towering red barn. "My father raises cutting horses," she said. "Some of his horses are champions. It's his passion."

The drive curved past more paddocks and a modest white ranch house. "Home, sweet home," she said, slowing in front of the house. "I'd take you in and introduce you, but my father is at a sale over in Farmington today."

"It looks like a good place to grow up." He glanced at her. "Were you happy?"

"Yes. Even though I don't want to live here right now, I love having this place to come back to. I never understood Metwater's followers wanting to come together to make a kind of fake tribe," she said. "I didn't think it could possibly be anything like the real tribe I was a part of. But then, when I went to live with them for a few days and really got to know them, I realized they were searching for what I had already found. Their makeshift family might be a substitute for the real thing, but it was better than whatever they had had before. I saw the strength in what they were trying to do—the courage it took to trust others enough to build something that had been handed to me for nothing and with no effort on my part. It made me a little more compassionate, I think."

"My mother has a real family," he said. "Me, my sister, and her parents and brothers and sisters. She's hurt them, but I believe they still love her. I want us to try to be a family again. That would be better for Sophie than any fake family led by a pretend prophet."

"I hope your mom will give them a chance," Carmen said. She turned toward him. "What do you want to do now?"

He wanted to prolong the time with her and see more

of this personal side of her. Driving through this ranch, he could imagine her as a girl, riding a horse across the pasture, her long hair streaming behind her. "Show me your favorite place on the ranch," he said.

She hesitated, then nodded. "All right."

She drove past the ranch house and turned down a road that was little more than two ruts winding up a steep hill. At the top, she parked the car beside a stack of boulders and got out. Jake followed her to a twisted pine, where the land fell away in a steep cliff, the valley below a patchwork of plowed fields, pastures and homes. "When I was growing up, this was my whole world," she said. "This was my kingdom, and I was the queen."

He put his arm around her, and she leaned in to him. "I could see you as queen," he said. "You've got the attitude and the courage."

"Some men have a problem with the attitude," she said. "They say they admire strong women, but they don't want to be with them."

"I'm not one of those men." He turned her toward him, so that they stood face to face, hip to hip. "Why did you bring me here?" he asked.

"Because you asked. And because I wanted to do this." She cupped his face in her hands and pulled his mouth down to hers, the kiss as strong and confident as the woman, a meeting of their lips that was as much mental as physical. He lost focus on anything else as he wrapped both arms around her and pulled her close. He flashed back to the first day he had seen her, striding across the prairie, beautiful and wary as a wild horse. Holding her now, he still felt that wildness, an energy beneath his touch that reminded him she was allowing him to be with her this way but might change her mind at any moment.

She pulled slightly away, and he looked down into her eyes, trying to read the emotions there. "That wasn't just a kiss," he said and smoothed the pad of his thumb over her bottom lip.

"No," she said and moved closer, fitting her body between his legs, the soft fullness of her breasts pressed against his rib cage. He grasped her hips, splaying his fingers along their curves, letting her feel how much he wanted her. If she was going to run, now would be the time.

But instead of running, she pulled him down onto the soft bed of pine needles beneath the tree. He rolled onto his back, bringing her on top of him. She looked down on him and brushed the hair back from his eyes. "When I met you that first day near the camp, I was a little bit afraid of you," she said. "I still am."

He stroked her arm, a gentling motion. "You don't have to be afraid of me."

"Then maybe I'm more afraid of myself and what I might do with you."

"I can think of a few things I'd like to do right now." He stared into her eyes, losing himself in those brown depths, letting himself be that vulnerable. "One thing."

"I suddenly can't think of anything else." She kissed him again, a long, drugging kiss of tangled tongues and tangled limbs, her fingers moving along with her mouth, unbuttoning his shirt, her touch sending hot tendrils of sensation through him to pool in his groin.

"Are you sure this is what you want?" He made himself ask the question, though there was only one answer he wanted to hear.

"Oh, yes." She kissed his neck, then stroked her tongue across his pounding pulse. "This is exactly what I want."

They didn't talk much after that. Words seemed useless compared to the messages their bodies telegraphed. Though he would have kept some of his clothes on in deference to their exposed position, she insisted on removing every stitch, and he had to admit the sight of the sun gleaming on her body was one he would always treasure. When she took a condom from the pocket of her jeans, he laughed out loud. "So you were planning to bring me up here and seduce me," he said.

"Not planning, exactly." She held the packet up to him. "You might have said no."

"But you knew I wouldn't." He knelt in front of her and ripped open the packet. "You knew I couldn't." He sheathed himself, then lay back once more, pulling her on top of him. She held herself above him for a long moment, staring into his eyes, as if searching for something there. He didn't look away, trying to let her know without words how much she was coming to mean to him. Then he lost focus as she lowered herself over him and began to rock her hips gently, and then with more force, driving them both to a place he had been wanting to go since the moment he met her.

WHEN JAKE OFFERED to drive back to Montrose, Carmen let him. She didn't often surrender the wheel to someone else, but considering how much she had given to him already that day, driving seemed a small thing. She wanted time to think, without the distraction of steep mountain passes and narrow, winding switchbacks.

The man beside her was distraction enough. She

could still feel the tension of his muscles beneath his fingers, the strength of him as he lifted her up with each thrust of his pelvis. Making love to him in the open like that, she had felt so vulnerable and at the same time so powerful. She had never done anything so daring with anyone before—had never wanted to even. But Jake made her want to be daring, almost as if she was trying to prove something to him, or to herself. *Look how bold I can be! Look at the risks I'll take!*

But being with him felt like the biggest risk of all. He was so many things she had decided would make the absolutely wrong partner for her. First of all, he was a cop—a man with a dangerous job and lousy hours and a world view that required him to regard everyone with suspicion. Just because she understood what that was like didn't mean she wanted to live with it every day, no matter what her mother predicted.

Then there was his family. He didn't have an ex-wife or a kid, other *no-no*s on her list, but he had a teen-age sister and a mother who needed looking after. She liked Sophie, and she liked Phoenix, too, but relation-ships were tough enough without those kinds of per-sonal complications.

Jake was good at his job, willing to do what was necessary to conduct an investigation, even if it meant pretending to be someone else. She approached her job with the same kind of determination but, if a man was so very good at lying on the job, how could she trust him not to lie to her in real life? And would she be tempted to lie to him? Wouldn't it be better to avoid putting them-selves in a position where they would have to find out?

Safer, maybe. But that wasn't the same as better. With the scent of him still on her and the memory of his touch still tantalizing her nerve endings, she couldn't think of anything but how intoxicating being with him was—like a dangerous drug she could all too easily become addicted to.

Her phone beeped as they crossed the last pass. "We must be back in range of cell service," Jake said, pulling out his cell. "I've got a call."

"Me, too."

He pulled to the side of the road. "I'd better check this," he said.

She took out her own phone and called up voice mail. Marco Cruz's message was clipped and to the point. "You need to get back to Ranger headquarters," he said. "Daniel Metwater is here, and he's asking for you."

Chapter Eleven

Daniel Metwater paced the length of the conference room at Ranger Brigade headquarters, his dark, curly hair in disarray from continually raking his hands through it. He stopped and turned to face Jake and Carmen as they entered the room. "What took you so long?" he demanded.

"You could have returned to your camp, and we would have come to you there," Jake said. Metwater didn't look so in control of himself today. Dark circles beneath his eyes testified to a lack of sleep, and he stood with his shoulders hunched, as if anticipating a blow.

"It's not safe for me there." He jerked his head toward the door. "I've been trying to tell your colleagues, but they said I would have to wait for you."

Carmen pulled a chair out from the conference table. "Mr. Metwater, sit down, and we'll discuss this," she said.

He scowled at her. "If you'd been doing your job instead of spying on me and my followers, you could have prevented this," he said.

"Prevented what?" Jake sat across from the chair Carmen had pulled out for Metwater. "Sit down, and start at the beginning. We can't help you if you're not making sense."

The scowl deepened, but Metwater dropped into the chair. "I need protection," he said.

"Protection from what?" Carmen filled a paper cup from the water cooler by the door and slid it across to Metwater, then sat beside Jake.

"The people who killed my brother. They're after me now." He drained the cup, then crumpled it in his fist. "Killing Reggae was a warning to me."

"Who are these people?" Jake asked.

"Organized crime. Russian organized crime. The *Bratva*."

"The Chicago police suspected they were responsible for your brother's death, but they never found any proof," Carmen said.

"They killed him," Metwater said. "He was into them for too much. He was so reckless and stupid—he thought nothing could ever touch him. He embezzled almost a million dollars from our father, but it wasn't enough. He owed even more—gambling debts, women, drugs. If there was a vice, David had it."

"And you were the good brother," Jake said.

Metwater's eyes flashed with anger. "I wasn't a saint but, compared to David, I looked like one."

"Why do you think your brother's killers are after you?" Carmen asked. "They took their revenge out on him, and they've left you alone until now."

He raked his hands through his hair again. "I don't know why now. I thought that, after all this time, they were satisfied, that David's blood was enough for them. Then they killed Reggae…"

"We haven't found anything to link organized crime

to Reggae's murder," Jake said. "It's more likely that he died because he was involved with a man or men who are smuggling rare cactus off public land."

Metwater stiffened. "What men?" he asked.

"Do you know a man named Werner Altbusser, a German?" Jake asked.

"Do you think he killed Reggae?" Metwater asked.

"We don't know. Do you know him?"

Metwater's shoulders relaxed, though sweat beaded his forehead. "Not well. He came to my camp and asked my permission to recruit some of my followers to hunt for cactus for him. I told him I didn't care what they did. I don't control their lives."

"When did he ask you?" Jake asked.

"A few days ago. He approached me first about making a donation to my ministry."

"Did you accept the donation?" Carmen asked.

"The money was freely offered and freely accepted," he said. "There's no law against it."

"No, but I have to wonder if he was trying to influence your answer to his request," she said.

"My answer was immaterial."

"Was anyone else with Werner when you talked?" Jake asked.

"No. He was alone." He opened his fist and let the crumpled cup fall onto the table between them. "Werner isn't important. He didn't kill Reggae, the *Bratva* did. And I'm their next target. You have to protect me."

"I thought you had your own bodyguards," Carmen said.

He sent her another withering look. "The men who are after me are professional killers. I need professional protection."

"Then you should consider hiring private security," she said. "We can't devote officers to babysitting you on the basis of your own paranoia."

He shoved the chair back so hard it toppled as he stood, the sound of it striking the floor jarring. "You think I'm making this up—that I'm not in any danger."

"If you receive a threatening note or phone call, or have some other proof that your life is in danger, we'll work with you to keep you out of harm's way," Carmen said. "But we're not designed as a private security force."

"If you feel you're in real danger, perhaps you should relocate to someplace safer," Jake said.

"You'd like that, wouldn't you?" He leaned towards Jake, hands clenched at his sides. Jake braced himself for a blow, sure Metwater was going to hit him. But, at the last moment, the Prophet whirled away. "I should have known better than to come here for help," he shouted. "You'd be happy if I ended up dead!" He shoved past Jake and out the door.

Jake's ears rang in the silence that followed. He turned to Carmen. "What do you think?"

"I think he's really terrified," she said.

Marco and Ethan came in. "We heard part of the conversation," Marco said.

"You were listening at the door," Carmen said.

"It wasn't hard," Ethan said. "He was shouting half the time."

"Did anyone look into the mob angle?" Carmen asked.

"No one reported seeing anyone near the trailhead the morning Reggae was shot," Ethan said. "No suspicious cars."

"No swarthy men with foreign accents," Marco dead-panned.

"We had a botanist from Colorado Mesa University look at the cactus that were in the backpack," Ethan said. "Most of them were pretty common, but a few of them were rare enough to be of interest to a collector. So maybe Reggae knew what he was doing after all."

"Or maybe he just got lucky," Jake said. "Any sign of Werner?"

"All we can say is he hasn't visited the national park," Ethan said. "But that's the only place you need a permit to enter."

"He could be clear-cutting big swaths of the rest of the public land, and we'd never know about it if someone didn't complain," Marco added.

"It wouldn't hurt to run a few extra patrols around Metwater's camp," Carmen said. "See if you spot anything suspicious."

"And he can't say we're harassing him, since he practically begged us to protect him," Marco said.

"Carmen and I can check around there this afternoon," Jake said. "I need to talk to Starfall again, anyway. I want to know if she's made contact with Werner."

"Good luck getting her to admit to that," Carmen said.

He sent her a look that was supposed to communicate that he didn't care so much about Starfall—though he would talk to her. He needed to see Phoenix and Sophie and reassure himself that they were all right.

His cell phone buzzed, and he checked it but didn't recognize the number. Frowning, he answered the call. "Hello?"

"Jake, you have to come quick." A female voice sobbed out the words.

He gripped the phone tighter. "Sophie? Is that you?"

"Jake, you have to come. Mom fainted again, and it's really bad. I'm afraid she's dying!"

CARMEN GRIPPED THE armrest and tried to brace herself as the pickup truck jounced down the rutted road, yet with every bump she was thrown to the side or bounced in the air. "Wrecking your truck isn't going to get us there any faster," she said through gritted teeth.

Jake's grim expression didn't change, but he did let up on the gas a little. "I tried to get Sophie to call an ambulance," he said. "But she said Mom made her promise not to. If I have to, I'll put Mom in the truck and drive her to the hospital myself."

"How did Sophie manage to call you, anyway?" Carmen asked.

"She got Starfall to drive her to the café out by the lake, and she used their phone. She and Starfall are on their way back to camp now. I guess I owe Starfall for agreeing to take her. The poor kid was panicked."

"Maybe Starfall is trying to score points with you."

He glanced at her. "You're kidding, right? She hates me now that she knows I'm a cop."

"She knew you were a cop when she stole your badge, and that didn't stop her from pursuing you."

He shook his head, grinning.

"What are you smiling about?" she asked.

"You're jealous."

"I am not!" Just because the idea of Jake and Starfall together made her see red didn't mean she was jealous. She merely hated to see him taken in by such a manipulative woman. "I know Starfall doesn't do anything unless there's something in it for her."

"Maybe she likes my sister. Did you ever think of that?"

Carmen pressed her lips together. Sophie was certainly likable, but she didn't think Starfall had ever paid much attention to the girl. Better to let Jake think everyone loved his sister and wanted the best for her.

They arrived back at camp moments after Daniel Metwater. The Prophet turned to meet them, his expression guarded. "Have you decided to take my concerns seriously?" he asked.

"I'm not here for you," Jake said as he strode past Metwater. "I got a call from my sister that my mother fainted again."

Metwater hurried after Jake, with Carmen close behind. Asteria met them on the path. She grabbed Metwater's hand. "You're needed," she said and pulled him toward camp.

Jake put a hand on her arm to stop her. "Where's Phoenix?" he asked.

Asteria gave him a puzzled look. "She's in her trailer, I guess."

"What do you mean, you guess?" He looked as if he wanted to shake her. Carmen laid a pacifying hand on his arm, and he released the other woman. "Sophie called me in a panic. She said Phoenix fainted again."

"She did. But she's fine now."

"What did you need me for?" Metwater asked.

"There's someone here to see you. He's waiting in your trailer."

Metwater froze. "Who is he?"

Asteria glanced at Carmen and Jake, then back to Metwater. "He's a…a business associate. He was here once before."

Metwater turned to Jake and Carmen. "You have to come with me," he said.

"I have to see my mother," Jake said.

Metwater grabbed his arm. "You have to protect me."

"Protect you from what?" Jake shook him off. "Who is your visitor?"

"I think it's that German—Altbusser." He glanced at Asteria, and she nodded.

"You said yourself he isn't the killer," Jake said.

"Maybe I was wrong. Maybe he's an assassin, sent to kill me." Metwater's voice shook, and his eyes were wide with panic.

"Then don't talk to him," Jake said. "I have to see my mother."

Carmen hesitated, debating staying with Metwater or going with Jake. Jake looked back at her. "I need your help," he said. The worry and fear in his eyes won her over. Metwater's danger might be all in his head, but Jake had real reason to be concerned for his mother.

Sarah met them at the door of Phoenix's trailer. "She's better now," Sarah said. "At first we were so worried because, after she came to from this last fainting spell, she wasn't herself. She was running a fever and out of her head, talking nonsense. That's when Sophie insisted on calling you."

Jake moved through the trailer's small living and kitchen areas to the bedroom. Phoenix lay on her back in the middle of the bed, her arms folded across her chest and her eyes closed. Carmen bit back a cry—for a moment the older woman looked as if she was laid out for a funeral.

"Mom, it's me, Jake," he said softly. Carmen glanced at him and felt a tightness in her chest. In that moment, the scared boy showed beneath the surface of the tough, courageous man.

Phoenix opened her eyes. "What are you doing here, son?" she asked.

"Sophie called and told me you were sick."

"She shouldn't have done that." She tried to prop herself up on her elbows but fell back with a sigh.

Jake sat on the edge of the bed and took her hand. "Mom, you need to see a doctor," he said. "Fainting like this and being this weak isn't right. Sarah said you were delirious when you came to."

"I'm just tired, that's all," Phoenix said. "And I wasn't delirious. Sarah exaggerates." She looked past him to Carmen. "Hello, dear."

"Hello, Phoenix." Carmen drew closer. "I talked to my aunt this morning," she said. "She's a nurse at the Ute tribal clinic. She thinks you could just be anemic. It's easy to fix, but you need to see the doctor to make sure you get the right treatment."

Phoenix's lower lip trembled. "But what if it's not just anemia? What if it's something worse?"

"Then you'll get the right treatment for that." Carmen took Phoenix's other hand. "You're a very strong woman. Think of all you've overcome already. You're not going to let something like a little illness stop you."

"I don't feel so strong lately," Phoenix said.

"Please, Mom," Jake said. "If you won't go for yourself, do it for me and Sophie."

"You need to go to the doctor, Mama."

Carmen and Jake turned and saw Sophie standing in the doorway of the bedroom. Her face was pale, and she had obviously been crying. But now she looked angry. She glared at her mother. "You scared me. I thought you were dying, and there was nothing I could do. I don't want to lose you."

She choked back a sob. Jake stood and started toward her, but Phoenix managed to shove herself into a sitting position. She held out her arms. "Come here, baby," she said.

Sophie ran to her mother and buried her face against her shoulder. Phoenix stroked her hair. "It's okay, sweetie," she murmured. "You don't have to get so upset. I'll go see someone at the clinic in town." She looked up at Jake. "You can make the appointment for me. And I want you and Carmen both to go with me."

The request startled Carmen. After all, she wasn't family, or even particularly close to Phoenix. "Are you sure you want me along?" she asked.

"Absolutely." A hint of a smile curved her lips. "Someone has to keep Jake from getting upset about something and flying off the handle. You seem to have a calming effect on him."

Her eyes met Jake's, and she could tell he was thinking the same thing she was—that *calming* wasn't the word she would use to describe the effect they had on each other. *Ravenous* or *incendiary* might be better terms, considering the way they had gone after each other on the bluff on her family's ranch. Her face felt hot just remembering their lovemaking. She usually wasn't so reckless, but after a morning spent facing other people's expectations of her—her mother's and Rodney's and even Aunt Connie's—she had wanted to revel in the freedom of being with someone who had no expectations.

Jake accepted her as she was. To him, she wasn't the beauty queen or the tough cop or the obedient daughter or niece. She was merely herself. Someone he freely admitted he wanted to be with, someone with no ulterior motive or guile. He might be skilled at deceiving people, but she was pretty sure he wasn't being deceptive when he said he liked her and was attracted to her.

Somewhere between that first kiss and her crying out her climax, Jake Lohmiller had touched more than her skin. He had touched her heart.

Chapter Twelve

Jake told himself he ought to feel good about getting his mother to agree to see the doctor, but he couldn't shake off the pain of seeing her so frail and helpless. He didn't want to have to deal with that, so he tried to push the memory away. Time to focus on work—something he was better at controlling.

"We should stop by Metwater's motor home and see what Werner wants."

"I want to talk to Starfall first," he said. "It won't hurt Metwater to see that we're not at his beck and call. And we can see Metwater's motorhome from her tent. Werner won't leave without us knowing about it."

"What if Metwater is in real danger?"

"If I thought that was true, I would have been over there before now," he said. "But he hasn't given us one scrap of evidence to prove there's a real threat." He glanced around them. "Tony is supposed to be watching Werner, so he's probably around here somewhere. He'll act if there's trouble. And Metwater always has a couple of young guys hanging around as muscle, and we know he owns at least one gun. I think he can look after himself for a few more minutes. So he can wait."

He headed toward the white tent Starfall shared with

Asteria. Carmen followed. He couldn't tell if her silence meant she agreed with him or if she was only putting up with him because this was technically his investigation. She wasn't a person who wore her emotions on her sleeve, which he liked most of the time, but it did make it tougher for him to read her.

Starfall stepped outside, her baby in her arms, as the two officers approached. She said nothing, only glowered as they drew near.

"Thank you for helping my sister and my mom," Jake said. "I really appreciate it."

Her expression softened. She shifted the baby to one hip and some of the stiffness went out of her posture. "Is Phoenix going to be okay?" she asked.

"I hope so," he said. "She agreed to let me make an appointment at the clinic in town."

"What about Sophie?" Starfall bounced the baby. "She was pretty upset."

"She'll be okay, too."

"She's a tough kid. Like her mom." She sent him a sideways glance. "And her brother, I guess."

"Have you talked to Werner lately?" he asked.

The guarded expression returned. "I don't know anyone named Werner."

"Yes, you do. The German who asked you to collect cactus for him?"

"I don't see that it's any of your business who I talk to." The Starfall he knew best was back, all tough attitude and pout.

Jake ground his teeth in frustration. He couldn't tell her Werner was on his radar as a lawbreaker; he might have said too much already. And his original plan to pay Starfall for information about the German wasn't going

to work, either. She didn't strike him as the type to resist the temptation to double-cross. She would take his
money, then turn around and sell any information he
passed on to Werner for more money. Better to let her
go on working for the German and keep an eye on her to
see what she led him to. "I was wondering if he needed
any more cactus," he said. "I saw some good specimens
near where I was camped before. If you're still selling
them to him, you might look there."

Her eyes lit up. "Thanks. I may walk over there tomorrow and check them out." She shifted the baby again.
"Maybe you're not so bad—for a cop."

"Yeah," he said. "For a cop."

He turned to walk away. "Hey, Soldier Boy," she
called after him.

He looked over his shoulder at her. "What?"

"I hope your mom gets better soon."

The tightness in his chest returned—the pain that
he had felt when he'd seen his mother lying in her bed,
looking so small and frail and helpless. For all the mis-
takes she had made and the bad things she had done,
his mom had always been so full of life and energy. He
did love her. At times, he had thought he hated her. But
he had never been afraid for her, the way he was now.
"Thanks," he said. "I hope so, too."

He headed toward Metwater's trailer, Carmen beside him. She didn't have to say anything—just having
her there with him made him feel calmer. "Thanks for
telling Mom about what your aunt said," he told her. "I
think it helped."

"Maybe." She glanced at him. "This can't be easy
for you."

"Life with Mom has never been easy." He shrugged

off the memories. "But that's in the past. I just want to make the future better—for her, but especially for Sophie."

"You've already helped your mother and sister, by coming back into their lives," Carmen said.

"I hope that's true." He couldn't be sure. "I was away for too long," he said.

"My grandfather always said guilt was a prison you built yourself."

"Is that some bit of tribal wisdom?" Jake asked.

"I don't think so. I think he read it in a magazine or something."

He laughed, surprised that he felt so much better. "Mom was right about you," he said.

She looked wary. "What about me?"

"You know just how to handle me."

A pink flush warmed her skin, and he wondered if she was thinking of the way she had handled him earlier.

She was the first to look away. "Let's go talk to Metwater and his visitor," she said.

Asteria admitted them without comment. Metwater sat in his recliner, stiffly upright, while Werner sat on the sofa beside him. Jake was thankful he was in civilian clothes today. He only hoped Metwater wouldn't blow his cover by revealing he was a cop.

Werner started to stand, then sank back onto the sofa. For once, Metwater looked relieved to see the officers. "These are a couple of friends," he said by way of introduction. "Mr. Altbusser is an associate of mine who is in the area on vacation and stopped by to say hello."

Jake nodded to Werner. "Mr. Altbusser and I ran into each other when I was camping not far from here," he said. "How is your vacation going?"

"I may have to cut my visit short," Werner said. "But I appreciate the Prophet giving me another audience before I had to leave. I am very interested in his experiment in cooperative living here in the desert."

Jake supposed that was one way to describe what Metwater was doing out here in the wilderness. "Why do you have to shorten your visit?" he asked.

"A business crisis I must see to." Werner waved away the question. "I have already asked Mr. Metwater, but I will ask you, too. I was hoping to meet up with a friend of mine who I understand is also visiting in the area, but so far I haven't been able to find him. Perhaps you have seen him."

"Who is your friend?" Jake asked.

"He is a Russian. Taller than me, and broader. His name is Karol Petrovsky. We worked together once upon a time. I only just heard he was in the area."

At the mention of the Russian, Metwater paled. Jake ignored him and shook his head. "Sorry, I haven't seen him. He sounds like the kind of guy I would remember."

"Yes, he is very memorable." Werner shrugged. "If I do not find him, then perhaps it was not meant to be." He stood and offered his hand to Metwater. "I will not take up any more of your time," he said.

Metwater let the German take his hand, then Werner insisted on shaking hands with Jake and Carmen as well, before one of the bodyguards escorted him from the motor home.

As soon as Werner was gone, Metwater leaned toward Jake and spoke in an urgent whisper. "Did you hear him? This Russian must be the killer who's after me."

"Not every Russian is a member of the Russian mafia," Jake said.

Metwater glared at him. "You can't think this is merely a coincidence."

"Life is full of coincidences," Jake said. "But we will keep an eye out for this Russian. If the man was a friend of Werner's, he might be involved in the same smuggling operation."

"Was that all Mr. Altbusser wanted?" Carmen asked. "To ask about his friend?"

"What else would he want?" Metwater asked.

"Maybe he wanted to recruit more of your followers to find cactus for him," she said. "Maybe he even offered you a cut of the profits."

"I have better things to do with my time than dig up plants." He stood. "If you're not going to help me, you can leave."

That was fine with Jake. "Call us if Werner visits again," he said. "Or if you spot any Russians—mafia or otherwise."

He and Carmen left. He was silent until they were back in his truck. "Starfall won't be happy if she finds out she has to compete with other people for payment from Werner," he said.

"I'm guessing if Werner did make an offer, Metwater won't go for it now," Carmen said. "He's too afraid of Werner's friend, the Russian."

"There's something else about this whole setup that bothers me," Jake said.

"Only one thing?"

"One other thing," he said. "Where is Tony?"

"Tony?" she asked.

"He's the Fish and Wildlife agent who took my place. The man who's supposed to be shadowing Werner? I didn't spot him anywhere around camp."

"He's not supposed to let Werner see him," she said. "Maybe he was doing a really good job."

"I would have spotted him," Jake said. He pressed down on the accelerator, speeding up.

Carmen grabbed hold of the dash as they bounced over the rough road. "What are you doing?" she asked.

"We have to go to Werner's motel," he said. "Tony had a room there. We have to make sure he's all right."

SOPHIE KICKED AT the dirt outside the trailer. As soon as Jake and Carmen left, Sarah had sent her away. "Go play now," she said, shooing her toward the door. "Your mother needs to rest." As if Sophie was some little kid and couldn't help take care of her own mother.

Her mom looked bad. At least she wasn't out of her head, the way she had been when she first woke up after her fainting spell. At least Jake had been able to talk her into seeing a doctor. She sure hoped there was some medicine that could make her better. Sophie had never minded much not having her father around, but what would she do without her mother?

And, of course, doctors didn't work for free. They'd need money to pay for the treatments and medicine her mother might need. Maybe the Prophet would pay for them. He always talked about how they were a *Family*, and families shared everything and took care of each other. But sharing a pot of beans was a lot different from sharing medical bills. Her mother had signed over everything to him when they had joined the Family, but it wasn't like it had been a lot—an old car that wasn't even around anymore and the trailer they lived in. Her mother had never held a steady job, and they had never had any money. That hadn't mattered so much most of the time. She and Sophie had lived with Grandma and Grandpa, and then here with the Prophet. But medical bills were different. They could be hundreds, thousands of dollars, maybe even more. The Prophet might not want to pay that much.

She wandered away from the trailer, toward the center of camp. Times like this she missed having someone her own age around. When Jake talked of her going to school and having friends, it sounded fun. Back when she had lived with her grandparents, she had liked school, and she had been starting to make friends when her mother decided they should move. She imagined it would be like in books she had read—she would have two or three best friends, or even just one—and they would have sleepovers and stuff like that. It made a little ache around her heart when she thought about it, so most of the time she tried to put the idea out of her mind.

"Hey, Sophie! Come here a minute!"

She looked around and saw Starfall beckoning her from outside her tent. Sophie started toward her. She didn't really like Starfall all that much—she was too bossy and even mean sometimes. But her little boy, Hunter, was so sweet, and he liked Sophie a lot. He always smiled and held out his arms to her when she was near. Maybe Starfall wanted Sophie to watch him while she went off with her friends or some guy. Sophie usually didn't mind babysitting—it was something to do, after all. But this time, maybe she'd ask if Starfall could pay her. She needed to start earning money in case her mom needed it.

But Hunter wasn't with Starfall, who sat in a folding chair outside her tent, one foot propped up on the edge of the chair while she painted the toenails a bright pink. "What are you up to?" Starfall asked when Sophie stopped in front of her.

Sophie shrugged. "Not much. Do you need me to watch Hunter?"

"Not now. He's napping." She capped the bottle of polish and fanned her hand over her toenails. "Do you remember that cactus you found for me the other day? The day we were picking berries?"

"You mean the day the guy shot at us?"

Starfall frowned. "Well, yeah, that too."

Sophie wanted to laugh. How could anybody think cactus were more memorable than being shot at? But that was Starfall—she was going to make money off cactus, so that was what was most important to her. "Yeah, I remember," she said.

"Your brother said he saw more of them by where he was camped. Do you think you could find them for me?"

Interesting that Jake had been talking to Starfall. But maybe it was the other way around. Starfall liked to flirt with men. Maybe she had been flirting with Jake. But Jake was interested in Carmen—anybody could see that. Just another example of Starfall being clueless. "I don't know where he was camped," Sophie said.

"I do." Starfall lowered her foot to the ground and extended both legs to admire her freshly painted toes. "We can walk over there in the morning, and I'll show you."

"What will you give me if I find the cactus for you?" Sophie asked.

"Why should I give you anything?" Starfall asked.

"Didn't you say some guy is paying you for the cactus? If I'm doing the work, I should get part of the money."

Starfall narrowed her eyes, but she must have seen

that Sophie wasn't going to back down. "I'll give you five dollars," she said.

"I want ten."

"No way," Starfall said. "That's half of what I make. And I'm a lot older than you are."

"But I'm the one who'll be doing all the work—finding and digging," Sophie said. "Besides, with me along, you'll find more cactus. Maybe twice as much."

Starfall had to know this was true. By herself, she wasn't patient enough to crawl around in the hot sun and really look at the plants on the ground. She would much rather have Sophie do everything for her. The older woman looked sullen but nodded. "Okay. But you don't get the money until after Werner pays me."

Sophie would rather have had the money up front. She didn't trust Starfall not to "forget" to pay her. But if that happened, she would ask Jake to get the money for her. She doubted very many people would say no to her brother when he was angry. Mama always scolded Jake for having a bad temper, but maybe sometimes it was a good thing. "All right," she said.

"Good. Meet me back here after breakfast," Starfall said. "Bring something to dig with and a sack to put everything in."

Sophie could have argued that if she was going to do all the work, she shouldn't have to provide the tools, too, but since she was getting ten dollars, she kept quiet. "All right. I'll see you in the morning." She turned away, not letting Starfall see how happy she was. She would find as many cactus as she could tomorrow. Ten—maybe even twenty. That would be a couple hundred dollars to help pay her mom's doctor bills. Jake would be so impressed. He wouldn't treat her like a baby who couldn't be counted on to help out when it really mattered.

JAKE BROKE EVERY speed limit on the way to the motel where Werner and Tony were staying—the motel where Jake had also stayed in order to shadow Werner until Tony had taken over that job. He circled around to the back of the motel and cruised past the room where Werner was staying—151. Tony would be in Jake's old room, 153, right next door. "That's Werner's rental," he said, indicating the red Jeep parked in front of 151.

"Do you see Tony's car?" Carmen asked.

"I don't know what he's driving. But he wouldn't have it parked in front of his room, anyway. He wouldn't want Werner to see it and recognize it, if he had to follow the suspect later." He parked his truck facing a fence across from the two rooms and shut off the engine, then sat, his hands on the steering wheel, eyes fixed on the image of the two motel-room doors in his rearview mirror.

"What now?" Carmen asked.

"I can't risk Werner seeing me and wondering what I'm doing here," he said. "Maybe you should go knock on Tony's door, see if he's in."

"Werner has seen me."

"But not for long." He reached behind the seat and pulled out a Houston Astros ball cap. "Stuff your hair under this, and keep your sunglasses on. Slouch or shuffle or something to change your gait. Approach the room from the side, so Werner can't get a good look at you out the window."

She took the cap. "What do I do if Tony answers? How will I even recognize him?"

"He's shorter than me and stockier. Balding. Crooked

nose where it was broken a long time ago. Tell him you're with me, and ask him to meet us somewhere near here in half an hour."

"All right." She gathered her long, black hair at the nape of her neck and twisted it into a coil, then covered the coil with the cap. This exposed her neck, and he fought the urge to lean over and kiss that long, smooth column. She put her hand on the door to open it, and he reached out and squeezed her arm.

"Be careful," he said. "If you see anything out of line, get out of there ASAP."

"I know the drill," she said. "I've been a cop a while now."

"Right." He let go of her. He forgot sometimes that she had more experience than he did.

He kept her in view as she moved behind the line of parked cars, then crossed the parking lot and walked toward Tony's room, approaching it from the direction opposite Werner's door. She pulled the hat lower over her eyes, then knocked on the door of 153. She waited a long minute. Jake gripped the steering wheel, counting off the seconds. If Werner was in his room—and the presence of his Jeep indicated he was—why wasn't Tony answering his door?

Carmen lifted her hand to knock again, and at that moment the door to the room swung inward. A man ran out, knocking Carmen back onto the sidewalk. She struggled with him as Jake bailed out of the truck, reaching for the gun tucked into the back of his jeans.

The man, a bulky build whose face was turned away from Jake, hauled back and punched Carmen in the face. Jake felt the punch in his own gut and raised his gun. "Stop! Police!" he shouted.

Carmen's assailant didn't even look his way. He jumped up and ducked behind the nearest car, then took off running. Jake pursued, his feet pounding the asphalt lot, but the man was too far ahead of him. He didn't see his quarry get into a vehicle, but the roar of an engine and the squeal of tires announced his getaway as he sped out of the motel lot and into traffic on the highway.

Jake stared after the fleeing vehicle—a dark SUV with heavily tinted windows. Mud on the license plate made it impossible to read. By the time he reached his truck to chase him, the man would be long gone. He turned and jogged back toward Carmen, picking up speed when he saw her still lying on the concrete. His heart battered his ribs as he threw himself down beside her. "Carmen, are you okay?"

She opened her eyes and looked up at him. "Did you get the linebacker who ran over me?" she asked.

He laughed—a sick sound full of relief and agony. "He got away," he said. "Are you okay? Should I call an ambulance?"

"He just knocked the wind out of me." She tugged on his hand and pulled herself into a sitting position. She touched the corner of her eye, which was already swelling and darkening where the assailant had hit her, and she winced. "I think it was Werner's friend—the Russian. The description fit, anyway."

Jake looked back at 153. The door stood open, the interior of the room in deep shadow. "I don't have a good feeling about this," he said.

"He was in a hurry to get out of there." Carmen tried to stand and swayed a little.

Jake jumped up and held onto her. "You should sit down."

"I'll be fine." She swatted him away. "We'd better call for backup."

"You call." He made sure she was braced against the side of the building and released her. "I'm going to check inside." He wasn't going to stand around waiting when Tony might be still alive and hurt, needing help right away.

She pulled out her phone. "All right. But be careful."

The same words he had used with her. Words cops said to each other all the time, overstating the obvious. They were always careful—but not too careful. Part of the job was taking risks most sensible people wouldn't take.

Avoiding touching anyplace that might retain prints, he nudged open the door with the toe of his boot. Sunlight arced into the small room, revealing an overturned chair and an unmade bed, the flower-print bedspread half-trailing onto the gray-green carpeting. He pulled out his phone and used the flashlight app to illuminate the rest of the room. He stilled on a bright red smear on the far wall and followed it down to the floor—and the body of Field Agent Tony Davidson.

Chapter Thirteen

Carmen ignored the aches and pains in her face and limbs as she stood beside Jake and watched paramedics carry Tony's body out of the motel room on a draped stretcher. His throat had been cut—a brutal, terrifying way to die. "I'm sorry about your friend," she said to Jake as the doors of the ambulance closed.

"He wasn't a friend. Not really."

"But another agent—they're a little like family."

"Yeah." He brushed his finger over the bruise on her cheek, and a shiver ran through her. "I saw red when that guy knocked you down."

"I'm okay. I've been hurt worse. I'm guessing he was the killer, but why?"

"I don't know. Tony was a good agent. I don't see how the Russian—if that was the Russian—could have made him for a cop. But I knew if he wasn't on the job, something must have happened to him."

"Did you think Werner did something to him before he headed out to see Metwater?"

Jake shook his head. "I didn't know. I just had a bad feeling. I was hoping we'd get here and find him sick with the flu or something."

She glanced toward the room next door. Jake had

pointed it out to her earlier as Werner's room. "Do we know Werner is in there?" she asked.

"We're pretty sure. That's his vehicle in front of the door."

"You'd think he would come out to see what all the commotion is about."

"He probably looked out and saw the police cars and is lying low. But I'd sure like to know how much he knows about all this."

"Then why don't you question him?" she asked.

"Because then he would know I'm a cop. When I called in to tell my boss what was going on, he told me to get away from here as soon as I could, and to not let Werner see me. He's hoping if I stay undercover—at least until they get an agent here to replace Tony—we can avoid aborting the investigation. We've been working on this case for more than a year and have poured thousands of dollars into it. We're really close to making a bunch of arrests."

"I can ask one of the other Rangers to question him." Carmen said. "He can say he's interviewing everyone near the victim's room."

"Good idea," Jake said.

"Let's call Lance Carpenter." She pulled out her phone. "Being with the Montrose Sheriff's Department, he won't look out of place."

Since the Sheriff's Department already had their investigative team on site, this made sense. Fish and Wildlife would assign someone to the case as well—maybe even Jake. But for now, they were relying on the local cops to secure the evidence on scene.

Carmen gave Lance a summary of what was going on, then passed the phone to Jake, who provided more background on Werner and what they hoped to learn from him. He gave Lance his contact information, then hung up and returned the phone to Carmen. "He's on his way. Let me take you back to your place. You need to put some ice on that eye."

CARMEN'S PLACE TURNED out to be half of a duplex not far from the national park. "We call this Ranger Row, so many of us live here," she said as Jake pulled his truck into her driveway. "Or used to. Marco and Michael and Randall have all gotten married recently and moved into town with their wives. But there are still some of us die-hards around."

He followed her up the walk from the driveway and waited while she unlocked the door. A loud yowl greeted them as they stepped inside. "I know, Muffin. I've been away forever." She stooped and gathered up a yellow tabby, who rubbed his head against her chin, then eyed Jake over her shoulder.

"You have a cat," he said, hanging back a little.

"I've had Muffin since he was a kitten." She cradled the cat in her arms and rubbed under his chin. The cat arched his neck and let out a purr that was audible across the room. She glanced at him. "You don't have a prob-lem with cats, do you?"

"I've never been around them much." Not at all, re-ally.

"Well, come and say hello."

Jake approached cautiously. Muffin watched him through slit, golden eyes. He held out his hand, letting the animal sniff him. That was what you were supposed to do, right? Then he let out a yelp as Muffin sank his teeth into Jake's thumb.

"Muffin, no!" Carmen scolded. She set the cat on the floor and turned to Jake. "Are you okay? I don't know what got into him."

Jake sucked him thumb and eyed the cat, who was stalking away, looking back every few paces to glare at Jake. So that was how it was going to be, was it? "I think maybe he's a little, um, possessive."

Carmen wrinkled her forehead. "Why would you think that?"

Because I'm the guy who wants to keep him from being the only male in your life. "I have no idea," he said. He walked over to a bookcase, where she had a number of pictures displayed in frames. Several showed her with various family members—her mother, a man he assumed was her father, her aunt and others. In one, she stood in the center of a group of women, all dressed in Native American dresses decorated with feathers and bells. "What is this?" he asked.

"I used to dance at powwows, when I was a teenager."

He grinned. "I'd like to see that some time."

He started to reach for her, but she turned away. "Do you want something to drink? I've got tea and sodas in the kitchen." She was already moving toward the kitchen, and he hurried to catch up with her.

Like the rest of the house, the kitchen was small but neat, decorated in red and yellow. She was opening a can of cat food when he entered the room. "I'd better feed Muffin before he starts complaining," she said.

At the sound of his name, the cat came into the room, again glaring at Jake as he passed him. Jake liked that the cat saw him as a threat. Animals were supposed to be sensitive to emotions, right? So maybe he was picking up on Carmen's feelings for this intruder. Or maybe that was Jake's wishful thinking.

Cat fed, she moved to putting ice in glasses. "Would you rather have a beer or something?"

He put his hand on hers to stop her. "I don't need anything," he said.

She looked up, her eyes big and dark. Her hand trembled a little. "You're nervous," he said, the idea shocking him. He moved his hand away and stepped back. "Why?"

She ducked her head, her hair falling forward in a silken curtain that hid her expression from him. "I guess I'm feeling a little…vulnerable, having you here."

"Do you want me to go?" His stomach knotted, but he forced himself to keep his voice even.

"No!" She turned away from the counter and reached for him.

He slipped two fingers beneath her chin and tilted her face up until he could look into her eyes. It bothered him a little to see the one eye swollen shut. "We forgot the ice for your eye," he said.

"A little late for that now. It's okay."

"Then want to tell me what the problem is? Why do you feel vulnerable?"

She blew out a breath. "I'm a cop. And I work with men all day. The criminals I deal with are mostly men. To deal with that—to fit in and do my job—I've learned to be tough. A little hard. And it's a side effect of the job that I tend to deal with all people that way. Makes it hard to date but, I figure, if a guy wants to be with me, he's got to accept that."

"You don't seem hard to me." He traced his finger along the underside of her jaw, and the soft, satiny skin there. She closed her eyes and leaned into his hand—not unlike her cat had done with her earlier.

"That's just it—you've made me let my guard down. Something I didn't see coming. I'm not sure I know how to handle it."

"You're doing a good job so far." He kissed her cheek, and then her smooth, warm throat, slipping one hand around her back to draw her snug against him.

She looked into his eyes, searching. "Part of me says not to trust you."

That hurt to hear, but he wasn't going to run from it. "Why is that?"

"Because you're not like any other man I've known. You don't have ties to a group of people or a certain place. You have your mother and sister and your job, but you still seem so alone."

"I am alone, but I'm trying to change that. I came to get my mother and sister to change that. I think I'm attracted to you because I want to change that."

"Can you change?" she asked. "Can a loner become part of a group? Part of a family?"

"If it's the right group. The right family." He kissed her temple, and she closed her eyes, then stood on tiptoe and pressed her lips to his.

"Then I want to help you try," she whispered. She took his hand in hers and tugged him away from the counter.

She led him out of the room and down a short hallway to her bedroom. He had an impression of soft blues and muted light before she closed the door behind them and gathered him in her arms.

"Just so you know, your being tough never put me

off," he said. "It's one of the things that attracted me to you from that first day."

"I figured most men like to play Big Strong Rescuer." She smoothed her hand down his back. "More than one man has told me I'm too intimidating."

"It can be an ego stroke to save someone but, you know, I did enough rescuing of my mom. I like a woman who can stand on her own feet—or who could rescue me, if that's what I needed." He kissed the corner of her mouth. "Or, as my mom pointed out, one who can keep me in line."

He liked the way her eyes crinkled when she smiled. She grasped the pull of his zipper. "I like keeping you in line," she said as she slowly lowered it.

He caught his breath as she freed him from his jeans and underwear, then he began undoing the buttons of her shirt. "Can't let you have all the fun," he murmured.

Their first lovemaking had been hurried, almost frantic in the rush to satisfy their pent-up need. This time, they savored the experience, undressing slowly, becoming acquainted with the curves and planes of each other's bodies. He measured the weight of her breasts in his hands and the curve of her hip against his palm, savored the taste of her skin and the sound of the breathy moans she made as he kissed his way down her body.

In turn, she skimmed her hands along his shoulders and down his back, her touch sending shock waves of sensation through him. He focused all his attention on her, on her pleasure. Some of the urgency of that first time returned. Her climax was still shuddering through her when he levered himself over and into her. She wrapped her long legs around him and rocked with him in a rhythm that soon had him panting and on the edge of losing control.

She opened her eyes and met his gaze. "Let go," she whispered, and he did, waves of pleasure rocketing through him until he was utterly spent.

Afterwards, they lay together, his head resting on her shoulder, her fingers idly combing through his hair. He had never felt this close to anyone before—maybe he hadn't allowed himself to be this close. "Thank you," he said.

She rolled toward him and looked into his eyes. "What are you thanking me for?"

"For trusting me enough to let me into your life. I know it isn't easy. It isn't easy for me, either."

She rolled back. "You're tough to resist," she said. "And I usually have a lot of willpower."

He was trying to think of the right response to this when his phone rang. "Is that yours?" she asked.

"Yeah." Reluctantly, he got up and found his pants on the floor and retrieved the phone. "Hello?"

"It's Lance. I thought you'd want to know the results of my interview with Werner Altbusser."

The fog cleared and he tensed. "Tell me."

"About what you would expect—he doesn't know anything, he didn't see anything. But it's clear he's terrified of something. He was packing to leave when I got there. I told him that we needed him to stick around for a few days as a potential witness. I didn't come out and say we wouldn't let him leave, but I gave the strong impression, so I think he'll stay put. Just in case he decides to bolt, I alerted all the airports in the area, and the Amtrak station in Grand Junction. If he tries to leave that way, they'll hold him for us."

"Thanks," Jake said "Did anybody else see the guy who did this?"

"No. Most of the rooms on that side of the motel are empty, or the occupants were out. No security cameras focused on that area, either. We've got an APB out with the description you gave us, but so far no one has spotted him."

"Werner mentioned this guy was camping in the wilderness area," Jake said. "If he wants to hide, it would be easier to do it there."

"We'll do some extra patrols and alert the park rangers and Forest Service people, too."

"Thanks."

"No problem. We want this guy as much as you do."

Jake ended the call with Lance and hit the number for his boss. Ron Clark answered on the second ring. "What have you got for us?" he asked.

He gave him a summary of Lance's report. "I was hoping you would have something," he said.

"We have a tentative ID on the Russian." Jake heard the tap of computer keys. "Karol Petrovsky. Originally from Vladivostok, but he's lived in Tokyo for the past ten years. We suspect he was Werner's Asian distributor. As far as we can determine, Petrovsky has never traveled to the United States before—he left that side of the business to Altbusser."

"So what is he doing in the States now?" Jake asked.

"We don't know. Maybe he wanted a bigger cut of the profits. Or maybe he suspects Werner has been cheating him."

"Werner seems afraid of the guy," Jake said. "Like maybe they aren't friends anymore."

"Maybe he wants to eliminate Werner and get all

the business for himself," Clark said. "It's a profitable market, but a relatively small one—not room for a lot of players."

"He must have killed Tony because he made him as a cop," Jake said. "And he probably killed Reggae as a warning to Werner, or maybe he thought he was eliminating more competition."

"Apparently, he did time in a Russian prison for knifing a guy he thought had crossed him in a different business deal," Clark said.

Jake's stomach churned. "We've got to stop him."

"Watch your back," Clark said. "Clearly, he's ruthless. Keep tabs on him, but don't be a hero."

"Right." That was the sensible way to approach this. But anyone who knew Jake would vouch for the fact that he wasn't always sensible, especially when it came to righting a wrong or protecting those he loved.

Chapter Fourteen

The next morning, Sophie set out with Starfall to look for cactus. Starfall led the way toward the canyon where they had picked raspberries. "I thought we were going over by Jake's camp," Sophie said as they trudged along.

"That was too far to go this morning. We'll go tomorrow."

"I'm hoping tomorrow Jake will take Mom to the doctor." Phoenix was out of bed and said she felt better today, but Sophie didn't think she looked much better.

"We'll go the next day, then. Now hurry up." Starfall marched along the edge of the canyon, whacking berry vines out of her way with a machete she must have taken from the communal tool shed.

"But we already looked here," Sophie said. "That day we picked berries."

"We didn't look very long," Starfall said. "We were interrupted, remember?"

"Yeah." Sophie wasn't going to forget that. "Why do you think someone was shooting at us?"

"Your brother's the cop. Doesn't he know?"

"If he does, he didn't say." She bit her lower lip. "I wonder if it's the same guy who killed Reggae." She shivered, the thought both horrifying—and a little exciting.

"Well, he's not going to care about us." Starfall nudged her. "Don't worry about that. Look for cactus."

Sophie focused her eyes on the ground, searching for the little spiny plants. The sheet of paper Starfall had shown her earlier indicated they could be as small as a quarter, and almost the color of the soil. No wonder they were hard to find. "What are you going to do with the money you get for selling the cactus?" she asked.

Starfall shrugged. "I don't know."

"I thought maybe you were saving up to leave the camp."

Starfall crouched to examine the ground more closely. "Why do you think that?"

"I don't know." She turned over a fallen branch with her foot and studied the beetle that crawled from beneath it. "You're not like some of the others, making such a big deal over the Prophet. You seem more, I don't know, independent."

"I'll take that as a compliment," Starfall said. She rose and walked on. "Sometimes I think about traveling, or maybe starting my own business. But for now, I have it pretty good. I always liked camping, and the Prophet leaves me alone. He knows I'm not one of his groupies."

Sophie guessed that meant her mom was one of the Prophet's "groupies." It made Sophie feel a little icky to think about it. "Mom says he wants to marry me when I'm older." It was one of the things her mom had said when she was delirious after the last time she fainted, so Sophie didn't know if it was true—she hoped not.

Starfall gave her a hard look. "No offense, but your mom is dreaming," she said. "Daniel Metwater has no reason to marry one woman when he can have all the women he wants."

"I think it's creepy that a man as old as he is would even be interested in a fourteen-year-old," Sophie said, relieved to be able to say the words out loud. "But Mom doesn't see it that way."

"Your mom is a dreamer," Starfall said again. "Some people are like that. Maybe real life is too hard for them, so they make up a better one in their head. And I don't know—maybe she has the right idea. Everybody copes in her own way."

"Yeah, I guess so."

Starfall nudged her. "Your brother, now, he's the practical sort," she said. "He's not going to let the Prophet marry you, no matter what your mother says."

"Yeah. Jake is pretty great. I like Carmen, too."

"I don't trust Carmen, but then I don't trust most people."

"You don't trust her because she's a cop," Sophie said. And maybe because Carmen and Jake were a couple—or, at least, Sophie was pretty sure they were—and Starfall was jealous. Even a fourteen-year-old could see that.

"Whatever." Starfall looked at her. "What about you? What are you going to do with your share of the cactus money?"

"I need the money to help pay for Mom's doctor bills." She knelt and pointed to the ground. "And there's our first one."

Starfall took a trowel from the bag she had slung over her shoulder and handed it to Sophie. "One down, more to go."

In the next hour, they found only one more of the kind of cactus the German wanted. "I don't see what difference it makes what kind we get," Starfall said when they sat to rest in the shade of a rock. "They all look pretty much the same to me—ugly."

"I guess it makes a difference to whoever he's selling them to." Sophie tugged on the end of her braid and squinted across the empty landscape of rocks and juniper. "It's kind of creepy out here, don't you think?"

"What do you mean?"

"I don't know. It feels like someone's watching us." She shivered and rubbed her shoulders.

Starfall looked around them. "I don't see anyone," she said.

"If someone is spying on us, he wouldn't want us to see him, would he? It just doesn't feel right out here today."

"You've been listening to too many ghost stories around the campfire." Starfall stood and patted Sophie's shoulder. "Come on. We only have another half hour or so before we have to get back to camp, and we've only found two cactus. If we're going to make any money, we'd better get busy."

She started to tell Starfall that, if they wanted to make any money, they needed to get lucky, but she kept quiet. After all, it wasn't as if either one of them had hit the jackpot when it came to luck in their lives.

CARMEN HAD BEEN sure that by the next morning she would be over having a man in her house—making a mess in her bathroom, spilling coffee grounds on the counter, pacing her bedroom naked while he was on the phone. Okay, maybe that last part wasn't annoying at all, just incredibly distracting. But, except for the fact that Muffin hissed and headed the other direction anytime Jake came within view, having him around hadn't been a bad thing at all. Was it a haze of sexual attraction making her overlook the disruptions to her calm little world—or was it that part of her recognized she might be overdue for a little disruption?

She was pondering this over the remains of the omelet Jake had cooked for her (the man had mad kitchen skills—who knew?) when her phone rang. Did mothers have some kind of Mom Radar, that she was calling on this particular morning? "Hi, Mom," Carmen said, prepared to lie and say she was alone if her mother asked. She wasn't ready to be that revealing about her private life.

"We had a really strange visitor here at headquarters," Wilma Redhorse said after she and her daughter had exchanged pleasantries. "Something I thought you might like to know about."

"Oh?" Carmen laid down her fork and looked across the table at Jake, who had picked up on her shift in attitude and was watching her intently. "Who?"

"A Russian man made an appointment with the chairman," Wilma said. "He said he had a business proposition for the tribe. We get that from time to time, especially from Europeans who are looking for new places to invest their money. Most of the time nothing comes of it, but the chairman has a policy that he will hear everyone out."

"What was the business proposition?" Carmen asked.

"He wants to grow cactus. Some kind of rare cactus that other Europeans and Asians will pay a lot of money for. He wanted permission to survey tribal land for the presence of rare species—which I'm thinking means he wants to see how much he can steal out from under our noses." She made a snorting sound. "Not that I'm cynical or anything."

"What was this Russian like?" Carmen asked. "What was his name?"

"He gave me a card. Let's see…his name is Karl Petrov. Big guy—looked a lot like your uncle Ed. As for what he was like—you know the type. Someone whose only knowledge of Native Americans is from bad western movies." She chuckled. "You could tell he was seriously disappointed when the chairman came out of his office and was wearing a suit instead of a loincloth and feathers."

"What did you tell him?" Carmen asked.

"We told him *no*. We don't do joint ventures. We have our own businesses. The chairman also let him know that, if he is caught trespassing on tribal land, he will be arrested and prosecuted. He muttered something in Russian that sounded like curses, but then a lot of foreign languages sound like that to me."

Carmen gripped the phone tightly. "Does his card have any contact information on it?" she asked. "A telephone number or email? Did he mention where he was staying or how to get in touch with him?"

"No. It's just a plain card with his name in English and Russian lettering. We didn't have any desire to talk to him again, so we didn't ask."

"And I guess you didn't get the license plate information on his car? Or security-camera footage that would show that?"

"We don't have security cameras. And why would we get his plate number?" Wilma said. "What is going on here?"

"That man is wanted for the murder of a federal Fish and Wildlife officer," Carmen said. "If he comes back there, please contact the police and one of us right away.

Don't try to hold him yourself, just call us. He's very dangerous."

"All right, dear. But I don't think he's going to come back. The chairman can be pretty fierce when he wants to be, even without a war bonnet."

She hung up the phone. "Karol Petrovsky was at Ute tribal headquarters," she told Jake before he could ask. "He wanted to look for cactus on tribal lands."

"So maybe he is trying to cut out Werner and handle all the business himself," Jake said.

She tucked the phone back into the pocket of her jeans. "I don't like the idea of that killer being so close to my mother."

"Is there any reason to think he'll come back?" Jake asked.

"No. And he didn't leave any contact information. He was using the name Karl Petrov, but I'm sure it was the same man."

"I'll let people know to be on the lookout for that alias. Do you want to go out there and talk to your mother?"

She nodded. "I should interview her and our tribal council chairman to find out what else they can tell us." But more than that, she needed to see for herself that her mother was all right.

"Do you want me to go with you?" he asked.

She shook her head. "You stay and work on things from this end. I'll go by myself." The time with family would do her good, help clear her head of Jake for a while and allow her to think about how she really felt about him—and where she wanted those feelings to take her.

CARMEN WORE HER uniform when she went back to the reservation to interview her mother and the chairman.

She needed that symbol of authority to remind her that she was in control. A killer was out there, but she and the other officers hunting for him were going to find him and stop him. And the uniform helped her be in better control of herself and others on the reservation as well. In uniform, she wasn't Wilma and Jim Redhorse's daughter, she was an officer of the law.

She had arranged to meet her mother and the chairman in the tribal council offices, but Rodney Tonaho greeted her when she entered council chambers. "I wanted to get your take on what we're dealing with with this guy," he said. "In case he comes back."

"I doubt he'll come back but, if he does, don't confront him," she said. She looked over her shoulder in time to see her mother and the chairman, Greg Fossey, emerge from the chairman's office. "I want to know exactly what he said to you," she said, hurrying to her mother. "Did he threaten you in any way?"

Wilma waved away her daughter's concern. "He was very polite and respectful," she said. "Persistent, but I admire that in a person."

"He didn't want to take *no* for an answer." Chairman Fossey took Carmen's hand. "It is good to see you again," he said.

"Has the Fish and Wildlife man moved on?" Wilma asked.

"He's still working on the case in Montrose," Carmen said, though she suspected that was not the question her mother had really been asking.

"Why don't we sit down and talk?" Wilma pulled out a chair at the meeting table. "Carmen, you can sit next to Rodney there."

Ignoring her, Carmen took the chair next to her

mother. For the next half hour, she went over everything they could tell her about Karl Petrov/Karol Petrovsky. Her mother and the chairman were good at supplying details, but none of it added up to anything that could really help her figure out where Petrovsky was now or what his next move might be.

"We'll keep an eye out for him," Rodney said, standing. "I'll put a deputy on patrol in the area he was interested in, in case he tries to sneak back in."

"Thanks." Carmen stood and shook his hand. "That could be very helpful." She shouldn't let her distaste for her mother's matchmaking get in the way of accepting help from a fellow law enforcement officer. "I'll let you know what we find out."

Rodney left, and the chairman excused himself for another meeting, leaving Wilma alone with her daughter. "That was smart, telling Rodney you'd let him know what happens," she said. "It will give you an excuse to see him again."

Carmen sat back down and faced her mother. "Mom, I'd like you to listen to me," she said.

Wilma widened her eyes. "I always listen to you."

"Then pay special attention now, and remember. I am not interested in Rodney. Not romantically."

Wilma pressed her lips together, then opened them to speak, but Carmen cut her off. "I have a job I love, and I'm not interested in working for the tribal police. I love to come back to the reservation to visit—but not to live."

"You say that now, but you could change your mind," Wilma said.

"I don't think I will but, if I do, it won't be because you keep pressuring me. That isn't going to work."

"I'm not pressuring you. I would never do that."

Wilma's expression showed sufficient outrage that Carmen believed her. Her mother didn't see anything heavy-handed in her attempt to persuade her daughter to move back home and take a job on and marry a man from the reservation. Carmen took her hand and squeezed it. "Mom, I'm not going to leave you. Just because I don't live down the street doesn't mean I'm not just a phone call away. But I need to choose my own place to live and my own job, and I need to choose my own man."

Wilma squeezed her hand, hard enough that it hurt, but Carmen didn't pull away. "Who is the man?" she asked.

Carmen blinked. "What makes you think there's a man?" she asked.

"You're my daughter. I know you. There's something different about you lately. Less…tense. Happier. Connie saw it, too. She called me right after you left here yesterday."

Aunt Connie, who thought she could "see" things about people. Carmen swallowed. "I've been seeing Jake. I like him. A lot."

Wilma nodded. "He has a very strong personality. Maybe that's what you need. It probably doesn't hurt that he's good-looking."

"Mom!" Carmen didn't know whether to be horrified or amused.

"I'm your mother—I'm not dead."

"You're not going to lecture me about marrying someone in the tribe?" Carmen asked.

"Are you going to marry this man—Jake?"

Carmen couldn't keep the heated flush from her face.

"I… I don't know." She was a little afraid of how much the idea appealed to her.

"Of course it would be ideal if you married another Ute. But, over the years, it's not as if there hasn't been plenty of marrying outside the tribe. Connie's husband is white, and Veronica's is Mexican, and they're both good men." She took her hand from Carmen's and cupped her daughter's cheeks. "I want you to be happy. And yes—I want to keep you close. I'd hate it if this Jake took you back to Texas or wherever he's from, but it probably wouldn't kill me."

"I don't know what's going to happen, Mom," Carmen said. "But you don't have to worry about me. I want to be happy, too."

"Good. We both want the same thing." Wilma gave Carmen's cheek a little pat, then sat back. "Rodney is going to be disappointed," she said.

"Rodney could have his pick of half the women on the reservation," Carmen said. "Maybe if he knows I'm not available, he'll open his eyes and notice some of them."

"Maybe he will. In the meantime, what about Jake?"

"We're taking things slow." She stood. "I'll let you know. But first, I have to catch a killer."

Chapter Fifteen

"Do you think this dress is all right? Maybe I should change." Phoenix tried to fluff up her limp hair with shaking hands.

Sophie grabbed her mother's wrist and clasped her hand. "You look beautiful, Mom. It'll be okay."

"I don't like doctors," Phoenix said for probably the tenth time since Jake had sent word yesterday that he and Carmen were coming to take her to the clinic the next morning. "I never understand what they're saying, and they rush over my questions."

"Maybe this doctor won't be like that," Sophie said. "And Jake and Carmen will be there with you. They'll make sure your questions get answered." At least, this was what Sophie hoped would happen. She hadn't been to a doctor since a school physical years ago that her grandparents had taken her to. That visit hadn't been so bad. The woman doctor had been friendly, even, and afterwards her grandparents had taken her for ice cream. "Maybe after the visit you can go for ice cream or something," she added.

A knock on the door interrupted before Phoenix could respond to this suggestion. "They're here." She fluttered her hands. "I'm not ready."

Sophie opened the door. Jake's smile made her feel a lot less nervous about this morning—she hoped it did the same for their mom. Jake was so strong and solid and steady. She believed him when he said he was going to take care of them. After all, he had fought the enemy overseas when he was a soldier, and he worked now to fight bad guys as a law enforcement officer. He wasn't about to let anything bad happen to his mom and sister.

"Are you ready to go, Mom?" he asked.

"You look very nice," Carmen said, and Phoenix gave her a grateful smile.

"I'm not ready," Phoenix said again. She smoothed her skirt. "But I'm going to go anyway."

Jake turned to Sophie. "We shouldn't be too long," he said. "You'll be all right here on your own?"

Sophie stared at him. "I'm going with you," she said.

"No!" Phoenix's voice rose. "I don't want you there, Sophie. You stay here where I'll know you're safe."

"Why wouldn't I be safe with you and Jake and Carmen?" Sophie frowned at her mother. "I want to go with you."

"I think it would be smart if you stayed here," Jake said. "Especially if it makes Mom feel better to know you're here."

"But I want to go!" She knew she sounded like a whiny little kid, but how could they possibly think it was right to leave her out of this? "I want to hear what the doctor has to say to Mom."

Carmen put a hand on her shoulder. "I promise I'll tell you everything he said." She met Sophie's gaze and held it. "I promise."

She started to protest again, but a look from Jake silenced her. "I promise to bring you a treat when I come back," Phoenix said.

"I'm not a baby," Sophie said. "You don't have to bribe me."

Hurt filled Phoenix's watery blue eyes. "You'll always be my baby," she said.

Sophie turned away. She couldn't believe after all the time she had spent worrying about her mother and taking care of her when she didn't feel well, they were going to leave her behind. She would have to rely on them to tell her what they thought she ought to know about her mom's medical condition—which wouldn't necessarily be everything the doctor said. So she wasn't going to pretend she was happy about any of it.

She stayed inside the trailer until she was sure they were gone, then she left and headed to Starfall's tent. "Do you want to go hunt cactus this morning?" she asked when Starfall answered her knock on the tent pole.

"I thought you were going to the doctor with your mother and brother," Starfall said.

"Yeah, I decided not to go." The lie was easier than telling the truth. The last thing she wanted was for Starfall to feel sorry for her or anything. "I'd rather stay here and make some money."

"I like the way you think." Starfall said. "Give me a minute, and I'll be out."

Five minutes later, she emerged from the tent with Hunter in a sling. "If he gets fussy, maybe you can carry him for a while," she said. "He likes you." She handed Sophie her backpack. "You can carry this."

The day was bright but breezy. The wind was cool and carried the scents of sage and creosote—the perfume of the high desert, Sophie thought. She would miss that smell if she and Mom went to live someplace else with Jake. But there would probably be good smells there, too. Pine trees or flowers and things like that. Or maybe cars and smog if they went to live in a city. Still, she hoped they could live in the country or a small town. Mom didn't like cities—and cities might make it easier to fall into her old life, with drugs and the wrong kind of friends. But she might be happy in the country, with flowers and a garden to tend.

Starfall led the way across the prairie, away from the ravine where they had picked berries to a plateau, where the wind had carved sandstone into towers and arches, and big boulders looked like fantastic sculptures that sparkled with glittery pyrite and quartz. "Is this where Jake was camped?" Sophie asked.

"Somewhere in here." Starfall adjusted Hunter in his sling. "I guess he's in town now. Or shacked up with Carmen."

Sophie wasn't about to speculate on that, so she slipped off the heavy backpack and started searching the ground for cactus. She found lots of wildflowers and weeds, and spotted a couple of horned toads, which looked like miniature triceratops crouched in the dried grass, staring up at her with shining eyes. Why was it so hard to find those little cactus? Then again, if they were easy to locate, they probably wouldn't be worth twenty dollars each to the German.

"When are you supposed to meet with that German guy again?" she asked as she and Starfall searched around the rocks.

"I told him I would have some cactus for him tomorrow," Starfall said. "He promised to bring the money, so we need to fill up that backpack."

"Maybe Jake was wrong about there being any around here," Sophie said. "I haven't seen—wait." She knelt, and a thrill of excitement bubbled up through her. "Wow—there's three of them right here!"

"Then, get digging." Starfall handed her a trowel, and Sophie carefully dug around the little spiny balls.

"I can't believe people collect these," she said as she loosened first one cactus, then a second. "I can think of a lot better things to spend money on." If she had a lot of money, she would buy lots of books—and a puppy. She had always wanted a puppy, but they had never lived anywhere she could have one. Maybe Jake would let her have a dog when they moved in with him…

A scream tore at the morning stillness, high and piercing. Sophie dropped the trowel and spun around to stare at Starfall. She stood a few yards away, clutching Hunter to her chest and staring at a big man who had a big gun trained on her.

The man swung the gun to point at Sophie. It was a handgun, but the barrel was long, and the opening looked to Sophie as big around as a half-dollar. "What do you think you're doing, scaring us this way?" she yelped. Maybe it wasn't the smartest thing to say to a guy with a gun, but Sophie couldn't think of anything else to say.

"I need you to come with me," the man said. He spoke good English, but with a heavy accent. Russian, maybe?

"What are you going to do with us?" Sophie asked.

"Get up!" the man shouted.

Sophie stood. Starfall was frozen in place. She must have been squeezing Hunter too tight because he began to wail, the sound setting Sophie's teeth on edge. She stared at the man. He didn't look friendly, and she didn't think he had anything pleasant in mind. Her stomach heaved at the idea, but she tried to ignore the sick feeling.

"Quiet!" he barked. Starfall flinched, but Hunter kept wailing.

"You scared him," Sophie said, drawing the man's attention once more. That was what she had to do, she saw now. She needed to distract the man and give Starfall a chance to get away. She could protect Hunter and go for help at the same time. She could drive to town and get Jake. Sophie would be all right until he came for her. "What are you doing out here, scaring people?" she asked the man.

He kept looking at her. She put her hand behind her back and made a shooing motion she hoped Starfall would notice. *Get out of here while you can*, she thought, trying to telegraph the words to Starfall. *Take Hunter, and run!*

"What are you doing out here?" the man asked.

The question surprised Sophie. She had been expecting another order. "We're looking for cactus." She held out her hand, one of the little cactus balanced on her palm. "Do you want to see?"

The man didn't come any closer, but he kept his eyes on Sophie. "You work for Werner, don't you?" he said.

"I'm collecting cactus to sell," Sophie said. "I don't care who I sell them to. If you want to pay me for them, I'll sell them to you." She didn't look toward Starfall and Hunter. She kept her eyes locked on the man's, making sure he didn't look over in that direction, either. "I have more here, if you want to see them." She reached to pull off the backpack, but the man jutted the gun at her. "Don't move."

Sophie held out both hands. "Okay, okay. Do you want to look or not?"

"Turn around," the man ordered.

Sophie turned, still avoiding looking toward the rocks. She hoped Starfall wasn't standing there like a statue. At least Hunter had stopped wailing. The man approached, focused, as Sophie had hoped, on the cactus. He opened the backpack and looked inside.

Then he shoved hard. Sophie landed on her hands and knees in the dirt and rocks. "Ouch!" she wailed, maybe a little louder than necessary. "What did you do that for?" She looked over her shoulder at the man.

"There are only two cactus in there," he said. "I need more than that. Many more."

"You interrupted me before I had been hunting very long," she said. "If you give me time, I can find more for you."

"I have other things in mind for you." He motioned with the gun. "Get up."

Sophie stood and brushed off her knees, which stung from their impact with the hard ground. "Where are you taking me?" she asked.

But the man didn't answer. He had turned toward where Starfall and Hunter had been standing—except now there were only piles of rock. Starfall was gone. Now Sophie was alone with the big man and more afraid than she had ever been in her life.

CARMEN HAD VOLUNTEERED one summer at the tribal clinic where her aunt worked—or rather, her mother had signed her up for the job, then told Carmen it was her duty to help out. She had spent most of her time escorting elderly men and women into the exam rooms, filing charts and cleaning up rooms between patient visits. Not difficult work, but not very exciting, either. And while her aunt had tried to interest her in assisting with blood draws and learning how to bandage wounds, Carmen had decided very quickly that she wanted nothing to do with the messy, bloody side of medicine.

So she couldn't say she was completely comfortable with the idea of escorting Jake and his mom to Phoenix's appointment at the Montrose clinic. But however ill at ease she felt, it was nothing compared to the grim expression on Jake's face and the look of abject terror in Phoenix's eyes. As the three of them walked into the clinic, Phoenix took hold of Carmen's hand and refused to let go.

Jake let the receptionist know they were there, then settled into a chair that looked too small for him, hands gripping the arms white-knuckled. Carmen wanted to swat his arm and tell him he wasn't helping his mother by looking as if he was waiting for his turn in the torture chamber. "My aunt's clinic is a lot like this," Carmen said, trying to sound a lot more cheerful than she felt. "She's been working there so long she knows the name of everyone who comes in the door. Sometimes it's more like a reunion than a doctor's visit, what with everyone catching up on each other's news."

"I want you to go into the room with me," Phoenix said. She still had a death grip on Carmen's hand.

"Oh. Well, I—" Carmen shot a desperate look to Jake. "Wouldn't you rather Jake—?"

"He can't go in with me." Phoenix was clearly horrified at the idea.

"I can't go in with her," Jake agreed.

Okay. Maybe Carmen could see her point. What

woman wanted to wear one of those drafty gowns in front of her grown son? "All right," she said. "I'll go with you."

They didn't have to wait long. A woman in purple scrubs called for Phoenix. She stood, tugging Carmen up alongside her, and they followed the nurse or tech or whatever she was into an exam room.

Phoenix didn't let go of Carmen's hand until the woman in scrubs asked her to sit on the paper-covered table. Carmen took the only other seat in the room, a folding chair in the corner, and studied the artwork on the walls, while Phoenix submitted to having her blood pressure and temperature checked.

"Sophie wasn't too happy about being left at home," Phoenix said, when she and Carmen were alone again.

"She's worried about you," Carmen said. "She'll be fine by the time you get back to camp."

"She worries too much," Phoenix said. "I shouldn't have put her in that position. She's still just a kid. She should be focused on kid problems, not adult ones."

"She's very mature for her age," Carmen said.

Phoenix slumped, perched on the edge of the table, feet dangling. "I did that to Jake, too," she said. "He had to practically raise himself, I was so caught up in my own problems. But I've tried to be a better mother to Sophie."

"Jake turned out all right," Carmen said. More than all right, if things had been as rough as he had hinted at. "And he loves you and Sophie very much."

Phoenix sniffed. "He does, doesn't he? I don't really deserve it, I guess, but he does."

"Of course you deserve it," Carmen said. "You did the best you could."

"But sometimes my best wasn't very good at all." She plucked at the edge of her blouse—they hadn't asked her to change into a gown after all. "I don't want to leave the camp. I know it's hard for him to understand, but I like it there. I feel safe."

"Jake would do his best to keep you safe wherever you went with him," Carmen said. "And if you need more medical care, it would be easier to get in a town. And Sophie could go to school and have friends her own age."

Phoenix sighed. "That's what Jake says. I don't know. I've never set a lot of importance on doing things just because they were easy or what other people thought was normal."

Carmen was saved from having to make a reply by the entrance of the doctor, an efficient, middle-aged woman who introduced herself, then conducted what seemed to Carmen's eyes to be a thorough exam. After several minutes of probing and asking questions, she stepped back. "The first step is to do some blood work," she said. "I wouldn't be surprised if you're a little anemic, and we might spot some other insufficiencies, but we'll wait until we get the results back in a day or two and address those." She patted Phoenix's arms. "After we draw your blood, I want you to go back home and rest, and try not to worry."

Phoenix sat up straighter, a little color in her cheeks. "You're not going to put me in the hospital?" she asked.

"I don't see any need for that," the doctor said. "Do you want to go to the hospital?"

"No!" Phoenix shook her head. "I want to go home to my daughter."

"You do that, and I'll be in touch with a plan once I see the blood work."

"Thank you," Phoenix said. She turned to Carmen. "I can go home."

Carmen hugged her. "That's great news."

A medical assistant came in and drew Phoenix's blood, then Carmen walked with the older woman to the waiting room. Jake stood to meet them "Well?" he asked.

"She drew some blood, and she told me to go home and rest," Phoenix said as she moved past him toward the door.

"But what did the doctor say?" He followed his mother and Carmen into the parking lot. "What does she think is wrong?"

"I might be anemic. It might be something else." Phoenix grabbed the door handle of the truck. "Unlock this so we can go home."

Jake unlocked the truck and hurried around to the driver's side. "That's it?" He looked to Carmen for confirmation.

"That's about it," Carmen said. She slid into the passenger seat, with Phoenix between her and Jake. "She'll know more when she gets the results of the blood tests."

"Okay." He sagged back against the seat. "So now I guess we wait."

"Now we go home." Phoenix prodded him with her elbow. "Start the truck, and let's go."

He turned the key in the ignition. "Do you want to go somewhere for lunch or something first?" he asked.

"No. I want to go home."

Jake looked across at Carmen and shrugged, then put the truck in gear and backed out of his parking space. No one said much on the way back to camp. Carmen thought Phoenix might have nodded off. Poor thing probably hadn't slept much last night.

The ring of Jake's phone was jarring in the silence. He hit the button to answer the call. "This is Jake."

"It's Marco at Ranger headquarters." Marco Cruz said. "Can you head this way?"

"What's up?" Jake asked.

"Starfall just showed up here in a panic. She says some Russian guy has your sister."

Chapter Sixteen

Cars filled the parking lot at Ranger headquarters. Jake even spotted a TV-news van. "How did the media get wind of this already?" Carmen asked, as Jake slid into a spot at the back of the lot. He had his door open before the engine had even fallen silent. Carmen was right behind him, one arm around Phoenix, who looked as if she might collapse any minute. Carmen hadn't said much since Marco's call, but her presence steadied Jake. She wasn't freaking out about this, so neither would he.

At least a dozen people waited at headquarters, and everyone seemed to be talking at once. At Jake's entrance, the noise level dropped. Marco hurried to him. "Starfall is back here," he said, motioning toward the conference room. "I'll let her tell you what happened."

Starfall sat at the conference table, flanked by officers Ethan Reynolds and Simon Woolridge. She cradled her baby, murmuring softly to him. When Carmen, Phoenix and Jake stepped into the room, she rose. "I wouldn't have left her with him if I had had any other choice," she said. "I had to go for help. You see that, don't you?"

The idea that she had left Sophie—a child—at the mercy of a strange man made Jake's vision cloud. He took a deep breath, fighting for control. He couldn't help

Sophie unless he stayed calm. "Tell me what happened," he said and sat in the chair across from her.

Starfall's gaze shifted to Carmen, who was settling Phoenix in the chair next to Jake, and her bottom lip trembled, but she sat and made an effort to control her emotions. "Sophie came to me this morning, after you left to take Phoenix to the doctor. She asked if we could go look for cactus."

"We should have taken her with us," Phoenix said. "She wanted to go and, if we hadn't left her in camp, this wouldn't have happened."

"This is the kidnapper's fault, not yours," Jake said. He turned back to Starfall. "Why did she want to look for cactus?"

"I promised her ten dollars—half of what Werner said he would pay me—for every cactus she found," Starfall said. "She wanted to earn money to help pay Phoenix's medical bills."

Phoenix broke down sobbing. Carmen comforted her. Maybe Jake should have been the one to try to calm her, but Sophie needed him more now. "I told her I'd pay for everything," he said. "She didn't have to worry about that."

"I don't know anything about that," Starfall said. "Anyway, we set out. I was carrying Hunter and Sophie had my backpack. We headed toward the area where you were camped before. I remembered you said you saw some of those cactus there."

Jake glanced at Ethan and Simon. "I don't know what the area is called, but I can show you on a map," he said.

Simon nodded. "We'll get Randall and his dog out there. If Lotte can pick up a scent, she might be able to lead us to him."

"You don't even know what you're looking for yet," Starfall said. "Do you want me to finish my story or not?"

"Go ahead," Jake said.

She settled back in her chair. "Sophie found some of the cactus and was digging them up, when this big guy steps out from behind a rock and points this huge gun at us. He had a Russian accent, and he told us if we tried anything, he would kill us. I think he would have, too."

"How do you know the accent was Russian?" Simon asked.

"Because it was. I mean, it wasn't German like Werner's, or French or Spanish. It was Russian." She looked to Jake again. "He was really big—over six feet, with broad shoulders. But he had a gut on him, too."

"How old was he?" Ethan asked.

She wrinkled her nose. "Maybe fifty? Not young. He was really solid."

"What did he say?" Jake asked. "What did he want with you?"

"He asked about the cactus. Sophie told him we were collecting them to sell to Werner, but he could have them if he wanted. I thought maybe we could make a deal and he'd let us go, but that didn't work."

"How did you get away?" Carmen asked.

"Sophie started talking to him, keeping his attention on her. But she motioned to me behind her back. I was so frightened it took me a little bit to realize she was motioning for me to run away. I didn't want to leave her, but I had my baby to think of and, if I got away, I knew I could get help."

"What did you do?" Carmen asked.

"At first, I ducked behind the rock. When he didn't

react, I started moving away, going from rock to tree, trying to hide. Every second I kept expecting him to shoot me in the back. But he never did. When I was far enough away that I was sure he couldn't see me, I took off running. I ran to camp, got my car and came here."

"You did the right thing," Carmen said. She looked at Jake when she said the words, and he nodded. If Starfall hadn't run when she had the chance, Jake probably still wouldn't know that Sophie was missing. The Russian would have an even bigger head start.

"What did this Russian say he wanted with you and Sophie?" he asked.

"He didn't," Starfall said. "He just said he had plans for us." Her eyes shone with tears. "You don't think he'll hurt her, do you? She's just a girl. A very brave girl."

"Jake, what are you going to do?" Phoenix clutched at his arm. "You can't let him hurt her."

Jake leaned across the table, his eyes locked on Starfall's. "Did this Russian have a car? Did you see one anywhere nearby?"

She shook her head. "All I saw was the gun. And a backpack!" She sat up straighter. "He was wearing a backpack. The big kind, like campers use, with a bedroll and other stuff tied on it. Does that help?"

Jake nodded. "Werner said the Russian was camping. If he had to hike a ways to get to a car, that would slow him down. We might even get lucky, and he's still in the area."

"Then you can find her," Phoenix said. "She'll be all right."

He patted his mother's arm. "That's the plan." No point mentioning that Sophie and her captor might be anywhere in the thousands of acres of wilderness in the area. Finding them wasn't as simple as heading to the nearest campground.

A commotion outside the conference room distracted him. Marco was already moving toward the door when it burst open, and Daniel Metwater stumbled in. "I came as soon as I heard," he said.

Phoenix rose. "I should have known you'd be concerned about one of your disciples," she said.

Metwater ignored her and turned to Jake. "I told you the Russian mafia was after me," he said. "Why wouldn't you listen? You've got to stop him, or I'll be next."

"Why do you think this has anything to do with you?" Jake asked.

"Isn't it obvious? They knew Sophie was special to me, so they took her. It's the way they do things—they want to send me a warning. To make me afraid."

Jake hadn't even realized he had made a fist and had his arm drawn back, ready to punch Metwater, when Carmen took hold of his arm. "He's not worth it," she said softly.

Jake studied the so-called Prophet, his hair a tangle, his shirt half-unbuttoned. He was so focused on himself, he couldn't even find concern for a child who had been kidnapped. But he might be useful to them after all. "Have you had any other 'messages' from the Russian?" he asked. "Any communications at all—letters, visits?"

Metwater shook his head.

"What about Werner Altbusser?" Carmen asked. "Have you talked to him since he was in your camp the day before yesterday?"

Metwater flicked his gaze to her. "Werner has nothing to do with this," he said.

"Maybe he and the Russian are working together," Starfall said.

Everyone turned to stare at her. "It makes sense," she continued. "Werner didn't want to pay me for the cactus, so he sent the Russian to collect them."

"But you offered to give them to the Russian, didn't you?" Jake asked. "Why bother kidnapping Sophie?"

"She told him we would sell him the cactus," Starfall said. "Of course, since he had the gun, we would have had to give them to him. Werner would have known that—the big cheat."

"I told you, he took Sophie because of me," Metwater said. "Why are you standing here wasting time? You have to go after him."

"We're getting together a search party to go out now," Marco told Jake. "Do you and Carmen want to come?"

"I'll catch up with you in a little while. I have something else to do first." Jake turned to Carmen. "Can you take Mom back to the camp for me?"

"Of course." Carmen looked into his eyes, searching. "What are you going to do?"

"I'm going to see Werner. He knows this Russian better than any of us. He might have an idea where he's camping."

"That's a good idea," she said. "Do you want me to go with you?"

He shook his head. "I need you to look after Mom. And I know Sophie trusts you. In case they find her before I get back, I'd like you there with her."

"All right." She gripped his hand. "Be careful."

"I will." But he wasn't going to leave Werner until he knew everything the German could tell him about his Russian "friend."

SOPHIE TRUDGED ALONG in the hot sun, her gaze focused on the broad back of her captor. When he had discovered Starfall had run away, he had yelled a lot—some in English, and some in what she guessed was Russian. Sophie watched him rant and didn't say anything. He waved the gun at her a lot, but he never actually shot it. She knew that he could—that he might shoot her still. But for now, he had only tied her up, then tied one end of the rope around his waist and led her off across the wilderness. He muttered a lot under his breath—words she couldn't understand—and, every so often, he glared at her over his shoulder and tugged on the rope to make her go faster, as if she was a dog.

"Where are you taking me?" she asked.

He didn't answer.

"Who are you?" she asked. "What do you want with me?"

Still no answer. Her gaze shifted to Starfall's backpack, which he had tied to his own pack. "I can find some more of those cactus for you, if you want," she said.

He still didn't say anything, but his head came up, and she could tell he was listening. "Why are people so interested in those little cactus, anyway?" she asked. "I wouldn't pay a quarter for one."

"Everything is worth what people will pay for it," the Russian said. "People will pay a lot of money for all kinds of cactus. I have made much money over the years, selling them what they want."

"What does any of that have to do with me?" Sophie asked.

The icy look he gave her made her want to throw up. "Some people will pay money for girls, too," he said.

"You do what I tell you, or I might decide to sell you to one of them."

She swallowed hard. "Is that why you kidnapped me? To s-sell me?"

He kicked a rock, sending it careering and bouncing across the rough ground. "Why can't you be quiet?"

She stuck her chin out. She wouldn't let him see she was afraid. "Because I want to know. Why can't you just tell me?"

He lunged back toward her. She tried not to flinch, but she couldn't help it. "Do you know how to make someone do what you want them to do?" he growled.

"H-how?"

"You take something of theirs. It causes more pain than if you broke their knees or cut off their hand. If you choose the right thing to take—the right person— then you will have them completely under your power."

His words made her feel cold all over. "Who are you trying to control?" she asked. If he said *Metwater*, she would scream. She wasn't his, no matter what anyone else said.

The Russian narrowed his eyes. "Don't pretend to be stupid, when I can see you are not. Your brother is a federal agent who has been following that idiot, Werner. Werner is too stupid to recognize him for what he is, but I can spot the police from two blocks away."

"What do you want from my brother?" she asked.

"I want him to go away. Tell his superiors he knows nothing about me. He can arrest Werner if he likes, that useless cheat. He thought I was so stupid I couldn't see he was keeping most of the profits from the cactus for himself, even though I did all of the work of finding the buyers and selling to them. I took all the risk, yet he ex-

pected me to be happy with the scraps he threw to me."
He spat in the dirt.

"If Werner is the one you're mad at, why not kidnap
him?" Sophie asked.

"Because he could still be useful to me. He is trying
to make a deal with the leader of that commune you live
in—that so-called Prophet. He wants this 'Prophet' to
tell all his followers to collect the cactus for Werner. If
they agree to this arrangement, I can step in and take
over. Then maybe I will get rid of him."

"Did you kill Reggae?" she asked. Her throat hurt,
thinking about the dead man. He had always been
friendly to her, and the way he tried so hard to get Starfall to notice him was kind of sweet. "Why? He never
hurt anyone."

"I wanted Werner to know that I meant business by
going after one of his workers. If he didn't turn everything over to me, I would kill everyone close to him,
until he was all alone. And, finally, I would come for
him." He smiled an awful, cold expression that made
Sophie's stomach hurt.

He straightened and glared down at her. "Your brother
will come after you, no?"

She nodded. Of course Jake would come after her.

"You'd better hope he does," the Russian said. "If he
doesn't, I will kill you. Even if you are a smart girl."

JAKE SPED INTO the lot of the motel, parked behind Werner's rented SUV, blocking it in, and stormed up to the
door of Werner's room. He pounded on the door, rattling
it in its frame. "Open up, Werner! If you don't, I swear
I'll kick the door in."

"Who...who is it?" The German's voice quavered.

"Someone you don't want to cross," Jake said.

The chain rattled, and the door eased open. Jake grabbed the German by the throat and shoved him back into the room, kicking the door closed behind him. He forced Werner's back against the wall. "Tell me where the Russian is camping. Your 'friend,' Karol Petrovsky."

Werner's pupils dilated, and his skin was the color of mashed potatoes. "I… I don't know what you're talking about."

"Don't lie to me!" Jake tightened his hold. "He has my sister, and I need to know how to find him."

Werner muttered something in German that might have been a prayer. "Where is he?" Jake demanded.

"I don't know for sure. I only suspect."

Jake released his hold on Werner and shoved him onto the bed. "What do you suspect?"

Werner rubbed his neck. "Why do you think I know where he is?"

"That day I caught you in my camp—you were looking for him, weren't you?"

Werner's face drooped, making him look much older, and he nodded. "A mutual acquaintance had told me he was in the area."

"What is he to you? Your friend? Your partner?" Jake shoved his hands in his pockets. He couldn't let his temper and his worry over Sophie get the best of him. He had a job to do, and that meant keeping his cool.

"Not my friend!" Werner shook his head, adamant. "We were partners at one time—business partners."

"But you aren't now?"

"No. We had a disagreement over how profits should be divided."

"When was the last time you talked to him?"

"Months ago. Six months ago. I don't want to talk to him. Not ever again."

"Yet you were looking for his camp that day."

"Yes. But that was before he killed that young man. And then he killed the man who was in the room next door." He pointed to his left.

"How do you know it was him?" Jake asked.

Werner looked away.

Jake took his hands from his pockets and leaned toward him. "Tell me."

"I saw him. I looked out the window and saw him. I thought he was coming for me. To kill me. But he went into the room next door instead."

"Why? Why would he kill that man instead of you? Why would he kill that kid?"

"He must have seen me talking to them. He thought they were working for me. That is how they do things, these Russians that he associates with. They attack people close to you first, to send a warning. They want to make you so afraid that, by the time they get to you, you will do anything they ask."

"What does Petrovsky want from you?"

"He wants to take over my business."

"What business is that?"

Again, Werner's gaze shifted away. "It does not matter."

"It does matter." Jake leaned toward him again so that the German leaned back on the bed. "You're illegally exporting cactus from the United States to Europe, including a number of endangered species."

"They are only little cactus," Werner protested. "And there are so many of them. What difference does it make to you?"

"Then you admit that's what you've been doing here?" Jake said. "You were paying people like the young man who was killed to collect the cactus for you?"

"What if I was? Who are you to care?"

Jake pulled his credentials from his pocket. "Officer Jacob Lohmiller, US Fish and Wildlife." He shoved the wallet back into his pocket and took out a pair of flex cuffs and grabbed Werner's wrist. "Werner Altbusser, you're under arrest." He recited Werner's rights and confirmed that Werner understood them.

Jake braced himself for a struggle, but the German merely slumped onto the bed again. "I am ruined," he said. "I was ruined before you came here. Karol is taking my business. I will be lucky if he doesn't take my life."

"Tell me where to find him, and I'll lock him up, too," Jake said as he fastened the cuffs. "If you get lucky, you can work a deal to testify against him."

This idea seemed to bolster the German's spirits. "I will tell you what I know," he said. "But I don't know if it will be any help. Who did you say he has taken?"

"My sister. She's fourteen years old."

Werner's eyes widened. "That is bad. Very bad."

"Tell me where he is. Where is his camp? Is it near where I was camping? Is that why you were looking there?"

Werner shook his head. "I never found it, but I was looking there because last year he insisted I bring him with me on my collecting trip to the United States, and that is the area where we camped. I thought he would go back there because it was familiar to him."

"Come on." He pulled Werner with him toward the door.

"What are you doing? Where are you taking me?"

"You're going with me to find Sophie."

"But I told you—I don't know where Karol is."

"Then you had better hope you get lucky."

Chapter Seventeen

"Tell me again where you were when you and Sophie were taken." Carmen put her face very close to Starfall's. She could smell the tomatoes the other woman had had for lunch and the coppery tang of sweat and fear. "Exactly where you were."

"I don't remember exactly." Starfall looked over Carmen's shoulder, at the other searchers who had assembled outside of Metwater's camp to look for Sophie. Carmen had given Starfall a ride back to camp with her and Phoenix. "We were somewhere near where Jake was camped," Starfall said. "There were a bunch of big rocks. And some of those cactus we were looking for."

Carmen suppressed a groan of frustration.

"This place is crawling with rocks and cactus," Simon, who was standing behind her, said. "And Jake isn't here to ask where he was camping. Why is that?"

"He went to talk someone who knows the man who took Sophie," Carmen said.

"Who probably isn't going to tell him anything," Simon said.

"I don't know about that," Evan said. "Something tells me Jake can be pretty persuasive when he wants to be."

"You have to find her." Phoenix stood with Daniel

Metwater and some of the other women at the edge of the parking area where the searchers had assembled.

Simon turned toward Phoenix, but Carmen answered first. "We're going to find her," she said, with more conviction in her voice than she really felt. The Russian had already left two dead men in his wake. Why would he want to be burdened with a fourteen-year-old girl?

"Let's get going!" Simon directed the searchers, who planned to cover the area in a grid pattern. Carmen stayed back in case Phoenix needed her. Starfall put a hand on her arm.

"I just remembered something," Starfall said.

Carmen waited, saying nothing.

"We were really near that place where we were all picking berries the first day Jake came into camp with you," Starfall said. "There's this high point there that kind of overlooks the whole area. The Russian must have been hiding up there, watching us."

Carmen felt a rush of recognition. She had a clear picture of Jake lying prone, field glasses focused on the little group of women and the girl, while she circled around to confront him, the first day they had met. He had chosen the perfect vantage point to surveil them— something the Russian must have realized as well. "Can you stay here with Phoenix?" she asked.

Starfall nodded. "Of course."

"Thanks." Carmen hurried to catch up with the searchers. They had set out fast and were already some distance ahead, traveling in the wrong direction. She would have to catch up to them, then waste time persuading them that she knew the spot where they should look.

She turned away and set out on her own toward Jake's

lookout point. He was only one man, with one girl. She was a trained officer, with her weapons, and a personal stake in saving the sister of the man she had fallen in love with. What men might offer in power she would make up for with finesse and determination.

Fifteen minutes of alternately walking and running brought her to the spot Starfall had described. She spotted a small trowel and a half-excavated clump of cactus beside it. The trail was easy to follow from there—two sets of prints in the fine desert dust, broken branches and disturbed rocks. Tracking them was so easy, Carmen knew the man wanted to be followed. He expected he would be found, which meant he would be waiting for her.

But would he expect a woman to come after him? Carmen asked herself. Probably not. Maybe she could use that to her advantage.

She slowed her pace, moving stealthily and keeping to cover. When she spotted the narrow box canyon shielded by a growth of trees, she stopped. The canyon would provide a perfect camp, with shelter from the wind, shade from the worst of the afternoon sun, perhaps fresh water from a spring or creek and, most important, only one way in or out. It was the perfect place to hide—and the perfect place to set a trap.

Instead of approaching the canyon directly, she veered to one side and began climbing up above it, working her way up the increasingly steep slope, stepping carefully to avoid dislodging loose rock. When something burst from the brush to her left, she had her weapon drawn and aimed before she could even process the thought, and stood, panting, heart pounding, her gun aimed at a startled mule deer, a trembling half-grown fawn at its side.

Shaking from the flood of adrenaline, she holstered the gun and watched as the deer ambled away. As soon as her legs felt steady, she set out again.

When the ground leveled out once more, she moved to the canyon's edge and looked down. But trees and rocks blocked her view. If she was going to find the Russian's camp, she would have to move lower.

She climbed down, keeping to the cover of trees and boulders, moving laterally as she descended, so that she moved further and further into the canyon. She estimated she had been traveling perhaps five minutes, when a flash of something pink made her freeze. She held her breath, waiting, and Sophie shuffled into view, her hands and feet shackled.

Three feet behind the girl was the Russian, a long-barreled revolver in his hand. Carmen drew her own weapon and sited in on him. She would need to wait until Sophie wasn't so close to him. Right now, it would be too easy for him to use the girl as a shield or even kill her before Carmen could react.

Sophie sat down on top of a blue and white picnic cooler. The Russian moved past her to a green nylon tent that was almost invisible in the underbrush. With the girl shackled, he had no fear of her running off. He was waiting for the searchers to come to them. Maybe they were why he had taken Sophie in the first place.

Or he wanted to get the attention of one particular searcher.

Daniel Metwater? Carmen shook her head. Though the Prophet was clearly terrified of the Russian, she didn't buy Metwater's story that he was the real target. If that was the case, why not go after Andi Mattheson who, as Asteria, lived with Metwater and was clearly closer to him than a fourteen-year-old girl?

That left Jake. It wouldn't be the first time a criminal had tried to get to a lawman by threatening his family. But this time it wasn't going to work. Carmen tightened her grip on her weapon.

After a glance over her shoulder toward the tent, Sophie stood and moved to the edge of the growth of trees where Carmen hid. She peered intently into the underbrush, and a smile transformed her face when she recognized Carmen. Still perfectly silent, she held out her manacled hands in a pleading gesture.

Carmen frowned. She didn't have anything with her to remove or sever the shackles, which appeared to be made of metal. The Russian had definitely come prepared. They wouldn't be able to run from him with Sophie hampered in that way. Their only hope was for Carmen to subdue him. She would have to catch him off guard and away from Sophie.

She motioned the girl back toward the cooler. Sophie frowned and didn't move. *Go!* Carmen mouthed, but still the girl remained rooted in place.

"What are you doing up?" The Russian's voice was loud, with a heavy accent. Sophie stumbled backwards and almost fell over. The Russian moved in behind her and took her arm, while Carmen retreated further into the underbrush. She didn't dare try for him now, not with his hands on Sophie.

He led the girl back to the cooler and shoved her down once more. Sophie kept looking toward Carmen. *Don't look at me*, Carmen silently pleaded. The Russian would figure out she was here.

She took a step back, thinking it safer to put extra

distance between herself and the camp. She didn't see the rock that moved under her feet, rolling down the hill and into the camp, sending her falling with a flailing of arms and a crack of branches.

Seconds later she was staring into the barrel of that revolver, pointed at her head. "Hello," the Russian said, his tone light, almost conversational. "Drop your weapon, and stand up slowly."

She did as he asked, gaze shifting between his eyes and the gun. Neither offered any comfort. The gun and the eyes were both cold and lethal. He made a grunting noise as she stood. "I recognize you," he said. "You are the girlfriend. The other cop."

She said nothing. What would be the point?

The Russian nodded and motioned her toward the camp. "You could be useful," he said. "If your game-warden friend doesn't respond to his sister's distress to meet my demands, I can cut off your head and send it to him to drive the message home."

WERNER DIRECTED JAKE to the forest service road where Jake had been camped. "We camped along in here last year, but I don't remember exactly where," Werner said.

"Why aren't you camping this year?" Jake asked.

"Camping was Karol's idea," Werner said. "I prefer to stay in hotel. But he likes to pretend he is a pioneer outdoorsman. Plus, he is cheap, and camping like this is free."

They set out walking, searching for some sign of Petrovsky and Sophie—or anyone else. "There was no one else camped here when we were here, either," Werner said. "Karol liked that. It went along with his fantasy of being a wilderness explorer. He has a great fascination with the American West."

"I heard he approached the Southern Ute tribe about raising cactus on their land," Jake said.

"Except collectors don't want farmed cactus," Werner said. "The ones who will pay the most money—collectors in Japan and Germany—they want wild plants. I told you Karol is fascinated by the whole mountain man, cowboys-and-Indians thing. He thinks, because he isn't from the United States, he really understands Native Americans. He thinks they will accept him as one of their own. I tried to tell him he was full of it, but he's crazy. He gets an idea in his head and decides that it's right and there's no talking him out of it."

"What idea made him kidnap my sister?"

Werner looked more woeful than ever. "I am sorry, I do not know. I truly believe he is crazy."

Jake might go crazy if anything happened to Sophie. Werner stopped at a pull-out alongside the road. "We camped in a place very like this, but I don't know that Karol would come back to the same place. It was only a hunch." He looked around them. "I'm sorry. I don't know."

"Let's walk a little farther," Jake said. They were very near where he had camped when he had first come to the area to look for his mother and Sophie. So much had happened since then—he didn't even feel like the same man. He had had a mission then, but the mission had changed to one that was so much more important. He was still on the trail of a smuggler, but his sister's life was at stake. He couldn't make any wrong moves.

He studied the terrain, searching for anything familiar, and tried to put himself in the crazy Russian's head.

That's what they had taught him in the military—*think like the enemy.*

Petrovsky would want a good position from which to hold Sophie but also a camp that enabled him to see anyone coming, without being seen himself. He was a fan of cowboys-and-Indians stories. Where had the cowboys always holed up? Jake's store of cowboy lore was painfully small, but hadn't there been something about Butch Cassidy and the Hole-in-the-Wall Gang making their camp in a box canyon? The Russian would like that—only one way in, and he could look out on the world from safety.

Jake pulled out the map they had brought along, spread it out and studied it. After a few minutes, he found what he was looking for. He put his finger over the squiggly line that outlined the box canyon. "That's where I think he is," he said.

"What do we do now?" Werner asked.

Jake folded the map and stuffed it into his pocket. "Come on." He traveled away from the canyon, then circled back to approach it from the side. Behind him, Werner, hands cuffed in front of him, panted and puffed, occasionally stumbling and grunting, but the German made no protest. When they were at the rim of the canyon, Jake stopped. "Sit here and don't make a sound while I check things out," he said.

Werner's face drooped. "At least remove the cuffs," he said. "I will do whatever I can to help you save the girl."

"I don't take chances." Jake moved toward the rim of the box canyon, crouching, and finally dropping to his stomach and crawling the last few yards. His hunch about this place had been right—someone had set up camp down below, with a tent tucked into the cover of trees, a campfire ring and various supplies scattered about. As he scanned the area a slight figure emerged from the trees—Sophie. She was bound hand and foot, her head down, shoulders slumped. The sight rattled Jake—it took all he had in him to push aside the rage and fear that threatened to crowd out everything else in his head. He had to keep it together if he was going to save her.

Another figure emerged from the woods behind Sophie. Carmen walked with her head up, her expression fierce, and Jake had to bite the inside of his cheek to keep back a roar of rage. He had expected to find Sophie here and had prepared himself for that. But seeing Carmen held prisoner touched something deep inside of him, a core need to protect the woman he loved, whatever the cost.

He hadn't let himself admit he loved her until that moment. He had been on his own since he was a teenager. He didn't need other people. He certainly didn't need a woman. Yet right now, at the very core of his being, he needed Carmen. He needed her faith and trust in him, and he needed to be the man he saw reflected in her eyes when she looked at him with love.

He crawled back from the edge of the canyon, then stood and raced back to Werner. When he pulled out his knife, the German shrank back, wide-eyed, but Jake only cut the plastic cuffs, then pulled out the keys to his truck and pressed them into Werner's hands. "Do you remember where I parked?" he asked. "Can you get back there?"

"Yes, yes."

"Drive to Ranger headquarters. Let them know where I am."

"You have found him?"

"Yes. Can you give the Rangers directions to this place?"

"Yes. What are you going to do?"

"I'm going to keep an eye on him until you bring help." He put a hand on Werner's shoulder. "I'm trusting you on this. If you steal my truck and drive away without getting help, I'll spend the rest of my life hunting you down."

Werner nodded again. "I will bring help, I promise."

"I'm counting on it." He clapped the older man on the back. "Now go."

As soon as Werner was out of sight, Jake moved back to the canyon rim. Stealthily, he dropped down, moving from the cover of rocks to trees to shrubs, until he was only a dozen yards above the trio in the camp and could hear them clearly. Then he settled in to wait for either the Rangers or the Russian to make a move.

CARMEN WORKED TO keep her expression calm and impassive as the Russian talked on and on about first one subject, then another. She had met his type before—give him a captive audience, and he would recite the history of the wrongs that had been done him. Since she was Native American, a member of another oppressed group, she was supposed to sympathize.

Beside Carmen, Sophie sat very still. Carmen worried the girl was in shock. She hadn't said a word since they had returned from a short trek into the woods, where Petrovsky had allowed them to relieve themselves, Carmen standing as a shield for the girl. When the Russian turned his back for a moment, Carmen tried to catch

Sophie's eye. She gave her a look that was meant to be encouraging, but the girl didn't respond.

"The people in the United States still see Russia as their enemy," Petrovsky said, turning back to them. "They look at every Russian as if he is a criminal, and they don't want to do business with me.

"Your people—" he pointed to Carmen "—they are different. They are outsiders, too. I think we could do business. I have experience they could use. I know how to get back at the Americans who have taken advantage of us for too long."

Carmen could have pointed out that the Southern Ute were not a bunch of naïve savages but successful businessmen and -women in their own right. They didn't need to take revenge on anyone. But arguing with the Russian wouldn't gain anything. She needed to stay in his good graces and watch for the opportunity to flee with the girl.

"My stomach hurts."

The sudden outburst from Sophie startled Carmen and cut off Petrovsky in mid-sentence. "What?" he barked at her.

"My stomach hurts," she said. "I have to go to the bathroom again."

"No!"

"Please!" She doubled over, hugging her stomach. "I have to."

"Do you think I am stupid?" Petrovsky asked. "If I let you go off in the woods again, you will try to run away."

"No, I won't," Sophie said. "I promise."

Carmen studied the girl. Something in her tone didn't ring true. Petrovsky was probably picking up on that. She was a terrified fourteen-year-old—Sophie gave her props for trying. But what had prompted her sudden acting job?

A flicker of movement in the bushes over Petrovksy's shoulder caught her attention. Someone was up there. No wonder Sophie had felt the need to cause a distraction. "I think she's telling the truth," Carmen said. "You'd better let her go."

"Please let me go!" Sophie wailed.

Carmen squeezed her hand, both to signal that she should tone down the overacting and to distract her from looking behind Petrovsky, where Jake was visible through the trees, moving stealthily toward them. But he still had a ten-yard gap of open space to cover to reach them.

"What are you looking at back there?" the Russian demanded. He drew his pistol and whirled, just as Jake stood and aimed his own weapon.

Carmen pulled Sophie down on the ground beside her, out of the range of fire. She heard a barrage of shots—maybe three or four—and the grunt of someone who had been hit. "Jake!" Sophie cried.

Carmen looked over her shoulder in time to see Petrovsky take aim at a large tree Jake must be using for cover. The Russian was hurt, blood running from his left shoulder, but the hand holding the weapon was steady. Sophie tried to break free of Carmen's grip. "We have to help Jake," she sobbed.

Petrovsky glanced back at them. When his eyes met Carmen's, she felt the cold of them clear to her heart. She pulled Sophie behind her and started backing toward the cover of the trees, even as the Russian swung around and aimed at her.

The shot went wild, the report of the bullet merging with the sound of the shot that brought him to his knees. He toppled over, dead from the bullet Jake had fired. Jake emerged from behind a boulder, the smoking weapon still in his hand. Carmen tried to walk toward him, a sobbing Sophie clinging to her, but her legs didn't want to work. She could only stand in place while he came to her, and the three of them embraced.

"I was going to wait for help," he said into her hair, between kissing it and stroking her shoulder. "But I couldn't be sure anyone would come, and I was too afraid to waste any more time."

"I knew you'd come." Sophie looked up at him, tears still streaming down her face.

"I wouldn't leave you." He wiped her tears away with his thumbs. "I won't leave you ever again."

She nodded and buried her face against his chest. He shifted his gaze to Carmen. "I won't leave you, either," he said. "If you're willing to let me stay."

"Just try to get away, Soldier Boy," she said and kissed him, the kind of kiss that said more than words and promised a lifetime of such kisses.

Epilogue

"Maybe I should have brought a gift or something." Jake tugged at the collar of his white Western shirt and loosened the turquoise and silver slide on his string tie. "A bottle of wine, or maybe some flowers?"

"There's no need for that." Carmen reached over from the passenger seat of her SUV and took his hand and squeezed it. "This is just a family dinner, nothing formal."

"A tribe is a kind of family, isn't it?" Phoenix spoke from the back seat. Carmen half turned to address the older woman. She had more color in her cheeks now, since she had completed the interferon treatments for her hepatitis C. She had put on a little weight and definitely had more energy. With proper care, she could remain in remission for years, possibly forever.

"A tribe is a real family," Carmen said. "One where people are related to each other by both blood and tradition."

"Are there any girls my age there?" Sophie asked. "Cousins or something?"

"I have a couple of cousins who have kids close to your age," Carmen said. "Girls and boys."

Sophie smiled shyly and smoothed the sides of her hair, which she had had cut last week into a fashionable, spiky bob. That and her new clothes made her look like any other teen girl, something Carmen knew delighted her almost as much as it worried Jake.

"Is Captain Tomato going to be there?" Jake asked.

"Chief Tonaho will not be there," Carmen said. "But, even if he is, I expect you to act like a gentleman."

"I'm getting better at controlling my temper," he said. "But you can't expect me to keep quiet if anyone says anything about him being your family's first choice for you."

"I do expect it," she said. "After all, you're my first choice, and that's all that matters."

Still holding Carmen's hand, he rubbed a finger over the large chunk of polished turquoise set in a wide silver band that she had selected instead of a diamond for her engagement ring. "Yeah, I guess you're right," he said.

"Will we get to see the place where you're going to have the wedding?" Sophie asked.

"Of course," Carmen said. "After dinner, we'll walk up there. You can see most of my family's ranch from there. I'll show you exactly where you'll stand during the ceremony."

"I can't wait," Sophie said. "Don't you wish you could get married today?"

"There's a lot to do to get ready for a wedding," Phoenix said. "The next two months will fly by."

"The main thing I'm waiting for is all the paper work to go through for my transfer to the Grand Junction field office," Jake said. "Ron Clark promised me it would be ready next week."

"You don't think anything will happen to hold it up, do you?" Phoenix asked.

"No. Clark is only too happy to get rid of me after he spent months—and a lot of resources—making a case against Werner Altbusser and ended up with nothing to show for it. With Petrovsky dead, his bosses didn't even think they had enough to go after the international organization and, by the time they got back to Werner, he had gotten rid of any of the cactus he'd collected on that last trip and was safely back in Germany, lawyered up and declaring his innocence."

"I hate that you worked so hard and have nothing to show for it," Phoenix said.

"Oh, I wouldn't say that." Jake slowed for the turn into the Southern Ute Reservation, and his eyes met Carmen's. "I'd say I got a lot out of this case. More than I'd ever bargained for."

She reached over and clasped his hand again. "I guess we both came out winners in this case," she said. All those years she had been so focused on proving herself, yet with Jake she didn't have to prove anything. She only had to love him, and be loved in return.

* * * * *

Look for the next book in Cindi Myers's
THE RANGER BRIGADE: FAMILY SECRETS
series, MISSING IN BLUE MESA,
available next month.

And don't miss the previous titles in
THE RANGER BRIGADE: FAMILY SECRETS *series:*
MURDER IN BLACK CANYON
UNDERCOVER HUSBAND
MANHUNT ON MYSTIC MESA

Available now from Mills & Boon Intrigue!

"Maggie."

Matt's voice was deep. Smooth. The only sound in her world at that moment. "I think you're the center of it all and that message might have just proven it."

"How?"

She needed the truth. She needed it so badly that she moved closer to the man. On reflex she tilted her head back to meet his stare easier. Had they ever been this close before?

And was it her imagination or did he look down at her lips?

"The message," he repeated, derailing her unwelcome thoughts. "It proves that whoever wrote it either *knows* you or researched you well enough to get really personal information."

"But why? Why would I need a reminder if I know him already?"

Maggie already didn't like what he was going to say. A storm seemed to start up in his eyes. Deep eyes, drenched in mystery.

"My guess? He's saying that he doesn't just know you. He knows your past and your present." She watched as his jaw hardened. "It's a threat, Maggie. A personal one."

FORGOTTEN
PIECES

BY
TYLER ANNE SNELL

First Published in Great Britain 2018
By Mills & Boon, an imprint of HarperCollins*Publishers*
1 London Bridge Street, London, SE1 9GF

© 2017 Tyler Anne Snell

ISBN: 978-0-263-26457-9

46-0118

Printed and bound in Spain
by CPI, Barcelona

Tyler Anne Snell genuinely loves all genres of the written word. However, she's realized that she loves books filled with sexual tension and mysteries a little more than the rest. Her stories have a good dose of both. Tyler lives in Alabama with her same-named husband and their mini "lions." When she isn't reading or writing, she's playing video games and working on her blog, *Almost There*. To follow her shenanigans, visit www.tylerannesnell.com.

This book is for Kortnie B.
and every other ER nurse out there.

I can't imagine what you all must go through during
every shift but I am immensely grateful that you do so
with courage, wisdom and compassion.

You're the real superheroes.

Chapter One

"What's a seven-letter word for a man who is an all-around donkey to the people who are just trying to help him?"

Maggie Carson shifted her weight to the other foot and blew a frustrated breath out. It moved a wayward spiral of hair out of her face. She tried to tuck it back into the makeshift ponytail holder but it was a no-go. Like her it was probably done with the flip-flopping, hot-and-cold weather. Humid to the point of feeling like you were swimming standing up and then nothing but a dry chill. It was like south Alabama had a fever. Not that she was overly concerned about the weather.

At least not when she was in the process of breaking and entering.

Or *attempting* to break and enter.

"Not going to answer me, huh?"

She gave the man crouched down next to her, fiddling with the lock, a look that would have done her reputation for being a handful proud. Except the man wasn't having any of it. He kept his eyes straight ahead and his fingers working.

Those fingers.

Those hands.

Oh, Lordy, what she could do with those.

Maggie shook her head, and the thought, away, surprised it had sprung up in the first place. Sure, Detective Matt Walker was a twelve on a ten-point scale of yummy—there was no denying that—but he was also still *Detective Matt Walker*. A man who had once called her a no-good ambulance chaser, pot stirrer and a scourge against society without an ounce of regret or shame. Not that she blamed him. She *had* accused him of murder. His wife's murder, to boot.

But she *had* apologized for that.

"Fine, I'll tell you," she said, bending at the waist to keep her volume low. The smell of some generic cologne wafted up to her. The image of his hands came back. Maggie powered through it. "The magic word is *jack*—"

The lock unlatched, distracting her from her insult. For now.

"Tricking me into coming over to break into your house because you got locked out isn't helping me," he deadpanned. "In fact, that's making a false report and is punishable by law." He stood tall and brushed off his jeans. "And I'd be lying if I said I hadn't fantasized about carting you off to jail before."

A smirk pulled up the corners of his lips—the bottom one plump and ripe for the taking—but Maggie knew he was telling the truth without his snark. Which was why she'd kept her distance for the past five years. Still, it seemed there might not be enough time in the world to put their particular stream of water under the bridge.

"It's not considered tricking if it's the only way I can get the lead detective to come here," she pointed out. "Also, I really did lock myself out. Two birds, one stone."

Matt crossed his arms over his chest. For what felt

like a long moment but she doubted stretched past a few seconds, Maggie took stock of the changes that had happened to his appearance since their last blowout years before. His hair was still a shade of dark dirty blond but now it was shaved short on the sides while the top had more length. It was a more controlled and clean look—probably part of being one of the county's most beloved detectives—and paired like a fine wine with the dusting of facial hair he also, no doubt, kept maintained to the point where no one could ever complain that he was unkempt. Not that she'd seen him be anything but proper and in control during his career with the Riker County Sheriff's Department. She might have been trying to avoid him but that didn't mean she'd missed newspaper articles and stories of cases he was involved in on the local news.

However, in person, Maggie had to admit there were a few points that had been lost in the media's translation of the man in front of her. The first and foremost was a pair of blue-gray eyes that always carried a hawk-like intensity. She imagined if she had the time she'd still not be able to put their level of intrigue on a scale. It was like looking into a spring and feeling its chill before ever even dipping a toe in the water. Then there was that jawline. The description of *chiseled* didn't do him, or any woman caught staring at him, justice. It was so perfect that Maggie's hand was itching to run along it before stopping just below his lips. For all she cared the rest of the man could have been a stick figure and she'd still rate him at an easy eleven. But it certainly didn't hurt his cause that he was tall and had muscles peeking through his button-down. *That* was a change from the last time she'd seen him in person. He'd been more lean and less toned. Then again, she wasn't surprised.

Everyone worked through grief differently.

Some people started a new hobby; some people threw themselves into the gym.

Others investigated unsolved murders in secret.

"And why, of all people, would you need me here?" Matt asked, cutting through her mental breakdown of him.

Instead of stepping backward, utilizing the large open space of her front porch, she chanced a step forward.

"I found something," she started, straining out any excess enthusiasm that might make her seem coarse. Still, she knew the detective was a keen observer. Which is why his frown was already doubling in on itself before she explained herself.

"I don't want to hear this," he interrupted, voice like ice. "I'm warning you, Carson."

"And it wouldn't be the first time you've done so," she countered, skipping over the fact he'd said her last name like a teacher readying to send her to detention. "But right now I'm telling you I found a lead. A *real*, honest-to-God lead!"

The detective's frown affected all of his body. It pinched his expression and pulled his posture taut. Through gritted teeth, he rumbled out his thoughts with disdain clear in his words.

"Why do you keep doing this? What gives you the right?" He took a step away from her. That didn't stop Maggie.

"It wasn't an accident," she implored. "I can prove it now."

Matt shook his head. He skipped frustrated and flew right into angry. This time Maggie faltered.

"You have no right digging into this," he growled. "You didn't even *know* Erin."

"But don't you want to hear what I found?"

Matt made a stop motion with his hands. The jaw she'd been admiring was set. Hard. "I don't want to ever talk to you again. Especially about this." He turned and was off the front porch in one fluid motion. Before he got into his truck he paused. "And next time you call me out here, I won't hesitate to arrest you."

And then he was gone.

THE RIKER COUNTY Sheriff's Department was quiet. Not that that was a bad thing but after the morning he'd had, Matt was itching to work a case. Anything to distract him from the storm of emotions raging through him. If he was being objective, he knew he'd be surprised at how one woman could affect him so completely. Then again, that woman *was* Maggie Carson. If she was good at anything it was leaving lasting impressions.

Without opening the bottom drawer, he imagined the picture within it. Erin Walker, smiling up at him. His beautiful wife. Unaware that a year later she'd be in the wrong place at the wrong time.

Matt fisted his hands on the top of his desk.

"So you're ticked off, huh?" A knock pulled his attention to the doorway and the man standing inside it. Sheriff Billy Reed wasn't frowning but he wasn't smiling, either. "I heard you answered a suspicious persons call on your way in this morning. A potential breaking and entering?"

Matt opened his hands slowly. He sighed.

Billy wasn't just his sheriff, he was also one of Matt's

closest friends. There wasn't any use trying to hedge around the truth. Or flat out lie.

"The only suspicious person was the woman who called in the false report to get me there in the first place. I should have let a deputy handle it but she asked specifically for me. It was a trap," he admitted, earning an eyebrow raise from his boss, "set by Maggie Carson."

Billy's demeanor shifted to understanding. He might not have been sheriff five years ago but that didn't mean he'd missed what had happened. Or why Matt had such an issue with Maggie.

"What did she want? I thought she hasn't tried to talk to you in years."

Matt tried to keep his rising anger in check.

"She said she had a lead that proves Erin's death wasn't an accident."

Billy scowled, disapproval shrouding his expression. "What's the lead?"

"Hell if I know. I didn't give her the chance to tell me," he admitted. "She doesn't have the best track record with me."

"I thought she would have moved on from the case," Billy said. "I wonder what it was she thought she found." Behind his words was a new curiosity. And, if Matt hadn't been so close to the situation, he would have listened to his own need to know. However, he *was* too close. And apparently, unlike Maggie, he had moved on.

"Maybe she's tired of writing magazine fluff pieces," Matt offered. "And now she's trying to claw her way back to the news spotlight by digging up the past she has no business digging up."

Billy stepped into the office. It was small and the bull pen of deputies started a few feet away. The sheriff must not have wanted them to hear what he was about to say, though. He lowered his voice.

"But what about the anonymous tip we got six months ago? Maybe it wouldn't hurt to hear her out?"

Matt started to bristle. He'd been completely blind-sided when he'd received a call from a man who claimed the same thing Maggie had. That the car accident that had killed Erin and one other pedestrian, hadn't been an accident at all. At the time the anonymous caller refused to identify himself unless Matt drove to Georgia to meet him. He'd only told Billy and the chief deputy, Suzy Simmons. They'd gone to the meet location together, only to find a note left with a waitress that read "I'm sorry." Matt and Suzy had stuck around to try to track down the man but they hadn't had any luck.

"That man could have been unstable or bored or both," he said. "For all we know Maggie could have orchestrated the whole thing." Even as he said it, Matt doubted his words. Whatever his issues with Maggie, he didn't think she was that malicious. He let out another long breath. "I just—I've finally gotten to a good place with what happened to Erin," Matt admitted. "And until I find some hard evidence that the accident that killed my wife wasn't an accident at all, then I'd prefer to not start up and drag another investigation along."

Billy nodded.

"And I don't blame you for that," he said. "If Maggie gives you any more trouble, let me know." He cracked a smile and tapped the badge on his belt. "I'm not afraid to use this thing."

Matt thanked him and spent the rest of the day avoiding any and all thoughts of Maggie, anonymous tips that led nowhere and an investigation he had drowned himself in years before. It wasn't until he had left the department and was driving home in the setting sun that he didn't have to distract himself from his thoughts. Instead, when his phone rang and the caller ID read "Dwayne," Matt felt his lips pull up into a genuine smile. It had been months since he'd talked to the retired detective and, if he was being honest, his mentor.

"Well, it's been a hot minute," Matt answered, forgoing any formal greeting. He'd once spent an entire week fishing with the man. Any need for formalities between them had sunk to the bottom of the river along with the faulty lures Matt had purchased. "How've you—"

"Don't," someone yelled. But it wasn't Dwayne and it wasn't into the phone. Instead, it was in the background. And it was a woman. "Don't do it!" A scream tore through the airwaves and, even though Matt couldn't tell who it was, he made a hard U-turn.

"Dwayne?" he yelled into the phone. "Dwayne!"

A *thud* that made Matt's stomach go cold preceded the phone call ending.

Matt called the number back. It went straight to voice mail. His car filled with obscenities in between calling dispatch and navigating to the outskirts of the city of Kipsy, right in the middle of the department's jurisdiction. Matt had been to the former detective's house on more than one occasion so when he pulled up and cut his engine, he knew outside the phone call that something was really wrong.

The screened-in front porch—a point of pride from the man, so mosquitos couldn't eat him up while he enjoyed a beer or two—was left open, the door to it off its hinges. The wicker furniture was scattered around the space. Nothing else on the outside looked disturbed but what he'd seen was enough.

Without waiting for backup, Matt got out of his car as quietly as he could. If he hadn't heard the woman scream he might have been more cautious. But he had. Which meant his gun came out and his attention turned to the house.

A small SUV he didn't recognize was parked at the side but Dwayne's truck was nowhere to be seen. Lights were on inside the house but as Matt got closer, he didn't hear any voices or movement. The darkness of night had fallen around him, offering cover, but it also might give an assailant the same advantage. It was a thought that made him slow as he got to the front door. It was cracked open. Something Dwayne would never do.

Matt held his gun high and pushed the door the rest of the way open, adrenaline spiking and ready to confront whatever had gone wrong.

Or so he thought.

"What the hell?"

The room looked like a tornado had torn through it. Furniture was overturned, books and trinkets were scattered and, with a drop of his gut, Matt realized blood was smeared across parts of the hardwood floor. Which shouldn't have been surprising, considering Dwayne was lying in the middle of the room, beaten badly, bloodied and unmoving.

What Matt couldn't have prepared himself for was the body next to Dwayne's.

It was Maggie. She was holding a bat covered in blood in one hand while a folder was next to the other. Matt felt like he was dreaming as his eyes focused on the name written across the top of it.

It was *his* name.

Chapter Two

It was her college graduation party all over again. Or, rather, the aftermath of it. Maggie's head was pounding. Worse than the hangover she'd had after her roommate, Barb, had decided bringing cake-flavored vodka was a good idea. While it had been a hit at the time, Maggie had felt like she was the one who had been hit the next day.

Which was how she felt as she sat on a hospital bed, staring at an IV in one arm and a pair of handcuffs around her other wrist. It connected her to the hospital bed and, according to a deputy she didn't know, had been an order. It was one of many things that had confused her since she'd come to in an ambulance, staring up at a woman asking her what her name was and if she could hear her.

While Maggie knew the hospital staff was doing all they could to make sure she was getting the treatment she needed, they sure as heck hadn't bothered to fill her in on a few details. Like why she'd wound up in an ambulance to begin with, where she had been before the ambulance had been called and why she was barefoot. That last detail, of all things, irrationally bothered her more than the rest. Because, much like the aftermath of her graduation party, she seemed to be missing a chunk of memory. This time, though, she hadn't the faintest idea what had prompted it.

A knock sounded on the door before a nurse pushed it open.

"How are you doing, Ms. Carson?"

A redheaded woman with bold lipstick and an easy smile slid into the room. When her gaze went to the handcuffs that smile tightened. Maggie decided to address the obvious.

"I'd really like to not be handcuffed," she said. "And to not be in the hospital. Neither were on my to-do list today. Or, at least I don't remember them if they were."

The nurse gravitated over to the IV.

"The cuffs I can't help," she admitted. "But what I can do is ask how your head is feeling. So, Ms. Carson, how is your head?" She met Maggie's stare. It was a look that was equal parts concerned and authoritative. She was trying to do her job and Maggie was being snarky. She sighed.

"There are few people in this world who ever use my last name and usually it's when they're about to yell at me. So, please, call me Maggie. But on the head-hurting front, it's throbbing. Not as bad as before, but it's there."

The nurse looked at Maggie's chart.

"And you're still having trouble with recall?"

Maggie nodded. It hurt.

"I'm also having trouble understanding why my head hurts in the first place." Maggie lowered her voice, trying to convey something she often tried to hide. Vulnerability. "Because no one, and I mean no one, has told me what happened to me since I woke up in an ambulance with my shirt and bra cut open and monitors stuck to my chest. So, please—" Maggie glanced down at the woman's name tag "—Nurse Bean, give me *something*."

For a moment the nurse looked like she was going to shake her head and try to offer another polite smile. Instead, she surprised Maggie by answering.

"To be honest, I just started my shift so I don't know all of the details. What I do know is that you being knocked out wasn't an accident." Her lips thinned. "But as for who did it, why and where… I'm sorry. Those are questions I can't answer."

Maggie's stomach turned cold. She knew she shouldn't have been surprised that she had been attacked since it wasn't every day she lost hours of memory, but having a nurse say it aloud was on the surreal side of uncomfortable.

"Well, I guess I'm glad to know I didn't wind up this way after tripping and bumping my head or anything," Maggie deadpanned. Sarcasm was her safety blanket. The throbbing from her head now made a fraction of sense. That in itself should have been comforting. But it wasn't. "Thank you for leveling with me," she added on. "I don't want to say I'm scared but, well, it's not a good feeling to be me right now. Thanks."

The nurse gave a quick nod and smile of acceptance.

"Like you, I prefer to go by my first name. So call me Kortnie." She took the chart and started to turn away. "I'll be back in a few minutes to check on you."

Maggie was ready to let her go and wait for someone who did know the inside scoop but then the cold steel of the handcuffs against her skin brought her attention to one more question.

"You have to at least know why I'm handcuffed, right?"

Kortnie's smile faltered.

"That's a question you should ask Detective Walker."

"Is he going to make it?"

Matt roused from the large square tile he'd been standing on for what felt like hours. It was outside Dwayne's room and was better than standing and staring inside it. Matt didn't like hospitals. Or, really, he didn't like the helplessness that came with them. He couldn't help Dwayne in his current condition. He couldn't make him heal any faster. He couldn't make him survive. All he could do was help from where he hovered and tried to puzzle out what had happened the night before. Not that he'd had much success in that department.

The sheriff repeated his question with an added inflection of empathy. He wasn't as close to the retired detective as Matt but he knew him well enough to grab the occasional drink or watch a football game or two together.

"He's out of the immediate woods but his injuries are extensive," Matt answered, dragging a hand down his face. "He still hasn't woken up and, if I read the doc's body language correctly, there's a good chance he might not. Or, if he does, he might not be the same Dwayne we knew. There was some bleeding on the brain." Billy cursed beneath his breath. Matt let him finish before he continued, "So unless the crime scene yielded some incredible results, our only way of knowing what happened might be down there. And, like I told you on the phone last night, according to *her* doctor she's having short-term memory issues."

He pointed in the direction of Maggie Carson's room. She'd been transferred out of the ER a few hours ago.

The sheriff followed his finger.

"Have you talked to her yet?" Billy asked.

Matt shook his head. Frustration, anger and more frustration sprang up at just the thought of the woman.

"When we first came in I stuck with Dwayne," he admitted. "By the time he was stable and put in his room, she was getting CAT scans. Then she was out, thanks to some pain meds. I was going to wait until the morning to talk to her." Matt really took in the sheriff's appearance. He couldn't help but smirk. "And considering there's applesauce on your blazer, I'm assuming it's morning."

Billy looked down at the smudge and sighed but in no way seemed angry.

"What can I say? Alexa and I have a routine. She wakes up early and we negotiate how much applesauce she's going to eat." He motioned to the stain. "It's a messy business. I've dealt with seasoned criminals that were easier to crack than this toddler."

There was pride clear and true in the way Billy spoke of his daughter. It matched his unconditional love for his wife, Mara. Which was one of the reasons so many residents of Riker County took a shine to him. He was a good family man who worked hard to provide and protect. He was the straightest shooter Matt had ever known in law enforcement. Something that had not always been the case for everyone he had employed.

Matt watched as Billy sobered.

"I would tell you that going home to get some sleep might be the best course for you and that I can handle talking to Maggie," he started. "But—"

"It's Dwayne that got hurt and I won't back off yet."

Billy nodded.

"Then let's go talk to Maggie."

They marched down the hallway and knocked on the door. Matt spied the clock on the wall. Hours had indeed passed. It was almost seven in the morning.

"Come in!"

Matt took his attempt at a calming breath and followed the sheriff inside.

If he thought they'd be met with guilt or shame, he was wildly mistaken.

One look at him, and Maggie's big green eyes got bigger. Her lips didn't have time to purse. They were too busy parting to yell at him.

"I know you have your issues with me, but *this* is ridiculous, don't you think?"

She shook her left arm.

Matt walked to the side of the bed as if he was going to inspect the cuffs. Instead, he crossed his arms over his chest.

"Considering the nature of what happened, we deemed it necessary."

Maggie looked like a fish out of water, opening and closing her mouth, trying to find the right words to fight him with, no doubt. Billy, however, stepped in. He closed the door behind them and cleared his throat.

"Let's calm down and talk," he said.

"Can we talk about how I've been cuffed to a bed for the entire night and no one, until now, has decided to come and talk to me other than doctors?"

Maggie's cheeks were flushed, Matt noticed. For the first time he realized there was a light dusting of freckles across her nose.

"Yes," Billy said, channeling the calm that Matt had heard him use throughout their careers. "But first, tell us the last thing you remember."

Maggie let out a breath of frustration.

"Sneaking off to my couch in the middle of the night because I couldn't sleep. I channel surfed until I fell asleep in front of the TV."

Matt shared a look with Billy.

"In the middle of the night," Billy repeated. "And by *night* you mean…"

Maggie sighed.

"By *night* I mean Tuesday night." She held up her hand in a stopping motion. "And, before you question my sanity, yes, I know that today is Thursday."

"You're missing more than twenty-four hours," Billy spelled out. Maggie nodded. Matt noticed she was more inclined to look at the sheriff with controlled emotions. When she looked at him, he could see the fire burning behind her eyes. Not that he could blame her. The phrase "poking the bear" came to mind. Not that Maggie Carson in any way looked like a bear.

"So you don't remember your conversation with Detective Walker yesterday?" Billy added on.

Maggie's eyes widened.

"No?" Her eyebrow rose as she looked at Matt for an explanation.

He didn't want to give it. He was too frustrated.

"Well, isn't that convenient?" Matt muttered.

The comment didn't go unnoticed. Maggie whipped her head around to Billy and then back to Matt.

"Hey, what's that supposed to mean? Do you think I'm making this up? Why would I even do that?"

"Oh, I don't know, covering your a—"

"Detective," Billy interrupted, voice sharp. Matt felt anger surge again. If he was honest, it was misplaced. While he did have issues with Maggie Carson, he had never pegged her for a violent woman. Aggressive with her words, sure. Stubborn to the point where he really had fantasized about arresting her a few times, absolutely. But was she capable of beating a man in his sixties to the point of potential brain damage? No. He felt it in his gut, whether or not he wanted to absolve her of the accusation that she'd done it.

Still, the only witnesses that they knew of were both in the hospital. One might never wake up. The other was claiming memory loss. That was a tough pill to swallow no matter who the two were.

"I'm sure the doctor would be happy to talk to you about it." Maggie cooled down as she spoke to Billy. "But I would like to know why you thought I would make it up."

She kept her eyes firmly on Billy. He squared his shoulders.

"What's your relationship with Dwayne Meyers?"

Matt watched closely as Maggie's expression turned to confusion. Her eyebrows drew together. She tilted her head ever so slightly to the side.

"I wouldn't say we have one," she answered. "I mean, we know each other and I've interviewed him before. But other than that I don't think you could even classify us as friends. Why do you ask?"

"Because I found you at his house," Matt said.

Again Maggie tilted her head to the side. Like the movement would shake loose a memory that would make the puzzle whole. Then her face lit up.

"Well, then, did he tell you who did this to me?" She

motioned to the back of her head where the initial blow that had knocked her unconscious had happened. While waiting for the ambulance Matt had inspected the injury in an attempt to understand the situation a little better. It hadn't helped. "Unless… Did *he* do this to me?"

"That's what we're trying to piece together," Billy hedged.

"Why not ask Dwayne?"

Matt took another step forward. He knew Billy was trying to ease the woman into the information to see how she reacted but Matt was tired of it. Tired in general. It was time to cut to the chase.

"Because you weren't the only one I found," he started. "Dwayne was beaten badly with, as far as we can guess, a baseball bat. One that you were holding when I found you."

A crinkle began to deepen between Maggie's eyebrows. She took a moment to respond with notable reserve.

"You think someone attacked us both and left the bat behind?"

"Or it was you who attacked Dwayne," Matt offered.

That crease turned from concern to something he couldn't read. It caught Matt off guard.

"I might not remember an entire day or so, but I wouldn't hurt Dwayne Meyers. In fact, I wouldn't *use a bat* to hurt anyone unless it was self-defense," she said, voice even. "And, even if I had, what do you think happened? You think I used him as batting practice and then knocked myself unconscious? What would I gain from any of that?" This time her eyes found Matt's and hunkered down on them. "I know you don't like me but do you really think I'm capable of that?"

Matt remembered the first time he'd seen Maggie Carson. Her thick, wavy hair had been short then, but still wild. Despite five years it was the same dark oak color with a few new spots of lightened brown from, he guessed, days spent outside in the sun. She was still slender, as she had been back then, but not as rigid. When she'd first introduced herself Matt remembered thinking she looked very much like a woman with the world on her shoulders, forced to struggle to keep them upright. He'd never stopped to think about the woman's personal life much past that, considering she had been there to question him about Erin's death. But now?

Matt caught himself wondering about the life of the woman staring up at him with true, forest green eyes. Ones he realized he'd never really forgotten.

Ones he realized he believed.

But then what had gone on in that house?

Chapter Three

Matt opened his mouth to answer Maggie's question when a knock on the door interrupted his thoughts. The three of them turned just as it was opened.

A young woman, maybe early twenties, flushed at the sight of them.

"Oh, I—I'm sorry," she said hurriedly, eyes bouncing across each of their faces. "The nurse said you were awake and we could come back."

No sooner than she'd said the word *we* did a boy with round glasses pop his head around her hip. His gaze went straight to Maggie's.

Out of Matt's periphery he saw her entire demeanor change.

"Well, hey there, little dude," she exclaimed, voice softening.

The boy, perhaps five or six, beamed. Then, just as quickly, he shrank back and looked up at the men. He was shy.

"It's okay," Maggie coaxed. "These are Mommy's friends."

Mommy? Matt thought, surprised. He hadn't known she had a kid.

"We can come back," the younger woman blurted

out, face now completely red. Her gaze shifted to Maggie again and then dropped down to what must have been her wrist cuffed to the railing. "I—I can skip class today," she offered.

Matt took a step to his right until he was touching the bed. It effectively cut off everyone's view of the cuffs.

Billy cleared his throat.

"I don't think we've met," he said, stepping forward with his hand outstretched. He moved into the woman's and child's sightlines, also blocking Maggie from view. "I'm Sheriff Billy Reed."

Matt turned, pulling his handcuff key out. Maggie remained silent as she watched him uncuff her as quietly as he could. She met his gaze and gave one small nod.

A silent thank-you.

It, like the boy, caught him off guard.

He returned it with a nod of his own.

Like she said, he might have issues with her, but he wasn't heartless. The boy was probably already freaked out that his mother was in the hospital.

But where was his dad?

Matt turned back to the sheriff and his conversation, trying to move past thoughts of Maggie's love life. He had bigger things to worry about.

"I'm Larissa. I babysit Cody occasionally."

"So then, you must be Cody," Billy said. Matt watched him kneel down in front of the boy. He nodded. "And I'm guessing you are ready to hang out with your mom for a bit." Again the boy nodded. "Well, why don't I make you a deal? You go grab a quick hug from her and then you can walk with me to the vending machine down the hall for an early-morning candy bar while my friend Matt finishes talking to your mom." Matt didn't have to be next to Cody to see his face light up at the mention of a candy bar. Billy turned to Maggie. "If that's okay with you?"

"Only if you save half of it for me," she said with a grin. Another expression Matt wasn't used to seeing from the woman.

Cody nodded, raced forward and jumped on the bed for a hug. Maggie winced but kept smiling. Even with the meds she was being fed there must have still been some pain from the hit that had knocked her out. She returned the hug with a few words in the boy's ear Matt couldn't hear. He giggled and then was off with the sheriff. Larissa followed, still flushed.

"If you needed a reason to believe I didn't attack Dwayne, then that boy is it," Maggie started. "I don't need to be able to remember the last day to tell you with certainty that I wouldn't jeopardize his life by suddenly being a violent and callous woman."

"Then give me a reason why you *were* at Dwayne's," Matt said. "Because I can't accept that everything that happened in the last day came out of nowhere. If you weren't friendly with the man, then you must have been talking to him about something."

That crease between Maggie's eyebrows came back in force. Her eyes unfocused and her normally plump lips thinned. She was thinking. About what, though, he'd pay good money to be in on.

"I have had no reason to talk to Dwayne in years," she finally said. "Whatever the reason was, it must have happened yesterday." Matt was about to open his mouth and vent his frustration when Maggie continued. This time, however, there was a different tone to her words. "*But* the last time I talked to him, years ago…"

Her gaze slid up to his. Slow. Almost sheepish.

Matt didn't have to be a detective to figure out what she was trying to say.

"The last time you talked to him was after my wife died," he inserted. Even as he said it the old ache of loss sounded in the distance. "And then yesterday you tried to tell me you could prove Erin's death wasn't an accident."

He read surprise clearly on the woman's face. If she was faking it, she was doing a damned good job.

"Let me guess, another thing you don't remember."

Maggie shook her head.

"No but yes," she said. "I *was* looking into the accident again but I definitely didn't have any proof."

Maggie sat up straighter. Again her gaze found his. Even with her makeup washed off, there was an almost-open kind of beauty about her. Like she had nothing to hide. But he knew better. Not only did she have something to hide, she'd also hidden it well from him for years.

"Matt," she started, unblinking. "I know you have a hard time believing this but I think I might have figured out who killed your wife."

"I'm going to release you from custody for a few different reasons and with a condition or two."

Sheriff Reed had his arms crossed over his chest but didn't look like he was being pained to talk to her. Unlike the detective. After she'd dropped her bombshell, she'd more than expected him to give her a weighty, anger-filled lecture. Instead, he'd excused himself and gone into the hallway. Now she was staring at the sheriff, wondering if he knew what she'd admitted to the detective.

"Okay, I'm listening," she added when she realized Sheriff Reed wanted a confirmation.

He held up his index finger and ticked off his points as he made them.

"One, where you were struck with the baseball bat suggests that someone swung and hit you from behind." He held up his other hand to stop her questions and continued, "Based on the angle of the wound, it would have been nearly impossible for you to have been able to hit that spot with enough force to knock yourself out cold. Which means we're looking for a third person who was in that house. Detective Ansler is on scene and CSU will get back to us when they find something. For all we know you walked in on a robbery in progress. Two, your doctor has cleared you health-wise so I don't see a reason to force you to stay in one of these rooms when I know exactly where you live. And some of your neighbors, too. Including a very observant Deputy Carrington." There was a warning beneath the words. Or maybe it was a promise. It was the sheriff's way of flexing his connection muscles.

Basically he was saying, "Don't try to run or do anything stupid because I have eyes and ears almost everywhere in town."

But Maggie had no reason to run. However, doing something stupid was an entirely different ballgame. She preferred the phrase "risk taking."

"Three," he continued, holding up three fingers. "As much as I dislike the digging that you've done into the life and pain of Detective Walker, it's highly likely that the circumstances surrounding your and Dwayne's attack could be related to you digging into Erin's death and not just random. That's too much of a coincidence for me to ignore. I want to see what information you *do* have on the case. And why someone might want that information, if that's what they were after." Sheriff Reed sobered. "But you *will not* continue to look into Erin's death, understood?"

Maggie liked to think she could read people. Or at least, know what they *really* meant when they said something. That was how she knew that the sheriff meant every word of the command. And there was nothing she could say to him in that moment to convince him otherwise. So she decided to lose this battle.

But not the war.

"Understood."

Sheriff Reed nodded. His shoulders loosened considerably.

"And the last reason is your son, Cody," he said. "I hadn't realized his father wasn't in—"

"He doesn't have a father," Maggie interrupted so quickly she surprised herself. The sheriff amended his statement.

"I hadn't realized you were a single parent with no immediate family in the area who he could stay with until this is all figured out. A hospital is no place for a kid to hang out unless absolutely necessary."

"Normally, I'd agree," Maggie said after a moment. "But if my being at Dwayne's was because I was *investigating*, then what if that third person in Dwayne's house decides to come after me? Surely I've seen their face. Cody will be in danger."

"Which brings me to my two conditions," he said. "I

want you to keep to your normal routine, including his, until we have this sorted out. Send your son to school today. I know what it's like to disrupt a kid's routine when they're young. He'll be safe there and in the meantime we can make sure your house is safe just in case. I would also like you to not talk about what happened to you until we have a better handle on the situation. That includes the media… And no personal reporting of any kind. This story, you need to keep under wraps. It'll be a whole hell of a lot easier getting information when we don't have to sift through a county's worth of theories on what happened. Not yet at least."

"Okay, I can do that, I guess," she said. Though she could feel the prickling sensation of curiosity trying to expand within her. She wanted to hit the street, ask questions and get answers about what had happened to her. What had she found? How did Dwayne fit in? Or maybe she'd simply been in the wrong place at the wrong time. Still, that left the question of who had attacked them. One she wanted answered, even if it had nothing to do with her personal investigation. Plus, the sheriff was probably right. Lying low might be the best thing for her. Maybe her memories would return if she took it easy.

Ha. Easy. Like I've ever done what's easy.

Before the sheriff could read any mischief in her expression, Maggie sat up straighter and cleared her throat.

"So what's the last condition?" she asked. "Because I'd really like to leave this charming place as soon as possible."

The sheriff definitely wasn't smirking anymore. In fact, he almost looked hesitant.

"What happened could have been a case of you seeing something you shouldn't have by accident, caught as an innocent bystander and targeted for that reason. But we have no proof. Just as we have no proof that your life could be in danger. So for the public's safety and your own, I am relinquishing you into the custody of Detective Matt Walker effective immediately."

Maggie opened her mouth to argue but the sheriff was faster on the draw.

"Until we find out what happened in that house, Ms. Carson, this decision is final. Arguing with me won't work."

Maggie lifted her chin a fraction. She crossed her arms over her chest.

"No offense, Sheriff, but you've never heard me argue before."

Chapter Four

There were a lot of questions but not many answers. At least none that led Matt to a clear picture of what had happened at Dwayne's house. Although Maggie had admitted to looking into Erin's accident, she'd gone tight-lipped as they left the hospital. Then again, that might have had more to do with Cody being caught between them as they got into Matt's off-duty, dark green Jimmy. The six-year-old had kept his eyes wide as Maggie talked to him in the back seat. She reminded him of a lesson she'd already taught him.

Don't talk to strangers.

In the rearview mirror Matt could see the boy took the conversation seriously. He watched Maggie with concentration that furrowed his brow. When she was done that concentration turned to worry. He didn't understand what had changed. From what they'd pieced together from Billy talking to Larissa before she left for the community college was that everything had been normal the day before.

Larissa lived near Cody's school and often picked him up and watched him until Maggie was with work between four and five. Around four thirty Maggie had texted and asked if she could watch the boy until eight. After that she'd called from the hospital. Larissa had offered to keep him for the night. She hadn't told Cody why the impromptu sleepover had happened.

And now, sitting in the back seat, Matt could almost see the boy trying to figure out what had changed their normal routines to include a last-minute stay with his babysitter, a trip to the hospital and a talk about strangers.

Maggie must have sensed it, too. Matt glanced into the mirror in time to see her press her thumb between his eyebrows. She rubbed the crease gently and smiled.

"Wrinkles are for me, not you," she said. "Don't worry, little dude. Everything's going to be okay. I promise." Her voice had gone gentle, maternal strength backing up each word. It was such a contrast from the woman he knew that it surprised a smile out of him. Thankfully she didn't see it. "And if *you* promise not to worry, I'll see what I can do about taking you, Josh and Emily to the science museum in Kipsy sometime soon."

Matt didn't have to see the boy's face to know Maggie had just hit negotiation gold. A quick intake of breath from him was followed by a bigger smile reflected on his mom.

"I can show Emily the tornado ride," Cody exclaimed. "And we can play with the burp machine!"

"And don't forget the puzzle room," Maggie added on.

Cody squealed and launched into his favorite things he'd done the last time they'd been there. Along with the tornado ride, burp machine and puzzle room, he'd had fun in the music house where the floor was a keyboard. Judging by the quick sigh Maggie let out, she had *not* been a fan of the music house.

She caught Matt's eye and shook her head.

"That place is the devil," she supplied, in no way stopping the boy's conversation. He stared out the window, still counting off the different rides, exhibits and interactive experiments the museum had. "Imagine a marching band forced into one room and each one is playing a different, horribly out-of-sync tune. I'd rather take another bat to the head."

Despite himself, Matt almost smiled.

The pleasantries ended after they got to the school. Matt talked to the principal about keeping an eye out for anything or anyone suspicious, just in case, while Maggie sweet-talked the boy's teacher into dropping the mark against him being late. Or intimidated the teacher. Matt didn't know. The Maggie he'd met years ago was starting to look like a different Maggie now.

When they rendezvoused back at the Jimmy, however, it was all business. Another surprise, considering Maggie had been the one to start it.

"Okay, we need to retrace my steps from yesterday." She jumped in and buckled her seat belt but gazed straight ahead. "Let's start at my house and see what we can find there."

"You may have been released into my custody but that doesn't give you the right to issue orders," he reminded her. Though he agreed with her idea. He navigated out of the parking lot and pointed the SUV in the same direction he'd headed the day before.

"Sorry, I just assumed you'd want to figure out what happened," she said. The gentleness she'd used with her son had definitely gone to school with him. "I didn't realize you had something better to do."

Matt muttered some bad things beneath his breath.

All of which Maggie didn't comment on. She was a smart woman. She knew which buttons to press. And when to stop pressing them altogether.

Or, at least, he thought she had. The fact that she was still trying to make something of Erin's death proved otherwise.

"So what do we know so far?" she said when he'd found a more peaceful state of mind. "Has CSU found anything helpful at Dwayne's house yet?"

Matt didn't like that he shook his head.

"Detective Ansler is supposed to update me when he gets more information on the prints found at the scene but I *do* know that a partial was found that didn't belong to you or Dwayne. Other than that, nothing of interest has been reported so far. You could tell a struggle had taken place but other than that I didn't have a chance to really investigate. I rode with Dwayne to the hospital when the EMTs got there. The sheriff and Ansler took over."

"Then why don't we go now?" Maggie asked, sitting up straighter.

"You want to go back to the scene of a crime where you're one of the suspects?" he had to ask. "That definitely isn't going to fly."

"I'm also one of the *victims*," she argued. "And how are we supposed to figure out what happened if you just admitted you didn't even have enough time to *really* look at the house? Plus, maybe something will jog my memory!"

It was a good idea, he had to admit, but he'd been burned by Maggie Carson's enthusiasm one too many times.

"How about you just leave the police work to the police? Despite the thoughts that I'm sure fill your head, last I checked you weren't law enforcement. In fact, last time I checked, you weren't even a reporter."

Maggie bristled. Her lips thinned. The air in the SUV seemed to go arctic.

And just like that Matt found a way to shut Maggie Carson up.

THE HOUSE AT the end of Birchwood Drive had a yellow door that stood out like a sunflower among a bucket of weeds. The moment they turned on the street, her eye was drawn to the door like there was a bull's-eye painted across the front. It made Maggie feel a touch of warmth just looking at it.

Because man, had she fought tooth and nail with the homeowners association about it.

The memory of fighting for something, even as small as the color of a door, made the detective's words' sting lessen. But not enough to press him further about going to Dwayne's. Instead, she decided to focus on another mystery.

Like what she had done after taking Cody to school the day before.

Her thoughts stalled when she realized something she hadn't even thought about until the house was right in front of her.

"The sheriff said my car was at Dwayne's but empty," she said when he cut the engine in the driveway.

"Yeah?"

"Including my purse, which also wasn't in the house." Matt nodded.

For the first time that day Maggie let her shoulders sag. "So along with my car key, it's safe to assume my house key is no longer in my possession." Matt turned to the front door. He hadn't thought about that detail, either. Maggie sighed. "You said you picked my lock yesterday morning? Another event I can't remember. Think you could put on a repeat performance?"

The detective led the way to the backyard and to the back door with notable tension lining his shoulders. He kept his left arm tucked close to his stomach. Ready to unholster his gun, she bet. Something she might have deemed unnecessary under different circumstances.

"Give me a heads-up before you crack the lock," she said at his elbow as they walked up the steps. "I might not remember what I did yesterday but I never leave the house without setting the alarm. I'll need to run to the front door and disarm it once the door is—" Maggie watched, confused, as Matt opened the back door with no problems.

"Do you normally leave your doors unlocked?"

Maggie didn't answer right away. She was listening for what should have been a familiar sound.

"Not on purpose," she finally said. "But again, I always turn on the alarm before I leave. Or at least I thought I did." She motioned to the house and met the detective's eyes. "The alarm beeps until you disarm it and—"

"And there's no beeping," he finished, turning back to the open door. He unholstered his gun. "Anyone else live here?"

"No. Just me and Cody."

"Anyone else have the code?"

"Only Larissa but she has classes until two today."

Matt gave one curt nod followed by an equally curt order.

"Stay here."

"Yes, sir."

She moved to the side of the doorway as Matt held out his gun and went inside. Despite his order and her common sense, Maggie wanted to follow him. She wasn't a stranger to taking risks, though admittedly she had taken a good deal less of them since Cody had arrived, but leaving the door unlocked *and* the alarm off? That didn't sound like her. Not even memory-less her. Something must have made her leave in a hurry.

Or someone.

That thought was the glue that kept her feet in place while the detective spent the next few minutes going through the house. During that time she revolved through question after question in her head. No matter which mystery popped up about her blank yesterday, she never reached any memories. No leads. No answers.

"No one's in here," Matt said, reappearing in the doorway. His eyes found hers with a notable amount of suspicion. If it was directed at her she didn't know. "Nothing jumped out at me that might shed some light on everything but then again, this isn't my place. I don't know what to look for."

They walked into the house, both uneasy. Maggie felt her defenses—and sarcasm—rising. In the past few years her social life had declined. The people who frequented her house were few and far between. Not that she was unhappy with her life. She just wondered what conclusions the man had drawn from his pass-through.

He followed her as she went clockwise through the house, starting at the kitchen and ending in the living room. It was the heart of their home and most lived-in. Stranded toys mingled with books and blankets and other odds and ends that never seemed to get sorted to their rightful places outside the room.

The detective stood sentry next to one of the large windows at the front of the house. His gun was back in its holster but his hands hung at his sides, ready to do whatever was necessary.

Maggie took a moment to watch the man. She'd be lying if she said she hadn't thought about him off and on throughout the years. Mostly when a case he was working crossed over the media airwaves. She might have switched from a reporter to a magazine writer but that didn't mean she'd stopped reading the paper. But there had been moments, quiet moments, where the detective had crossed her mind without her conscious volition.

He'd just be there. Like he was now.

A man she barely knew.

A man who loathed her.

A man seemingly always in sync with the world.

Except when it came to her.

Maggie cleared her throat. She wasn't about to give herself permission to think about the detective as anything but a pain in her side. No. She wasn't allowed.

"Okay, so as far as I can tell the house is how I would normally leave it."

"Other than the unlocked door and the disabled alarm," Matt supplied.

"Yeah, except those. Everything else, though, looks like it did before the memory loss." To prove her point further, she turned to the couch. "See, my pillow from the other night is still there—"

Maggie's eyes caught on to a few details she'd missed. The strangeness of what she was seeing must have shown in her expression. The detective's body language became more open. He faced her with a look split between curiosity and concern.

"What is it?"

Maggie walked to the coffee table and paused. She pointed to the contents on its wooden top.

"Those are my keys," she said, thoroughly confused. "My house and car keys." She started to pick them up as if the physical contact would somehow answer the questions starting to spring up in her head when she noticed something else between the table and the couch. "And this is my purse."

"What?"

Maggie picked up her bag. She pulled out her wallet and flipped it open. Her ID, credit cards and money were inside. The same as she remembered it from before her memory blanked out.

"Everything's here."

It was a statement but even to her ears, her confusion was still running rampant. The half-filled cup of coffee with lipstick marks on its edge didn't help.

"You may think I'm a lot of things but let me tell you, messy isn't one of them."

"But you *and* your car were at Dwayne's," Matt added. "How did the keys end up back here?"

Like someone had flipped a switch, a new theory blazed across Maggie's mind. She turned around and walked straight to the kitchen. Matt's boots were heavy against the hardwood as he followed.

"Do you remember something?"

Maggie rounded the breakfast bar and made a bee-line for the three metal canisters on the counter next to the sink. The one labeled Flour was open, its lid next to it. She was sure of what she *wouldn't* find within it but still had to look. After she did she turned, confused.

"It's gone."

"What's gone?"

"The spare key to my car." She motioned to the canister. "I kept it in there."

Matt looked between her and the tin for a moment.

"So let's assume you used your spare car key to drive your car to Dwayne's," he said. "Why would you need it when your original car key is in the other room? And why not take your purse?"

"Why leave a half-filled cup of coffee out? Why leave the back door unlocked and not the front? And why not set the alarm?"

Matt's eyes widened. Like her, his switch had flipped.

"Because you needed to leave in a hurry," he guessed. "But why not grab your things?"

Maggie walked to the door that opened into the kitchen. From where she stood she couldn't see the living room. But she *could* see the back door.

"I'm not one to make baseless guesses, despite your personal opinion of me, but I think someone was with me here yesterday," she started. A knot of cold began to form in her stomach. "And whoever they were must have said or done something I really didn't like."

Chapter Five

"It's a theory," Matt reminded the sheriff. He was standing in the living room, phone to his ear, and looking down at Maggie's key ring. After she'd become convinced of what had happened, he'd had to reel her in a bit. She'd excused herself to shower, not that he blamed her with dried blood caked on her head and a hospital stay that had extended through the night. Now he was bringing Billy up to speed. "But I have to agree it may be right on the money. I mean it looks like she just got up and got out. It's not adding up."

"Then we must not have the right numbers," Billy said. The background noise of the department filtered through the phone. It reminded Matt that he hadn't been home since he left for work yesterday. "I'll keep things going on my end while Ansler runs point on the investigation."

"You're giving lead to Ryan?" Matt asked, surprised. He was head detective in the sheriff's department and had been employed with them for four years longer than Ryan Ansler. Not to say that Matt didn't like the man. He was just more invested in figuring out what had happened thanks to his friendship with Dwayne.

Which, he realized two seconds too late, might have been the problem.

"You need to figure out Ms. Carson's part in all of this," Billy said. "Whether or not she was in the wrong place at the wrong time, at the right place at the wrong time, or did exactly what she wanted to do. Finding out what happened with her is the key to solving this case. Trying to juggle everything at the same time won't help Dwayne. Getting answers about what happened at that house might. Let Ansler and me cover the other details and questions. You focus on Carson."

Billy was right. Like always.

Matt ended the call and decided to explore his surroundings while he was alone. It was less curiosity and more of an attempt to keep his mind from settling until he could ask Maggie some *real* questions. Ones that she did have answers for. Like the investigation into Erin's accident.

He imagined his late wife as he often did. Years later and he could still trace every curve of her face in his mind. Bright eyes, button nose, all smiles. He felt more at home in those snatches of memories than he ever had since the accident. Matt didn't know if that was because he'd moved on or that he hadn't.

Depending on the day he could give an answer one way or the other.

Today, though?

He wasn't sure.

The inside of Maggie's house was surprisingly cozy, all things considered. Beige and white, linens, blue and yellow pops of color and various pictures of Cody, herself and a few people Matt didn't recognize. He didn't know what he had expected of the ex-reporter—maybe newspapers and magazines scattered around or a bulletin board filled with pictures all connected by strings—but normal hadn't been it.

He moved from the living room to what he guessed was a converted dining room currently being used as an office. At least this room looked more like the speed of the Maggie he remembered. Surrounding her computer was a sea of notebooks, papers and empty coffee mugs. A small filing cabinet was tucked next to the desk, partially hidden by a wooden side table standing over it. Matt walked closer to inspect it. There was a lock on the bottom drawer.

A treadmill was tucked in the corner and against the left wall, while a small bookcase stood on the right and seemed to be dedicated to Cody. Colorful spines filled the openings while toys were interspersed between some of the covers. Matt paused at one and smiled. It was a toy cop car.

From there his attention roamed over the pictures hanging on the wall in this room. A collage of more unfamiliar faces hung above the desk while a picture of a newborn Cody sat in the center. He'd had a lot of hair as a baby and was swaddled in a blue blanket, filling up the entire image.

And then there Erin was. Heralding a memory of the first time they'd talked about having kids. He'd just joined the Riker County Sheriff's Department and she was working through nursing school. They'd decided to wait until their life became less hectic.

Now here he was, years later, standing in Maggie Carson's house wondering what his own child might look like.

It was another question he didn't have an answer to.

However, it shepherded in a thought that had been in the back of his mind as he moved around the house, looking at pictures.

"Investigating and snooping are separated by the finest of lines, Detective Walker. I thought you of all people would know when you're toeing it."

Maggie came to a stop at Matt's side. A sweet aroma wafted off her, filling his senses before he'd known what hit him. Shampoo or soap or perfume. He didn't know which but it didn't matter. It caught him off guard all the same.

"Don't worry, I know the urge to not answer a question is hard to resist," she continued. "Did you finally get some insight into me? Find anything interesting, Mr. Keen Eye?"

She was teasing him. There was a small smile pulling up the corners of her lips. It caught his attention and held it for a few beats too long. It also applied pressure to the idea that he despised the woman next to him. That she was nothing more than a pain in the ass. *His* ass.

Maggie put a fist on her hip. She must not have liked his slow response time.

"Oh, come on, Detective," she said more harshly. "Make an observation about me based on what you've seen. Wow me with your skills."

"It's not as loud as I thought it would be," he started, rising to the challenge. "The house I mean. With how you present yourself in public *and* one-on-one I assumed this place would be…more chaotic. Instead, it's pretty calm. Ordered. Except in here."

He motioned to the desk and the scattered papers around her computer.

"But I bet my badge that all of those are just for

show. I can't imagine someone like you would leave any important documents out like that. Even in your own house. I imagine those are tucked inside that filing cabinet." Matt motioned to the coffee cups next. "I also assume you work at home, considering the amount of coffee cups on your desk and the treadmill. I bet you use it when you get tired of sitting around all day. Unless I'm wrong and you work late nights instead." He walked over to the toy cop car. "And if I had to take a stab in the dark about *this*, I would bet you tried to talk Cody out of this toy, explaining that cops are too by the book for your liking."

Maggie's eyebrow stayed high. She raised her hands in mock defense.

"Your words, not mine," she said. "But anyone could have drawn the same conclusions if they'd just walked through the house. Especially if they already knew me or, at least, *of* me. It's not a hard stretch to see a treadmill and coffee cups in an office and guess the person works at home."

There was no smugness there but Matt did recognize a challenge when he heard one. Maggie was baiting him to prove himself.

So he did.

Dropping any hint of a smile from his lips he walked back over to her desk. He pointed to the baby picture of Cody. Her smile wavered before he even spoke.

"You adopted Cody," he said simply. "The house is filled with pictures of him as a toddler but this is the only one I've seen of him as a baby. And it's cropped, which means you weren't the one holding him."

Like a candle that had been lit, Matt could almost

see her intention to tease him start to burn away. She crossed her arms over her chest.

"I suppose if you make enough guesses you're bound to get one right." Her smile had dwindled down to barely there but he wasn't reading anger from her. "The first time I met Cody he was three." She motioned to the picture of him as a baby. "That was the only picture that had been taken of him until he was placed in foster care. I make sure he knows that even though I wasn't there, I still like to look at how cute my baby boy was."

"He knows he's adopted, then."

Maggie nodded.

"There's nothing wrong with being adopted," she said, resolute. "And I wanted to make sure he knew that at an early age. I'm sure he'll have more questions when he's older but so far, he's never had any problems calling me Mom. Even if I tell him it's a little too formal sounding. But he's a mini genius so I guess that comes with the territory."

This time the smile grew. Love. Pure and genuine.

Matt might not have known Maggie Carson as well as he'd once thought but in that moment he knew one thing for certain. She loved her son with all of her heart.

He opened his mouth to say something when his ringtone went off. The caller ID read "Ryan Ansler."

"That was fast," Matt muttered. He looked at Maggie before pressing Accept. "Give me a minute."

THE DRIED BLOOD had washed away easily enough in the shower but that didn't mean Maggie wanted to push her luck by blow-drying her hair. The gash left by the bat wasn't bad enough to need stitches but it was still throbbing enough to be uncomfortable. She stood across from her reflection in her en suite, trying to see if the past two days were showing.

She felt tired and her legs were a little sore. The former could have been attributed to the sleep she'd gotten off and on in the hospital but the latter was troubling. Matt had been right about her working from home and using the treadmill when she felt too cooped up or restless. She wasn't ready to knock out any marathons but over the past few years she'd gotten into fairly decent shape.

So why were her legs sore?

Had she walked around a lot the day before?

Had she run?

Maggie raked a hand through her hair and blew out a sigh. She'd always loved puzzles. Mysteries had to be solved. Questions had to be answered. That was all she'd ever wanted to do when she was little. Find the truth that people—bad people—tried to hide.

But now that the new mystery involved her?

She hadn't asked to lose a day's worth of memory. And well, she didn't like the feeling.

Just as Matt hadn't asked to lose his wife. Or have Maggie start her own investigation during what must have been the worst low of his life like some dog after a bone.

Again she sighed.

"You in here?"

Maggie straightened as the detective called into her room. One last look at her reflection and she nodded.

"Yeah," she answered, walking out to meet him in the hall. His eyes were wide. Something had happened. "Was that the sheriff?"

"No, Detective Ansler. But we do have some new information."

Again, Maggie searched his expression. It was troubled. The cold knot that had formed in her stomach earlier started to expand.

"And I'm guessing it's not the answers to all of our questions."

Matt shook his head.

"CSU reported in," he started. "Your prints and Dwayne's were found on the bat. A partial print was found on the inside of the screen door near the handle. And that's it."

Maggie felt her eyebrow rise.

"What do you mean *that's it*?"

"I mean those are the *only* prints in the entire house."

Her eyes widened.

"And that's not normal."

Matt shook his head. Again, he didn't like what he was saying.

"No, that's not normal for a lived-in residence," he replied. "Unless Dwayne has a serious case of OCD, that house should have been covered in his prints at the very least. Which means one of three possibilities."

Maggie held up her index finger, much like the sheriff had done earlier in the hospital.

"One, that Dwayne wiped down the entire place after he was beaten into unconsciousness." Maggie held up another finger. "Two, *I* wiped the place down before I did my own unconscious dance."

Matt held up his finger in lieu of her ticking off her third.

"Three, whoever attacked both of you wiped the

place down, erasing any evidence linking him or her to the house. And to you and Dwayne."

That cold in the pit of Maggie's stomach was starting to unravel to the point of becoming flat. She had no sarcasm or joke to replace it. There was no denying she was caught in the middle of something.

And she needed to figure out what that something was fast.

Maggie gave the detective one decisive nod. He must have seen the intent in her eyes. Ever so slightly he tilted his head to the side. The human way to silently question something that was a mystery.

Under different circumstances, she would have liked to have been a mystery that the handsome Detective Matt Walker tried to solve, but now she was afraid the question mark she had been branded with was dangerous.

"Okay, then we only have one option." She brushed past the man and headed for the living room. He followed her, his stare burrowing a hole in every step she took. He kept quiet as she grabbed her purse and dumped its contents on the floor next to the couch. "Let's figure out what I did yesterday."

His eyes didn't leave hers for a moment. Then he nodded.

"I agree. I also want to call in CSU to dust for prints here. They're still working on the partial, but considering how quickly you appear to have left yesterday, maybe if you did have company, we can at least find out who it was."

"Good idea."

Maggie was still trying to ignore how freaked out it made her feel to know someone or something had spooked her enough to run from her own home. Her eyes started to skirt over the various pieces of her life that had made up the inside of her purse when she realized Matt wasn't moving.

Maggie looked up and met his eyes.

Trying to solve another mystery.

But not one that had to do with her.

"After I make this call you're going to answer a few questions before we do anything else." His voice was cold. She could almost swear she felt its chill from where she sat on the floor. He wasn't going to let her off the hook this time. She'd run out of wiggle room.

"Sounds fair."

Matt pulled out his phone but kept his eyes on her when he spoke again.

"And we'll start with why you think my wife was murdered."

Chapter Six

Erin Walker had been walking out of a three-story parking garage when the truck popped the curb and hit her. She was a tall woman and her height was the only reason she went over the top of the truck instead of under it. Though that stroke of luck wasn't enough to save her. She was gone before she hit the ground.

Maggie had been working for the *Kipsy City Chronicle* at the time. She'd been gunning for the news editor position that was about to open up when she heard the accident over the police scanner. Wanting to get the scoop before another reporter who'd shown interest in the promotion did, Maggie had grabbed a notepad and pen and drove like a bat out of hell to get to the parking garage. The drive hadn't been a long one. She arrived before any patrol officers, just after the EMTs.

That was when she saw Erin for the first time. From a distance she looked like she was sleeping. Like she'd decided, instead of going wherever it was she had started to go, that she'd lie down on the side of the street, wrapped up in her long blue coat and ready to fall asleep beneath the stars. Then the rest of the details had begun to filter in. Erin hadn't been the only hapless victim. An older man who'd had the misfortune of being on the side of the road next to the opening of the parking garage had also been struck. He, however, was surrounded by EMTs. His name was Lowry Williams. He survived for two days before he succumbed to his injuries. According to everything she discovered, he was a good man.

And also the reason Maggie didn't let go of what happened.

"Lowry Williams passed away before he was able to talk to anyone other than the emergency responders and hospital staff," Maggie started. She really didn't need to remind Matt about that. The detective might not have believed her back then or even now, but he'd done his due diligence and learned every angle of what had happened. Or so he thought. "Except that he did talk to someone. Me. Lowry didn't have any family so I pretended to be a friend. I'm not proud of the lies I had to tell to convince a nurse to let me see him but it worked. He let me slip in to see him before he was wheeled out to surgery. It was the last time Lowry was conscious. Afterward the nurse realized I was a reporter and, to cover his hide, told me to leave. I imagine he never mentioned me to anyone else to, again, save his hide."

Matt's expression was blank.

"And what did Lowry say?" he asked, voice void of any notable emotion.

"He was in a lot of pain," she reminded him. "He spoke in broken thoughts and I can't even be sure my questions were understood by him. But there was something he said twice that stuck with me after I asked what happened. 'She waved at him.'"

Matt's body shifted. He dropped his hands to the top of his belt.

"She waved at him," he repeated. "Who waved?"

"He was in so much pain but I assumed he meant Erin." Maggie wanted to look away from the detective, to give him privacy with his thoughts at the mention of his late wife, but she had to press on. She had to make her point now that he was willing to listen to her. Even if it was only because it might be dangerous not to know. "It was such an odd statement that I couldn't let it go. I went back to the parking garage and tried to track down the security footage from either the parking garage camera or the one across the street. But the parking garage tape had already been taken by the police and the one across the street had a ticket in for repairs." Maggie cut her gaze downward for an instant. The detective might not like her next admission. "So I decided to take a closer look into Ken Morrison to try to find a connection." Matt's body tensed enough that Maggie knew just saying the name of the driver who had killed Erin was dangerous. Even if Ken was no longer living.

"Since they spent that night trying to stabilize him after his overdose, getting into the hospital to talk to him was a no-go," she continued. "And then, after he passed, I spent some time tracking down relatives and friends, trying to find a connection between him and Erin. Trying to figure out why she would wave to him."

"I'd never met him or heard of him before the accident," Matt interrupted. "Erin's coworkers and friends also had no idea who he was until that night."

"But I kept looking anyway," she admitted. "I just… I started looking into Erin instead."

Matt's face drew in, his lips pursed and his eyes turned to slits.

"You started looking into Erin?"

Maggie knew now was not the time to back down from what she'd done. From the decisions she'd made. From the detective. So she rallied herself, shoulders going stiff and back straightening.

"I started with her coworkers first and then friends. I looked at her online profiles. I was just trying to find a connection to Ken outside of the accident. One that would explain why she recognized him and waved to him before everything happened."

"And did you find one?" Matt forced out each word. "After you decided to pry into my wife's life for some damn story, did you at least find a connection?"

Maggie tried to hide the sting she felt at his accusation but she didn't correct him. It wasn't important now why she'd done the things she did then. Her intentions changed nothing. She shook her head.

"No, I couldn't find a connection. For all I knew he could have waved to her and she did it in response. But it didn't matter because although that's what grabbed my attention, it was what I found next that held it." Maggie grabbed her keys off the coffee table and got up to lead the detective back to her office. She unlocked the bottom drawer of her filing cabinet and began to rustle through it with one file in mind.

However, it wasn't there.

"What the heck?" she muttered, going through the files again. Matt moved around to her side and peered into the drawer. "I had it here," she explained. "A folder containing everything about what happened. But it's not here."

"It was a folder?" Matt asked. Maggie nodded. She turned her attention to the detective when he swore beneath his breath. "And did it have a name on it? The folder?"

Maggie didn't like the look he was giving her but she nodded.

"I always intended to take the information to you when I had something. Something *concrete*. It has your name on it."

Matt pulled out his phone. He swiped through a few pictures until he found the one he wanted. Maggie inhaled as he turned it around for her to see.

The picture was of her, unconscious and on the floor. A bat was in one hand and a folder was next to the other. She didn't have to use the zoom function to read the red print across the top of it. She knew what it said.

"That's the folder I'm looking for," she said. "Do you know where it is now?"

"In evidence." Maggie started to sigh in relief. Matt ruined it. "But by the time I got to Dwayne's house the folder was empty."

Maggie froze.

She might not have her memories of what had happened but she knew one thing for sure.

"I decided a long time ago that the only reason I'd take that folder out of this house was to bring it to you." Her hands fisted at her sides. "But now I don't know what I figured out!" Anger was starting to burn through the outside edges of her chest, coming closer to the heart of her. Where it was born from, she couldn't tell. But she didn't like it. Maggie turned her full gaze on the detective. "Do you know what the truth is, Detective?"

Matt raised his eyebrow.

"The truth is I gave up on this case within the first year of the accident," she continued without waiting for him to respond. "I was tired of being the only one who thought there was another layer to it. That there was some kind of conspiracy going on. That Ken Morrison wasn't just some drug abuser who destroyed the lives of three people, including himself. I was tired of everyone hating me for believing there was more." Maggie threw her hands wide, motioning to the house around her. "So when I hit too many dead ends, I stopped looking. I stopped asking questions. I got a new job. I started a family. I tried to redeem my image from, as you've said and as I've done, an ambulance chaser. I even joined a book club. *I stopped looking.*"

Maggie felt her anger turning to something else. A raw emotion she hadn't realized was waiting to be unleashed. She took a step to the side and glanced at the filing cabinet.

"Something must have happened yesterday that was big," she said. "I wouldn't have brought this all up again if I wasn't sure I'd found something."

Fear.

That was what she felt. Beneath the surface of sarcasm and sass, fear was lurking. Sure, throughout the past four years she'd thought about Erin's and Lowry's deaths but she'd kept those thoughts private. After she'd confronted Matt about her suspicions back when it had happened, she'd created a county of enemies. It had made her reevaluate her life. Her drives, her goals, even her career. But to bring the case back to the front lines? That was dangerous, not only to her emotions but also to the life she'd spent the past few years building. To a life she had fallen in love with. To a son she would cross oceans for.

She turned her gaze back to the detective. He

searched her face. She hated how vulnerable she felt at that moment. How could she complain about what she'd lost when he'd lost the woman he loved?

"What *did* you find back then?" he asked after a moment. "What was in the folder before yesterday?" His voice was like velvet. Smooth and strong and fluid. He took a step closer. It helped pull Maggie out of her widening hole of anger and fear.

She took a deep breath and answered, "A list of names."

"Names? What names?" he started. "And where did you get the list from?"

Maggie wished she'd had her files now. It would have made her explanation easier. Still she straightened her back again and got ready to try to convince the detective that the list was not only important, but might have been the key to that night years ago, too.

However, Maggie didn't get the chance.

The world around them filled with a nearly deafening sound. Maggie instinctively tried to escape it by ducking her head and covering her ears. The detective wasn't far behind, throwing his body around hers. Maggie gasped into his chest as another burst of sound sliced through the air.

This time Maggie could place it.

It was glass. Shattering glass.

Someone was breaking the living room windows.

MATT'S HAND WAS on his gun as soon as the noise stopped.

"Get away from the windows," he barked, already pushing Maggie back. He didn't want her out in the open if the next one was broken.

He unholstered his gun and moved into the living

room, senses on high alert. Both windows were broken and glass was scattered on the floor. In the middle of the shards next to the window that looked out to the street sat a brick, highlighted because of how out of place it looked against the light carpet.

Matt's gaze snagged on movement outside the front window. Right through to a van at the curb. And getting into that van was a man wearing a baseball cap.

"Hey, you!" Matt yelled. "Stop right there!"

Matt flung open the front door just as the van's door slammed shut. The tires squealed as the van began to peel away.

It presented Matt with a choice.

He could leave Maggie and chase the man who may or may not have been behind the attack on her and Dwayne or he could stay with her and call in the fleeing culprit. The first ran the risk to himself and to Maggie. The second ran the risk of letting their only lead get away.

Matt holstered his gun and hesitated.

And then Maggie ran up behind him and grabbed his hand.

"Come on," she yelled, moving out the door and trying to tug him along. "We'll lose him if we don't hurry!"

"We can't go!" Matt yelled. "It's too dangerous!"

But Maggie wasn't having it. She paused only long enough to look him square in the eye and say one sentence with absolute conviction.

"Matt, my son could have been in there!"

That was all it took to push his good sense to the side.

Maggie must have seen the change in his expression; she continued to pull him to his car.

This time he let her.

Matt had the pedal to the floor as soon as they were in, trying to eat up the gap between them and the van, but the closer they got the more erratic the driver became.

"Call this in to the Darby Police," Matt said as their mystery perpetrator took a turn out of the neighborhood so fast he popped the curb. The driver overcorrected and clipped the neighborhood welcome sign at the corner. It splintered but didn't break apart. The van kept going like it hadn't hit it at all. "This guy's driving is going to get himself killed."

"Just make sure it's not us who get killed," Maggie replied. Even in his periphery he could see her leaning forward, tensed, while her hand clung to the handle above the passenger-side door. He was feeling it, too. Danger and adrenaline. Both mixing together to feel like an odd form of excitement. That feeling was starting to pull out an unintended reaction in him. The corner of his lips quirked up.

"With my driving skills? I don't think so." He eased them out of the neighborhood without losing much speed. The van was hauling down a two-lane that stretched straight for a few miles before getting into the thick of Darby. No cars were on the road, which probably was normal for this time of day during the week, but that didn't mean they were in any less danger.

"Was that Detective Walker being cocky?" Maggie asked with a nervous laugh as Matt tried to gain back some speed. He hated to admit the sound bolstered him.

"That was Detective Walker being confident in his abilities," he responded. "But still we need to call this in." He fished out his phone and tossed it to her. "Call 911 and put it on speaker so we can tell—"

Matt cut himself off as the van slammed on its brakes. He followed suit, lurching both him and Maggie forward. The space he had just been trying to close between the two vehicles disappeared so rapidly that by the time the Jimmy came to a stop they were within throwing distance.

"What's he doing?" Maggie asked, all traces of excitement replaced by caution. In the next second the man answered. His reverse lights blinked on. "He's going to hit us!"

The van lurched backward so fast that by the time Matt put the Jimmy in the same gear, the driver had already changed his course again. He cut his wheel so the van turned, giving Matt a clear view of the driver's-side window. It was rolled down. Which gave the man pointing a gun at them an uninhibited view.

"Get down!"

Matt threw his arm out to make sure Maggie stayed down just as the windshield shattered over them. Another shot sounded. The Jimmy sank to the left. Before Matt could bring out his own gun to the party, the sound of screeching tires squealed away.

"Stay down," Matt barked. He pulled his gun out and up, ready to return fire but the van was already booking it in the opposite direction, dust kicking up behind it.

"They're fleeing," he said with a few added words that would have made his mother angry. "Are you okay?"

Maggie popped up like a spring flower.

"We have to follow him," she yelled. "We can't let him get away!"

Matt knew now that the right thing would have been not to bring Maggie along. Just the option of staying at the house after someone had thrown a brick through the windows until backup arrived would have been risky before. Now the option of following had proven to be far too dangerous. To keep following would be nothing less than reckless. But he wasn't about to spell that out for her. Not when she wanted blood.

Instead, he reached over and grabbed his phone. She started to argue again that they needed to continue the pursuit but he ignored her until the local police dispatcher picked up the phone. Even if Matt agreed with her and decided to risk her life further, the fact of the matter was whoever it was they had been chasing wasn't just some petty criminal fleeing a crime scene.

Matt looked out the window at his front tire. Their perp had shot it flat.

Whoever the man was he had a lot of guts. And determination.

Matt glanced back at his deflated tire.

The man knew what he was doing.

Which made him even more dangerous.

Chapter Seven

An off-duty Riker County Sheriff's Department deputy was the first to arrive at the scene. He parked his car on the shoulder behind where Matt had moved the Jimmy off the road.

"You're fast," Matt greeted the man. His name was Caleb Foster, and while he'd had a rocky start when he'd first transferred in, he had earned the respect of the department. And a lot of their friendships, too. Matt hadn't had the chance to really get to know him but he knew that would change soon. Especially since Billy had suggested the man try for a future detective's spot opening thanks to a growing county.

Caleb raised his eyebrow.

"If the sheriff called you roaring like he was, you'd get to where he told you to as fast as you could."

"You're right about that," Matt agreed. He'd called Billy after he'd gotten off the phone with the Darby PD. To say the sheriff had retained his calm and cool composure after finding out someone had shot at one of his people would have been a bald-faced lie. No one attacked one of his own. Not without incurring his wrath.

"I wasn't too far away, though. Just dropped the dog off at the vet for a checkup." Caleb walked closer and lowered his voice. He motioned to Maggie, who was on the other side of the car, facing the trees that lined the road. She had his phone up to her ear. "How's she doing?"

"Have you ever met her before?"

"No. Can't say I have."

Matt let out a long breath.

"I don't think I've met a more stubborn woman in all of my life," he said. "I'm sure she's only rattled when she wants to be."

He glanced over as Maggie turned, her face in view. She'd been cut by the windshield's glass in two different places. When he'd first asked about them she'd shooed away the concern. Seeing her hurt, though, even if the cuts were small, filled him with more anger than he thought was possible.

"But I'm not above admitting I don't like this situation," Matt added. "We need to figure out what the hell is going on. Fast."

Caleb agreed and together they recapped what they knew until the Darby PD showed up. Two officers relayed the infuriating information that the van and the driver hadn't been found. There was an all-points bulletin out, and officers were looking but so far all they had was a big bag of nothing.

They needed another lead. Another angle that might shed light on what was going on. A wish they got when Caleb drove them back to Maggie's house while another deputy stayed with the Jimmy when it was being towed.

Caleb whistled low, pulled out his gun and followed Matt around. Together they cleared the house for the second time that day and waved Maggie in. She hadn't said much since they'd been stranded but after the high of being in a pursuit had worn off she had asked to call Cody's school to make sure he was okay, just in case.

Now her lips were downturned, her eyebrows drawn together and an emotion he couldn't pin was brewing behind her eyes. Her hands were on her hips as she walked through the front door and turned toward her living room and its floor littered with glass shards. The defensive stance only strengthened an impulse within Matt he had been trying to ignore.

He wasn't angry at Maggie Carson. He was angry *for* Maggie Carson. A change that he would have laughed at had anyone suggested it was possible the day before.

"Didn't you call in a CSU crew already? Before the bricks came flying in?" Caleb asked, actively trying not to touch anything while still looking around. Matt had explained their theory about Maggie leaving the house the day before in a rush. He didn't combat it with a different one after seeing her car keys on the table.

"Yeah, Sheriff Reed said he was going to personally call them when we got off the phone earlier." Matt shared a look with the deputy. They both knew that meant that the crew would be there sooner rather than later. "So until then we have to be careful with what we touch," he added on for Maggie's benefit.

She was standing next to one of the bricks, leaning over to get a better look at something. The movement caused her hair to fall over her shoulder. It created a backdrop of curls that somehow made her profile even more appealing. He shook his head a little, hoping the deputy hadn't caught the lingering look. Since when did he focus on Maggie Carson like that? Especially in the middle of an active crime scene?

"What if there's a piece of paper on the other side

of the brick?" Maggie's eyes stayed aimed downward. "And what if we aren't patient people and want to see what that paper says right now?"

That definitely caught Matt's attention.

"There's paper under the brick?"

Maggie nodded.

"I'm assuming the message is meant for me, seeing as there's a rubber band around it and the brick. Not to mention it crashed through *my* window into *my* house."

True to her word there was a piece of paper bound to the brick. Matt turned to Caleb.

"Do you happen to have any rubber gloves in your car?"

The deputy shook his head.

"I'm driving my girlfriend's car while mine is in the shop."

"I'm almost afraid to ask if you have any," Matt said to Maggie. She raised her eyebrow but then cut off whatever she was about to say by holding her index finger up.

"Would a plastic sandwich bag work? They're pretty useful, you know."

Matt smirked but was weirdly proud of the suggestion. He nodded and a minute later he was navigating the rubber band off the brick and holding up a letter, sandwich bag on his hand.

The note was written on stock printer paper and torn in a few spots but the message across its middle was clear enough. At least the first part. Understanding it was a different story.

CHRIS LESLIE RYAN was written in small, neat black print. An equally small line in red ran through the name.

But Matt still didn't understand.

"Who is Chris Leslie Ryan?" he asked the room, though really it was rhetorical in nature. He didn't expect Maggie to react. Not as much as she did, at least.

In another moment of open vulnerability, her hand went up to cover her mouth and her eyes went wide. They met his gaze with a surge of nearly tangible fear. For that one second every part of Matt felt drawn to those green eyes, felt compelled to replace the fear with anything else.

"Who is Chris Leslie Ryan?"

Maggie shook her head and lowered her hand. As if she couldn't believe the answer she had.

"It's not one person," she said. "It's three."

MAGGIE FELT HERSELF shutting down, freaking out and attempting to keep her chin up all at the same time after she escaped to her bathroom. The thick skin she had cultivated when being a cutthroat journalist had been her greatest goal in life, and had apparently grown paper-thin over the past few years. Or she'd finally come up against something that was sharp enough to cut through it.

She looked at her reflection in the bathroom mirror for the second time that day and tried to grab some piece of solid ground from the day before.

Nothing but a headache and sore legs.

The sound of strangers in her house clobbered through the sanctuary-like feeling her bedroom and en suite used to hold. She finished patting water off her face and paused next to her bed. Before she had a chance to explain the note, a CSU crew had arrived. Even without being a part of Matt and the deputy's

inner circle she knew that the sheriff must have been
the devil that was nipping at the crew's heels. They
were already apologizing for the delay before they'd
even hit the front porch.

It was all good timing, though. As soon as she'd seen
the names Maggie knew she needed a moment to collect herself. Seeing how the detective's expression had
changed after *she* had read the note had proven that she
hadn't been wearing her game face. And that was what
she needed if she was going to survive this situation.

She needed to stay strong.

She needed to stay steady.

She definitely didn't need to lose her mind. Again.

Heavy footsteps echoed down the hallway. Maggie
pulled a smile out of her arsenal, hoping it would provide cover for her actual feelings. Detective Walker
came into view.

"You look grumpy," she couldn't help but say.

Matt didn't even skip a beat.

"Why do you think Chris Leslie Ryan is actually
three people?"

He stopped just inside the doorway and crossed his
arms over his chest. Maggie wondered when the last
time he slept was. He looked like a man who was ready
to fall face-first into a bed.

The bed next to her suddenly felt like it was on fire.

Maggie angled her body slightly so she couldn't see
it.

"Because I don't know a Chris Leslie Ryan," she answered. "But I do know a Chris, a Leslie and a Ryan."

The detective shrugged.

"Those are pretty common names," he pointed out.
"I also know a person who goes by each."

He was trying to make Maggie create a solid case for herself. It was an effective way of getting answers without asking any questions. She understood the tactic. But that didn't mean she liked feeling as if she was blowing something out of proportion. Not again. Not by Matt Walker.

Like her mother before her, to make her point more *pointed*, Maggie's hands gravitated to her hips. She even felt her chin tip up. All business.

"Well, unless you were married to a Chris, adopted a child from a Leslie and currently work for a Ryan, then maybe my Chris, Leslie and Ryan are a little more relevant than yours. Don't you think? Not to mention, once again, the brick went through *my* window."

The detective's expression gave away only one clue as to his first thought. Surprise. But at which point, she didn't know. Then, like watching a clock, she saw the gears starting to turn. His eyebrow rose and he stood straight.

"When's the last time you saw Chris?"

Maggie hoped she hid the involuntary twinge of pain at how casual the question sounded. Chris Bradley wasn't the happiest of memories for her.

"When we signed the divorce papers," she said, trying to maintain an even voice. "Four years ago. Give or take."

He glazed over the admission to his next question.

"And Leslie?"

"She helped navigate the ins and outs of adoption but she relocated shortly after the adoption was finalized. The last time I saw her was maybe two years ago?" Maggie held up her hand to stop the question before he asked it. "Ryan is the owner of the magazine I work for.

I mostly work out of my home but stop by the office at least once or twice every month. I saw him last week."

"So there's no connection between these three people?"

Maggie shrugged.

"The only connection I know is that they've been part of important life moments for me," she admitted, a knot beginning to form in her stomach again. "If there's something else that ties them or us together, I don't know it." Maggie's air of calm ran out. She took a step forward and lowered her voice so the team in the living room couldn't hear her. Not that she distrusted them.

Maggie realized the movement might simply mean she *trusted* Matt.

Maybe.

"Everything that's happened in the past two days," she started. "Surely it's not all a coincidence? There has to be *something* connecting everything together that we're not seeing. Right?"

The detective didn't answer right away. He was still searching for something. The answer? Or the right way to say the answer?

"Maggie." His voice was deep. Smooth. The only sound in her world at that moment. "I think it's you. I think you're the center of it all and that message might have just proven it."

"How?"

She needed the truth. She needed it so badly that she moved closer to the man. On reflex she tilted her head back to better meet his stare. Had they ever been this close before? And was it her imagination or did he look down at her lips?

"The message," he repeated, derailing her unwelcome thoughts. "It proves that whoever wrote it either *knows* you or researched you well enough to get really personal information."

"But why? Why would I need a reminder if I know him already?"

Maggie already didn't like what he was going to say. A storm seemed to start up in his eyes. Deep eyes, drenched in mystery.

"My guess? He's saying that he doesn't just know you. He knows your past and your present." She watched as the detective's jaw hardened. He was angry. "It's a threat, Maggie. A personal one."

Chapter Eight

His plans changed as soon as he said his theory out loud. Again. Right in that moment, standing so close to Maggie Carson that he could smell her shampoo. Someone was sending her a message and, while he didn't know exactly what it meant, he wasn't going to stand for it.

He was going to protect Maggie and her son to the ends of the earth if he had to. No discussions. No hesitation. No second thoughts.

"Pack a bag for you and Cody," he commanded, hoping the authority in it would keep her from arguing with him the way only Maggie could argue with him. Still, he added on an explanation to move things along. "If someone thinks he knows you and your life, then we're going to do some things you don't normally do."

Maggie's eyebrow quirked up so quickly that he realized what he'd said sounded charged with something other than protectiveness. He took a step back to create some distance between them, playing it off like he was getting ready to go into the living room.

"And that would be?" she asked, looking down at his feet for a second as he moved away.

"We're going to get you out of here for one. You two aren't staying the night here." He motioned toward the front of the house when her mouth opened to interject. "Unless you want Cody to stay here. In the house that the gun-wielding, brick-throwing perpetrator has already targeted and perhaps even been inside."

"Of course I don't want him to stay here," she snapped. "I just—I don't have anyplace for us to go." Like a match had been struck, Maggie's cheeks turned red at the statement. The sight surprised him. He felt his expression soften. If only for a moment.

"Don't worry," he said. "We'll figure it."

There was no snappy reply; Maggie simply nodded.

Half an hour or so later and Billy didn't have good news. Matt shouldn't have been surprised. Not with how everything else had been going.

"They found the van you chased behind a Walmart in Kipsy. It had been set on fire. By the time first responders arrived the car was covered." Billy's jaw was tight. The three of them stood in the kitchen, just out of earshot of two CSU team members who were finishing up. "There was no security footage around that got a good shot of where it happened but there was definitely no body in the vehicle."

"So the gunman who charmed his way into my house via bricks isn't some first-time criminal, I'd guess," Maggie piped in at his side. "He knew how to cover his tracks."

Billy tipped his head to the side in agreement.

"I wouldn't count his intelligence out," he concurred. "But I also wouldn't say he's making all smart decisions. Instigating an attack in broad daylight against a law enforcement officer isn't the best course of action."

"He probably didn't know that he was a detective," Maggie said, jutting her thumb over to Matt.

"Which means that, while he might be familiar with you, Ms. Carson, he's not familiar with Detective Walker here."

"He at least didn't know my personal vehicle," Matt agreed.

"Which makes me feel inclined to agree with your plan." Billy lowered his voice again. "We'll set you and Cody up in a hotel in Carpenter, a few minutes' drive from the department, and put a guard on you."

Matt saw the slight shift in Maggie's demeanor. She was uncomfortable. And Billy didn't seem to catch it. His expression didn't change as he spoke directly to her.

"Do I know this guard?" she asked, eyes sticking to Billy's.

Was that what was making her uncomfortable? Who the guard would be?

Billy motioned to the front yard.

"Deputy Caleb Foster has offered. When you head over to the hotel he'll meet you there." Billy glanced at Matt. "Once you all are there Detective Walker *will* go home and get some rest."

That was an order, given in a no-arguments tone by the sheriff. It kept Matt quiet. This time Maggie looked at him. She didn't say anything, either.

"Until then, we need to get a better handle on this situation," Billy continued. He dug into his pockets and pulled out his keys. He tossed them to Matt. "Take the Bronco and see if you can retrace any of her steps before Cody gets out of school."

"Shouldn't we get him now?" Maggie jumped in. "If our mystery person knows me then he definitely knows where my son goes to school."

"Which is why Cody has his own guard. Do you know my chief deputy?"

"Suzanne Simmons," Maggie said with a nod. "She had an impressive résumé even before her promotion when you took over as sheriff."

Billy smirked.

"That's her. Impressive to the teeth. Great at her job. Cutthroat when needed." He sobered. "She's also the godmother to my kid. Not to mention she's a mother, too. She won't let anything happen to Cody."

Maggie visibly relaxed a fraction.

"Detective Ansler is still working this case," Billy continued. "You keep him in the loop. And, Matt, you call in at any sign of trouble. You *do not* take off after it. Am I understood?" Matt nodded. "Good. I don't need to send the Bronco to the body shop again. I'm still in the doghouse for slamming it into a house last year."

"Hey, I appreciated that."

They turned as Deputy Foster walked over. Billy was referring to when he'd intervened in a wild rescue of Caleb and his now girlfriend. Both men shared a quick smile.

"All right, let's go pick up your dog and then head back to the station," Billy said, conversation over. Caleb pulled out a card from his back pocket and handed it to Maggie.

"Call me if you need anything before we go to the hotel."

Maggie took it and gave a small smile.

"Okay."

Matt didn't know how it happened but there it was. Jealousy. Just sitting there in the pit of his stomach, unhappy at the idea of passing Maggie off to someone else.

Someone who wasn't him.

Get it together, Matt scolded himself.

But still that feeling stuck even as Caleb and Billy walked off.

"Wait!" All three men turned to Maggie. She was looking at Billy. "I know enough about the sheriff's department and the people who work there to know that you consider them more than just colleagues. And you and Matt are friends. Good friends." She hesitated. It was a strange reaction to see in her. Even stranger was the look she gave Matt before continuing. "He doesn't like me. A lot of law enforcement around here doesn't. So why are you doing all of this? Most people would have kept me in cuffs in the first place and now I'm going to ride in your personal vehicle while the godmother to your child watches mine? I get that you're the sheriff but that seems a little bit beyond the call of duty. Why help me, of all people, like that?"

Another feeling Matt didn't like replaced jealousy. He didn't have time to address it before Billy answered.

"You already said it. I'm the sheriff and you're a resident of Riker County who needs help." Billy flashed a genuine smile. "There's nothing that I won't do to help my people. It's that simple."

MAGGIE WAS GRATEFUL for the sheriff's candor. She wasn't special in his eyes, which was somehow comforting. It was like she had a clean slate again. Like she hadn't fallen in the eyes of Riker County law enforcement yet. Now she was just a resident of the county who needed some protection.

And answers.

However, those were trickier to get as proven by the

stoic set of Matt's shoulders as he walked from the spot on her front porch to the Bronco she was sitting shotgun in. He left behind a man from CSU who disappeared back into her house to finish whatever it was that he was supposed to be finishing.

"What did he say?" Maggie greeted. Matt answered by swearing.

"Let me guess, they didn't find anything. Again."

"They found the prints they believe to be ours from today," he said, voice constricted with frustration. "But like Dwayne's house they are almost positive your place was cleaned. Where there should be prints of you and Cody there are none. Which doesn't help us."

Maggie's stomach turned.

"I'm now one hundred percent for staying at a hotel with a guard," she decided. "This is getting too creepy."

"We can go there now, you know," he replied matter-of-factly. "To be honest it would be much safer for you than running around the county grasping at straws until school lets out. Detective Ansler and I will keep looking for leads no matter what."

It didn't sound like a dismissal but Maggie still felt the sting as if he was trying to get rid of her. She bristled at the thought.

"Listen, I might not be a cop but I did *something* yesterday that created chaos for everyone. Whether we like it or not that everyone *includes* you and myself. That means we have a better shot at figuring this thing out. Together. So even though you'd rather be detecting with someone else, it's me you're stuck with for now. Okay?"

To her surprise Matt chuckled.

"You sure are bossy for someone who technically is still a suspect."

"By *bossy* I'm sure you mean *determined*," she replied, pushing her shoulders back. Her attention went down to the purse in her lap. She'd started to go through its contents when the man had stopped them from leaving the house to update Matt. CSU had allowed her to take the bag and the contents she'd poured out onto the floor. Now she was sifting through the items in hopes of finding a clue.

"So is there anywhere you think we should go?" Matt asked. She could feel him watching her. "Anything in there jumping out at you? Anything bringing back some memories?"

Maggie cycled through scraps of paper and cards that had been in her purse for upward of two years.

"I'm remembering all of the times I promised myself I would clean this thing out." She set the stack of scraps on her thigh and picked up a new handful of odds and ends. "Yesterday apparently wasn't the day I decided to follow through."

The detective laughed again. This time it was softer.

"Erin once lost her engagement ring in her purse. She forgot to take it off before work and had to drop it in there."

Maggie kept her gaze down. She didn't want to spook the man from opening up. No matter how much it shocked her. Whenever they had talked about Erin in the past it had been one-sided with her trying to get him to agree with her theories on Erin's death. And that at that time, Maggie was positive his beloved had been killed on purpose. Targeted by Ken Morrison. Not just a random victim. Maggie was more than happy to hear nice stories rather than speculation of the reason behind the young woman's death.

"How long did it take her to find it?"

"Two days. I kid you not. We turned that thing inside out and still managed to miss it until we thought it was long gone. Then *bam* she reaches into her purse for some gum and comes out with the ring. I couldn't believe it had been there all along, but she said the Bermuda Triangle is at the bottom of every woman's purse. How things disappeared and reappeared there was a mystery."

Maggie didn't have to see his smile to hear it.

"Well, she wasn't wrong." Maggie was smiling, too. Though she knew her patience was about to turn tail and run. They needed a lead. Not to bond.

Matt kept the car in Park as she continued to sift through the remnants of her life that had never made it back out of her bag. Old receipts, notes for work, a few fast food napkins, a pack of tissues, five pens, allergy medicine, two canisters of lipstick and four plastic dinosaurs that Cody had insisted they take with them to the park one day last month. Nothing out of the ordinary...

"Wait."

Maggie pulled out a card she almost mistook for more paper scraps and notes. Her handwriting on the back didn't help.

"'Two-hundred-one,'" she said, reading the card before flipping it over. "This is new."

Her eyes traced the words but no sparks of recognition flared.

"Looks like we're going to a hotel after all," she continued. "Just not the one the sheriff had in mind."

She handed him the card.

"Country Heart Hotel," he read. "In Kipsy. What's there?"

Maggie shrugged.

"Hopefully answers."

He turned over the ignition and started their drive away from her home. It bothered Maggie more than she thought it would. It wasn't like she was leaving the house forever. Then again, someone didn't like whatever it was that she'd found out. What if the next time the unknown man came back he issued more than just a threat tied to a brick?

Thankfully she didn't have to dwell on that thought for too long. The detective handed his phone over and told her to call the hotel.

"We need to see if that room is occupied. If so, then we're calling for backup," he explained. So she sweetened her voice, called the room and, when no one answered, called the front desk and asked if the guest had already checked out.

"He did," the man at the front desk confirmed. "Would you like to book it?"

Maggie politely declined at the detective's insistence.

"He said *he*," Matt pointed out.

"So do you think I met the mystery man there yesterday?" Maggie was relieved in part that she hadn't been the one to book the room. "And what? Now he's trying to threaten me?"

Matt shrugged.

"Maybe you tried to get the information to someone else after I wouldn't bite."

But who would that have been? Maggie wondered as silence stretched between them for a few miles. Matt finally broke it.

"The list of names you found," he started. "We got

interrupted before you could tell me who they were and where you got them."

Maggie felt around inside her purse again until she found a pen. She took an old sticky note with her grocery list on one side and flipped it over. Taking in a deep breath, she jotted out three names, then she let that breath out slowly.

"I might not have the original list but I won't forget their names," she explained when he gave her a questioning look. She traced her handwriting before continuing, "I researched them for almost a year straight. And I asked *you* about them, too, but it probably wasn't the best time to do it. I doubt you remember them."

Matt's hands gripped the steering wheel for a moment. Then they relaxed.

"After the funeral." It wasn't a question. How could either forget that afternoon? Regret filled Maggie's chest.

"I'm sorry," she answered instead. "I should have approached you somewhere—*anywhere*—else. I—I just felt like I was running out of time. I was desperate. But still I shouldn't have—"

Matt held one hand up to stop her. Maggie quieted.

"We can't change the past," he said, voice thrumming into a low octave. Not a sensual tone but a decisive one. "But we might be able to right some of its wrongs. Now, tell me about the names and where you got them. And maybe we can solve this damned mystery and let everything get back to normal."

Maggie wanted the same thing but couldn't deny she once again felt a surprising sting. Their normal was two different paths. Without any intersecting points.

Completely separate from each other.

That had never bothered her before. But now, for some reason she had trouble understanding, it did.

Chapter Nine

"Joseph Randall. Jeremy Pickens. Nathan Smith."

Maggie waited to see if the detective recognized any of the names. He shook his head. "There's quite a few of each in the United States as you can imagine. And definitely more than a few in Alabama."

"Feels a lot like grasping at straws."

"And that's how I felt until I found news stories on all three names." That got the detective's attention. He kept his eyes on the road but she could tell he was focused on her. "Without going into all the research I had to do and all the phone calls, emails and lies I had to tell to get the information, here's the basics. Joseph Randall, early thirties, died in a head-on collision in Florida almost a decade ago. Jeremy Pickens, also in his thirties, died in a fire started by faulty wiring at his home in Georgia eight years ago. Nathan Smith, forty, was hospitalized after a mugging turned more violent. He succumbed to injuries in the first few hours of being admitted to the hospital. That was six years ago in Tennessee."

Matt didn't say anything right away. It gave Maggie a moment to look at him in profile. Strong jaw. Prominent nose. Stern lips. Those same lips were downturned. He hadn't known about the list and he didn't know about the men on it. She wished she could hear his thoughts. Instead, she'd have to settle for another one of his questions.

"And where did you find this list?"

Maggie sighed.

"You're not going to like this answer," she warned. A muscle in his jaw jumped.

"Maggie."

"It was taped to the top of Erin's locker at work. Which is probably why you didn't see it when you cleaned it out."

Matt went tense again. She couldn't blame him.

"And the hospital just let you back into the nurses' locker room?"

Maggie looked at her hands.

"I might have done some sneaking around."

Matt said some not-so-great words. She waited for more but was surprised when it was himself that he cursed.

"*I* should have found the list."

Maggie started to reach out for the man, to try to comfort him, but caught herself. They could talk about all the things they should and shouldn't have done later. Right now they needed to focus.

"I contacted a friend up north in law enforcement and, as far as he could tell, there was still no connection between the names on that list and Erin. Or Ken, for that matter. Why she had those names and where she got them from, I never learned." She blew a breath out. "And to be honest, that's when I started hitting all of the road blocks. A wave and a list of names taped to the top of a locker does not a conspiracy make."

"But now that list is missing and there's a very real person threatening you to be quiet," he added.

She nodded.

"There is that."

They lapsed into another silence. This time it wasn't that bad. Maggie chalked up the detective's quiet to him silently processing the new information. Most likely trying to track back memories of his wife to figure out why she had the names in the first place. Or maybe his lack of sleep was starting to get to him. He wasn't sitting as tall as he had been on the ride over from the hospital. Either way, Maggie watched out the window as the small town of Darby was replaced by the much larger city of Kipsy and tried to give him privacy. She felt the weight of weariness starting to press on her bones, too. Even though it was barely afternoon, it felt like days had passed between the hospital and walking through the back door of her house. An ache had begun to beat in her chest as she thought about Cody at school, oblivious to everything bad that had happened. Maggie prayed they could find the answers they needed before the three-o'clock bell rang.

It wasn't until they pulled up to a two-story building that didn't look like it had more than two stars, let alone five, that Matt broke the silence with a low whistle. He pulled into a Country Heart Hotel parking spot next to the front doors and cut the engine. Worry started to fill Maggie's gut.

"Are you sure this might have something to do with your investigation?" Matt asked. "And not something... well, else? You know, something *personal*?"

Maggie turned on the man like he'd thrown a bucket

of ice water on her. She felt heat scorch up from her belly, across her neck and into her face.

"And what exactly are you trying to suggest, Detective Walker?"

Matt held his hands up in defense.

"Nothing illegal or anything like that," he answered. He jabbed his finger out the window. "I just meant this place kind of looks like the type where a person might meet a special kind of person when they wanted some alone time. I didn't know if you had someone like that in your life right now."

"And you thought that if I did, that yesterday, the day I potentially made some big discovery in an investigation that destroyed my reputation, that I decided to visit some imaginary—what?—*lover* here instead of at my house or his?"

"Hey, you said you can't remember anything from yesterday."

"Still, I'm pretty sure I didn't have a rendezvous with a secret lover," Maggie said. "Considering I'd need a secret lover to do that." The detective lowered his hands and for a split second Maggie thought she saw relief in his expression. It made the heat in her cheeks reach a new height. "And if that was your way of trying to see if I have a boyfriend, next time just *ask*."

The detective's lips thinned. For a moment Maggie wondered if she'd crossed some imaginary line between them. It was pretty foolish for her to think, even for a second, that Matt Walker was relieved she was single.

What was also foolish was to admit she liked the idea that *he* might be relieved.

What am I, in high school? she thought.

Wanting anything beyond their forced proximity acquaintanceship wasn't just barking up the wrong tree, it was barking up the wrong tree in the wrong park. Plus, she'd only spent less than *one day* with the man. Why was she entertaining *any* thoughts about him like that?

Those storm-fueled eyes found their way to hers.

They were grounding, an anchor that kept her still.

Oh, yeah, she thought. *That's why.*

"The one fact that we have to work with is that you don't remember what you did yesterday," he said. "I'm trying to cover all of our bases. Even the personal ones. Remember that, other than Cody telling us you made him breakfast and took him to school, no one can account for you yesterday. I'm just double-checking there isn't someone who *could* and you haven't brought it to our attention."

Maggie's dichotomous emotions of anger and, dare she think it, latent desire started to dissolve. Maybe she was reading too much into one look. Matt *was* just doing his job. She took a small breath.

"No, the list I gave you in the hospital contained the only people who I might have talked to or seen on a normal day. Even abnormal, if I'm being honest." Maggie handed Matt the hotel manager's business card that she'd found in her purse. "I think I came here because someone asked me to. There's no other reason I would be here or take a card with me and write down a room number. I've never been here before. I wouldn't have picked this as a meeting place unless someone else picked it."

Matt held her gaze for a bit longer. He must have believed her. He nodded.

"Then I want you to stay here while I go talk to the manager and staff." Maggie opened her mouth but Matt hurried on. "We have no idea what went down here yesterday. Your presence might distract them. Plus, I can't imagine you'd stay quiet long enough for me to even ask the right questions."

"That's insulting," she tried, knowing it really wasn't. Because that was exactly what she would do.

Matt pulled out his phone, clicked a few buttons and held it up in front of her.

"That's the truth and we both know it. So I'm going to take a picture of you and show it around instead."

Maggie narrowed her eyes at the phone.

"Now, smile for the camera, please. We don't want to scare them. We just want to question them."

Maggie changed her frown into what she hoped was a smirk to end all smirks. A *click* sounded as the picture was taken.

"How'd I do?" she asked, half sarcastic, half curious.

The detective snorted.

"You look like a pain in my side." He cut her a quick grin. "And I wouldn't have expected it any other way."

TECHNICALLY, MATT WAS off duty but the hotel manager named Luca, a small man who appeared to be in his fifties, didn't know that. He looked up as Matt walked in and his eyes immediately went to the badge around his neck. Matt rarely wore his credentials like that but he'd found that when the badge was hanging in view that most people remained pleasant during questioning. Luca, however, looked at the badge once before his eyes glued to Matt's face. He was already fidgeting by the time Matt walked up to the front desk.

"Hey there. I'm Detective Matt Walker from the Riker County Sheriff's Department and I'd like to ask you a few questions, if that's all right," he greeted, cutting out any pleasantries.

Luca nodded his head so hard that Matt was afraid it would come right off.

"Yes, sir, whatever you need!"

The way he spoke was an immediate red flag. He was nervous. *Really* nervous. Matt had gone from asking some simple questions to mentally preparing for the fact that he might have to unholster his gun. Something wasn't right. And he was about to find out if it had to do with a brunette ex-reporter currently confined to the sheriff's car.

"Were you working yesterday?" Matt started off.

Luca nodded. "I run the hotel during the weekdays."

"And did anything out of the ordinary happen here yesterday?" Matt followed up. "With any of your guests? Or staff?"

"Out of the ordinary? I don't—I don't think so. Can you give me an example?"

Luca's eyes widened but he seemed not to have expected the question. Which was good news for Maggie. She apparently hadn't done anything that was outrageous during her time there. At least, not publicly. Matt pulled out his phone and the picture he'd just taken of Maggie.

"Have you ever seen this woman before?"

Luca squinted his eyes. He nodded a few seconds later.

"Yeah. She was in here yesterday."

"She checked in?"

"No, she bought a sandwich."

He pointed to the corner of the lobby. A counter containing a coffee maker and foam cups stood next to a vending machine and a small display refrigerator. Pre-wrapped sandwiches, cups of fruit and bottles of orange juice and water lined the three shelves. It was more than Matt had expected to see in the place.

"She bought a sandwich," he deadpanned. "And that was it?"

"She asked if she could have a Ziploc bag," Luca tacked on. "She said she wanted to save one half for later because she wasn't that hungry."

Matt kept from rolling his eyes. It was hard.

"No, I mean, did she check in or out or talk to anyone else while she was in here?"

Luca didn't have to think about it long at all.

"When she paid she said she was meeting one of the guests."

"Did she give a name?"

"No, and I didn't ask for one. To be frank, usually when a pretty woman like that meets someone here during the workweek there's a spouse, or two, out there who have no idea. I try to keep out of it." Luca's eyes widened. That nervousness that had greeted Matt came back in full force. "Is that your wife?"

Matt had done his fair share of interviews during his career with the sheriff's department. He'd been called names, insulted, questioned and even physically attacked. In each instance he'd kept his cool and responded without issue. However, the hotel manager's simple question had an unforeseen effect on him.

Was Maggie his wife?

In an instant two threads of thought wove together. One was of the wife he'd had for two years. The one he'd met in a grocery store in Carpenter. The one who laughed at all of his lame jokes, loved pineapple on her pizza and would fight anyone who disagreed, and who promised to love him always in front of a church full of people. The one who had called to remind him to do the laundry because she needed a fresh pair of scrubs for work the next day. The one who, an hour after that call, was gone.

The other thread, the one that caught him wholly off guard, was of a woman who had entered his life at its lowest. A woman who had ambushed him time and time again during that lowest part, trying to convince him that what he knew was a lie. A woman whom he'd denounced in front of a county's worth of people and publicly hoped he'd never see again. A woman who, years later, was still not giving up. A woman who had grabbed his hand and pulled him out into the world to chase a suspect, despite the obvious danger. A woman who had driven him crazy but now was surprising him more than he thought was possible.

Was Maggie Carson his wife?

No. But she was turning out to be much more than an ex-reporter running after a story.

In fact, Matt was starting to see that maybe he'd misjudged her all along.

MAGGIE WAS BORED. Or, rather, impatient. While the detective did his detecting inside the lobby, she kept her word by staying put in the car. From her seat she'd taken in everything in her view from the rocks lining the flower beds to the flagpole that needed a good deal of repair. She'd even watched as a giggling couple dressed in workday best made out next to their cars before getting into them and driving off in separate directions.

After that Maggie realized her listening to Matt Walker's commands wouldn't last.

She opened the door, got out and quietly shut it back. Instead of going into the lobby, she decided to pass through the breezeway that led to the courtyard that all room doors faced. Since it was a weekday and barely afternoon to boot, there was no one lounging in the pool or on the slightly rusted-out patio furniture around it. She turned around in the courtyard and read the second-floor room numbers until she saw 201.

"I hope there's something in there that will make sense," she mumbled to herself, rounding the deep end of the pool to head for the stairs beneath an awning.

However, two steps along the pool's side, something caught her attention in the water. Thinking it might be trash, or maybe just her imagination, she paused and bent over the edge to get a better view.

The pool probably wasn't the most used part of the hotel but it was still kept up enough that the water wasn't cloudy. Something *was* at the bottom of the pool, resting near the drain in the middle of the deep end. Whatever it was it looked to be the size of her palm, maybe a little bigger, but the depth and water warped the image. She couldn't tell what it was but it didn't look like trash.

It looked like something in a bag.

A jolt of adrenaline made Maggie stand tall.

"No way," she said to herself, glancing up at room 201 and then back at the breezeway that led to the lobby. She would have had to cross right by the pool to get to the room and to leave it. Her heartbeat sped up as she looked back down at the object in the pool, but she already knew she'd made up her mind.

Now she needed to be fast.

Chapter Ten

Luca conveniently couldn't find the guest book. He also had a hard time remembering who the man who'd checked into 201 was. The only details he could cobble together were that he walked in the morning before six, paid in cash and left his key at the front desk while Luca was in the bathroom around ten. When Matt pressed for anything else, the hotel manager began to sweat. The man nearly seemed to have a heart attack when Matt asked if he could see the security footage for the hotel.

"Do—do you have a warrant?" he asked. "Because I—I don't think you can unless you have a warrant."

That was when Matt figured out why he was so nervous at law enforcement being in the hotel.

"Listen, I'm going to level with you, Luca," he started, leaning on the counter, trying to appear casual. "I've been on the job long enough to know what kind of establishment you're running here. On the outside this hotel looks normal, a little run-down but still good for a night or two. A good place, as you said, for cheating spouses to meet secret lovers. I get that. I do. But considering how nervous you seem to be, I'm pretty sure you play to the rougher crowds rather than to unhappy men and women in business suits. Maybe drug dealers or buyers? Sex that's paid for? You might even be in on the action. Either way I'm sure all your loyal customers pay in cash while you conveniently lose the guest book a lot. Am I right?"

Matt's hunch was confirmed. Luca's face went beet red. He opened his mouth like a fish out of water but Matt didn't have the time to listen to lies.

"If today were any other day I wouldn't be standing here, asking for your cooperation. I'd be telling you," Matt continued. "But today's timeline is a little tight. Instead of calling in my friends at the local office, who maybe even know you already, I'm going to leave. Only after I get to look at the security tapes for yesterday. I'm looking for one man and one man only. You can keep your tapes afterward. So what do you think? Are you going to help me out or is this place about to be swarming with black-and-whites?"

Matt wasn't planning on calling in anyone if Luca refused to let him see the security footage. He couldn't just waltz in and demand them without a warrant. But if you said something with enough confidence then sometimes that did the trick.

And it sure did it on the hotel manager.

"I—uh—I'll get them," he said after a moment. "It might take a minute."

Matt pushed off the counter and smiled.

"Good. While you do that I'd like to go ask your staff about the occupants of 201." Matt paused and dropped his smile. "If that's okay with you?"

The question seemed to ease the man a little. It gave him the illusion of control. It made him stand taller as he nodded.

"Yes, sir."

He saw him out and told him that housekeeping might still be in the laundry room preparing the new towels before they made their rounds. The handyman wouldn't be in for another hour.

Matt took off his badge and placed it in his back pocket. If there were any guests with an aversion to cops he didn't want to find out by being ambushed. He'd rather blend in. Maggie, on the other hand? He almost laughed at the idea of telling her to try to keep a low profile.

And then he cursed under his breath.

Maggie wasn't in the Bronco and he didn't know why that surprised him at all. He sighed, turned on his heel and headed through the breezeway. Knowing her, she was either already asking the staff questions or trying to break into room 201.

Matt scanned the courtyard, ready to be annoyed when he found her, but was distracted by something that turned his blood cold. There was something in the pool. *Someone* in the pool.

He waited a beat to see if the person was moving, stilling every instinct he had to dive in, when he saw it. A cloud of brown hair.

Maggie.

Every part of his body seemed to react at once, leaving only thoughts of the woman behind. He tore off his holster and phone and was in the pool in what felt like a second flat. Diving into the deep end, Matt opened his eyes beneath the water.

And indeed confirmed it was Maggie.

However, she definitely wasn't in distress. In fact, she wasn't even in her clothes.

Oh, hell, he thought just as her eyelids lifted. Two

forest green eyes found his moments before she pushed off the bottom of the pool. Her body flew upward past his face. He followed her. He could already hear her yelling at him before he even broke the surface.

"What do you think you're doing?" she yelled, wiping water out of her eyes. "You scared the heck out of me!"

"Me?" he responded just as loud. "What are *you* doing? And why aren't you wearing any clothes?"

"I didn't want them to get wet," she countered. Like he was looking at some picture book, trying to find Waldo, he spotted her pants, blouse and shoes on the other side of the pool. "And I *do* have clothes on! I'm not crazy!"

Matt didn't know which part of her statement he wanted to dissect to try to make sense of the maddening woman treading water in front of him in nothing but her underwear.

"Then what are you doing in the damned pool?"

She raised her hand out of the water only to point down. On reflex he followed the silent order but his gaze got caught on a black lace bra he'd definitely not planned on seeing that day. It pushed up a fair amount of cleavage; even beneath the water it was distracting.

"There's something at the bottom of the pool I was trying to grab before you scared me half to death," she answered, unaware that his gaze and thoughts had strayed for a moment. "What are *you* doing in the pool in *all* of your clothes?"

Matt strung together a series of curses, his frustration at the woman almost a tangible object.

"I was trying to save you," he defended. "I thought you were drowning. One second you're in the car and the next I see you floating in the pool. Forgive me for jumping to an illogical conclusion."

Where he was sure Maggie would kick up a fuss or, at the very least, goad him, she instead seemed to lose her initial anger. Her expression softened. Somehow it had seemed to ease his anger, too. He looked back down at the object she'd pointed to, this time avoiding looking at her body.

"It's a clue," she said, answering his unasked question. "I think I threw it in here yesterday on purpose. To hide it. Or keep it safe."

Matt didn't need another word. He held his breath and went under. This time his descent didn't have his heart slamming against his rib cage. Instead, he scooped up the bag at the bottom of the pool and pushed while relief settled through him.

Maggie was okay.

Maddening, but okay.

"Well?" she asked as soon as he sucked in air. "What is it?"

A door shut somewhere behind them. Matt whirled around, trying to shield Maggie's body from view. A young man paused, eyes widening at the sight of them, before going to Matt's gun on the side of the pool.

"Take this," Matt muttered, pushing the bag back to her under the water. He misjudged where she was and his knuckles touched bare skin. She didn't make a fuss, though, and took the bag.

It freed up Matt's hand to pull his badge from his back pocket.

"Police business," he said loud enough to break the young man's gaze from his gun.

The man hesitated. Matt didn't break eye contact.

"Move along," he commanded. Even to his ears Matt heard the hammer drop in his tone. The young man didn't say anything but hurried past them and out of the breezeway.

"We need to get out of this damned thing," Matt muttered. "Come on."

Maggie didn't argue and together they waded to the shallow end of the pool. It wasn't until Matt was standing on the patio, picking up his gun and cell phone, that he remembered that he had been the only one fully dressed. He glanced back across the pool and froze.

He'd seen half-dressed women before. Lacy bras, sexy panties, bare stomachs, legs and more. But looking on as Maggie stood next to her clothes and stared down at the bag in her hands, Matt felt like he was seeing something new. Or, really, feeling it. Her face was angled downward, her wet hair dark against her sun-kissed skin. The little makeup she'd put on that morning had washed down her cheeks. Her brows began to knit together just as her frown deepened. Still, he couldn't ignore one truth about the woman any longer.

Matt might have thought a few bad things about Maggie throughout the years but he realized he'd never once thought she was anything other than beautiful.

Even when she was being a pain in his ass.

"Maggie, put on your clothes," he chided, breaking out of his epiphany. He rounded the pool, already annoyed at how his clothes clung to him.

Maggie didn't move. At least not toward putting on her clothes. She held the bag up to him instead.

"It's a key," she said.

"What does it open?"

For the first time that day Maggie looked tired. She shrugged.

"I have no idea."

THE SECURITY FOOTAGE was grainy and only covered the main entrance of the lobby, not the lobby itself.

"That's convenient, considering there's a side entrance," Maggie muttered.

Matt leaned his head to the side.

"Convenience is this hotel's biggest selling point." Normally that was the point of a hotel but judging by his tone, Matt didn't seem to be a fan of the establishment.

The mystery man who booked room 201 wasn't seen by the lone working camera. However, Maggie was. She pulled into the front parking lot around ten in the morning in her personal car and left fifteen minutes later.

Maggie didn't like what she saw in the footage, but kept quiet until they were back in the car. Alone.

"I was scared, Matt. In the security footage I looked scared."

Matt started the engine.

"I know."

Maggie looked at the hotel one more time as they pulled away, trying to grasp the memories she'd lost by sight alone. Instead, she decided she didn't like the place at all. She wasn't alone in that opinion, either. Matt had had a private chat with the hotel manager while Maggie dripped water in the middle of the lobby and it had been clear neither enjoyed it. She wouldn't be surprised if Kipsy PD made a stop by the hotel sooner rather than later.

"So we have to talk about that bag in the pool." Matt was going in the opposite direction of Darby, which probably meant Carpenter, and the hotel was their destination. At this point Maggie didn't mind. She had her packed bag with her and was ready to rinse off the chlorine and change. Considering the detective was still dripping a little, she imagined he, at the very least, needed a good towel. "How did you know it was you who left it? Did you remember doing it?"

Maggie readjusted in her seat to sit taller. She was quite proud of herself in this instance.

"When I transitioned into working for the magazine, I toyed with the idea of trying my hand at starting a book, true crime. A nonfiction book about cases in Riker County—because you have to admit we've had some doozies around here." Matt inclined his head. He couldn't argue with that. No residents could. "Anyway, I ended up spending basically two years with my head in other true crime stories and learned a lot of interesting things. Including how this man almost got away with murder by wrapping a piece of evidence in a plastic bag and dumping it in the pool. Two days later, when he was alone, he came back for it and tried to dispose of it. He was caught and eventually went to jail. I in no way condone him or what he did *but* the idea of what he did never really left my mind. I've actually always wanted to try it, just to see if it really does work, but we don't have a pool and it's not like I'm about to go to the community one with a sandwich bag, rocks and a mystery item to test it. Today I noticed the rocks outside the hotel and so I figured I did yesterday, too. I don't know where I got the bag from, though. Unless I brought it with me."

Matt held up his index finger.

"I think I can help with that."

He told her about the sandwich she'd purchased with the cash she'd had on her, according to the hotel manager. Plus the Ziploc bag.

"Ten bucks you only wanted the plastic bag," he continued. "You must have sneaked around, grabbed some rocks and tossed it in. None of the hotel staff said they saw anything."

Maggie looked down at the bag in her lap. A handful of small rocks and one small silver key.

"But why did I hide it? I arrived at the hotel alone and I left alone. Why not just take it with me and hide it somewhere that wasn't in a public place?" Maggie ran her hand through her hair. Wet tangles fell against her shirt.

She glanced at the man next to her as he laughed.

"Listen, if there's one thing I've learned in the past—" he made a show of looking at his thankfully waterproof watch "—four hours or so is that Yesterday You is a mystery wrapped within a mystery and crammed into another mystery. I think we're better off working with what we have instead of trying to retrace your steps."

Maggie sighed.

"Not that we have much of a choice." She shook the bag. "This is the only concrete lead we have now... And it's a small key that leads to where? I don't know."

"Could it fit your filing cabinet?" Matt offered, coming to a stop at a light. They were definitely headed toward Carpenter. In front of them was the county road that transitioned from downtown to the rural edge of the neighboring town. "Didn't the drawer that originally had the file in it have a lock?"

Maggie shook her head.

"The key to that is gold *and* on my key ring. I never went to great lengths to hide it because I never thought anyone would ever look for it." Matt reached over and took the bag from her. He lifted it up to look at it more closely.

"It could go to an actual lock. Is there anywhere you might have one?"

Maggie shook her head again. She hated not having better answers.

"Unless I bought one yesterday, no."

They sat in silence as the light turned green. Maggie was trying to list the ways she would use a lock that fit the key.

"What if this isn't mine?" she asked. It was more to herself than the detective. "What if I got this from our mystery man somehow? I'm almost scared to think what it might be used—"

Maggie didn't have time to scream.

Something slammed into the driver's side of the Bronco.

And then the world flipped.

Chapter Eleven

The world was dark. At least Matt's world was.

It also was painful. His entire left side ached, including his head. It was throbbing.

But why?

He opened his eyes slowly and didn't understand right away. Instead, he blinked at broken glass and metal. He was lying on his side. Glass and metal beneath him there, too.

What had happened?

Noise began to filter in as his head swam, lost in a sea of confusion.

Someone was screaming.

"Matt! No!" It was a woman. *"Matt!"*

The fog of confusion lifted in an instant and he knew what had happened. Someone had hit them, they'd flipped and now the Bronco was lying on its side, the driver's-side doors pinned against the ground.

And the woman screaming was Maggie.

Matt turned his head so fast the pain tripled. He fought the urge to get sick. Though the empty passenger's seat hanging above him wasn't helping. The door was also missing.

"Matt!" Maggie shrieked in the distance. She sounded terrified.

What was going on?

Matt tore the seat belt off him—probably the only reason he was still alive—and scrambled to pull himself up to stand. Pain surged across him. Not only was his left side hurting but so were his ribs. He sucked in a breath, grabbing his side on reflex. His hand brushed against the butt of his gun. Thank God for holsters.

"Help! Matt!"

Maggie's yells were pitching higher.

Matt readied to answer when a new voice entered the mix.

"Shut up or I'll go back and kill him," a man yelled. It seemed like their mystery man had found them.

Again.

Matt grabbed the passenger seat, pain no longer something he cared about, and pulled himself up through the truck. The fact that he was having to use the Bronco as a jungle gym meant that they had indeed flipped after the initial hit. And the fact that the passenger's-side door was completely gone meant that it had been violent. No wonder he'd lost consciousness.

He hoped Maggie hadn't been seriously hurt.

Matt unholstered his gun and used the seat as a foothold to push himself out of the vehicle. The Bronco was in the middle of the intersection. No other cars were around but one. It was a truck and Maggie was being pulled toward it.

Matt threw his legs over the side of the Bronco and jumped to the ground. The noise caught the man's attention. He whirled around, pulling Maggie against his chest like a shield. Matt's gun was up and aiming within a heartbeat.

Immediately he noticed two things that weren't great.

The man had his own gun and it was pressed against a wincing Maggie's stomach. She looked at Matt with fear clear in her eyes and blood across her face. A new cut had stretched above her right brow and was bleeding at a good clip. It had to have been stinging her eye.

The second detail that kept Matt's stomach tight was the fact that he could see the man's face clearly. He wasn't wearing a mask. Nothing to obstruct their view. Which was never good for a hostage. And that was exactly what Maggie would be if Matt didn't stop him.

"You move any closer and I'll shoot her," the man yelled. "I mean it!"

Matt didn't lower his weapon. But he also didn't move from where he'd stopped at the front of the Bronco.

"If you shoot her, I'll shoot you," Matt replied. "Simple as that. So let her go."

Matt clocked the man's age as midforties. He was tall but broad; Matt guessed he would be able to do some damage if he had to go one-on-one. His hair was thick and black, his skin tan, and he was dressed not unlike Matt was. He looked like an everyday man. One whose hand was steady.

He wasn't nervous.

Which made him even more dangerous.

"I'm not going to do that." His voice carried over the few yards between them with ease. Like he was a man used to talking to people. Maybe even giving them orders. There was no awkwardness in the way he addressed Matt. Perhaps he'd even done this sort of thing before.

"And I'm not going to let you take her," Matt promised. The man wasn't the only one with a steady hand.

"Then we have a problem."

He pressed his gun harder into Maggie's stomach. She winced. Matt reacted on instinct and took a step forward. The man pulled Maggie a step backward.

"What do you want?" Matt tightened his stance, already contemplating if he could get a clear shot without harming Maggie. "Who are you?"

"It doesn't matter who I am, but what I want is *simple*." The man pulled the gun up to the side of Maggie's head. Her eyes locked with Matt's.

"To be left alone," he bit out. "Once and for all."

Matt shook his hand.

"Listen here, buddy. You're the one who's been following us. You threw the first stone. Brick, if you want to get technical. You can't blame us for trying to find you."

The man snorted. Matt was too far away to hear it but he saw the expression of disbelief clearly enough.

"Considering this one here hasn't let me go in five years, I'm afraid I can't shoulder the blame of starting things first."

Matt's blood went cold.

"Five years?" he asked. Maggie's eyes widened. "What do you mean by that?"

The man's face went blank. Like an invisible hand had taken an eraser to the emotion that had just been there and scrubbed it clean. He didn't answer and for a few seconds the only noise in the intersection was the sound of two broken vehicles whining. It wouldn't be long before some motorist came along. They were in a slow part of town for the time of day but not that slow.

"Let her go," Matt repeated. He didn't like the change in the stranger. If he was becoming unbalanced then that only lessened Matt's chances at getting Maggie back unharmed. "Let her go and we can talk."

Maggie opened her mouth to say something but Matt gave her a look that kept her quiet. The man's eyes narrowed.

"I know her." The hand gripping Maggie's arm must have tightened. She winced again. "She won't let *this* go." For the first time the man's gaze shifted away from Matt. He looked down at Maggie, his expression still blank, but she only had eyes for Matt.

They widened and then trailed to the side, away from the man and to the ground. Before he could question it she did it again. Eyes on him and then jumping to her side. All within the space of a few seconds. By the time she started to do it again, Matt realized what she was trying to tell him.

"Maggie," he warned. But he should have known better. When their mystery man's attention went back to Matt, the infuriating woman went into action.

She stomped down on his instep with a small war cry. The man matched it as he howled in pain. It was enough of a distraction to take advantage of. Maggie threw all of her weight to the side she'd been looking toward. She broke free of the man's grip.

Then everything seemed to happen in slow motion.

The man recovered enough to know he needed to do one of two things. Shoot or run. Fight or flight.

Matt had to make the same choice in less time. To fight was to put Maggie, who was out in the open, in danger. To flee was to leave her in danger. Two roads but the same scenery.

If Maggie was at risk either way, then Matt was going to choose the former.

He needed to stop the man once and for all.

Matt stepped forward and pulled the trigger.

The man didn't have time to retaliate. Instead, he tapped into his flight reflexes and moved. Still, the bullet found his arm. He yelled out in pain but kept his head. As he turned to run he shot back blindly.

"Matt!" Maggie yelled out.

Pain burned across his thigh as a bullet must have grazed him. He didn't have time to check. He dived to avoid another shot and fired back. The man, however, was faster than Matt would have thought. He made it to the cover of the truck.

"Maggie, run!" Matt yelled, moving full tilt toward the vehicle. There wasn't much else in the way of cover unless he wanted to fall back to the Bronco. And he didn't want to create distance; he wanted to close it.

Out of his periphery Maggie did as she was told but not without making a little noise.

"He took the key, Matt," she yelled back as she ran. "He took the key!"

Matt almost stuttered in his movements. Not only had this man repeatedly put Maggie in danger, but he also potentially held the literal key that could help explain Maggie's theory about Erin's death.

He made it to the truck without another shot being fired. Matt didn't have to be a mechanic to know that the vehicle was a lost cause. The man wouldn't be able to drive it anywhere, let alone use it to escape this situation.

"Come out with your hands up!" he yelled.

The sound of a car door slamming behind him drew

Matt's attention. An elderly man was standing beside his car, stopped at the intersection next to the Bronco.

"Get back in the car!" Maggie yelled, changing direction to go right to him.

Another noise brought Matt's attention back to the truck. Footsteps. *Retreating* footsteps.

Fed up with hide-and-seek, Matt rounded the front of the truck with his gun raised just in time to see the man running over the sidewalk and to one of the buildings by the intersection. It was two stories and run-down, abandoned, he'd guessed, since no one had come outside at the sound of the crash or the gunshots. Or maybe they were playing it smart and were staying put. Hopefully calling the cops while they were at it.

"Stop," Matt yelled. "Stop or I'll shoot!"

The man sidestepped around the front of the building until he disappeared along its side. He didn't shoot but that didn't mean that Matt wouldn't. If he got another clean shot, he'd try to take the man down. To temporarily disable him so he couldn't run anymore. This needed to end. For Maggie. For Erin. For the truth.

Matt paused at the corner of the building and looked around the edge, keeping his head low. The man wasn't anywhere to be seen. Matt cursed beneath his breath as he tried to catch up.

His adrenaline was on high, surging through every muscle in his body. When a door at the back corner of the building flung open, he nearly shot the teen who walked out.

"I—I heard a—" He started to stutter, stopping so quickly that he nearly toppled over. He was looking at the gun as if it was the first time he'd ever seen one in person. And maybe it was. Either way, Matt hoped it would be the last. At least for the day.

"I'm a cop. Get back inside," Matt barked, lowering the gun. "Lock this door!"

The boy didn't have to be told twice. He scurried back into the building in a flash. Matt kept his gun low just in case more civilians were about to spring out at him. He'd never accidentally shot a civilian and didn't want this to be his first time.

The building led to an alley that opened back out into the street. Matt paused, heart slamming against his chest. The man could have easily gone around the next building or out to the road. He didn't want to lose him. He couldn't.

A scream cut through the air, making the choice for him.

"Maggie!" he yelled, running full tilt down the alley. How had he already gotten to her so fast? Matt didn't think his lead had been that large.

He skidded to a stop the moment he hit the sidewalk along the road.

It wasn't Maggie who screamed.

"Stop or I'll shoot!" the man yelled, opening a repeat of their earlier conversation. However, this time the scene had changed. The man was standing next to a running car, the driver's-side door open and the driver standing at the end of his gun. He must have made her stop and pulled her out.

Matt had to admit, it was a good move as far as escaping was concerned. Especially considering the woman he had at gunpoint was pregnant. Young, too. Her eyes were saucers as she looked at Matt.

"Whoa, whoa," he said. "Easy there."

The man's calm was gone. He didn't seem shaken, but angry was definitely on the table.

"We're not doing this again," he growled. "You drop your gun and let me leave or I'll show you what I'm capable of."

"Let her go so we can talk," Matt tried.

The man moved the gun from the expectant mother's side to her protruding belly. She had to be at least eight months.

Matt needed to tread carefully.

"You don't know this about me so I'll go ahead and tell you," the man started. "But I don't kill women. However, I'm not above hurting them." He pushed the gun into the woman's belly. She whimpered. "Now, I won't say it again. Drop the gun. Or I'll give you something to regret for the rest of your life."

Matt didn't try to get any more information. He wouldn't take the chance. Slowly, he dropped the gun on the ground and then nudged it away with his foot. He placed his hands in the air.

The man also didn't waste time. He pushed the woman away from him. She turned tail and ran toward the intersection in the distance. Then the gun was pointed squarely at Matt. He was at the mercy of the stranger.

"Were you responsible for the death of my wife?"

Matt hadn't realized how much he believed Maggie's theory until the moment he asked the question. He'd tried to stay objective, following potential leads that connected Maggie to what had happened to Dwayne. But somewhere in the past few hours, he'd gotten in line with her idea that Erin's death was no accident. That it had been a part of a larger picture. That Ken Morrison hadn't just popped that curb because of some ill-fated destiny.

The man kept his gun steady. His words matched.

"If I were you, Detective, I'd find another case." He lowered himself into the car but kept the door open to give Matt one last message. "*I* don't kill women. Don't make me start."

Chapter Twelve

The pain in Maggie's leg was nauseating. Not to mention there was a growing list of other aches radiating throughout her body. Her hand was already covered in blood after swiping at the stream coming down into her eye from the cut across her forehead. It stung something awful, but that didn't stop her from running toward Matt as he jogged into the intersection.

"Are you okay?" she asked. Her run was more of a gaited hobble. It took everything in her not to cry out. "Are you hurt?" She didn't wait for an answer, giving him a once-over until her eyes caught on his leg. Blood stained his pants at the side of his thigh. "Matt!"

The detective reached out, wrapping his hands around her upper arms. He was steadying her, something she realized she needed.

"It's a graze," he answered, making sure to bring her eyes back up to his. "I'm fine. I promise. Has anyone called the police?"

Maggie nodded. It hurt.

"Jerry did when he drove up." She pointed back to the older man whom Maggie had yelled at to get into his car. He was now out of said car, trying to console a pregnant woman who had run to them. Maggie had already confirmed the expectant mother, Lea, was physically fine but understandably terrified. "What happened to the man?"

Anger squeezed his face. Maggie had to shut her eye as blood stung it again. Matt didn't miss it. He released her arms and grabbed the bottom of his shirt. With one quick movement he ripped off a strip.

"Here, use this," he offered. "It's still wet from the pool."

Maggie took the strip and ran it over her eye while Matt surprised her again by running his thumb across the skin between the cut and her eyebrow. When he pulled his finger away it was covered in blood.

"We need to get you out of here," he said, concern clear in his voice. It resonated within Maggie more than it should have. "Let's see if Jerry doesn't mind you using his car to rest until first responders get here."

Maggie didn't want to but she had to agree.

"Can I stay right here instead?" She looked down at her leg. Now that the adrenaline was starting to wear off, it was really starting to throb. "I—well, I just hurt."

"We need to get out of the open, just in case he comes back." Without saying anything more he put one arm behind her and then bent to put the other under her legs. One moment she was standing and the next she was in the detective's arms.

"Never thought Matt Walker would sweep me off my feet," she joked, trying to ignore how her eyes watered as the ache in her leg lessened but the one that reminded her she'd been in a car accident came to the forefront.

"It's been one heck of a day," Matt agreed. He walked them over to where Jerry and the woman were standing. "Jerry, is it? Why don't we let the ladies take a seat in your car while we wait?"

Jerry zipped to attention like Matt was a drill sergeant. Maggie half expected him to salute before he went about helping Lea into the back of the car. Matt stopped next to the other side and let her down gently.

Maggie kept her arm around his neck longer than was necessary, she was sure, but being so close to him—both wet and bleeding—something in her shifted.

"Thank you."

His eyebrow quirked up.

"For what?" he returned, voice low and filling with anger. "I let him get away. Again."

Maggie didn't have to force her sarcasm to stay away. She meant every word before she said it.

"For trying to save me at the hotel." Maggie was whispering now. "And for waking up when I called for you." She pulled her arm from around him but stayed close. "After the crash, when everything stopped moving—" Maggie paused as she felt the same panic again. Tears pricked the insides of her eyes. She didn't know where the emotion was coming from but she didn't try to fight it. "You stopped moving, too. He pulled me out before I could check to make sure you were—" Maggie cut her words off. She gave him a small, grateful smile. "Thank you for waking up."

Matt didn't return the smile but he answered her in a matching whisper. Like they were sharing secrets in their own little bubble.

"All thanks go to you," he said. "You're what woke me up."

Just like that Maggie's attention changed directions. From trying to cobble together a thank-you to her savior to glancing at his lips so close to hers, her aching body betrayed her mind. In that moment Maggie knew exactly what the new feeling was that swept through her.

She wanted to kiss Detective Matt Walker.

Because he'd tried to and actually had saved her. Because her breath had caught when he'd run into danger and her body had sagged in relief when he'd come back alive. Because he was the most handsome man she'd ever met. Because Maggie just wanted to feel his lips against hers.

Period.

But what did Matt want? Her? Or had she truly burned that bridge years ago?

Sirens sounded in the distance.

It burst their private bubble.

Matt reached around her and opened the car door. He remained gentle as he helped her into the seat. Then he rejoined Jerry outside at the front of the car.

He never met her eyes.

"Knock, knock."

Maggie looked up from the magazine she'd been pretending to read and was surprised to see a familiar face.

"Nurse Bean," she started, then corrected herself. "Kortnie, I mean."

The ER nurse nodded with a smile. She was wearing her scrubs but her name tag was off. She thumbed at the spot it had been clipped to the night before.

"I just finished a double," she explained. "Was on my way out the door when I heard another fuss being kicked up with your name in the center. I have to admit I was hoping I wouldn't see you again. At least, not this quickly."

Maggie raised her hands in defense.

"I swear I'm not doing this on purpose. Trouble seems to be my middle name as of late is all."

Maggie had been ordered to go to the hospital as soon as the first local police officer had shown up on the scene. Once she'd finally been able to see herself in a mirror, she'd realized why. She looked like she'd been dropped into a blender with some rocks thrown in for good measure. Blood and cuts and the weight of pain had created a startling image. Matt wasn't much better. She had a sneaking suspicion that he would have refused the ambulance had she not been around, staying at the crime scene until the sheriff arrived. Instead, he'd sat in the back of the ambulance with Maggie as the EMT rattled off a series of questions.

Now, two hours later, and Maggie had been left in a room to wait for Matt's meeting with the sheriff to come to an end. They were down the hall. Both refused to go any farther than that, considering their mystery man had shown up twice in one day.

Kortnie walked in with a chart, head bent and ready to read it but Maggie beat her to it. She pointed to the cut above her eyebrow.

"It bled a lot but was superficial. No stitches, thank goodness, because I already look like a disaster. I might have a small scar, though." She pointed down to her leg raised up on the bed. "Pulled a muscle. I'm supposed to take it easy for a few days. Or a week. But who has time for that?" Maggie motioned to her body as a whole. "And last but not least, bruising plus the occasional laceration."

Kortnie smirked and crossed her arms over her chest. "And the old noggin?"

Maggie sighed. It still hurt.

"I'm not missing any more memories," she said. "But I didn't remember anything from yesterday, either."

"Even still, let's hope you can avoid any more traumatic events, okay?"

Maggie shrugged.

"I'll really try. I promise. Maybe."

Kortnie laughed and the two dived into small talk that surprisingly wasn't forced. Maggie didn't have the best track record with female friends so the company was unexpected but pleasant. Maggie brought up Cody and how she missed him despite seeing him that morning which turned into Kortnie bringing up her own son. From there they talked about their respective jobs and were about to get into the politics behind PTA when Maggie was reminded that her life had become more complicated than normal. Matt walked in looking more world-weary than he had that morning.

"And that's my cue to go home and sleep," Kortnie said before the detective could ask for some privacy. She rummaged through her purse and pulled out a card. "On the off chance trouble finds you for a third time today," she said, handing the card over, "I was a hospital administrator before I switched back to my nursing roots and the ER but my number is still the same."

Maggie smiled at the thought.

"Thanks. I'd give you one in return but, to be honest, I have no idea where my purse is right now." Her tone let Kortnie know it was okay to laugh and soon the nurse was saying goodbye. Matt didn't talk until the door shut behind her.

"I chased down your doctor," he started, sinking into the chair next to the bed. "We can leave when you're ready." His eyes went to her leg but he kept quiet about it. He hadn't left her side until she'd been checked out when they had first come in. Which meant he knew she'd been asked to keep off it. There was no point lying.

"It hurts but not as bad as it did. The medicine for inflammation helped."

He nodded. He looked lost. Tired.

"Matt, what did the sheriff say?"

The detective ran his hand down his face.

"The APB is still out for our perp and this time we know what he looks like and the exact make and model of the car he took so that should help. Local PD are co-ordinating with the sheriff's department to work every angle available to try to get this guy. They're retracing *our* steps to see if anyone saw anything helpful, and Detective Ansler is probably dissecting the truck as we speak." He opened his mouth and then closed it.

"What?" she prodded.

"Something our mystery man said is bothering me. He said he didn't kill women."

Maggie felt her eyebrow rise.

"Last time I checked that was a good thing."

Matt gave her a dry look.

"It is. *But* it was the way he said it that was off." He sat up straighter. "Like he was saying *he* didn't kill women but—"

"But someone else did," she interrupted.

He nodded.

"There's already so much about this man we don't know. Can you imagine if we were really dealing with *two* people?"

A shiver ran up Maggie's spine at even the hint of

more than one bad guy who wanted to keep whatever secret she'd uncovered a secret. Especially when the maybe accomplice wasn't above killing women.

"Hey, either way," Matt said, scooting to the edge of his chair, "you solved this thing once already. There's no reason we can't do it again."

Maggie couldn't help but smirk at that.

"Every time we team up, a man in a van or truck appears," she pointed out. "Maybe we should table our investigation until we at least get some better pain meds."

The detective snorted and, once again, ran his hand down his face. It worried her.

"Billy is going to take us to the hotel where we're going to lie low for a while. I've been officially benched and *I'm* officially benching you. I should remind you the doctor will back me up on this."

Maggie rewound and settled on the first part.

"We? I thought Deputy Foster was being assigned to watch Cody and me?"

"He is but, while I trust him, I don't think he can handle you on his own." A small smirk crossed his lips but a smirk nonetheless. It made their darkening conversation brighten a moment.

"You act like I'm some wild creature. The past few days are not an entirely accurate representation of my life."

He snorted.

"The past few days might not be your normal speed but in just one morning I've been witness to you wanting to chase a man who threw bricks into your home, strip in public to retrieve a clue you *hid at the bottom of a hotel pool* and break out of a gunman's grip with ease after riding out a crash that was like being tossed in the spin cycle. Yeah, I don't think I can accurately warn Caleb what you're capable of." He got to his feet. It was a labored move. She'd overheard the nurse chastise him about moving around so much. His ribs weren't broken but they were bruised. And had been already when he'd carried Maggie across the intersection, worsening his pain to help alleviate hers. In the same gentlemanly fashion, he held his hand out to her now.

"But I thought you were benched," she added, hesitating from taking it. "You know, since you're hurt and haven't slept in a few days and people tend to need rest."

"Billy can bench me all day long but what I do in my spare time is my business. Now, you want to get out of here or what?"

Chapter Thirteen

The hotel was definitely a step up from the one Luca was running. That was for sure. Maggie followed Matt and Sheriff Reed up to the third floor where they'd already booked a room for her and Cody. It was nice and not too small. There were two double beds, a love seat and a TV. The view from the window showed the top of an office complex next door and, if you knew just where to look and squinted, you could just make out the corner of the Riker County Sheriff's Department.

The building's proximity did little in the way of easing any part of Matt's or the sheriff's minds. They spoke to one another, quickly and quietly, heads bent together, while Maggie unpacked the bag she'd made for her and Cody. A little less chaos was what she needed right now. She even took out his favorite books and toys and positioned them on one of the beds, hoping that their presence would make the fact they were in a hotel room and not home a little less jarring.

"I'm going to go to the school now, Ms. Carson," the sheriff said just as Maggie was putting her clothes in the dresser. "After everything that's happened I want to provide extra backup for Cody, just in case."

Maggie nodded.

"I won't argue with that."

"Good. I'll give you a call once I get to the school to let you know we're on the way back." The sheriff turned to Matt. "Deputy Foster should be here in a few minutes with a bag from your place."

Matt's eyebrow rose. Sheriff Reed held up his hand to stop him.

"I don't have to be a detective to know you've already made up your mind about sticking around," he said. "Which is why I also booked the adjoining room for you."

They turned to the door next to the dresser.

"Deputies Mills and Grayson came out here earlier to check everything out," he continued. He pulled a key out of his pocket and handed it over. "It's technically two doors so if you want to open it, you each have to use your own key to do so."

Maggie watched as the detective's expression turned to one of appreciation. She couldn't help but mimic the feeling. Having Matt close by was one of the few thoughts that made her feel more secure.

"Let me know if you need anything," the sheriff said, already walking to the door. "Try to rest while you can. *Both* of you. I'll call you as soon as I get to the school."

Maggie thanked the man and shut the door behind him.

Leaving her alone with Matt.

In a hotel room.

Oh, how strange this day was.

"Well, I don't know about you, but I think I need to get a quick shower so I don't have to explain to my son why I look like a zombie and smell like a pool."

Matt beat her to the bathroom, turned on the light and did a quick search. It was unnecessary, she believed, but touching.

"Do you mind if I keep the adjoining door open until Caleb gets here?" he asked, unaware that he'd unintentionally ignited a bit of heat within her. "I'd rather not break down all of these doors if something happens."

Maggie laughed and tossed him the key card the sheriff had given her.

"I'd rather we not break anything else today if possible," she said. "I still feel really bad about the Bronco. Even if we didn't ask to be bulldozed by some deranged stranger."

Matt caught the key and went to open both of the doors. It was like looking into a mirror, an identical room reflected back beyond it. He put her key on the dresser and paused in the doorway.

"Are you okay for now?"

His eyes went to the lone crutch beneath her arm. She waved him off.

"Nothing I can't handle," she assured him. "But, Matt, maybe after the deputy gets here you should think about taking a nice long shower." She cracked a grin. "I also don't want to explain to my son why the normally good-looking detective looks like he's visited the inside of a blender and *also* smells like he's switched his cologne for chlorine."

Matt smirked.

"I'm going to take the compliment of 'good-looking' away from that and move on."

A little bit of heat crawled up Maggie's neck. She hadn't realized she said he was good-looking.

Although, she wasn't about to take it back, either.

THE SHOWER MIGHT have been difficult to navigate since almost every part of her body was hurting, but Maggie couldn't deny that the hot water pelting her felt amazing. However, when it was time to dress herself she encountered more of a problem.

Pulling her hair up in a loose, wet bun, she shimmied into her bra, blouse and panties. Then, with a little more trepidation than she was used to feeling, she cracked the bathroom door open.

"Uh, Detective?"

She pressed her face against the inside of the door until she heard movement.

"Yeah? Is everything okay?"

Maggie felt the blush before the heat ever reached her skin.

"Yeah," she called back, clearing her throat. "Are you alone by chance?"

There was a pause.

"I am."

Maggie took a small breath.

"And we're both adult enough to admit you've seen me in my underwear already, right? And we were both really professional about it?"

The pause was longer this time.

"Matt?"

"Yeah," he replied. "What are you getting at?"

With her free hand Maggie finagled the crutch beneath her arm and opened the door all the way. She held her chin high as she walked out into the middle of the room, nothing but her blouse and a pair of black panties on.

"Now, before you think I just like showing you my unmentionables," she said quickly, stopping at the foot of the closest bed, "I want to remind you that I've been in the ER twice in twenty-four hours and my body has finally decided to let me know how much it dislikes that. It stages its own little protest every time I try to put on my pants."

Matt's eyes stayed on hers as she spoke. Like she was the most interesting woman in the world and every syllable was as good as a tied football game in the fourth quarter. When, really, he just didn't want to look down. Maggie didn't know if she should be offended or not.

"The medicine they gave you isn't helping?"

Maggie shrugged.

"Yes and no. I mean I'm not feeling like I'm going to be sick when I move but everything feels stiff and uncomfortable." She gave him a look that she hoped expressed just how much she'd love for him to agree to help her put on skinny jeans.

He sighed.

"All right. Are they in the bathroom, then?"

Maggie nodded and laid her crutch on the bed. She remained standing until Matt was in front of her. He crouched down and Maggie felt a flame ignite just south of her waistline as he passed her panties. Apparently, she wasn't the only one. A glance down showed the detective's face was as red as a cherry. Which was a sight in itself. Even his ears were turning scarlet.

"Never thought I'd see Matt Walker blush," Maggie couldn't help but say. What was the point of being quiet if the situation would have still been just as strange as it was with no talking? "It's like you've never been asked to help a girl get dressed before."

The man was holding her jeans like a matador holding a red flag. That made her the bull in the scenario but it was the only image she could imagine, looking at the detective's expression when he met her gaze.

Caution.

Suspicion.

Focus.

And a dash of cockiness.

"When it comes to women, I've only ever been asked to help take clothes *off*."

Maggie's blush seared across her skin. It didn't help that the back of his hand skimmed the side of her leg as he tried to steady her. Good thing she'd been able to put on her shirt. The two of them might have been stained tomato red otherwise.

"Now, hold on to me," Matt ordered. "Last thing we need is you falling over and earning us a one-way trip right back to the hospital. Three times in twenty-four hours might get you thrown in a padded room somewhere. Just so you don't hurt yourself."

Maggie laughed and followed Matt's command with little to no grace. She held on to his shoulders as he navigated one pant leg halfway up and then moved to the other one to do the same. The pain wasn't as bad as it had been thanks to the lingering medicine from the hospital but when she'd stepped out of the shower and tried to work the material around her bad leg, she'd been met with surprising resistance. It was like her entire leg had been frozen stiff, refusing to bend with her.

She hadn't thought to involve the detective until three attempts ended with the rest of her body reminding her it had been beaten up, too. Now the dull throb that blanketed her was only being interrupted by the burn of her blush...and something else. It wasn't a mystery what that other thing was, either. Every time Matt's skin came in contact with hers, no matter how innocent, it was like he was lighting matches along her body. Trailing them from one spot to the other until it went out and he struck up another one. The detective was touching parts of her skin that hadn't been touched by a man in a long time.

It completely distracted her to the point he had to repeat himself.

"Lift your other leg," he said. "Unless you want to explain to Cody why you can't do it yourself."

Maggie cleared her throat. The longing for the man at her feet quieted as her thoughts moved to her son.

"While he's mature for his age I *would* like to avoid that particular conversation," she admitted. "He's already been through enough in his young life. I'd like to keep him a kid as long as possible."

She winced as she put weight on her bad ankle for a second. Matt looped the pant leg under her foot as fast and gently as he could. He pulled up until it slid to above her knee.

"You got it from here?"

Maggie nodded. She grabbed the waist of her jeans as he turned away to give her privacy to pull them the rest of the way up and button them. Not that it was needed. He'd already seen her.

"And who said chivalry is dead?" she joked, lowering herself onto the bed when she was done.

Matt snorted and walked over to the window. He moved the curtains back, letting light stream through. It lit up his hair.

Golden.

Beautiful.

Worthy of a pair of hands running through it.

The cut above her eyebrow stung.

Maggie sighed.

All jokes and sarcasm aside, she couldn't ignore how horrible she felt. Which had to mean that her steadfast companion must have felt worse. He had, after all, not slept in nearly two days as far as she knew.

It was a painful reminder that one man had put them through the ringer within the span of one morning. Suddenly, she didn't feel so jovial.

"Did you know I was married before all of this happened? I mean before I told you I'd been divorced?" The question surprised her. Matt turned to listen. But to what? She wasn't sure. In a flash she went from feeling lust and humor to something much more dangerous. Overwhelming vulnerability.

"No," he answered stoically. "I didn't."

Maggie exhaled a long breath.

"I interviewed him when I first started working at the paper in Kipsy. It was some fluff piece about a diner being renovated after fifty years of serving the community. Chris was a lawyer, family law, but loved the diner so much that every Wednesday he'd go to work an hour early so he'd have a longer lunch break to fit the extra twenty-minute commute." Maggie felt herself smile a little. She knew it was broken. All the happy memories of her ex were still there, in her heart, but just off enough that reliving them brought a twinge of pain. "He loved that place," she continued. "And that's where he told me he loved me. He asked me to marry him in the booth we sat in during that first interview. I know it sounds cheesy but at the time it was perfect. *We* were perfect."

Maggie brought her hands up to help illustrate a point she'd already made to herself in the past several years. She laced her fingers together, pushing her palms flush.

"We fit together like this—so snug, so great—but as time went on, I realized that this—" she shook her clasped hands "—this isn't perfect. Because, if you look down, you'll see that one of the two hands is on top. One thumb over the other. Not equal. Not in sync. No matter how great it might look at first."

Maggie let her hands fall to her lap.

"I didn't realize that our marriage wasn't the way it should have been until life really started happening. I may have been—and still am—difficult and aggressive and intrusive and a list of other adjectives that you'd use to define people who usually end up alone, but even I, with all my flaws, thought I deserved to try to be happy. And that *desire* ended up eating its way through my chest and then into other parts of my life until I had nothing left to distract me from it." She gave him an apologetic look. "Becoming, for lack of a better word, obsessed with cases and stories that I had no business getting attached to, for instance."

Matt kept quiet. Which was fine. For some reason Maggie realized she needed to get some things off her chest.

"Adopting Cody, I can see now, wasn't about just saving him. It was about saving me, too." Tears began to prick the insides of her eyes but Maggie didn't stop. Not when she was so close to making her point. "See, I come from a small family. Two parents, an idiot brother who does idiot things and an aunt I saw once a year until she remarried and moved across the ocean. They loved me, my family, but in a detached way. Not the most in-volved bunch but they call on birthdays and holidays and even sometimes try to fit a visit into their schedule. It's just who they are and have always been. It's how I grew up. I can't fault them because I had a good, healthy childhood. We loved each other but... Well, we weren't *a team* like so many other families seem to be." Maggie felt her lips pull up for a moment. "The first month Cody lived with Chris and me, he got sick. You know, I knew what you were supposed to do when your kid gets sick. Take them to the doctor, give them the medicine, watch over the kid until they're better. But things in theory are always easier, aren't they? At first I was doing fine, sticking by the book on how to help him. But one time when I touched his cheek to see how hot he was, he looked up at me with these round, innocent eyes, and I swear I felt that fever in my bones."

Maggie knew why the vulnerability was there and why she had felt the need to tell the man a few feet from her everything. Why she wasn't the same woman he'd met years ago. Why she'd really put the case away. Why she needed them to solve it now.

"It was in that moment that I knew I *finally* had a team." She smiled and felt the tears slide down her face. She didn't care. She wanted him to know the bottom line. "We can't let anything happen to that boy, Matt. He's my entire life and then some. We have to finish this thing. Whatever it is."

The detective stayed right where he was but that didn't lessen the severity of his response. Despite the distance between them she felt as if he was close enough to kiss.

"We might have been banged up today, Maggie, but I promise you, Cody will never be hurt." His voice was steel. "And just because this case is difficult doesn't mean it's impossible. I believe in the sheriff, the department and even local PD." A smile carved itself out of his frown. It was small but effective. "I even believe in us."

Maggie didn't bother wiping at her cheek. She felt a surge of relief wash over all the pain and doubt and worry. It might not last but she welcomed it.

And was thankful for the man who had given it to her.

She smiled.

"You better be careful, Detective. You keep talking like that and I'll start to think you actually like me."

Matt snorted.

"Well, we wouldn't want that."

Those blue-gray eyes found hers.

"No, we wouldn't want that."

Chapter Fourteen

Maggie might have started to cry when she opened up to him, but when Cody finally arrived she managed to hold it together remarkably well. However, she wasted no time in wrapping him in her arms as if he were a life preserver in choppy waters. Cody, more curious about their new surroundings, returned the hug. Then squirmed when Maggie had a hard time letting go.

"Mom," he whined. "You're crushing me!"

Maggie laughed but didn't pull away until she gave one more squeeze. She looked up when she was done and met Matt's gaze through the open adjoining room door.

"I finally had a team."

Matt broke the stare and let Maggie's words echo one last time through his head as he took his bag to the bathroom to shower and change. He tried to coax his mind into going blank so he could enjoy the quiet, especially after everything that had happened. Everything he thought he'd known. Everything he'd learned. But the thoughts came hard and fast.

Ken Morrison might have killed Erin because of their mystery man with a moral code that included not killing women.

But why? What was the point? And what did it have to do with the list of names Maggie had found?

Matt let the hot water run across his face and down his body.

Erin.

The ache of loss started to spread. His fists balled. He'd already done this. He'd already fallen apart, felt destroyed and lost. He'd already done the horrible dance of burying a loved one. A wife.

It was hard but he'd tried his best to move on. He'd grieved. He still did in his own way when he was reminded of the once-little things that seemed so big and empty now. Whether it was the side of the bed that remained cold, the fact that the shampoo and soap in the shower were only his, or the at times startling realization that he'd never again see her use the chipped New Orleans mug he'd bought her on their honeymoon, Matt had tried his best to heal the ache. Or at least embrace it until it eased.

Now, though, how could he do what he always had if Erin's death had been intentional?

Matt opened his hands. Thinking of Maggie, he pressed them together without lacing his fingers.

Equal. In sync.

They'd both lost someone they had hoped would be a partner for life.

Matt sighed into the steam.

The weight of exhaustion was finally starting to crush him. He finished his shower, dressed and sat down for the first time in what felt like days. The door between their rooms remained open.

Matt fell asleep to the sounds of laughter between mother and son.

IT WAS SOMEWHERE between dreams and reality that an answer found its way into Matt's head. He opened his eyes, blinking the sleep away, and felt a wave of disorientation. A dim light was in the distance but everything in his immediate area was dark. For a moment he forgot where he was and a sense of panic seized him.

A noise followed by subtle movement at his side turned that panic into action. He reached out and caught someone's wrist. They tried to resist and soon he felt the weight of a body on his.

"What the heck, Matt?"

The voice and body pressed on top of his belonged to Maggie. He took a deep breath, trying to calm his racing heart, and reached out toward the lamp on the nightstand. He remembered now where he was. But couldn't imagine why Maggie was on top of him.

The light wasn't great but it showed him a red-faced woman struggling to roll off him. It was distracting to say the least. Here he was trying to concentrate on reorienting himself and instead all he could seem to focus on was the heat of Maggie's body pressed against him. Her curves and softness. Moving against him.

As swiftly as she'd fallen over, Matt realized he needed to focus on anything other than the woman or else she would know exactly what he thought of her body. What *his* body thought of her body.

"Maggie," he whispered through gritted teeth. "Just roll over."

"You act like that's *easy* with the list of injuries and pain meds," she bit back, sounding as irritated as he did. Though he doubted she was fighting her body's responses as hard as he was at the moment. "Walking like five steps over here was difficult enough."

Matt grunted to no one in particular and decided to move the woman himself. He tried to sit up and roll her over on her back next to him. His body went from registering desire to handling a wallop of pain. He winced but followed through on his original plan until Maggie was lying in the bed next to him instead of on top of him.

For a moment they were quiet, both catching their breath and waiting for their various pains to ebb.

Maggie was the one who broke the silence.

"Well, I can't say that's how I imagined getting you into bed." There was the normal Maggie snark in her tone.

"You always have a response for something. Do you realize that?"

They both kept their gazes to the ceiling. Still, he saw her shrug.

"I do what I can."

"And what exactly were you doing just now?" he asked. "Before you fell over onto me."

"To be fair, you scared me so the falling part is on you." Her voice softened. "But originally, I came in to check up on you. You've been asleep for a while now."

Matt grabbed at his side and fought through the pain to grab his phone off the nightstand. It was a quarter after nine.

"Honestly, I think you need *more* sleep," she said. "I just wanted to make sure you were all right. But I guess it's hard to sneak around with a crutch. Sorry I woke you."

There were no missed calls or texts on his phone. Which meant there had been no breaks in the case while he'd been asleep. It was frustrating, to say the least.

"Is Caleb still outside?" he asked. He'd been so tired he'd barely spoken to the deputy earlier.

She nodded.

"I let him know when I was putting Cody to bed. I gave him a stern, motherly warning to not disturb us unless something big happened." She flashed him a smirk. "And even then be quiet about it. If there's one thing I'm proud of about my kid, it's that he sleeps hard. But Heaven help us if he *does* wake up. I'm pretty sure I've learned the skills of an expert negotiator because of that boy."

Matt smiled and shifted his gaze until he saw Cody's sleeping form through the open door. His mouth was open and his arm was hanging halfway off the bed.

"I envy how easily kids can sleep," he admitted. "The older we get the harder it becomes."

He hadn't meant to take the conversation down a more serious path but suddenly it felt like he had. Silence moved between them until Maggie let out a breath that dragged down her body, despite the fact she was already lying down.

"It's because we know the truth about nightmares," she whispered. "They can be all too real."

Matt angled his head to get a better look at the woman. Green eyes met his. Within them a nearly imperceptible shift happened.

The two of them whispering in the dark suddenly felt right. Them, so close together he could still feel the warmth of her body, felt right.

Matt glanced down at Maggie's lips.

Suddenly, he felt like the two of them hadn't just been trying to solve a mystery all day but also building toward something.

"Maggie," he started but she didn't let him finish.

With an almost-apologetic smile she pulled herself

up until she was sitting with her back against the head-rest. He could tell the movement was painful but she didn't complain.

"Sorry again for waking you up. But now that I know you're alive and well, I think it's time I made the long trek back to my room."

The moment, whatever it was, dissipated.

Maggie was back to being the woman who had found herself in the middle of trouble.

And he was back to being the detective who needed to figure out who was behind it all.

IT WASN'T UNTIL he awoke the next morning that Matt remembered what his dream had told him the night before. A part of him wished Maggie was still in bed with him. Rolling over to tell her his theory would have been a lot less painful.

He felt like he'd been hit by a truck. Well, he really had been. The side of his body was an ache he couldn't escape. One that whined as he tried the simplest of tasks. Never mind his ribs. The doctor had confirmed they had been bruised. The adrenaline had masked that particular nuisance after the crash but now there was nothing dulling it. Apparently, Maggie was having the same issues.

He looked through the open door between them after he finished changing and caught her eye. She was sitting up in bed, her foot propped up on some pillows.

"*Not being broken* isn't the same as *feeling okay*," she called. "At least if something's broken, they give you more pain medication." Her brow was furrowed. She uncrossed her arms to wave him in. The bed next to her was disheveled but empty. The bathroom door was open but empty. She followed his gaze to it. "Cody's in the hallway talking Deputy Foster's ear off. I didn't want Cody to go to school, considering Brick Thrower made a point to let us know that he's familiar with my life. On the off chance he still wants me after getting that key, I don't want to give him the opportunity to grab my son."

"Speaking of the key, I realized something about it." Maggie's entire body perked up.

"Yeah? What?"

"It was a small key, right? Probably to a lock?" Maggie nodded.

"And what do people nowadays really use those for?"

"Other than bikes and maybe the occasional shed, I don't know."

A thread of excitement started to wrap itself around Matt's gut. The idea of a lead, no matter how theorized, was one of the best parts about his job. It pushed them closer to the truth, to completing the puzzle.

"Storage units," he answered. "You rent a unit and bring your own lock."

Maggie's eyes widened. Then she was smiling right along with him, catching on to his excitement. However, it didn't last.

"But whose storage unit would it go to? And why would that guy yesterday want it?"

Matt had already had the same questions. He pointed to her.

"I don't know but *you* did at some point. Why else would you have hidden it?"

"The operative word is *did*," she pointed out. "Now? Not so much."

"If you could figure it out once, you can do it again."

The hotel door opened. Cody walked in, looking thoughtful. Deputy Foster nodded to Matt before shutting the door behind the boy. When Cody saw Matt he hesitated.

"Cody, you remember Detective Walker?"

The boy's eyes were wide. Such acute concern seemed to cross his face that Matt felt his face draw in, too.

"You got hurt like Mom," the boy said. "You have cuts on your face."

Matt had forgotten that beyond feeling bad, he also looked it. Maggie, on the other hand, had lessened the intensity of her appearance with makeup. But no amount could cover up everything. Matt wished he'd thought to ask Maggie how she'd explained what had happened to the boy.

"I did," he decided to tell the truth. "But it's not that bad."

Cody looked him up and down. Then he nodded, apparently accepting Matt's statement as truth.

"Okay." The boy turned to Maggie. "Mom, I'm hungry."

Maggie laughed. She shared a look with Matt.

"He really does care," she promised. "Just not a lot until he gets some food."

Matt put his hands on his waist and turned back to the boy, serious.

"Well, I can't blame him. Us men need nourishment."

Cody nodded, mimicking Matt's stern expression.

"Yeah, Mom."

Maggie held her hands up.

"I guess I can't argue with that logic."

Chapter Fifteen

It wasn't until Tuesday afternoon that something shook loose with the case. By that time it had been four days of hotel living. Four days of fast food and room service. Four days of being cooped up and slowly going stir-crazy. Four days of forced proximity with a man Maggie had spent five years avoiding.

The first day Matt had kept his distance after breakfast. He'd kept the door open between their rooms but worked on his laptop and phone, out of sight at his desk. The only conversation she'd heard was him checking on Dwayne's condition at the hospital. Maggie had tried to eavesdrop on more of his calls, or when Sheriff Reed or Detective Ansler had stopped by, but Cody had made that difficult. It was like she had a toddler all over again. His books, toys and the television did little to ease his restlessness. It wasn't until day two that Matt was able to ease some of the pressure.

"Want to explore the hotel for a few minutes with me?" he asked after they finished off our lunch at the lone table in her room. "I was thinking about stretching my legs."

Cody had lit up like a Christmas tree. He was still working through his shyness with Matt but the offer had been too good for him to stay silent. His little eyes found their way to hers and he'd started in with a chorus of "Please, Mom" and "Pretty please."

Matt's "I won't let him out of my sight" was what really did the trick.

The two had marched out of the hotel room with purpose and they'd come back in with smiles. Apparently, Matt had regaled the boy with watered-down police stories full of action and mystery. So much so that they'd taken another walk that night—and every day since. It became a little ritual, one Maggie couldn't join in on.

While she was itching to stretch her own legs or to track down and follow any bread crumbs that could lead to lost memories, Maggie was grateful for the break. Her leg, along with all the other postaccident pain, had been given time to heal. Or at least get to the point where mobility without cringing was possible.

She'd used the downtime to drag out her own laptop—grabbed by the sheriff and his wife, who had offered to pick up extra clothes for her and Matt and Cody—and revisited her original investigation into Erin Walker's death. Afterward, she'd made a list of everything they knew from recent events. Including his interest in the key she'd hidden at the hotel. Following Matt's theory that it could belong to a storage unit had focused her attention on the several in Kipsy and the rest of the county. She'd stared at the new and old information until her eyes crossed. Until she felt like she was going crazy. Nothing was adding up. Not *one* damn thing.

That is until Tuesday afternoon when a news story popped up on the *Kipsy City Chronicle*'s Facebook page. It was a link to their crime blog but it was the caption that made Maggie stop scrolling.

The Kipsy Police Department is asking for the public's help in finding a suspect in a recent break-in at a local storage-unit facility.

Maggie clicked the link, heartbeat already speeding up. A picture of a Danny's Storage Facility billboard was at the top of the page. The press release beneath it was short. However, it was enough to get Maggie going. She grabbed the pen and hotel notepad and scribbled down Danny's Storage Facility's address. When she was done with that, she focused on her leg.

The swelling had gone down but there was still some soreness. She'd spent the past few days testing the limits of her mobility and could, at the very least, walk without her crutch. It just hurt a little and was less of a walk and more of a limp.

Now she tested her leg again, moving around the room in search of socks and shoes and lipstick. The lipstick wasn't necessary but Maggie still grabbed the tube and put it on with conviction. She was excited and wanted Matt to get on the same wavelength. Plus, she hoped putting on lipstick showed him without her having to say it that she meant business. Maggie straightened her back, held the piece of paper in her hand like it was the track-and-field baton and waited to pass it off to the detective the moment he came through the door.

Luckily, she didn't have to wait long.

"We saw a squirrel jump off the roof," sang Cody, riding his own wave of excitement into the room. Maggie paused only long enough to get an explanation for that.

"One of the rooms was open and we scoped it out,"

Matt jumped in. "Through the window we saw a squirrel jump off the roof next door onto a tree."

Cody made a stretched-out scoff.

"That's what I *just* said!"

Matt laughed and held up his hands in defense.

Maggie used the opening to push the paper into the palm of one of them. It confused the detective but he read it regardless.

"And this is?"

Maggie was brimming with excitement now. It showed her how stir-crazy she'd actually become being cooped up in their two rooms for days.

"Cody, why don't you go see what's on Matt's TV?" she answered instead. "Channel 14 has an all-day marathon of *Bill Nye the Science Guy*."

Maggie didn't have to tell the boy twice. He was already singing the theme song before he even made it through the adjoining room's door. Matt, however, was waiting with his eyebrow raised.

"That's the address to a storage-unit facility in Kipsy," she started. "There was a break-in, but they don't have any leads as to who was behind it."

It was as if someone had sprinkled Miracle-Gro over the man. He perked right up.

"This could be our guy."

Maggie nodded but held up her index finger to keep his attention.

"*But* the break-in happened *last week*," she corrected. "They just didn't catch it until this morning."

His eyes widened.

"So barring coincidence, this break-in could have been—"

Maggie couldn't help herself. She cut him off.

"Me! It could have been me. The timing lines up with my missing chunk of memory. I hid the key before lunch in the hotel room. So maybe I took Cody to school and went to the storage unit afterward. Then took the key with me to meet whoever gave me that card for the hotel but then I, for whatever reason, felt the need to hide it. And well…"

"But why? What did you find that led you to the key in the first place? And when did you leave your house without your purse or keys?"

Maggie's thread of excitement began to unravel.

"I don't know," she admitted with a shrug. "But that storage unit may or may not hold the answer."

Matt eyeballed the address again.

"Did you tell anyone else about this?"

"No. Just you."

He ran his hand through his hair.

"I need to call Billy. Get someone out there."

Maggie held her hands up in a stopping motion.

"*Or*, hear me out," she said. "*We*, me and you, go check it out first and let them keep following whatever leads they're following."

Matt raised his eyebrow and snorted.

"I'm not about to welcome trouble by walking straight into it. That's not good police business, or any business really."

"But we don't even know where our mystery perp is," she pointed out. "Last time we saw him, you shot him. There's a good chance he's long gone or at least lying low." Maggie swept her arm backward, motioning to the room as a whole. "As much as I've enjoyed our nose-to-the-grindstone, operating-out-of-a-hotel-room methods of investigation, we haven't gotten anywhere in days. Neither have the rest of the department or the local police. And again, as much as I've enjoyed our nonangry meals and our nightly game show viewing, we can't stay in this hotel forever." Maggie lowered her voice, hoping Matt caught her shift from optimistic to the direct opposite. "Eventually, we'll all have to go home. Our separate homes. But right now *this* is the only lead we have. And I want—need—to see it for myself. To see if any of it is a missing piece to what I did during the span of one lousy day." Matt kept his eyes on hers as she took a small step closer to him. "Please, Matt, I need to do this. Help me do this."

For one long moment Maggie was sure he'd say no. Then cite off all the reasons—all legitimate, too—that the two of them going back out into the field, busted and partially broken with a target on her back and a child hidden in a hotel room, was a no-good, very bad idea.

But he didn't.

Detective Matt Walker actually grinned.

"I think I've finally accepted the fact that you're just the most persistent pain in the backside I'll ever know."

Maggie felt herself beam. She placed a hand over her chest and upped her Southern accent to classic Scarlett O'Hara.

"Why, Detective, I do think that's just about the nicest thing I ever did hear."

DEPUTY FOSTER HAD been on guard duty every day since they'd first come to the hotel. His partner, Dante Mills, took the night shift so he wouldn't be run ragged. Though Matt almost wished the deputy was a little slow on his feet that afternoon. Because he might have swallowed their story a little easier. Instead, his eyebrows rode high and his questions swung low.

"And why can't we just send Detective Ansler out there?" he asked, circling back to his original objection of the two of them leaving.

Maggie opened her mouth to, no doubt, argue her points again, but Matt gave her a look that doused that particular flame. She let him do the talking, though he could tell she was ready to jump in at any moment she thought he was failing. So he decided not to fail.

"Listen, Caleb, there are lines," he started.

"Lines," the deputy repeated.

"Yeah, lines. There's a misconception about lines. On account of there's not just one of them," he continued. "There are tons of them. Boatloads of them. And they all separate *something you haven't done yet* from *something you shouldn't do at all*. The moment you cross any line, you can't go back. There's just another line now, in front of you, that you shouldn't cross, either. So in our line of work, it's important we don't cross the lines. And if we do, that we don't cross so many that we stop seeing the new ones that pop up." Matt squared his shoulders. He liked Caleb and didn't want to lie to him. So he was taking the direct approach, flowered by some blunt conversation. "In my career I've crossed a few. Ones that I didn't realize were even there until I'd jumped clear of them. And I know you can agree with me on that."

Caleb had more demons than most in his past. So he kept quiet on the point. He certainly couldn't dispute it.

"But I'm here to tell you right now that I know this is a line I'm crossing." He motioned to Maggie. "But it's worth it if we can finish this damned case. You just have to trust me on that."

Caleb looked between them. Matt wondered if he was thinking about the lines he'd crossed to help his now girlfriend, Alyssa, when she'd found herself with a wild target on her head, too. He'd had moments of going rogue in his tale to save the girl. And that was probably what helped him agree.

Though it took a few beats before he answered.

"Fine. But you gotta tell Billy. You need backup, no matter how good your intentions. You know the sheriff will argue but he won't stop you from going." Caleb grinned. "Especially if you give him that ridiculous speech you just gave me."

Matt snorted.

"Hey, I thought it was pretty eloquent myself."

"It was sure something," Maggie piped in. It made Caleb all out laugh.

"Okay, you two, get it all out," Matt said, waving them on. "We have serious work to do, so go ahead and get all of this mess out of your systems."

Maggie burrowed into a series of laughs before coming to a stop. She nodded. Caleb, too. It was a nice stress release, Matt realized. The three of them had been wound tight, ordered to stay on their toes for whatever attack may come. Matt also realized it would have been nice of him to talk to the deputy more during his posts.

"Thank you, Caleb," he said, sobering. "I know this hasn't been the most exciting detail."

The deputy fell back into his deputy composure.

"You don't hear me complaining," he assured. "You two be careful. I'll make sure Cody stays safe." He said the last part to Maggie. "Only a few of us even know you're here. If we do get any trouble, though, I swear to you nothing will happen to him."

Maggie nodded, all traces of humor gone from her expression.

"Matt trusts you, so I trust you."

It was a simple statement but said with such basic honesty that Matt was taken aback.

Maggie didn't just trust him, she trusted his word. His instinct. On voucher alone she trusted a stranger to protect her child, her entire life, as she'd said earlier. A slow yet nearly overwhelming emotion started to slip into the detective's heart.

Pride?

No.

Gratefulness?

Not quite.

Affection?

Maggie found his gaze. Beautiful, trusting, determined eyes.

Qualities that easily described her, as well.

For days they had been trapped together within their rooms, connected by a door that had stayed mostly opened. Now, looking at a woman he used to loathe, Matt realized something had shifted between them in that time. Or, maybe, something had been building. Something they'd been trying to ignore or resist. Something unspoken.

Something coming to a head.

With every conversation, every wayward glance, every subtle touch, Matt had struggled to stay focused on the case and only the case. Instead he'd found his eyes straying to Maggie's lips, his thoughts hovering on her laughter, and his mind being filled with images of what could be between them.

It had been nearly impossible to stop.

It was distracting.

It was dangerous.

Yet, Matt couldn't help but wonder...

What would happen after the case was finished?

Chapter Sixteen

Danny's Storage Facility was near the city limits of Kipsy. It needed the room to stretch, taking up half an acre of indoor climate-controlled and outdoor non-climate-controlled units. No other businesses butted up against the place, but an old T-shirt press sat abandoned across the road.

Maggie wondered what kind of shirts they used to make as Matt drove their third car in a week up to the main office, the only building on the outside of a gate that closed in all the units. Matt's eyes were taking that gate in when he finally spoke.

"The buildings in front look brand-new," he noted, driving along the gate until they were in the parking lot. "How long did you say this place has been here?"

"At least a decade, I think." She pointed in the direction opposite them. "The article said they've recently been renovating. I assume out that way are the older units since you can't see them from the road. Still, there seems to be a lot of security here. At least around the gate."

Maggie tilted her head to the side, trying to size up what she would do to get inside, which would basically entail breaking and entering.

"I'd probably cut a hole in the fence before I'd attempt to climb that sucker," she said out loud. It earned her a questioning look from the detective. "I was just thinking about how I'd try to break in to this place. The answer would be cutting a hole somewhere in the fence. It looks like it's almost eight feet tall. No way I'd climb that. I may be fearless but I'm not stupid. My clumsy self would fall and break something."

Matt laughed and joined her looking out the windshield at the tall compound-like fence.

"But why would you break in if you have the key?" he pointed out.

"Maybe I wasn't supposed to have the key in the first place?"

Matt sighed and started to get out of the car.

"I'm going to be really glad when we can hang out and not just sit and ask each other questions we don't have the answers to."

Maggie grinned.

"Are you telling me we're going to hang out when this is all done with?" she teased. It was half-hearted. Her nerves were starting to mount. They'd already told the sheriff where they were going and had a car in the area just in case they needed help. But still, they'd thought they had a hold on everything earlier that week…right before they'd been bulldozed in the middle of an intersection. Sarcasm and teasing were an easy way to distract at least some of that tension. Plus, Maggie couldn't deny there was some curiosity there, too. "What would you even talk to me about if you couldn't question my motives?"

Matt snorted and led the way to the front door.

"I'd probably just tell you that you talk too much."

He grabbed the door handle and pulled. "Or finally just arrest you like I've always wanted."

His lips had pulled up into a dazzling smile. Maggie shouldn't have been surprised that her body seemed to take a moment to appreciate how good-looking the man was again. A warmth and longing started below her waist and moved across her body until the warning of an incoming blush made her move past the man inside. She hoped he hadn't read the excitement in her expression. They didn't have time for that.

Though Maggie was starting to come to the realization that she wouldn't mind making time for it later.

The lobby of Danny's Storage Facility wasn't as sterile as she thought it would be. Instead of the whites and gray and shine on the outside, there was more warmth and color inside. Framed pictures of family members and employees hung on the walls, comfortable-looking furniture and a silver-haired woman standing behind a desk with a generous smile, all contributed to the warmth that was clearly lacking on the outside.

"Good afternoon," she greeted. "Welcome to Danny's! How can I help you two?"

Matt didn't lead off by showing the kind woman his badge. Instead, he pulled out a smile that would make any woman's knees weak. Maggie was amazed the older woman was still standing by the time they were in front of her.

"Howdy," the detective greeted, amping up his Southern drawl. It was smooth and thick like peanut butter. Tasty. "I'm a detective with the Riker County Sheriff's Department. My name is Matt Walker and this is my associate." He motioned back to Maggie, omitting her name on purpose, no doubt.

The woman continued smiling and nodded to Maggie. If she recognized her, she didn't show it in her expression. Her focus zipped back to Matt.

"Nice to meet you two. How can I help you, Detective?"

"We heard about the break-in you reported this morning. We were wondering if you could tell us about that. We think it might be linked to a current case we're working."

The woman's expression pinched. She twisted up like she'd tasted something sour.

"It's the first time in ten years we've ever had something like this happen," she started, riled up in an instant. "Someone breaking in to our legacy units."

"Legacy units?" Matt asked.

"The units at the back of the facility that have been with us for years but have no one currently paying for them." Her look of anger turned momentarily sheepish. "I won't let my son Ralph empty any of them out. Some of those renters have been here since the beginning and, without them, we wouldn't have been able to get to where we are now."

A man walked out of the next room, cleaning his hands off with a paper towel. He shook his head but kept a smile on his face.

"Where we are now is my wife, Emily, putting in overtime to try to hunt down the owners of those units and telling them to pay up or lose their things. She's been glued to the phone and internet at the house for weeks, trying to find people." He walked up to Matt and nodded to them both. "A thankless job if I ever did hear one."

"And you must be Ralph," Matt guessed. The man nodded.

"They're here about the break-in," the woman explained. Just like that her earlier anger transferred to her son. He shook his head in disbelief.

"I guess it was only a matter of time before someone tried to break in, but it still gets my blood going," he said.

"Do you know what was taken?" Maggie jumped in.

Ralph must have really taken a good look at her then. His eyes stuck to the cuts healing across her face. No amount of lipstick could distract from them.

"To be honest, I don't know," he admitted. "We have thirteen legacy units and never kept stock of what was inside each. I wouldn't even have known anything was taken at all if all the locks hadn't been cut."

Maggie couldn't hide her surprise.

"Wait. *All* of the locks?"

Ralph nodded.

"All of the legacy units had their locks snapped off. With a bolt cutter, if I had to guess."

Well, that put a wrench in their theory. If Maggie had a key to one unit then why would she have needed to destroy all of the locks?

"And the report said you found them this morning but suspect it happened last week?" Matt asked, no hint of confusion in his expression. He was keeping a tight lid on his thoughts in front of the strangers.

"Since working on the renovations on the front of the facility, we rarely go to the back." Ralph motioned out the window that showed the tall fence. "We've added security cameras and a gate code to the front and haven't had any issues of break-ins or vandalism since. The most trouble we get is someone trying to let their friends follow them in without reentering their gate code. And even then that's not a big deal. The only reason I went back there was to help my wife try to track down the owners of the legacy units or their kin. Before today, the last time I had to go into those units was last Tuesday."

"That's—what—about eight days between now and then?" Matt asked. "Why do you think it was done Wednesday?"

The mother and son duo shared a look.

Embarrassment.

"Because that's when we found the hole in the fence."

MAGGIE COULD BARELY contain herself. She bounced from foot to foot next to Matt as they stood in front of the new portion of the storage facility's perimeter fence.

"We didn't make a police report because I was afraid it would hurt business." Ralph rubbed the back of his neck, clearly uncomfortable with the choice he had made. "When I did a pass-through to see if anyone was around, there was no one and I didn't notice the locks had been broken. To be honest I didn't look that hard at first in the back since no one goes there. Again, it wasn't until my wife sent me after the legacy units that I saw the locks." He sighed. "I made sure to include that in my statement today with the police. We also ordered more security cameras for the few weak spots we realized we had." Matt glanced over at Maggie. Her eyes were wide, taking in the now-repaired fence.

The one she said she would have never climbed to break in. The one she said she would cut a hole in instead.

"Can we go see the legacy units now?" Matt asked.

"Sure thing."

Ralph started to walk away but Matt held back enough to grab Maggie's hand. She tore her eyes away from the fence.

"We still have questions," he said, voice low. "Not answers. Okay?"

It took her a second but then she nodded.

They followed Ralph. It wasn't lost on Matt that he held Maggie's hand longer than necessary. He also couldn't deny that if felt more right than he expected.

This case had been full of surprises, but Matt was starting to see it wasn't just the facts that were throwing him. It was Maggie herself.

Or, really, how he felt when she was around.

"This starts the lot of them," Ralph announced when they'd walked for a few minutes. It pulled Matt out of his head. "All legacy units are non-climate-controlled. The units on either side of the thirteen are empty. My brother is out getting new locks so, for now, they're open."

There were no clues outside the units that would lead them to any answers on why someone, possibly Maggie, would break all—or any, really—of the locks. The thirteen small units looked as normal as he would expect.

"Do you mind if we take a look inside them?"

Ralph shook his head.

"If these were normal units, I'd object, but seeing as no one has officially claimed them in years, have at it. Just please let me know if you want to take anything. Then we'll have to get into the details. I'm going to go check a few other empty units. Holler if you need me."

Ralph gave them space as Matt and Maggie started with the closest unit.

"Here we go," Matt said beneath his breath, becoming tense. Maggie gave him a quick smile. It actually helped.

HALF OF THE units were filled with boxes of odds and ends that had once meant something to someone. It felt eerie in a way to look at someone else's life, especially knowing that for whatever reason they hadn't come back to get or see about their things. Maggie tried to be respectful as they looked around each space, seeing if something jumped out at her. Nothing seemed disturbed and no memories surfaced for Maggie.

"Maybe this really wasn't you," Matt said when they were done looking in the eighth unit. "Maybe we've just been itching for a new lead so we fabricated this one."

He pulled an open box of trinkets closer to him. He peeked over the edge of the cardboard.

"There's too many coincidences," Maggie argued. She had to focus on not stomping out of the unit like some angry child. Her frustrations were starting to get the better of her.

Maybe Matt sensed that rising aggravation. He hung back as she went through the next unit. By the time she went to the twelfth, he had just gone into the tenth.

What if Matt was right?

What if they were creating more questions just because they couldn't find their answers?

It was a thought that almost cost Maggie the very thing she was looking for.

Unlike the other units, this one was less cluttered and more on the empty side. A few pieces of old furniture, a metal cabinet with a lock and boxes without labels lined the walls.

Maggie's attention zipped back to the lock. Her breath caught. It was the same type of lock that had been on the storage unit doors. But this one wasn't cut.

"Because you don't need to cut a lock when you have the key," she whispered to herself.

She took a step closer, trying to remember anything that would tell her what was in the cabinet, when a box next to it pulled her focus away.

And then trapped it.

"Oh, my God."

Maggie's heartbeat sped up like a racehorse out of the starting gate. Her hands nearly shook as she picked up the picture frame she couldn't take her eyes off or, rather, the picture in it.

"Did you say something?" Matt called out.

For the first time, Maggie felt like a fish out of water, gulping air while she tried to find the right words. At least the right way to say them.

They had finally found a lead. However, Maggie felt no joy in it. No excitement. Because, if she was right, there was a good chance that it was going to hurt the detective.

"Maggie?"

The concern in his voice only made her discovery that much more bittersweet, but she couldn't hide it forever.

"I did." She cleared her throat and spoke louder. "I found something."

Maggie turned toward the opening, ready to look at Matt Walker and tell him she was standing in his late wife's secret storage unit, when the calm breath she'd just claimed disappeared in a gasp.

Someone was standing in the walkway in front of the unit but it wasn't Matt. It wasn't even Ralph.

It was their mystery man.

He was smiling.

Though he could have been making faces and singing "Dixie," and Maggie wouldn't have cared. It was the gun he had pointed at her that made all the difference.

Chapter Seventeen

He was wearing clothes that were as average as they came, just as he had been the day he'd pummeled them with his truck. There were dark circles under his eyes and one heck of a bruise across his nose, but he seemed to be feeling better than they had been. Which probably meant he'd had his bullet wound in his shoulder doctored. He certainly didn't seem to have any issues holding the gun on her.

"Detective, I think it would be best if you put down your weapon. Or this time I'll do what the car crash didn't to Ms. Carson here."

Even though they were standing in two different storage units, concrete walls separating them, Maggie could imagine Matt's face as he realized their own personal nemesis was back. And had the upper hand again. The detective probably was as tense as she was, but sporting a more intimidating facial expression. Hard jaw, pursed lips, eyes a raging storm. While Maggie could barely keep the picture frame steady in her hands.

"I thought you said you don't kill women." Matt's voice was ice. The man's eyes stayed on him. The gun stayed on her.

"I did say that," he admitted. "But after the run-around this one has given me, I might reconsider if I don't get a win soon. So, please, drop your gun or I'll make sure her part in your investigating stops here."

Maggie wished the wall between them was gone. She wanted—no, *needed*—to see the detective. To know everything was going to be okay. To see those storm-cloud eyes and feel their power. Maybe it would make her feel less helpless. She glanced around the unit to see if there was anything she could use to defend herself. Or to attack.

"And what will you do with her if I follow your order?" Matt asked. "What stops you from shooting her now?"

The man actually grinned.

"Because I have a few questions only she can answer." His grin unhinged. His head tilted to the side like a dog hearing a foreign sound. Maggie didn't like the change. Or how fast it happened. "But you know, I can't really think of a reason for me to not shoot you."

Maggie took a small step forward. Her voice was louder than she thought was possible with the fear coursing through her.

"If you kill him then you'll not only have an entire county of law enforcement hunting you down, you'll have an entire *community* hunting you. And they won't stop until you're found."

The man glanced at her, the grin back. And just as sinister looking.

"You underestimate my power to disappear."

There was a clear point of pride in the way he said it. Maggie's stomach knotted.

"If you kill him," she started, slow but strong, "I'll fight until you have to kill me, too. Then I can't answer any of your questions."

The man didn't respond for a moment. Instead, he looked between them. Maggie wondered what Matt was thinking. Again, she wished the wall was gone.

"Oh, okay," he finally said. "I see. You two are a thing." He nodded in Matt's direction. "You're willing to die for her and she's willing to die for you. Looks like this investigation has been heating up while you two have been in hiding. How cute."

Maggie didn't have time to dwell on his words. All of his attention went back to Matt.

"So now we have another very real choice for you to make. You can put the gun down and let me take Ms. Carson here so we can have a little chat. Or you can not put it down and I'll just kill her and do what I do best and you'll never see me again or find out *any* truth whatsoever. Or, my new favorite option, I can just kill you now, which will force your girlfriend here to attack me until I kill her, too." The man laughed. "Now, if you ask me, the first option is the best bet, considering it's the only one where you both live. But I have to admit that while I might have known your wife, I don't know you, Detective. You might like having the women around you die." His lips pulled into a wider smile. It was downright sickening. "Everyone has their own secret kink after all. Maybe that's yours. Who am I to judge?"

The world around them disappeared. All Maggie could see and hear was a madman with a gun. It was like she was seeing him for the first time. He wasn't just a criminal, some unknown piece to a larger puzzle, he was the end game. Even without her memories, Maggie knew right then and there that she was looking at pure evil. Smiling like he was at the damn park or out with friends. Average looking in every physical detail while hiding a core dripping with evil. And she believed that evil.

Matt must have also believed it.

"Good choice, Detective," the man said, his eyes moving downward for a moment. Maggie heard metal hit concrete. He had dropped his gun. "Now, back up against the wall, Detective."

"Why?" Matt asked, voice still arctic.

"Don't worry, I'm just going to shut you in. I think it's time you took a time-out."

The man switched his aim from her to Matt and stepped out of view. The moment she heard the sound of the metal door shifting, Maggie made a split-second decision.

She ran.

Fast.

Moving out of the twelfth storage unit, she ran like there was no tomorrow to the corner of the building, only a few units away. It gave her just enough time to clear the corner before the man yelled.

"Stop!"

But Maggie wasn't going to stop. She wasn't going to let him use her against the detective anymore. Instead she was going to use the adrenaline coursing through her, dulling the pain and wounds she'd racked up over the last two weeks, and try to put as much distance between herself and the man.

If he really wanted her, then he was going to have to catch her first.

THE DOOR SLAMMED DOWN, sounding like a gunshot in the new night Matt found himself in.

"Stop!" the man yelled on the other side. For a moment Matt thought the man was talking to him. Confused, he paused to listen. Footsteps raced away. Two sets.

She ran, Matt thought, adrenaline rocketing through every inch of his body within seconds. He scooped up his gun and grabbed the bottom of the door. If he knew he had a clean shot at their perp, he would have taken it through the door. Instead, he held the gun ready and pulled the door up.

It rose an inch and stopped. Matt fell against it, confused. He readjusted and tried again. It stopped again. Hung on something.

A lock.

Their mystery man had come prepared.

Matt took a few steps back. The unit was bathed in darkness but that hadn't stopped him from taking stock of its contents when he'd first come in. There was nothing he could use to push the door off its tracks.

Nothing but himself.

He squared his shoulders, held his gun low and charged forward. The pain that shot through his body as he hit the aged metal, mingling with the soreness that was already there, meant nothing to Matt. The only detail he was focused on was the fact the door was still standing.

He backed up to the middle of the room and tried again.

The metal and his shoulder protested in sound and pain.

"You can do this," he said.

He took his spot back up again. He dropped his shoulder low, ready again, when a sound chilled him to the bone.

A gunshot.

He stepped back until he was touching the wall. Matt wasn't about to waste another breath on being in the storage unit. He ran at the old metal door, mind already on the layout of the outdoor units they'd passed coming in. Because he had no plans on staying in the dark anymore. Not when Maggie was out there.

His shoulder connected with the door. This time it didn't stop. The metal overhead buckled and then snapped off the tracks holding the top of the door in place. Matt fell forward, riding the door as it fell beneath him. Together they hit the ground in a loud tangle of metal, human and dirt. It wasn't a perfect kicking-the-door-down move but it got him out in the daylight. He scrambled to his feet, rolling off the door and pulling up his gun. He took a beat to listen. No one made a sound.

Matt ran around the building, toward the front. Toward where he thought the gunshot had gone off. The small road between each row of outdoor units was covered in dirt. Matt moved fast across it, slowing at corners but keeping his eyes on the ground. Three buildings over and he finally saw what he was looking for. Footprints, small footprints.

Maggie.

He followed them past a row of units to around the building's corner. There he froze. Matt wasn't just looking at dirt anymore. There was blood, too. A lot of it.

"No! *Matt!*"

Like a string was attached from her voice to every part of his body, Matt was propelled around the corner. The man was there. He had Maggie's hair by the ends, yanking her out of an open unit. There was blood caking her shirt.

"I'm not playing around anymore," the man yelled. "You're going to tell me *everything*!"

Maggie stumbled to her knees. It only agitated him even further. He put the muzzle of his gun to her temple.

"Stop right there," Matt boomed. He closed as much distance as he could before the man's attention switched to him. Maybe the sorry son of a bitch knew that Matt wasn't going to let him off the hook as easily as he had before. His confidence appeared shaken when he finally locked eyes with Matt.

"Why can't you let me take her?" he asked. "I told you that *I won't kill a woman*."

Matt planted his feet firm.

"But you said earlier you might," Matt reminded him. "And even if you won't, I bet you have friends who would." Matt took a tentative step forward. "I think it's time *you* put down the gun."

The man's focus scattered. He looked from Matt to his gun and then back to Matt. He was weighing his options. Judging by his widening eyes, he was realizing he didn't have many.

"If you take me in, you'll never know the truth about what happened to your wife," he said quickly. He shook his gun enough to make Maggie wince. Matt took another step forward in turn. "It's either her or the truth."

Matt didn't have to think about this choice. As much as he'd loved his wife, he'd accepted her death. He'd tried to move on. Just like she'd want him to do. And while he didn't want to lose the truth behind what had really happened, there was no way he was going to give up Maggie for it.

No, he would never sacrifice her.

Before Matt could let him know exactly what he thought about that choice, the man shook his head.

"Because I'm not going to jail, Detective," he said. "Not now. Not ever."

Matt believed him. So much so that his body reacted to the promise.

The promise of resistance.

When Matt spoke, he knew that one way or the other, it would be the last thing he said to the man.

"And she's not going with you."

The man's jaw hardened. His eyes narrowed. His brow creased. He swung his gun around, leaving Maggie in the clear, and tried to set his sights on his new target.

But Matt was faster.

His bullet found the man's chest.

It was all that was needed to take him down.

He hit the dirt. Hard.

Matt ran forward and kicked his gun away.

"Are you okay?" Matt asked, dropping down next to Maggie. Her eyes stayed on the man.

"He's trying to say something," she whispered.

Matt turned around. The man was looking at him, his mouth moving. They had to get closer to hear him.

"I t-told you," he whispered. "I—I don't kill women."

THE MAN DIED right then and there, in front of them both on the ground of Danny's Storage Facility. As far as last words went, his sounded movieworthy.

And unsettling.

Not that Maggie had the sanity to really think on

them. The detective was back on her within seconds of the man's last breath.

"Where are you hurt?" he asked. "Maggie! Where are you hurt?"

He grabbed at her shirt, trying to find the source of the blood. It shifted the cloth and its wetness to a dry spot of her skin. The contrast shocked Maggie back into action.

"It's not mine," she said, voice barely registering even to her own ears. She cleared her throat.

"What?" Matt continued to search her body. She took his hands before rocking up to her feet.

"The blood isn't mine."

Maggie turned on her heel and stumbled into the open storage unit. Ralph was propped up against a wall, at the end of his own blood trail, barely conscious.

"He was coming to check on us when I ran into him. He tried to find us a hiding spot and got shot. I dragged him in here."

Maggie sat down on the concrete next to the man. She applied pressure to the stomach wound and ignored how warm his blood was as it pushed through her fingers.

"It's going to be okay," Matt assured over her shoulder.

Ralph was barely hanging on but managed to ask about his mom as Matt stepped out to call in reinforcements.

Maggie put on a smile she hoped conveyed unyielding confidence.

"I'm sure she's fine. Just like you're going to be."

Maggie hoped she wasn't lying.

Chapter Eighteen

Ralph and his mother left in one ambulance together. She'd been ordered at gunpoint to open the gate but, thankfully, words were the extent of the gunman's attack. His focus had been resolutely on Maggie. And the contents of the locked cabinet. Neither of which he had been able to obtain in the end.

Maggie stood off to the side of the crime scene now being submerged in a constant wave of local PD and Riker County deputies. She watched as Matt was next to the gunman's body, talking to Detective Ansler. Without Matt she had no idea where she would be or if she'd even be alive. Their backup deputies had still been a few minutes out when Matt was finally able to call them in. That would have been a big enough gap for the man to take her away without anyone being able to follow.

The man might have said he never killed women, but the fact of the matter was that Erin Walker had been run over. As best as she could guess he had paid Ken Morrison to do it. In her book that meant he had no problem killing women, he just preferred outsourcing. Now with Ken and the man both dead Maggie was hoping for some peace. For all of them.

"How are you doing?" Maggie's heart jumped to her

throat. Sheriff Billy Reed immediately looked apologetic. "Sorry, I thought you heard me walk up."

Maggie took a deep breath and let it out.

"It's okay. I was just stuck in my own head," she admitted. "But I'm doing okay. Though I wish we had more answers."

The sheriff nodded.

"But at least we know a man willing to kill is now off the streets," he pointed out. "Even if we don't have all of the answers, that's enough to make me happy."

Maggie didn't skip a beat.

"But I need more. *We* need more."

Together they looked over at Matt. He was talking to Detective Ansler. His face was stone.

"He hasn't gotten the chance to look in the unit you were in earlier, has he?"

Maggie's gaze stayed on the detective in question. He'd chosen her over finally knowing the truth about his wife, unaware Maggie had already stumbled upon a new lead.

"No. We were focused on Ralph until the ambulance got here and then you guys showed up."

The sheriff surprised her with a small sigh. She glanced up at him. He looked tired.

"So he doesn't know that the unit you were in belonged to Erin yet."

Maggie shook her head.

"No," she confirmed. "He doesn't."

They were quiet for a few seconds. Maggie was reminded that Sheriff Reed wasn't just Matt's boss, but also his friend.

"He's not going to take it well," he finally said. "But maybe what's inside will give us answers we couldn't get from him."

Maggie looked back at the gunman. Dead. She felt no sympathy for him. He'd shot Ralph without provocation *or* hesitation.

"Are you going to tell him?" She angled her entire body in front of the sheriff, no longer able to bear the sight of the man's lifeless body a few yards away.

"To be honest, I think it should be you who does it," the sheriff said. "I feel like it would mean more."

That confused her.

"Mean more?"

He fixed her with a pointed stare.

"You never believed Erin's death was simple and were criticized for it. Still, you pressed on until the road dead-ended. Years later and, even with more to lose than before, you still never gave up." He gave her a small smile. "Going down the roads you two went down to find the truth, in my book, makes you like partners. And hard news, good or bad, comes easier from partners."

Maggie returned the smile, touched by the sheriff's gentle words. She didn't have to ask it and he didn't have to say it but Maggie felt like he had just apologized and forgiven her in one fell swoop. Where the sheriff saw redemption, the others in Riker County's Sheriff Department would, too. Eventually.

It made Maggie's heart feel lighter.

Finally, she'd risen from the actions she regretted taking five years ago. Or, at least, how she'd handled the beginning of looking into Erin's death. She never should have cornered Matt the way she had. Especially after the funeral. There had been better ways to go about it but Maggie had been single-minded, driven by an obsession and pushed by unhappiness in her own life at the time. Maybe now she could reform her relationship with the department and the detective himself.

Though when she met Matt's gaze after he was done talking to Ansler, she felt the weight of a different burden settle.

She left the sheriff's side and moved closer to Matt.

"Did our mystery man have the key on him by chance?" she started.

Matt nodded. He produced the key she'd hidden at the bottom of the hotel pool from his back pocket. It looked impossibly small in the plastic evidence bag it was in.

"It was the only item he had on him aside from a key to a stolen car out front."

"Good." She took a breath. "Because I need to show you something."

Matt didn't question her as she led him back to the twelfth legacy unit. She paused only long enough to look at the tenth's damage. The metal door was on the ground, bent awkwardly.

"Did you do that with your body?" she asked, surprised.

He nodded. No-nonsense.

"I had to get to you."

Maggie felt a butterfly dislodge in her stomach. It fluttered around, spreading warmth. She reached out and touched his hand.

But now wasn't the time to indulge in how Matt Walker made her feel.

Maggie left his side. She went for the picture frame she had dropped on the floor when she'd run earlier. Thankfully, it was still in one piece. She held it up to her chest but motioned to the locked cabinet.

"I think the key unlocks that."

Matt didn't need to be told twice. Still wearing the

gloves Detective Ansler had given him, he pulled the key out and put it into the lock. It came undone without any issues. Maggie took a step closer.

They remained silent as he handed her a worn notebook while he pulled out a stack of pictures and newspaper articles. Separately they examined their pieces of evidence before Maggie finally understood.

Which made things even harder.

"She was investigating him."

Matt looked up from the picture in his hands. Maggie recognized their gunman in the top one, younger but definitely still him.

"Who?"

Maggie put the notebook down and gently took the photos from his hand. She then handed him the picture frame.

"Erin," she answered. "Matt, I think this is Erin's storage unit. Which means she was investigating the man… And I think that's why she was killed."

Maggie had never seen him look so confused before. It pained her to see a man like him, one built up on confidence that rarely failed, looking so lost. That expression only became more pronounced when he looked at the picture between his hands.

It was of a young woman dressed in a graduation robe and smiling for all she was worth. Maggie might not have known the woman but there was no denying that it was Erin in the picture.

Once more Maggie touched his hand.

Then she left him alone with his thoughts.

ERIN WALKER HADN'T trusted the new janitor who had started working at the hospital. His name was Seth and whatever their initial meeting was, it inspired suspicion in her. Enough that she began to dig deeper into who he was. Which led to the list of three names Maggie had found in the woman's locker five years ago.

Joseph Randall, Jeremy Pickens and Nathan Smith.

How she had gotten from Seth to those men, Maggie didn't know by reading her notebook alone. However, she did understand the thread that wove all four men together.

Erin Walker had suspected that, not only had the hospital's new janitor assumed each man's identity, but he'd also killed them to get it. Joseph had been in his early thirties, Jeremy had been in his midthirties and Nathan had been forty. Each man resembled the next and, now that Maggie had met Seth in person, she couldn't deny how similar he looked to those men.

In her notes, Erin called him the chameleon killer.

Finding men who looked like him and causing their deaths to look like accidents. As hers had.

A chill ran up Maggie's spine at the moniker.

However, there was nothing concrete that proved Erin's suspicions, which made Maggie wonder if Seth had already taken care of that evidence or if Erin had still been looking for some when she'd died. When he'd probably realized what she was doing. Then he'd found a felon, Ken Morrison, and managed to get him to take Erin out of the equation completely.

But what had brought him out of hiding after all these years?

Matt opened the door as if he could hear her thoughts.

"Ralph is in surgery but the doctors are very optimistic," he said. "His wife, Emily, was calm enough to answer a few of the sheriff's questions about the twelfth unit after promising to keep us updated on Ralph's condition."

Matt settled into the driver's side of the patrol car they had driven over in. Maggie had been seated in the passenger's side for half an hour as Matt, Detective Ansler and Sheriff Reed had gone over every inch of the storage unit. He'd taken pictures of the pages in the notebook they'd found and given it to Maggie to look through while he finished up to see if she recognized or remembered anything. She hadn't. At least nothing they hadn't already figured out.

"The storage unit was under Erin's father's name," he started, turning over the engine and getting out of Park. Without the immediate danger of Seth he'd suggested they stop by her house to get cleaned up before picking Cody up from the hotel. Dried blood caked on her outfit wasn't the best accessory when greeting a young child. Or anyone, really. "Erin and her dad were never close and he passed away a few years before we got married. Almost everything in there is from when she was a kid with a few random pictures and memorabilia from her high school and college years thrown in. I don't think she used the unit often, if at all, except for what was in that locked cabinet." He navigated back to the main road and kept his eyes focused out the windshield. His jaw was tight. His entire body was tense. "After she passed away and the unit stopped being paid for, it fell into the legacy category. When Ralph's wife, Emily, started digging into who each of the units belonged to she couldn't remember Erin's name and called someone she thought might be able to help. Gabriel Thompson."

Maggie snapped her fingers.

"That's what changed," she exclaimed. "Gabriel

owns the *Kipsy City Chronicle*, the newspaper I used to work for. He knows everyone in the city, heck, the entire county. His family has been here for generations. He must have known Erin's father. When he got to Erin's name he called me?"

Matt nodded.

"Detective Ansler just got off the phone with him. He said that Emily left a message about the unit, hoping to find someone. He knew your history with Erin. He thought it might help bring you some closure for a case that made you lose your reputation. His words." He looked pained. Apologetic.

"It's okay," she assured him. "I made the choices I made and that's that. We can't change the way we handled the past. I'm happy with who I am now."

Matt kept his eyes forward. His sharp expression didn't lessen.

"Gabriel thought it might win you some points in my book if you were the one who gave me the news of a forgotten storage unit that might have things I'd want of Erin's. That was Wednesday morning." His fingers tightened around the steering wheel, turning white. "If I'd only listened to you that morning, then…"

Maggie reached out and, for the third time that day, placed her hand on one of his. This time, though, she didn't let go. Instead, she moved it to the middle console and held it there.

"You got him now," she said softly. "That's all that matters. Okay?"

He glanced down at their hands and then her face. He let out a short breath and nodded.

Maggie didn't let go of his hand.

"But I do wish I had a better idea of everything I

did that day. Like how did I get the key to the cabinet in the first place?" she asked. "And how did Seth hear about the storage unit anyway? Last Wednesday, without my memory, is still really confusing. Even if we know now that it started with a call from Gabriel, it doesn't explain why I broke into the storage facility, then took the key to the cabinet, went to a hotel room and hid the same key, and then at the end of the night, wound up at Dwayne Meyers's."

"That, I think I have a theory on," Matt said, coming to a stop at a red light. "Emily said a woman matching your description came in Wednesday morning and asked about the unit. You couldn't provide any ID showing you were related. They want to get rid of the legacy units but not without giving family who might be out there a fair shake first. She turned you away. So you took matters into your own hands and broke in." He gave her a sly smile. It was nice to see him smiling. Even though she'd had to break a law to get it. "The brand of lock that was used on the cabinet usually comes with a set of two identical keys."

"You think Erin left one of the keys *in* the storage unit."

Matt nodded.

"She didn't want me to know about the unit, so what better place to keep the copy safe?"

There wasn't any bitterness in the detective's tone but there was definitely a sadness there. A question. One he wanted to ask someone he couldn't. One Maggie couldn't answer.

While Erin's notes had given them answers, one she never wrote down was why she didn't tell her husband what she'd found. Maggie knew that question would weigh heavily on the man for a long, long time.

"So let's say I found the notes, decided to keep them in the unit because they've been safe there for years, and then what? I went back to my house then freaked out because Seth followed me? And who did I meet in the hotel?"

Maggie let out a long, long breath and dropped her head. It brought the blood on her blouse back into view. She let go of his hand. They didn't talk for a while.

Chapter Nineteen

Thanks to the Riker County Sheriff's Department, Maggie's front windows had been replaced and the inside of the living room cleaned. Matt looked out through the windshield and couldn't tell that anything had even happened. Let alone a madman had tried his best to scare Maggie away with the old brick-through-the-window trick.

Seth.

That had been his name. Or at least his current one. If what Erin had suspected was true—a fact that Detective Ansler had jumped on as soon as he'd shown him and the sheriff the contents of the cabinet—then Seth might have been the last man the chameleon killer had killed. And he had just been walking around pretending to be someone he wasn't.

Matt leaned back in the seat, making no move to get out of the car.

There was just something so surreal about feeling lost while knowing exactly where you were. Matt stared out the window but was now as blind as a bat to everything past the hood. Instead, he was cycling through memory after memory of his marriage.

Of Erin.

Looking beyond the pain of knowing she'd been intentionally killed to examining everything he thought he knew before any of that had ever happened. Trying to find the cracks in their marriage that he'd missed. The cracks his wife had fallen into while his attention had been on his job. The cracks that had created a cliff she'd been pushed off by a madman.

In hindsight it all made him feel like a fool.

And an even worse husband.

Why had she taken it upon herself to investigate Seth? Why not come to him?

"Matt."

Maggie's voice was becoming a normal part of his days, but the concern in the way she said his name was enough to break his trance. But not the lingering emotions attached.

He was mad, angry at himself and ashamed of what he hadn't seen all those years ago. What he hadn't done.

And what he had.

Looking into the green, green eyes of the woman who had fought harder than he had to solve his wife's murder. He'd been angry at her for such a long time and now he knew exactly why.

"Maggie, I was never really mad. Not at you."

Her eyebrow arched up in question.

"Back then, after Erin passed. I wasn't mad at you. I was mad at myself. I thought of a thousand different scenarios of how I could have saved her had I done *something* different that day. But in none of them did I think I could have changed her fate. Changed her being there when she was. Changed what happened. And because of that, I felt helpless. I thought that maybe that meant she was supposed to die there regardless of anything I did or could have done. That it was fate." Matt felt the hole he'd pretended didn't exist start opening up. That darkness he'd tried to ignore for years.

"That's a kind of helplessness that destroys someone. One I knew I couldn't live with. So I tried to move on. I tried to put it all behind me. Pretended to accept that my wife had died alone on a sidewalk," he continued. "But then there you were, accusing me of having something to do with her death and then asking questions I should have been asking myself. And it made me mad. *Angry*. But it wasn't just at you, it was at myself, too." He paused, searching for the words he'd never said out loud. "I didn't want to listen to you then because I didn't think I could handle what it would do to me if you had been right. If her death hadn't been an accident. I've seen good men and women become obsessed, losing themselves in cases that, more often than not, lead nowhere. The closer you are to what's happened, the more you can't see the damage it does to you. To the soul. And I—I didn't want to lose what little I had left in my life, my job included. It grounded me. It gave me purpose when I didn't even want to get out of bed in the morning." He gave her the smallest of smiles, comforting himself by explaining it to her. To Maggie. To the woman who had been fearless at his side. "They say people grieve in different ways. Trying to pretend I had healed was mine."

Maggie's expression softened, but he wasn't done yet. What they'd found in that storage unit had shaken him. He needed to get it out.

"But how did I think I could be a good husband in death if I wasn't in life? How did I not know about everything we just found?" He hit the steering wheel, more anger spilling over. Or, really, self-loathing. "How could I have not known my *wife* was tracking a serial killer? How could I have missed that? Tell me, how does a good husband lose that much perspective about his partner that I wasn't even suspicious of what she was doing? Tell me, Maggie, how?"

Maggie answered by opening her car door and getting out. For a moment he thought she was going to leave him, go into the house, done with his outburst. But then, she curved around the hood and came up to his door, opening it wide.

"Step out," she ordered.

He listened, though there was hesitation.

Maggie reached out and took his hands in both of hers, planting herself firmly in front of him. Her face was open but hard. Stern. Then she spoke with words that were sharp, cutting and very clear.

"You want to know why you, the no-doubt good husband, didn't know what Erin was up to?" She squeezed his hands. He couldn't look away from her. He was locked in. "It's because your wife didn't want you to know," she said. "And so you didn't."

It was a simple explanation that, he realized now, compounded an entire side of his wife's life that he never knew existed. And somehow, the way Maggie said it, or maybe the way she looked at him now with those big, true green eyes, that it was enough of an explanation. Still, she sweetened the pot of her argument. Her words were softer but still just as clear.

"Wives. Husbands. Detectives. Reporters. We're all just people in the end. People who make decisions. Erin made them, I made them and now you have a decision to make."

"I do?"

She nodded.

"You can beat yourself up for the rest of your days, doubting yourself, or you can take a breath and move on. Happy with the fact that you helped get a crazy man off the streets." She smiled. "And saved a crazy woman in the process. More than once. Now, I'm going to go inside and clean up. Come in when you've made your decision."

Maggie didn't wait for his response. She took out her house keys and started to open the door.

Despite himself, Matt smiled.

"Erin would have liked you," he called.

Maggie paused in the doorway, long enough to respond.

"I think I would have liked her, too."

MAGGIE WAS FEELING GOOD.

While they didn't have all the details, they'd still managed to stop Seth. She had the utmost confidence the sheriff's department could fill in any holes that remained. Eventually. Until then she was relieved that the target was off her, and her son's, backs, grateful to be able to help finish Erin's investigation, and happy that the detective had finally opened up to her. However, that feeling of everything starting to look up didn't last past her shower.

She sat down on her bed, wrapped in a towel, and caught a glimpse of the blouse she'd stripped out of on the floor. The dark crimson that stained most of it was dry but she still felt its wetness against her skin. She looked down at her hands, remembering how Ralph's blood had covered them. How he'd cried out when she pressed down on the wound. How he'd been barely hanging on to consciousness and still made sure to ask about his mother, worried she'd been hurt.

Maggie slapped a hand over her mouth as a cry escaped her throat. Her vision blurred. She thought about the car crash, the way Matt hadn't moved, lying against crushed metal and broken glass, and how Seth had dragged her away with no idea what would happen next.

Then all Maggie could think about was the blood on Seth's chest—and his lifeless body.

Maggie hung her head, burying her face in her hands.

The weight of everything had finally become too heavy. No amount of humor or sarcasm could hold it back.

Another sob racked her body; tears began to drench her hands; images she wished she could forget filled her mind.

She didn't even hear when Matt called out to her from the other side of the door. This was her breakdown. This was the price she had to pay to process the danger and fear she'd experienced in the past two weeks.

"It's okay. Let it out."

The bed next to her sank lower.

Maggie didn't look up as two strong arms wrapped around her. She felt embarrassed. Dealing with danger and death was part of Matt's job. She bet he'd never broken down. Not like this.

That embarrassment escalated as Matt turned her into his chest. Yet it somehow felt right. He just was there.

What felt like hours, but had to be only minutes, went by. Maggie slowly disentangled from the man. She hung her head and used her towel to wipe at her face. If there had been a mirror in front of them she was sure she wouldn't like her reflection. Swollen, red eyes plus cuts and bruising from the past week without an inch of makeup to lessen the marks.

"Sorry," she tried, voice cracking. Maggie cleared her throat and tried again. "It just finally caught up to me. Everything, you know?"

"I know."

Matt pulled away. It made her exposed skin, not covered by the towel, feel cold. Maggie looked up, not liking the contrast in feeling. Matt's gaze was already on her. His eyes locked within hers.

Suddenly, Maggie was acutely aware of several things.

Matt wasn't just *close*, he was touching her. His jeans rubbed against her bare thigh where the towel had ridden up. Which made the fact that the only thing keeping all of her from all of him was the cloth of her towel and the thin fabric of his clothes. Then there was the heat. Beneath her skin yet crawling over every inch. All within seconds. Starting below her waist and yet seemingly always there. Maggie couldn't help herself. Her eyes traveled down to his lips.

The world around them quieted to an impossibly loud silence.

"Maggie."

Her name had never sounded so good. Or different. All her life she'd heard it. From her mother, her teachers and colleagues, friends and even her ex-husband. But the way Matt pronounced those two syllables in that moment was like hearing it for the first time.

Her chest started to rise and fall faster. It was like

the air in the room had gone. Or maybe she was just trying to breathe in something else.

Someone else.

She met those eyes, those blue, blue eyes, and knew she was on the brink of everything changing. That nothing would be the same if she could just...

"Maggie." His voice was filled with grit.

It wasn't him repeating himself. No, it was different. It felt different. Like he was fighting her. Fighting himself. Fighting something.

He moved his hand, slow and precise, up to the side of her face. The tips of his fingers skimmed her jaw, his thumb brushing along her cheek. She leaned into his palm until his fingers found the back of her neck, his thumb stopping beneath her ear. He rubbed against her skin in an excruciatingly slow circle.

Maggie felt like she had just run a marathon. Her breath becoming harder to catch after every second that passed. She bit her lip to keep from trying to fill the silence. If remaining quiet prolonged Matt Walker touching her the way he was—*looking* at her the way he was—then she'd gladly never say another word.

Though she wasn't the one who broke that silence.

Matt leaned in, just as slow as his hand had cupped her cheek, until their foreheads were touching. She stayed locked in his gaze, his eyes never leaving hers for even a second, and almost moaned as his hand slid back across her cheek. This time his fingers tucked beneath her chin. His thumb, however, had its own agenda. It ran across her top lip, stopping at the edge until she let go of her bottom. She parted her lips as he traced both of them.

How could she ever breathe after this?

"Maggie?"

She heard the question. It was the reason she allowed herself to answer.

"Yes?"

She barely heard her own voice.

"Thank you."

Maggie was almost completely submerged in desire for the man touching her that she nearly decided to just accept his words, no questions asked. But desire, lust and even something stronger than the two—deeper than the two—aside, Maggie was still Maggie. Curious to the ends of the earth. She had to know why, out of everything he could have and could not have said, he chose *those* two words.

"What for?" she whispered.

He licked his lips. When he spoke Maggie felt pleasure in every part of who she was.

"For waking me up."

His lips turned up into a smile that she knew was real.

Then he wasn't smiling anymore.

He was kissing her.

And God, it felt good.

Maggie moaned as his lips went hard and fast against hers. No longer was it time to take things slow.

They both turned into each other. She let Matt take the lead. His hands went from her neck to her hair to pushing her gently onto her back. She'd been so focused on pulling him closer Maggie forgot about the very towel she'd been so aware of minutes ago.

It parted like the Red Sea as she moved. Cold air pressed against her exposed breasts.

Matt broke the kiss and gave her a look she could

only describe as unsure. It was endearing. So much so that Maggie found herself smiling.

"What?" he asked, propped up on his elbows, inches away from her bare skin.

Maggie couldn't help but laugh.

"It's just unfair." She glanced down at herself. "I showed you mine…"

That look of uncertainty the detective had been harboring evolved into a mischievousness she had always guessed was beneath his intense, cop-like surface. His lips quirked up into a smirk that simply smoldered. He dropped down, ran his lips against hers and then sat up.

"So it's only fair I show you mine, right?"

It was a question but he was already answering it. His boots thudded to the floor and his shirt found its way across the room. Maggie's heartbeat galloped at the sight of the man over her. Like a statue. She saw no flaws in him.

When he got to the button of his jeans, Maggie reached out and grabbed his hand.

"Let me help with that one, Detective."

Matt's eyes widened and then that smirk heated up.

"Yes, ma'am."

Chapter Twenty

Matt hadn't expected to kiss Maggie Carson. He wasn't going to lie, the thought had crossed his mind, but he hadn't thought he'd act on it. At least not *that* day. He hadn't even thought he would go inside her bedroom.

But then he'd heard her cry out.

Nothing could have stopped him from trying to comfort her—to ease the jarring reality she'd witnessed in the past few days—some way. Somehow.

Kissing her?

Not what he had expected.

Not that he was complaining.

Lying naked in Maggie Carson's bed, arms wrapped around the equally naked Maggie Carson herself, and there was no bad feelings for what they'd just done. And definitely no denying how good the two of them had been at the choice they'd just made.

"Well, that wasn't how I expected to get Matt Walker in my bed."

Matt chuckled into her hair.

"You always have to say something, don't you?"

Maggie moved her head back to look at him. He liked how good it felt having his arm hang over her hip, protective, with her bare skin against his.

"These are two things we've already said," she pointed out, grinning. "Does that mean we're beginning to be predictable?"

Matt couldn't help but laugh again.

"I think what we just did was anything but predictable."

She shrugged. Matt felt the movement against his body.

"Does that make it a good thing?" she asked.

"It definitely doesn't make it a bad thing."

Maggie smiled. She opened her mouth to say something else when Matt's phone started to go off. They shared a look.

"I'm putting my money on that being the sheriff," she said, moving out from under his arm. "Which means I'm going to step into the bathroom while you take that call."

Maggie slipped into the bathroom while Matt dashed across the room to his jeans. A wild, giddy feeling took over him. Like he was a teenager caught doing something he wasn't supposed to be doing. It made him smile. The first genuine smile he'd had in a long time. One that grew when he saw the call *was* from the sheriff.

"What's up, Billy?"

The sheriff didn't waste any time.

"I know I told you to take some time to get things back to normal…" Matt glanced at the bathroom door he'd just watched a naked Maggie run through. He didn't know if their being together was what Billy meant when he'd said *normal*. "But I thought this might help. All three of our cars are back in working order thanks to two very hardworking and fast mechanics in Kipsy."

"So the Bronco lives?" Matt asked, his day getting even better. Everyone knew that the Bronco had been Billy's late father's personal car and that Billy had loved his father dearly.

"Oh, ye of little faith," the sheriff responded with a laugh. "You can't kill the Bronco that easily."

"Glad to hear it!"

Matt moved around the room, collecting and putting his clothes on while getting into the more serious details of what happened next. Billy still insisted that Matt take a few days off to really rest, and his last task would be to bring Maggie to the hotel where both of their cars were being delivered.

"You're probably ready to sleep back in your own bed instead of being cooped up in a hotel," Billy commented before they ended the call. Matt agreed but didn't feel the relief he thought he would. While hotel living had never been on his to-do list, he had to admit he'd gotten used to seeing Maggie and Cody throughout the day. Eating with them, walking around with Cody and watching a game show or two with Maggie after Cody had fallen asleep.

The case might have been dangerous but it had also been an excuse. One that forced them together.

One that they didn't have anymore.

Matt finished dressing and relayed what the sheriff had said as the two of them made their way back to the car. If Maggie had any concerns about leaving the hotel for good, she didn't voice them. Instead, she kept the conversation light. She answered Matt's question about her job and, by the time he was parking outside the hotel, they were talking about a camping trip Cody's school was taking in a few months. Neither spoke of what they'd done, or what it meant for them now.

It didn't bother Matt. Not at first. He took one last walk with Cody around the hotel while Maggie packed their things. Then he threw his belongings in his bag and thanked Caleb again. But when he was standing in the parking lot, in front of both of their cars, Matt didn't like how final it felt.

"Well, Detective, I guess it's time to go," she said, twirling her keys in her hand.

Matt nodded.

"I guess it is."

The two of them stood there, quiet for a moment. Matt was reminded again of feeling like a teenager. This time an awkward one.

"All right, well, I'll see you later, then," Maggie said, finally breaking the silence. "Stay safe, Detective."

She gave him a small nod and turned away.

Matt watched her go.

But couldn't let her leave.

"Hey, Maggie?" he called.

She paused in the doorway of her car.

"Yeah?"

"I promised Cody that I'd still go exploring with him after all of this was over," he said. "And Billy says there's this park near here that has some really good trails." He smiled. "Maybe we can explore them sometime. You know, the three of us."

Cody was the one who answered.

"Yeah! Say yes, Mom," he yelled through the open door.

Maggie laughed.

"Well, I'd hate to make you break your promise."

She flashed him a smile. It was warm. "I guess I really will see you later, Matt."

"Yes, ma'am."

He watched as she drove off and then did the same.

It wasn't until he was out of the shower in his own house that his phone rang again. This time he didn't recognize the number.

"Hello?"

"Hi, is this Detective Walker?" It was a woman's voice, one he recognized but couldn't place.

"This is he."

"I don't know if you remember me but my name is Kortnie Bean. I'm a nurse at the Kipsy ER."

Matt pictured the red-haired woman with ease.

"The nurse who talked with Maggie *both* times we were there," he filled in.

"Yeah, that's me! And she's actually why I'm calling."

Matt's body tensed; his back straightened.

"What's wrong?" he asked, already eyeing his shoes across the room.

"Oh! No! Nothing," she replied. "At least I don't think so. See, I just worked on a man who came in with a gunshot wound and his mother mentioned that Maggie was with him when he was shot. She said she thought Maggie was okay but, well, with her track record, I thought I'd check in. I know you two have been together a lot and assumed you'd know for sure if she *was* okay."

Matt's body loosened.

"That's nice of you," he said, honest. "I'm sure Maggie will appreciate it, too. But yeah, she's fine. A little shaken up but this time no injuries."

"Good! I didn't like the routine the three of us were making in here," she said with a laugh.

"I'm right there with you, but that should be over with now. Hopefully no more hospital visits for a long time."

"So I'm assuming that means y'all caught your perp. That's great," she exclaimed. "That plus your friend waking up, and you must be on cloud nine right about now."

Matt paused.

"My friend?"

"Yeah, the man you rode in with last week? The one who was assaulted along with Maggie?"

"He's up?"

Matt grabbed his shoes.

"Yeah. A few hours ago! I heard he was lucid as could be. It's a miracle, really!"

Matt couldn't help but smile.

"This day just keeps getting better."

"KEEP LOOKING!"

Maggie dived into the cushions while Cody got on his stomach to look underneath the couch.

"I see it," he yelled. "I can't reach it!"

Maggie dropped to her stomach, moving through the new soreness that made her think of the detective— no matter how pleasant it was—and extended her arm until her fingers wrapped around the cordless phone. While she preferred her cell phone, her mother had always made the point that landlines still came in handy. Which was true, considering Maggie hadn't been able to replace her lost cell phone yet.

"Carson residence," she answered, rolling onto her

back. She trapped Cody beneath her in the process. He erupted in giggles.

"Hey, Maggie, this is Dwayne Meyers."

Maggie sat up, excited.

"Oh, my God, Dwayne! How are you? I had no idea you'd woken up!"

The man chuckled. It sounded familiar and foreign all at the same time. Years ago she'd asked the then detective about any connections he might know between Erin and Ken Morrison. He'd been nicer than most of the people she'd talked to but still, she hadn't been friends with the man. The last time she remembered talking to him had been in passing at a local football game. Then again, they knew for a fact she'd been at his house the week before. She'd been afraid she wouldn't get the chance to ask him why.

"I've actually been up since yesterday but the doctors didn't want to say anything until they had a better handle on my condition."

"And how is your condition?"

"Right as rain," he said, smile clear in his voice. "Just a little bruised and sore but nothing sleeping in my own bed won't cure."

That caught Maggie off guard.

"Wait? They're letting you go?" She wasn't a doctor but she doubted letting a patient who had been in a coma go home one day after he woke up was the best move.

"I'm actually already at home." He continued before she could express her concern. "To be honest, it took some pretty intense persuasion but at the end of the day the doctor admitted I was in good condition. He called it a miracle."

Maggie nodded to herself.

"It sure sounds like it," she admitted. "Have you talked to Matt already? I know he was really worried about you."

"I did. In fact that's why I called. The sheriff told me about what happened, you know, with your memory and I'm officially offering to fill in the blanks for you."

Maggie's heartbeat started to speed up.

"The blanks? You mean why I was at your house that night?"

"Not only that but before we got attacked, you told me everything. Everything you did that day."

Relief and excitement mixed together into an intoxicating cocktail. She turned and gave Cody a wide smile. He returned it.

"That's wonderful!"

"But if you wouldn't mind, I think it would be easier if we did this in person," he said. "I already got Matt and the sheriff on the way over. Do you mind coming out here?"

Maggie nodded profusely, already standing.

"I'd love that!" She held her hand out to Cody and then pulled him up. "I might be a bit, though. I need to get a sitter for my son."

Again she heard Dwayne's smile through the phone.

"I'm okay if you bring him out here," he said. "I have cable to entertain him while we all talk."

"Sounds great! We'll leave now!"

Maggie ended the call and looked at her son.

"Where are we going, Mom?" he asked.

"We're finally going to get the rest of the answers."

MAGGIE AND CODY sang to the radio all the way to Dwayne's. Neither knew all the words to any of the songs and, if she was being honest, they both could use some lessons. However, Maggie was finally feeling a weight lift at the realization she'd know what she'd done the week before. It made her happy. A feeling she was already experiencing thanks to a certain detective. Cody must have picked up on her mood. He mimicked the excitement all the way until she cut the engine outside Dwayne's house.

"Now, you make sure you behave while we're here," she said, helping him out and holding his hand. "We have some adult stuff to talk about that's important to me and Matt and the sheriff."

"Matt's going to be here?"

Maggie didn't miss the extra infusion of excitement at the mention of his name. Another point of endearment for the man she'd finally opened herself up to.

"Yes, sir! It looks like we beat him, though, so you're going to have to entertain yourself with the TV while I talk to Mr. Meyers, okay?"

"Kinda like I'm on a case?"

Maggie laughed. There was no mystery where that talk had come from. Or who.

"Yeah, kind of like you're on a case."

Cody nodded, serious. But then he lowered his voice. "Who is Mr. Meyers?"

Maggie opened the screened-in porch's door. She dropped Cody's hand to keep it from falling over. Someone had knocked it off its hinges.

Seth.

It reminded her that while she wanted answers, she'd forgotten the shape that Dwayne must have been in. How he looked. And how that might scare her son.

Maggie paused before knocking on the front door. She bent down and looked Cody in the eyes.

"I want you to know that Mr. Meyers might not look that great right now," she started, trying to choose her words carefully. "He got hurt recently and probably has a lot of bruises and cuts, but he's okay now. He just looks worse than he is."

Cody's innocent eyes widened.

"How did he get hurt?"

Maggie had always tried to tell the truth to her son and so she made no exception here.

"A bad man was angry at him."

"And he hurt him?"

"Yes, but the bad man is gone now. He won't hurt him or anyone else again. Okay?"

Cody nodded. Maggie kissed his forehead and stood tall again. She ruffled his hair and turned toward the front door.

"But why did he hurt him?" Cody asked.

Maggie froze, fist in midair.

"What?"

"Why did the bad man hurt Mr. Meyers?" he repeated.

Maggie opened her mouth but no answer came out.

She didn't have one.

Why *had* Seth beaten Dwayne?

She knew that Seth didn't kill women but why hadn't he killed Dwayne? Beating him to a pulp with a bat still riled up local law enforcement so why hadn't he just finished the job?

And why had she been at Dwayne's to begin with?

A sinking, sick feeling began to fill her stomach.

Maggie took a step back from the door as the one

lone detail from the week before filtered in. It wasn't a memory but it was a fact.

"Oh, God."

Maggie grabbed Cody's hand again and spun around. She pulled him along with her so hard that he stumbled. She didn't have time to explain to him why they were leaving when they'd just gotten there.

They just needed to leave.

Now.

Because Maggie knew without a doubt that Seth hadn't used the bat on Dwayne.

She had.

Which meant they hadn't been invited over for the truth. He'd invited her over to silence it. And she'd been stupid enough to fall for it and, worse, bring her son.

Maggie fumbled with her keys, her hands already shaking from the new dose of adrenaline raging through her.

But for the third time in one week, someone had a different plan for her.

She heard the footsteps too late.

The last thing she remembered before everything went black was Cody screaming.

Chapter Twenty-One

Light.

Bright, blinding light.

Maggie tried to blink it away. When that didn't work she tried to bring her hand up to shield her eyes. The movement almost made her sick. Not only from pain but from fear.

Because she couldn't move much at all and she couldn't understand why.

"And here I thought you weren't going to wake up."

Maggie blinked again until her focus finally adjusted. She was sitting on a bed, legs stretched out in front of her. She could move them but barely. Duct tape was wrapped around them, making her feel like she was in a cocoon. Her hands weren't better off. The unmistakable coldness of cuffs pressed against her wrists.

Those details alone would have put her in a panic but the way Dwayne Meyers was smiling at her, sitting in a chair in the corner, turned her body to ice.

"Where's Cody?" she rasped out.

How long had she been unconscious?

"Don't worry, he's in the guest bedroom watching TV. It was the only thing that would stop him from whining." There was such disgust in his words that Maggie panicked.

"Cody?" she yelled out. "Cody?"

"Mom!"

It was faint but he was definitely in the house.

"Are you hurt?" she asked, looking away from Dwayne's obvious annoyance.

"No," Cody answered. "I'm scared!"

Maggie's heart threatened to break in half at his words.

"Everything's going to be okay," she tried.

Dwayne let out a too-loud sigh. He leaned forward so his elbows rested on his knees.

"Now tell him if he doesn't keep quiet, I'm going to kill you in front of him," he said. "You don't have to say that verbatim but I suggest you run that point home." His words were less words and more of a hiss. A dark, evil hiss. One Maggie believed.

"Hey, little dude, I'm going to need you to be really quiet right now," Maggie said. Her voice wavered but she powered through. "So don't say anything else until I come in there, okay?"

"Okay," he answered. It was small. Scared.

The cold that permeated Maggie's body heated in anger at the sound. She turned her gaze back to the man who held the forgotten pieces of her memory.

She'd seen the pictures of Dwayne on the floor, bloody and unconscious, but it was nothing like sitting in front of the real thing. Bruises, dark and bright and varying shades between, covered his face, arms and neck. His nose had been broken and sat at an odd angle. He was still in pain. A lot of it.

That much she could tell for certain.

Which only added to the anger he seemed to have for her.

"You're admiring your handiwork right now, aren't you?" he asked, motioning to his face. The bruises there were the darkest. "You sure caught me by surprise when you decided to use me as batting practice. I didn't expect you to have any fight in you past your sarcastic comments."

Maggie took a small breath, trying to calm her racing heart. She needed to stay focused. Stay alert.

"I don't remember doing it," she said. "I don't remember last Wednesday at all."

The man snorted. Even that small bit of movement seemed to hurt him.

"That's what I heard. Apparently, Seth hit you a little too hard." He smiled. If you could even call it that. "Or not hard enough, if you ask me. The damned fool always did have a soft spot for women. I heard what happened to him, too. Can't say I'm sorry about it. Just another no-good killer off the streets."

That earned a few words from Maggie.

"And what are you?" she asked. "Are you a killer, Dwayne?"

He eased back in his chair, his smile sharpening.

"You really *don't* remember anything, do you?" He didn't wait for her to answer. "You couldn't let the truth go and then it let you go. How much fun is that?" He repositioned himself again, like he was trying to get comfortable. Maggie couldn't imagine that he could, given his injuries.

The injuries *she* had inflicted on him.

"You know you're a lot like her in that respect," he continued. "Erin, I mean. She also couldn't stop digging—couldn't let the truth go—and look where that got her. Dead on the side of the road."

"It was you," Maggie guessed. Dwayne didn't just have the missing piece, he *was* the missing piece. "Erin saw you in the truck before you went after her. She was waving at you."

Dwayne laughed. It was crude and cold and felt wrong in every fiber of her body to even hear.

"Which is what you figured out last week," he said. "In fact, we've already had this conversation. So let me skip ahead to answer a few more of your questions. It was me who was driving Ken's truck that night. It was me who ran her over. And it was me who framed drugged-out-of-his-mind Ken. Then I just walked away."

Maggie couldn't stop a small gasp from coming out. Picturing Erin's body lying in the street like some forgotten rag doll. He talked about killing her like she had been nothing more than a piece of debris that had fallen out of some truck's bed. And then he'd just walked away.

"You didn't look so surprised the last time I told you this," he continued. "But I guess this time you found a different set of clues. To be honest, I thought I'd gotten rid of all of Erin's evidence into Seth."

"So she figured out you were helping Seth, tried to take you both down, and you killed her for it."

"Oh, on the contrary, I didn't even know who Seth was until Erin came along."

"I don't understand."

Dwayne's smirk was back in full force.

"Erin was a very *singular* woman. She had this sixth sense about people. I swear, if you had a secret, she could sniff it out just from a few minutes of talking to you. So when Seth started working at the hospital, she started to suspect he wasn't who he said he was. It probably didn't help that he was a grade-A idiot when it came to keeping all of his identities in order. I mean, sure, the first two times he was okay but by the time he became Seth he was having some issues keeping all his lies straight." He shrugged, dismissive. Like it was no big deal he was talking about a serial killer taking people's lives and then *living* them. "Either way Erin asked to meet me one night in private. Matt was in the middle of helping with some stressful cases at the department, the kind that kept him up all night, and was strung out and sliced thin, and she said she didn't want to add to his stress until she had proof. Concrete proof. She was like that. Always worried about people worrying but also unable to let go of things she had no business grabbing in the first place. So she told me what she knew about the man and I told her I'd look into it."

Dwayne paused and cracked his neck. Although his tone was calm, Maggie could feel the mounting anger behind his words.

"And I did. I looked into it and went straight to the source. I cornered that weasel after one of his shifts and asked him everything I could. And by God if he didn't crack. Laid out the whole truth right at my feet." He chuckled. "I remember thinking, 'How can this guy, this little idiot of a man, pull off what he's been pulling off for almost a decade?' So I asked him. You couldn't find a more surprised man than me in that room all those years ago when he started talking about how he'd been living off his old identities' accounts, sucking them dry and then moving on." He rubbed the stubble on his chin. "He even showed me on his phone all the money he had earned being Seth. The man was nearly a self-made millionaire just by hacking and killing nobodies." Dwayne's nostrils flared. His lips thinned. His smirk long gone. He tapped his chest with his index finger. "When I'd been breaking my back for the department for years and barely getting by?" He shook his head. "No. Not me. Not anymore. Not then, not now, not ever again."

"He bribed you to keep quiet," Maggie whispered. She felt sick.

"No, ma'am," he was quick to respond. "I *took* what I was due from someone who found a way around the system. He didn't fight me and I didn't rat him out. We had an understanding."

"The only problem was Erin."

Maggie hated saying the words but knew them to be true. The reason she'd lost her life hadn't just been Seth's self-preservation. It had also been because of Dwayne's greed.

"She hadn't told anyone else and I already had what I thought was all of the evidence she'd collected. Plus, Seth was too weak to shut her up. So I did what had to be done." His anger ebbed. Maggie's stomach rolled when she recognized pride starting to bolster the man up. "I waited a few months, making sure *you* stayed in your lane and didn't find anything out, and then I retired. Easy as pie."

"How could you do that to Matt?" Maggie had to ask. "He looked up to you and still does. You're his mentor. His friend. How could you hurt him like that?"

"Listen, I still care about that boy," he said, hands up in defense. "Hell, I'm even going to feel bad about what I'm sure I'm going to have to do to him when I'm done with you, but back then? I wasn't about to let his nosy wife stop me from taking an opportunity I sorely deserved."

Maggie listened to every word he said but was still stuck on one part.

When I'm done with you.

It made the fear and anger in her chest turn to panic. Not for her but for her son.

And for Matt.

"He'll come for you. Matt will. He'll come for me and my son." Tears started to prick the edges of Maggie's eyes. Still, she persevered. "And when he comes, he'll bring hell to your doorstep for what you've done."

Dwayne didn't waste a breath.

He smiled.

"I'm counting on it."

MATT WASN'T SEEING RED. He was seeing blood.

After his call with Kortnie he'd barely made it out of his driveway before another call had come in. It hadn't been a good one. Apparently, Dwayne hadn't just woken up. He'd left the hospital, but not until he'd shot two people and killed a cop in the process.

Matt had called Maggie before he'd even processed the shock of the news. When she hadn't answered, he'd called in Deputy Carrington, who lived across the street from Maggie.

She wasn't home.

The house was empty.

Matt realized then that he already knew where she might be. Dwayne had played them. Something Matt guessed Maggie had figured out before she'd lost her memory. Which meant that Dwayne either thought he had a loose end to take care of before he bolted, or he wanted something else. Something more simplistic.

Revenge.

Matt slammed his hands against the steering wheel.

He couldn't pretend to know or guess at Dwayne Meyers's state of mind anymore. The man had been his mentor. That mentor had just shot a civilian and then killed a good cop. Which meant he was more than capable of killing a good woman.

And probably already had.

Erin.

Matt took a deep breath, trying to keep his rage under wraps. It was a hard feat, considering the car he saw parked behind Dwayne's house as he pulled up. It was Maggie's.

Suddenly everything felt different. *Looked* different. The house he'd once found comfort in at times when he needed a friend was now dark. Filled with an evil Matt had been too blind to see.

He cut the lights and stopped the Jimmy out far enough that it couldn't be seen from the front windows. He pulled out his phone and texted Billy that Maggie was there.

That she was with Dwayne.

A man neither of them knew anymore.

Matt pulled out his gun and checked the clip. His phone started to ring before he could open his door. It was Billy and Matt knew what he'd say if he answered.

Wait for us.

But Matt wasn't going to do that.

Instead, he left his car as quietly as he could and moved across the lawn, ready for anything.

The screen door on the patio was still broken. It would make noise if he moved it to get to the door. He knew Dwayne wasn't one to lock his windows, so he used that fact to his advantage. Slowly yet as quickly as he could, Matt went to the first window.

The living room looked the same as it had the week before when he'd first found Dwayne and Maggie unconscious. Neither were there now. He continued moving along the house until he was at the small bathroom window. With the foundation already raised a foot, he had to rise up on the tips of his toes to see inside. It, too, was empty. Next was the guest bedroom. It was small. Matt doubted if he was holding Maggie that he'd do it in there. Still, with the mind-set of no stone going unturned, he looked in through a part in the blinds.

Fresh rage nearly compelled Matt to fling the window open.

Cody was sitting on the bed, hands and legs bound. The TV in the corner was on. Maggie wasn't with him. Neither was Dwayne.

Matt knew that it might have been the wiser of choices to keep looking to see where Dwayne was. However, one look at Cody, small and with duct tape on his skin, and nothing could have made him leave. He only prayed the window was unlocked.

Chapter Twenty-Two

"I still don't understand what led me back here last week."

Dwayne stood, tall and proud despite his pain. Threats of Matt and the rest of the department swarming in had fallen on deaf ears. Though his distaste for what he was about to say was clear. His frown was deep as he explained.

"You found Erin's secret stash and started poking around Seth. He can kill people no problem, but the man gets jumpy when cornered. You asked a few too many questions and he went squirrelly. So he tried to convince you that Erin did suspect him but had it wrong all those years ago. He told you not to worry because I'd already questioned and cleared him before Erin's death."

"Which I knew was a lie," Maggie said.

He nodded.

"But you didn't suspect my involvement then. You just thought it was a piece of the mystery you'd somehow missed. I told you we needed to meet in person to get all the details ironed out. You weren't happy about my meeting place but you didn't argue, either." That's why Maggie wound up at the hotel. That's who she had been meeting.

"Why not shut me up while we were there? Why let me go?"

Dwayne cracked his neck again. Like he was gearing up for something. Maggie hoped she wouldn't have to find out what.

"You might not have suspected me but you didn't fully trust me, either," he said. "You kept talking about Erin's notes but refused to tell me where they were. I remembered how annoyingly determined you were when it all first happened so I couldn't take the chance that you had stashed it somewhere that might bite me in the ass down the line. I tried to convince you that you needed to tell me everything—to *show* me everything—but, in hindsight, I guess I pushed too hard. You got all weird, went to get food from the lobby and then came back with some excuse about having to leave. So I let you."

"Did you come to my house after that?"

Maggie still wanted to know why she'd left in such a hurry.

He shook his head.

"That would be the idiot. He tried to take a crack at *persuading* you to take him to what you'd found. You left. From there you disappeared for a few hours. So I came back here." His grin was back. "And who do I find snooping around my house? You didn't find any proof I was involved but, man, did you have a mouth on you." He shrugged. "A man can only take so much."

"That's when I attacked you," she filled in. "It *was* in self-defense."

A muscle in his jaw twitched.

"I should have shot you the moment I saw you," he growled.

Maggie knew it was only a matter of time before Dwayne was done entertaining her. In fact, she couldn't think of any reason why he was explaining everything that had happened to her in the first place.

"So what's the plan?" she decided to go ahead and ask. If they were getting to the end of his mental rope, then she wanted to prepare herself for what was coming. It was the only way she could try to think of a plan to get Cody out unharmed. The thought of him being hurt by the deranged man in front of her was too much. She couldn't let that happen. She *wouldn't*.

"My plan? It's simple." He reached into the back of his jeans and pulled out a gun. Maggie froze. She hadn't seen the weapon at all. "I'm going to kill you like I killed Erin. And then? I'm going to show Matt exactly what it feels like to have everything ruined. And then I'm going to kill him, too."

Dwayne lifted the gun, but before Maggie could scream, a shot rang out.

The man she guessed she would see in her nightmares for years to come, toppled over onto the bed. Maggie was stunned for a moment, confused as to why she wasn't the one who had fallen. It wasn't until she tore her eyes away from the dead body of Dwayne Meyers that she noticed the man standing in the hallway behind him.

Through the open door, Matt lowered his gun.

"I promise I didn't wait until he was done talking and then shot him for dramatic effect," he said. "It just took me longer than I expected to get Cody out of the house."

"He's okay?" Maggie rushed.

"Yeah, he's locked in my car. I wasn't sure how this would all shake out and didn't want him to be in any danger."

Maggie opened her mouth to thank him but all that came out was a sob.

Matt didn't waste any time taking her out of the bedroom. He found Dwayne's handcuff keys and unlocked them from her wrists. The moment Maggie's hands were free she threw her arms around the detective's neck and kissed him for all she was worth. He returned the favor in kind. They didn't speak while he cut the tape off her legs next. The moment they were free Maggie let them lead her outside and right up to Matt's car.

To say she cried the moment Cody was in her arms, unharmed, was an understatement.

To say her heart expanded to the brink of almost bursting when Matt put his arms around both of them, promising mother and child everything was going to be okay, was another giant understatement.

Together, the three of them sat in the back seat of his car and waited for first responders. It wasn't until the sheriff arrived that Matt left their side.

And even then he wasn't gone long at all.

MAGGIE SHOULDN'T HAVE been surprised when Kortnie met them at the ER doors. She might not have known Maggie that well but when she pulled her in for a hug, Maggie felt like they were old friends. The nurse looked exhausted and drained but still managed a joke.

"I think we might just need to get you a helmet," she said, walking them straight back to a room.

Maggie was surprised when Matt joined in.

"Don't worry. I've already thought about it."

He gave Maggie a small smile.

She might have been tired, too, but seeing him smile

gave her enough energy to be grateful. She mussed Cody's hair. A lot of things could have gone wrong that day. If Matt hadn't come…

Maggie didn't want to think about what *could* have happened. Instead, she went through the now-familiar routine of making sure her third blow to the head hadn't left any permanent damage. Thankfully, it hadn't. Though the doctor insisted she stay the night for observation. She wouldn't admit it but the idea didn't offend her. Cody had fallen asleep on the bed next to her and she wasn't far behind.

The only thing keeping her from giving in to the abyss of sleep was the need to talk to Matt. The sheriff had taken him outside to talk. It wasn't until a half hour later that he reappeared. He smiled. It was tired, but there. He took the chair beside her and glanced at the TV in the corner before starting.

"They found a note in the desk at Dwayne's," he said, voice low. "He never planned on trying to run. After he realized we were looking into Seth together and actually getting somewhere, Dwayne wanted me to pay for everything. For not stopping Erin or you back then and for not stopping you now. That was his final stand. He didn't write much else but I assume he would have tried to kill anyone who came. Even if it wasn't me who got there first." Maggie reached out and took his hand but he continued before she could try to comfort him. "You know, I thought about feeling guilty for a minute. About not being able to stop Erin or you, not being able to do what you two did instead and keeping you both out of danger." The corners of his lips turned up ever so slightly. "But the fact of the matter is I'm damned proud of you both."

Maggie returned the smile.

"And I'm sure Erin would be proud of you, too," she said. "Because I know I am."

A quiet moment passed between them. It stretched past their bruises, cuts and the damage that couldn't be fully measured or seen. They had been broken but had survived. Together. Now it was time for them to start to heal.

Maggie patted the spot next to her on the bed. Matt didn't question it. He slid in next to her, packing them in the hospital bed like sardines in a can. But it wasn't uncomfortable.

In fact, it felt just right.

Two months later and the twisted web that Dwayne Meyers and Seth Armstrong—whose real identity was now being looked into by the FBI—had woven had finally been mostly unraveled. The city of Kipsy and Riker County as a whole knew to thank Erin and Maggie for finding out the truth. Something that meant a great deal to the loved ones of Seth's known victims. Two of the families drove out to give their personal thanks while the rest wrote letters or called. Maggie handled each encounter with grace, telling them that Erin was the true hero of the story, not her.

But Matt and the rest of the Riker County Sheriff's Department didn't see it as one-sided. Billy made it known throughout the department and county that any old grievances they'd had with Maggie had been misplaced and were absolutely over. She even received a job offer back at the *Kipsy City Chronicle*, which she ended up turning down. The idea of finally going forward with writing her true crime novel had taken hold of her and wasn't letting go. Matt had already started helping her with research. It only made sense. They were, after all, spending most of their free time together. Although Matt knew, even without the excuse of work, being with her and Cody was just where he wanted to be. Period.

They'd fallen into their own little routine. One that felt right. One that felt whole.

While he never in a million years would have guessed Maggie Carson could make him feel that way, Matt couldn't deny that it had happened. It wasn't until one Saturday, after finishing exploring a trail with Cody and returning to the house, that he was able to finally put words to what he now had.

A team.

* * * * *

Look for the next book in Tyler Anne Snell's
THE PROTECTORS OF RIKER COUNTY
series,
LOVING BABY,
available next month.

And don't miss the previous books in
THE PROTECTORS OF RIKER COUNTY
series:

SMALL-TOWN FACE-OFF
THE DEPUTY'S WITNESS

Available now from Mills & Boon Intrigue!

MILLS & BOON®

A sneak peek at next month's titles...

LET'S TALK
Romance

For exclusive extracts, competitions
and special offers, find us online:

 facebook.com/millsandboon

 @millsandboonuk

 @millsandboon

Or get in touch on 0844 844 1351*

For all the latest titles coming soon, visit
millsandboon.co.uk/nextmonth